BOBBY MEHDWAN

Liberty One

60S

Previously published as Love or Liberty

Second edition

ISBN: 978-1-7398131-5-4

Editing by Anne Brewer

This book was professionally typeset on Reedsy.
Find out more at reedsy.com

For Nisha, Serena and Amar.
For the adventurer inside each of us.
For NASA and the other space programs which inspired us.
Keep looking up.

Contents

GET BLUE PANTHER

Read the prequel to *Liberty One.*

Get it at 60strategies.com/Blue_Panther

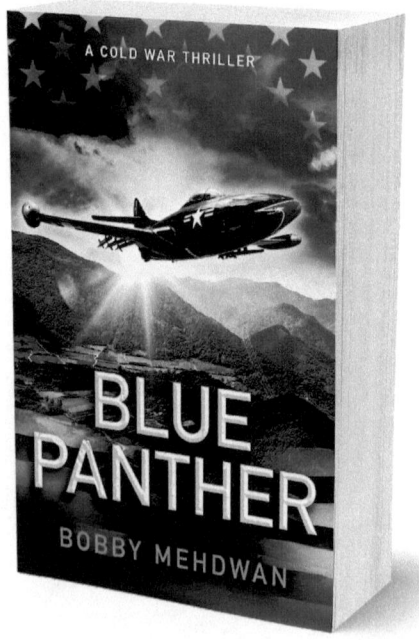

LIBERTY ONE

BOBBY MEHDWAN

About

A fictional story inspired by real events, people and places. Scroll to the back of the book to leave a review and join the newsletter to get free goodies.

* * *

Some timings have been adjusted for story-line integrity. Ethnic group name calling reflects character and period views.
Written in American English.

* * *

Get the playlist:
https://60strategies.com/LibertyOnePlaylistSpotify
See the history:
https://www.pinterest.co.uk/LibertyOneNovel/_saved/

* * *

For all mankind: We find peace through conflict.

Glossary

- 1-A Draft card designation: Available for military service
- CAPCOM: NASA Capsule Communication
- CCCP: Union of Soviet Socialist Republics (Soviet Union before 1991)
- CIA: Central Intelligence Agency
- CO: Commanding Officer
- CNO: Chief of Naval Operations
- DCI: Director of Central Intelligence
- EAFB: Edwards Air Force Base
- EVA: Extra Vehicular Activity (spacewalk)
- Excomm: Executive Committee of the National Security Council
- FBI: Federal Bureau of Investigation
- FLIGHT: NASA Flight director
- G4/5: NASA Gemini 4/5
- HHMU: Handheld Maneuvering Unit
- ICBM: Intercontinental Ballistic Missile
- JFK: President John F Kennedy
- KGB: Komitet Gosudarstvennoy Bezopasnost
- LBJ: President Lyndon B. Johnson
- LEO: Low Earth Orbit
- LK-3: Russian lunar lander
- LLRV: Lunar Landing Research Vehicle (Flying Bedstead)

- LOI: Lunar Orbit Insertion
- MLR: Main Line of Resistance (Korean war)
- MOL: Manned Orbiting Laboratory
- MSc: Master of Science
- N1: Soviet Soyuz N1 rocket
- NAS: Naval Air Station
- NASA: National Aeronautics and Space Administration
- OKB-1: Experimental Design Bureau in Russia
- PoW: Prisoner of War
- SAC: Strategic Air Command
- SAM: Surface to Air Missile
- SDS: Students for a Democratic Society
- SEAL: US Navy Sea, Air, and Land special operations
- Simsup: NASA Simulator Supervisor
- TEI: Trans Earth Injection
- TELEMETRY: NASA flight tracking desk
- TLI: Trans Lunar Injection
- TNT: Trinitrotoluene explosive
- U2/G: US Reconnaissance aircraft. G-variant for carrier operations

CHAPTER 1 - BLOCKADE

North East of the Bahamas, Tuesday October 23rd, 1962

"Landing a fighter at slow speed on a carrier deck on a stormy night is like throwing a brick at a moving postage stamp ten feet in front of you." That's how the instructor put it to Jim during his Field Carrier Landing Practice, back in his training days. "The A-4 Skyhawk, the US Navy's light attack workhorse, is unstable, so you can throw it around in the sky; but it's really just a pig with wings when you slow it down," the instructor had said.

Jim Cobb looked down through a break in the billowing cloud brought on by Hurricane Ella and caught a glimpse of the USS Essex through shafts of shifting moonlight somewhere off the coast of Cuba. The hole closed again and he continued through the white and gray tufts in search of the Enterprise, desperately needing to land his plane.

The instrument panel cast a faint glow across the dark, cramped cabin. "One hundred and sixty knots and about fifteen miles on the glide path. Low clouds," he murmured, tapping a gloved finger on the fuel gauge. It no longer gave a reading.

"Er, Big-E, this is Eagle Three. I'm out of fuel here and

it's, well, it's getting pretty hot in the cabin right now." Jim paused to consider his words, then took off his gloves to stay cool.

He pressed his microphone again and spoke more deliberately. "The cabin heat is jammed on and it's blasting hot air inside. I need to land this thing before I'm roasted alive up here." He waited for an answer, then looked out through the thick cloud cover at the vast North Atlantic and added with a sinking tone, "Or broiled in the soup."

"Roger, Eagle Three, we see you on the glide path now," came the reply. It was the familiar deep Texan voice of Captain Powell of the behemoth Enterprise, a floating nuclear-powered island of giant steel plates. She'd just returned from a round-the-world cruise in the Mediterranean and was heading straight back out of Norfolk on her first real mission to keep Soviet nuclear weapons out of Cuba. Powell spoke again. "Looks like you're still caught in the tail of the storm, Eagle Three. Don't screw up. I have something important to tell you when you get here."

Jim felt hot engine air seeping into the Skyhawk's cabin through the vents. He turned some knobs and looked around his little cocoon for a malfunction, something, anything he could switch that would make a difference.

The problem had to be the two single rifle shots from the Soviet container ship he'd just passed, low and starboard, practically on the water, though closer than he really needed to be. But it gave him a perfect view of the payload—huge tubes, perhaps missiles, laid out under cover across the long deck. He'd gotten close enough to see the patriotic crewmen under their little hats, one of whom had brandished a rifle and pulled the trigger on him like a giant clay pigeon. Were they careful or careless shots? He couldn't tell. It wasn't anything immediately lethal, and he was still in the air, though he wouldn't be doing that again in a hurry. He'd invaded their space and they'd beaten their little Red chests at him. The bullets themselves had pierced the tail somewhere he couldn't see, and must have hit an air duct or a valve or a gyro—something in the environmental control system. The plane flew on into the gusts of the storm. Two minutes later, the cabin had become unusually warm.

Now the heat just kept coming, and it was more than just tepid—the blasting air was already scalding hot. He wondered if he should just bail into the sea; Big-E could always fish him out. The Reds would be rolling around on their deck, laughing or terrified that they'd started mankind's final war. Still thinking, he tapped the stick gently to keep the nose on point. The plane bobbed in the air against raging gusts and lashing rain.

"A little left ... straight ... left again, then ... up," he muttered, trying to cheer himself. "Now ... straight," he added with his left hand on the stick. He took a quick look at his horizon and airspeed, then yelped, "Ouch, damn it!" and jerked his hand back from the hot stick like the head of a rattlesnake after a bite. He should have known not to remove his glove. He placed it back over the head of the stick gently and continued to poke it, steering the plane with his fingertips. He took a deep breath and loosened his zipper, then opened a small cold air vent in the glass canopy. The cabin began to roar with wind noise.

"You should be there somewhere," he murmured with a piercing look through the cloud, now high up again. Suddenly a clearing opened and cool blue moonlight flooded the cramped cockpit, giving him an immediate sense of space and calm.

Below, ships of the fearsome floating firepower of the US Atlantic Fleet, stretched out in a long arc across the ocean some five hundred kilometers off the Caribbean islands, guarding against Soviet ships reaching Cuba. Essex, which he'd just seen, was parked in a long line with Lake Champlain, Wasp, Intrepid, Randolph, Shangri-La, Boxer, Okinawa, Thetis Bay, Canberra, and Independence. The anti-submarine groups he had seen earlier were stationed at the southern and northern ends of the line.

It was just two weeks ago, on October fourteenth, that an American U2 spy plane detected Soviet medium-range nuclear missile launchers in Cuba. They were right on America's doorstep, pointed directly at it. Newly assigned to the Enterprise, which was leading the blockade, Jim was on a long reconnaissance mission over the ocean to locate several Soviet Foxtrot submarines. But they had remained submerged and out of sight, presumably with combat systems ready for all-out nuclear war.

But now he'd used up all his fuel, having taken a very long way around the storm to get back to the ship. He glanced down at the instruments again to see if any of the dials had moved, thinking he'd better not fall out of the sky into the sea only to embarrass himself and the might of the US Navy in front of the Soviets.

The de-icing vent continued to blast super-hot air against the metal frame of the canopy, and Jim got a nose full of burnt gloves the moment he touched it.

"Eagle Three, we have a visual," Big-E's controller said, to Jim's immediate relief. He pictured the binoculars on the bridge, trained on him like an insect in the sky with the landing gear down.

With even greater relief, he saw the ship's pulsating landing lights in the distance. "Big-E, you're like a beacon in the dark. I see you now. You could not have appeared too soon."

He flicked the gear lock into place, set the flaps, and pushed the throttle just a touch as a third vent, behind his legs, began to cane his calves with hot air. He spread them as wide as he could while keeping his feet on the rudder pedals. He began to worry that his suit might actually melt or catch fire.

With only a mile to go, a huge hook dropped under his tail like the hind legs of a mosquito ready to bite. He pictured the trip wire and the giant tennis net twanging into place on the ship's deck and gently nudged the throttle again. He reset the flaps. The plane slowed and bounced in the air, picking up extra wind noise, but dropped again as the headwind relented for a split second.

"We don't want to hit the front of the ship there, do we?" he muttered, holding the glove against the stick just as a bead of sweat rolled down his forehead and stung his right eye. He leaned forward and winced, feeling his suit already glued to his back.

Without warning, the glass of the altitude gauge shattered. He ducked as if his seat had been pulled out from under him and looked up and around frantically. Small pieces of glass remained around the edges of the dial, and some had fallen around his feet. A particularly long shard had lodged itself in the seat between his splayed legs. He reached for the display, but recoiled when he felt super-hot air blowing directly on it.

"Great! Guess the rate of descent now, Jim, just when guessing is the least useful thing to do," he muttered. His mind raced with the prospect of aborting the flight again, but now, with only a few hundred feet to the deck, there was only one choice.

"Damn Soviets." He sighed. "Too late for that." His eyes searched the darkness for a fixed point of reference, though the sea itself looked like a vast gray plain with the moonlit silhouette of Big-E bobbing around like a corkscrew. "Land this thing, or hit the carrier, or it's the drink. Take your pick, buddy."

With only a hundred feet to go, a headwind pushed the plane off the glide path. Jim quickly corrected it by pushing the nose down hard and aiming for the landing lights. The plane crabbed right into the headwind as the left wheel dropped. He pulled the nose up and maxed the flaps, which buoyed the plane again.

The final countdown began in his head. *Three ... two ... one.* He saw the landing signal officer's cut engines sign. The plane flared as the left wheel touched down first, smoking and spinning violently as it skidded across the deck. The right wing came down hard, shaking the whole plane as if it had been dropped from a great height. It bounced with the wind and began to float above the deck.

"Come on, catch the wire! Catch the wire!" Jim panicked, thinking he'd come in too high and missed the line, but the plane dropped and skidded like a crab.

"Net? Come on! Where are you?"

He put a hand back on the throttle for an emergency lift off. "Big-E, I'm going around!" He threw the lever forward, but nothing happened. "Come on!" he urged. He released the throttle and pressed it again, then began to pump, but the engine simply sputtered.

Just when it looked like he was about to plummet over the edge, Jim was thrown forward into his harness. The huge net and arresting wire had brought the plane from the speed of a bullet to a standstill in an instant.

Jim quickly unstrapped himself and looked out into the darkness. It was like staring at a charcoal painting with inky black objects in the foreground. Nothing moved for a moment and he couldn't even tell if he was falling or sinking. He looked around the cabin for water, but there was none. "God damn net—thank you!"

Barely able to breathe, he regained awareness of the cabin temperature, unfastened his harness, and released the canopy, pushing it back like the top of a fancy car. To his relief, there was definitely no moisture. He tore off his mask and paused for a lungful of cold air, then thanked the last gust of wind for lifting the plane on approach. But his thoughts were interrupted by a ramp man waving a glowing orange wand in a neck slit on the darkened deck. Jim reached down to flip the engine kill switch, but it had already stopped and the fuel gauge read empty.

"They're dead. Dead!" he yelled to the wand man. He stood up in the cabin and saw, out of the corner of his eye, new landing lights approaching in the sky. He clambered out quickly and hobbled toward the ship's tower in the moonlight, looking back to see if he could see any bullet holes. A tug emerged from a dark corner and grabbed his plane as he stumbled through an arch into a cold gray stairwell at the base of the tower. By the time he turned around, his battered plane was being dragged into the shadows by an array of multicolored wands and newly lit spotlights on the deck.

A light tap on his shoulder caught his attention. "Lieutenant Commander Cobb? Welcome," an officer said.

Still startled, Jim spun around and exclaimed, "Oh, that was close. You don't know how ..." He paused to look down at his suit and saw that the backs of his knees were browned and his sleeves charred. "Well, I was going to say how close that was."

Both he and the officer ducked as the Skyhawk's cockpit suddenly exploded into a fireball on the dark deck. Gusts of wind fanned the flames, but the ground crew scrambled and blasted their fire extinguishers at it, just as Red Three descended quickly and quietly like a black panther in the night. It was parked in line with the other tails in less than thirty seconds and disappeared below deck on a giant lift in under sixty.

Jim turned back to the officer, speechless. The man just grunted with a calm, wry smile. Still inspecting Jim's tattered suit, he said, "You'd better change quickly. The C.O. is expecting you in his quarters. You might want to think of a story." He glanced back at the burning plane. "You picked a bad day. He's not a happy man. Said he was about to lose one of his much needed new crew. But that might be a lot easier now."

Jim's eyes searched for an explanation. "I screwed up, didn't I?"

CHAPTER 2 - STONEWALLED

Moments later

Jim had already showered and changed into a new flight suit when he arrived at the commanding officer's door about twenty minutes later. He knocked twice, then turned the handle and saw Captain Powell sitting at his desk.

Powell pulled the phone from his ear. "Come in and take a seat, Jim. I'll be right with you."

He entered the room and settled at a round conference table overlooking the deck. The walls were wood-paneled and lined with ship memorabilia, gifts, and photographs of the captain with friends and colleagues on various vessels. A map of the world took up most of the wall, and a game of chess lay unfinished on a small round table in a corner to his right.

Powell hung up the phone. "That looked like a lucky escape."

Jim shot to his feet and turned to salute, standing as straight as a post. "Yes, sir!"

Powell rose and asked (as if they were genuine concerns), "Cold or something, were you, out there, Cobb? Far from home?"

Jim swallowed quietly. Powell was clearly toying. He must

have known the Soviets took pot shots at him—he'd reported it. Jim buttoned his lip, but Powell nodded that it was his turn to speak.

"Sir, the cabin heat was jammed. There was nothing I could do." Jim paused for a reaction, not daring to repeat the incident for fear of sounding insolent or shifting blame. "But I managed to save the plane. I mean, I didn't ditch, sir."

Powell said nothing at first, but walked around his desk and looked Jim straight in the eye. His tone changed. "You saved the plane, did you? I wouldn't have said that. It was burning on my deck and I don't have a spare for you." His remark hit Jim in the face, as if he'd been called out on a blatant lie. Powell walked back to his desk.

"Sir," Jim hesitated at first. "It was tricky. I was patrolling a wider area of the ocean, there was the storm ... the Soviet gunfire. I barely made it in. I'm sure there's an explanation."

"And, just what were you doing getting shot at, Cobb? You know as well as I do that we could be at war in a matter of hours. This lady may be about to see her first real action," he added, glancing around the room.

Jim didn't dare say that he shouldn't have flown so close to the Soviet ship and upset its crew.

"They're trying to get more nukes into Cuba. My crew can't be crippled at a time like this. Can you imagine that?"

Jim was silent, then said, "I saw it, sir."

"Saw what?"

"I saw what looked like missiles. I have to write my debrief."

Powell paused and considered his tone. "I want to see it on my desk before you leave."

"Yes, sir ... leave, sir?"

"At ease."

Jim's face remained taut from the reprimand.

"You've been reassigned to shore duty," Powell said, "but your plane is broken, so it'll be the transporter back to the dock. In one hour."

Jim stood there, stunned. He really had screwed up.

The captain looked him in the eye. "I had a call from the secretary and the CNO," Powell continued. "You, Cobb, are off this ship now."

Jim's face flushed as the words *what the hell?* rattled around inside his head. He swallowed hard.

"The thing is, the CNO and I have been asked to recommend you for a position at NASA." Powell handed him a sealed telegram.

Jim was astonished when he opened it and read, feeling like he'd just been fired. "But, sir—"

"This is not a regular procedure. You'll have to find out why. I can't tell you. I guess they don't take applications from, or talk to people that are not suitable. The stakes seem very high from what I can tell."

Jim held his tongue as his head whirled with mental calculations to figure out what was going on.

"What's on your mind?" Powell asked.

Jim glanced at the note again and replied firmly, "Sir, my job is to ... well, to protect our country. The blockade needs everything we've got. What's the point of going to—"

"Jim. I think I know what you're thinking—"

"Sir, my fight here is with the Communists. They fired at me. My role is here with you. I'm not ready to leave the battlefield just when I need to man the blockade—"

"I didn't give you permission to interrupt, did I?" Powell

walked back around his desk and said, "You've been a good pilot." He stopped abruptly and glanced out the window where Jim's plane would have been, then rolled his eyes and turned around. "And I've known you throughout your naval career. But I'd advise you to check it out before you react badly."

Jim felt silenced.

"I know you just got here, but it has to be now or never. Between you and me, there's no leaving this ship after today," Powell added.

Jim thought for a moment, relented, and simply replied, "I'll get my things, sir." He saluted again, then walked to the door, seeing that the conversation was over and thinking that he'd either gotten his orders or been sidelined for losing a plane. But it couldn't have been the latter—the telegram had already arrived.

Powell glanced up from his desk as Jim walked out the door. "By the way, you were looking at that chessboard over there."

Jim turned around. "Yes, sir, it looks like you've been, uh, stonewalled. I assumed you were black?"

"Stonewalled?" Powell muttered, glancing at the board as Jim closed the door and disappeared.

Still feeling irascible, Jim packed his meager belongings, quickly wrote his debrief, then climbed aboard the helicopter for shore exactly sixty minutes later. The sky had cleared and the moonlight was now full on. He opened the cool air vent above his head and sat down, feeling relieved to be the passenger this time.

The telegram crossed his mind again. It said he was to report to Ellington Air Force Base in Houston on Monday morning at eight in strict secrecy. He was not to reveal the order to anyone. And that was it. No clue what they wanted.

"You okay, buddy?" the pilot asked, stepping forward and interrupting Jim's thoughts.

He looked up. "Yeah. I, er, just need to get some real sleep. It's been a long day. And it looks like we're going to war with the Soviets, doesn't it?"

"It's looking grim. Are you on shore leave?"

"I'm going to, uh, Langley ... Field next week." Jim's tongue had just managed to keep the news from escaping his teeth, but he found Carl to be a smart cookie.

"Langley?" he exclaimed. "Are you going to the Moon or something? That's where all the space boys are stationed, isn't it?"

Jim bit his lip, then said, "I'll call you."

"Okay, buddy." Carl saluted and jumped back into the cockpit.

As they lifted off, Jim's mind returned to the standoff in the ocean below. The world, it seemed, was on the brink of another catastrophic conflict after World War II. If just one of the Soviet ships crossed the line, Kennedy and Khrushchev would fill the skies with nukes within the hour, and there would be no more NASA unless it jumped into one of its own rockets and shot off to the stars. And it was just possible that he wouldn't even make it back to shore to see JoAnn today. All it would take was one Soviet submarine captain to get an itchy finger or a rogue order so deep underwater that he probably wouldn't know what else to do.

Exhausted, he promptly sat back, though his mind continued to race. Powell began preaching in his head. "We don't ask soldiers which battles they'd rather fight. Choices are made for you, Jim, unless you're the one making them."

He was still agonizing over it all when he closed his eyes, tired and with a bruised ego from losing the second plane of his career that day.

CHAPTER 3 - STARS

The next day, Wednesday October 24th, 1962

Jim walked through the front door of his home outside Houston around dinner time the next day, having spent the previous night at Norfolk Naval Station Chesapeake Bay. He paused for a moment to take in the delicious smell of apple pie that hung in the air.

His first sight, after closing the door behind him, was of JoAnn watering pots of snake plant with a small hand-held canister. She was wearing a slim blue shirt and tight white pants, just as she'd dressed when they'd decorated the lounge the previous summer. Elegant, he thought, in its simplicity, neutral colors, not at all a mishmash of old rags, but chosen for the job. It reminded him of the white tail on an airplane before all the fancy logos and swirls were sprayed on.

He looked around for paint cans, but there were none. The room was tidy and orderly, and he felt satisfied that his own place in the world had some sanity, even if the outside didn't. To his right, next to the entrance, a wide wooden staircase led to the first floor. Immediately in front of him, he noticed that the white sofa had an assortment of new cushions, though clearly not all of them for keeps, as there was no more than an inch of actual seating space left. A matching footstool stood next to it on an orange patterned rug that hid a solid white tile floor underneath. Cream-colored armchairs were on the other side of the sofa, and a pedestal within arm's reach stood between them, holding an equally pale green telephone with a circular dial. Light streamed in through the blinds.

Jim put his keys and a book on a small round table by the door. With one hand still behind his back, he kissed JoAnn in the middle of the room and handed her a bouquet of red roses wrapped in green paper.

She looked delighted, put down the watering can and beamed at them. They hugged and she asked if he was all right.

Jim, still admiring her joy, shrugged and replied, "Yeah." With a big sigh, he added, "But I lost the plane."

She looked alarmed. "What happened? Was everything okay out there?"

Jim nodded. "It caught fire, but it's fixable. No one's hurt." Jim thought his plane was probably not written off, but it would be an expensive repair for the Navy. A nagging self-doubt remained. The investigation report might reveal something he did or forgot to do.

"And what about the ..."

Jim thought for a moment. "I'm sure the Soviets will get the message and this will blow over. They'll back down." He winced slightly.

JoAnn stopped and looked him up and down. "What? Are you hurt?"

Jim brought his hidden hand forward to reveal a medium-sized tub of ice cream, swapped it with the other, and felt instant relief. He held up the tub with a grin. "Something for later."

JoAnn relaxed again and laughed. "Let me see." She took it from him. "Chocolate chip? What's the occasion?"

"And I got a book about the stars, too." He pointed to where he'd left it by the door with the keys.

"Something going on?"

"Just, you know."

JoAnn looked at her flowers again. "Well, okay. I'd better put these in some water. Come on."

Holding his hand, she led him into the kitchen, just visible around the corner, and put the ice cream down while she got a vase from a cupboard. She began filling it with water at the sink.

Just behind her, he pulled the telegram out of his back pocket. "Take a look at this."

She turned with the flowers still in her wet hands, set them down, and dried herself on a dishcloth. She pulled the note from an envelope and read it silently. "Ellington? Monday?" She looked intrigued. "What is it?"

Jim hadn't shared that with her on the phone, knowing the line might not be private. Instead, he'd said his plane had broken down and he'd be home for a few days while they found him another. She knew that was baloney and code for something else.

"NASA," Jim said.

She was puzzled. "NASA? What do they want?"

"I'm not sure. That's all it says. Even Powell didn't know and he gave it to me. They didn't bother to mail it."

"That can only mean one thing, right? What else could it be?"

"I can't think. Testing equipment or something?"

She looked astonished. "Rockets? Astronaut? That's ... wow. Are you okay with that?"

"I don't know yet. Maybe." Jim's mind hadn't let go of having to leave the ship in the middle of the conflict. This was his second big chance, after Korea, to strike back at the Reds and stop their advance around the world. He had to avenge the loss of his father to the Soviets, and had to stay focused on the goal that had brought him to the Navy in the first place. How was he going to do that at NASA? And what if he got a desk job there, calculating flight paths or something? "Maybe when the blockade is over. We'll see what they want on Monday."

JoAnn was clearly intrigued. "Imagine that," she said, turning back to her flowers. She looked around the kitchen. "Good thing I cleaned this place up, if that's what it is. Can you imagine? They put cameras everywhere." She laughed at the idea, barely believing her words. "Are you okay with that?"

Jim thought she was getting a little ahead of herself, but let her play with the idea. The truth was, it might be cool some other time when mankind wasn't staring at its end. Sitting on a yellow bench in the diner-style booth to the left of the window, he said, "I'm a little camera-shy. That could be a problem."

"You'd have to get used to it." After a thoughtful pause, she added, "I'll need some clothes." She seemed to have an idea. "I could borrow some." She placed the flowers in the watered vase and asked, "So, what happens on Monday?"

"Honestly, I don't know. Maybe they're expecting a chimp or something with four legs to put to the test."

She dried her hands and walked over to him, placed the

flowers squarely in the middle of the table and paused to admire them for a moment. Then she sat astride him in the chair and looked into his eyes. "I can't believe it. I could have my very own spaceman here."

Jim thought she hadn't remembered all the rockets that had exploded on takeoff. That would certainly come to complicate things at some point, if that's what they had in mind.

They kissed. "Oh, what did you think of the colors?"

Jim said he liked the blue cushions on the white sofa, that there were too many of them, that they worked well, though in truth he had no idea, except that they didn't look bad. He also knew that she wasn't really asking for approval, she just needed to know that there wasn't a problem. She would set up their home and he would stay out of the way.

She continued, "I started moving furniture into the bedroom so we could start decorating. But it was too hot. I couldn't do much. I need your help."

"You started that already?" One of the smaller rooms needed repainting. "You should have waited."

She shrugged. "I had time. And you had another world war to stop." She smiled at him.

Jim put his arms behind his head and stretched. "I can't believe how hot it is out there. It's all because of Ella. I got caught in it on the way back to Enterprise." He looked out the window. " It must still be ninety out there. That's got to be a record for this time of year." He had a thought. "That's a nice baby name, don't you think?"

JoAnn laughed. "Ella?" She weighed it up and said, "Well, it would be nice to make some children before you go exploring the universe. We'd better get started."

Jim still had part of his mind on the war brewing in the

Atlantic, but he could see that she was imagining a new future in her mind as she kissed him again.

JoAnn sensed it and looked him straight in the eye. "Do you really think it's going to be okay?"

"Yes, I do," he reassured her. He really thought it would be, maybe because he couldn't imagine the horror of a nuclear war. "The Soviets must care about their children, too." He hugged her and silently prayed that he was right.

"Anyway, I thought we could go to that new place. Mexican, since you're home early," she said. "And I was going to ask Mike and Martha."

Jim had another idea. "Actually, can we just keep it to ourselves tonight? I don't have the energy. And I haven't seen you in weeks."

"Oh. Okay." JoAnn was surprised.

"We could do tomorrow."

"Sure, I'll call them and let them know we're busy."

"Why don't we just sit out tonight and look at the sky? I have that book on the stars and it's going to be a clear night. I should probably brush up for the NASA meeting on Monday. They might ask me something about the sky that I should have known in grade school."

"Sounds fun. I'll heat something up for dinner if that's okay with you?"

He kissed her again then said, "Maybe even sleep out, it's so hot. In fact, we could go beyond the city lights and make it a stargazing night."

JoAnn laughed. "Sure. Sounds crazy."

She warmed up dinner, and right after, they headed north-east, stopping near the southern tip of Lake Houston at a small hill with a wide-angle view of the night sky. Jim had come here as a boy with an astrology club. She laid out a picnic mat and spread a large blanket for cover, although it didn't seem necessary in the heat of the night. The ice cream tub came too. She opened it and handed Jim a spoon while he searched the pages of his book under a flashlight.

Soon they lay back and JoAnn began to feed him. He scanned the sky and pointed out what was what. At first, they were both speechless at the vast array of stars above them and the beauty of the Moon, low over the horizon. They wondered how incredible it must look from space, without dust or other lights in the way. Jim joked that the sky looked like a giant black bag that had been placed around the galaxy with pinholes for light to shine through. She pondered the crazy idea that the big omnipotent light bulb on the outside was God Himself.

Using the book and turning the flashlight on and off, then pausing for a few moments to let their eyes adjust, they quickly found the Little Bear with Polaris on its tail. Jim said it was also known as the North Star. That, he knew. Next they found Orion's Belt, which JoAnn had already spotted, then Aries—Jim's horoscope—which was a little more difficult. JoAnn raised her hand and drew an imaginary line from Polaris to Segin in Cassiopeia. She continued to double the distance while Jim read and told her what to do. Her finger ended at a cluster of stars, which may or may not have been the ones they wanted when they agreed they'd done a good enough job. Sagittarius, JoAnn's zodiac, came next, though ten minutes later they were still at a loss as to how to find it.

They lay still for a few moments and saw the flashing tail lights of an airplane high above. JoAnn asked if the Soviet Sputnik satellite was still up there. Jim said he didn't know, that things didn't necessarily stay in orbit for long without power, and that it had been a few years since it went up. He was sure it must have fallen from the sky.

"I tell you what, though. This is a good time of year for shooting stars."

JoAnn snuggled up to him and after a moment of silent searching, he said, "Let's make our own."

He turned to her and they locked lips just as a streak of starlight in the atmosphere flashed across the corner of his eye.

CHAPTER 4 - SPECIALS

Some days later, Monday October 29th, 1962

Arriving at Ellington Field, Jim was a little surprised to be directed to a Gulfstream which was standing alone in front of an open hangar. Slender, with bulbous, oversized engines, it was attached to a fuel bowser, with grounds men hurrying around it to make final preparations for flight.

He still had no idea what to expect when someone walked over from the other side and held out a hand. "Hi, I'm Tom Mitchell. Are you waiting for that plane?"

Jim nodded. "Yeah."

"Cape Air Force Station?"

"That's right. I'm Jim Cobb." They shook hands. "Is it just us?"

"I'm told there are a few other guys in there. I was just getting on board." Tom glanced at his watch. "I think we should be leaving soon. Any idea what this is?"

Jim looked up at the sky and grinned. "It just came out of the blue."

Tom stopped with a wry smile and Jim felt an immediate click between them, like a pair of wings being bolted together on a new airplane.

The fuel line was disconnected as they walked across the sunny tarmac and hopped up the small steps. They turned right into the tube and saw two other men already seated in the plush walnut and cream leather cabin.

The man on the left stood and shook Tom's hand as if they'd been friends for years. "What's up, buddy?"

"Bean!" Tom exclaimed. "I can't believe it. Have you *been* following me again?"

Tom introduced his buddy Fred. "He and I were in Flight Systems. Skunkworks."

Tom turned to the other man. "And ..."

"... Chris James." He stood up, too, and shook with each of them. "I'm just the NASA guy."

"Navy—Enterprise," Jim added.

Tom Mitchell was introducing himself as a Major from the 4028th Strategic Reconnaissance Squadron when the captain interrupted from the cockpit door.

"Gentlemen, please take your seats. We're about to push off."

They all sat quietly, faced forward and fastened their seat belts. The front door was closed and the plane began to taxi to the runway. Soon the big engines had pushed the plane eastward into the sky.

Chris looked to be the youngest of the four, maybe in his late twenties, thought Jim. He was also the tallest by almost a foot. He had a serious face with glasses that gave him the analytical look of someone who read a lot. To Jim, he was borderline money man. Buried in paperwork and barely speaking at the beginning, Chris came to life when they reached cruising altitude and the seat belt sign was turned off.

"Gentlemen, I want to welcome you to NASA. I'm sure

you're wondering why you're here."

They spun their spacious swivel seats to face him as he stowed papers and searched through the pile of paper. "Before we continue, I need you to sign something. Whatever we discuss here is restricted. I'm sure you understand that."

Jim, Tom and Fred looked intrigued as Chris handed each of them a document. "This will remind you of your national secrecy obligations."

They silently looked over them and saw that they were being instructed on the Espionage Act. They scribbled their signatures and handed them back.

"Tom, I was sorry to hear about Anderson. Do you know what happened?" Chris asked.

Jim knew that an American plane had been shot out of the sky over Cuba by the Soviets on Saturday.

They all looked at Tom for an answer. He said, "The plane is still missing. It's certain now that it didn't make it. As far as we know, the plane was hit by a surface-to-air missile. There were no other planes in the air."

"You knew the pilot?" Jim asked, surprised.

Tom nodded. "Same squadron, flying recon to check on Soviet missile buildup. He got caught, just like Powers in sixty. The warheads are out there, just like Kennedy said." He paused, then added, "I'm going to see Rudy's family next week."

Jim inhaled sharply and frowned, then leaned forward and, without realizing it, cupped his mouth. It was the dreaded "R" word again. His father, Lieutenant Commander Cobb, had been shot down on a reconnaissance mission when he'd discovered Soviet ICBM launch sites, SAM nests, bomber squadrons, and nuclear submarine production lines somewhere in Russia in fifty.

From what Tom hadn't said, Jim now understood that he was probably a U2 jock, assigned to pilot twelve-mile-high spy planes for the CIA, even though they didn't officially exist. The Kremlin had tried in vain to get the little black midges from the sky until they finally got one. Jim remembered the Russians looking as astonished at their success as the Americans had looked wide-eyed and red-faced when Gary Powers was brought down over the Soviet Union in sixty.

"Jim, are you okay? Did you ..."

Jim realized he had an audience. "No, no. I didn't know him. We just ... we can't lose this war." It felt to him, as it had many times before, that the Reds were closing in on all sides, getting closer and closer to destroying the free world, though he would never say that to JoAnn.

"Well, that brings me to why you're here. Let's talk about the space programme first. Gentlemen, in late fifty-seven, the Soviets launched their Sputnik satellite into orbit."

Jim thought back to how the world had changed that day. The war against communism, that he had pledged his life to after his father's death, seemed to have resumed after Korea, where it had never really ended. It meant that the scourge was no longer confined to a distant foreign land somewhere on the other side of the globe as people wanted to believe, but was now in their own skies. Sputnik was a new threat, and Americans were shaken by the object circling out of sight above their heads.

"That event alarmed the nation and prompted Congress to create NASA in fifty-eight. It inherited the Air Force's Man In Space Soonest project," Chris continued. "You know it today as Project Mercury. It launched Al Shepard into orbit last May."

Jim's mind flashed back to the first spaceman. In April of sixty-one, the world was stunned, when out of nowhere, Soviet Yuri Gagarin beat America's Alan Shepard by just three weeks, to become the first man in space. The rumor at the time was that Werner von Braun, the builder of America's rockets, was adamantly opposed to a faster launch which would have put America first.

"Then NASA sent John Glenn up earlier this year, in February. Mercury has more missions in the pipeline."

Jim had been following these events. Glenn had been the first American to orbit the Earth, but in August of that year the Soviets had usurped NASA again, with two record-breaking orbital missions at the same time, when one would have done. It seemed to have become a numbers race when American astronauts also began going up in twos.

"We've seen the Soviets moving into space at breakneck speed." Chris said. "They use six ICBM launch pads; two at a place called Baikonur and four at another place called Plesetsk. Right now they seem to be unstoppable and unbeatable.

"But we have Project Gemini, which will put our men in space for longer periods of time, laying the groundwork for President Kennedy's goal of putting a man on the Moon by sixty-nine. You heard his statement. About two years ago, the Marshall Spaceflight Center opened in Huntsville, Alabama, and is already building the rocket that will take us there. But more on that in a moment. We also have information that the Soviets are close to sending a man out into space, free floating, to begin preparations for a Moon landing. We, on the other hand, have some way to go before the Gemini project reaches the same point. So all indications are that they seem to have a big lead over us."

Fred glanced at Tom to see if he was going to react, but he remained focused.

"What do you make of all this? Do you think the American people will buy it?" Jim asked.

"I'd say so. They all think they're going on a great big adventure across the galaxy," Tom said.

"But by the end of the decade?" Jim asked.

"Sure, that seems like plenty of time," Tom replied.

Fred jumped in. "Well, you know the Soviets are already building the N1 rocket. It's a giant; have you seen it? I've seen aerial photos and it's an impressive beast. A real big fella."

"Yeah, so big they say it's visible fourteen miles up. It could be a giant elevator."

"Some say we're already out of time," Jim remarked, looking at Chris again.

"I'd say someone needs to fire a rocket," joked Fred.

"So how do we stop them?"

"Fire one of our own. Let them know we're on it," Jim said.

"Well, the Moon's on the line now. For freedom or tyranny?" Tom added.

"I sure hope the president knows how hard it is to point at a dime in the sky a zillion miles away. I bet he's worried about the Soviets claiming the Moon as Communist soil. Probably wants to secure it at all costs. I guess somebody told him they're planning to put nuclear weapons up there, too. Imagine that, hey: nukes hanging over our heads. He's right, we really need to get there first," Jim said.

Fred grimaced and added, "But some people say the Soviets can't even fund their program."

"Well, leaked memos show that they're actually planning to go all over the solar system," Chris interrupted. "And they seem to be making progress. It's been one thing after another since Sputnik. But that's not all. There are indications that they are already building a defensive capability in space. That's a threat to our nuclear response. That's why you're here today."

"The CIA has given us all a warning," said Tom. He recited: "An implacable totalitarian enemy with no rules of morality." He paused to let the words sink in, then added, "They kill and imprison their own people. You can read all about it."

Jim asked, "The CIA said that on morality? Was that before or after the Bay of Pigs?"

Tom grinned at the irony. "We have to protect our freedom. There are no rules with an enemy like that."

"You know, it looks like everyone's trying to get in on the space action. Strategic Air Command doesn't want the Air Force to let go. And the DCI's pulling in his direction, too. Vandenberg's in there somewhere," Fred added, looking out the window. "Up here's Air Force territory as far as they're concerned. Can't say I understand what NASA's going to do if everything goes south and a war starts up there."

They were all getting very excited when Chris stepped in again to bring the discussion back on track. "We also have reason to believe that the Soviets have a lunar vehicle being prepared to survey the Moon's surface in anticipation of manned missions. So, all in all, the truth is that we are a long way behind. But we are accelerating. And as Jim said, we can't let them win this race. So, the reason you are here is that each of you has been invited to join a NASA Special Operations program to train to pilot vehicles into space and defend our skies."

The trio looked at each other for reactions during the pause that followed, though they remained neutral and guarded.

"Don't you need test pilots? Or chimps?" Jim asked.

"They were requirements. But not anymore," Chris replied.

"Turtles? Grapefruit?" Fred asked.

"Nope. The payload's evolved."

"What about Apollo? Isn't that what it's for?"

"Apollo will get us to the Moon. But billions have been poured into NASA, and there is a high risk that it will be crippled in a nuclear exchange, allowing the Soviets to reach and dominate the Moon first. That would be a catastrophic outcome, setting us back years in the worst-case scenario, even if it were possible to catch up and regain parity. You all remember how close we came to annihilation in Korea against the communists from the north. And that wasn't even against the might of the Soviet Union. The stakes are high, and regaining a competitive position in space will not be easy. It may not be possible at all. We can't be second, not to a totalitarian regime, gentlemen.

"So we are setting up a Special Operations unit. It's a contingency in case things go wrong. As you can probably imagine, in the next fifteen or twenty years, we expect to be going to the Moon and all over the solar system, and whatever happens, it's going to take more than just a small handful of trained, experienced, capable pilots like those selected as the main NASA crew.

"Another launch site will be built, and you will be the backup. Some of you may even go on to the Apollo program, but that's another matter and remains to be seen. By the time you're called up, you'll have had all the preparation necessary for whatever eventuality we may face."

CHAPTER 5 - RACE

A moment later

"You'll train alongside the NASA crew," Chris continued. "You'll develop systems and missions and prepare to go to space. To get a feel for it, you'll meet the others who will also be invited to Special Ops at the Cape Air Force Station later today. The second launch site is still on the drawing board. You'll also meet a selection committee in about three weeks."

Jim had a question and ventured first. "But what do we do if people ask? What can we say?"

Fred and Tom were obviously thinking the same thing and looked eager for the answer.

"Avoid talking about it. There won't be any press. It's strict secrecy. You will not be announced to the public; just like the Soviets behind their Iron Curtain. NASA's Gemini and Apollo may be the show of the century, but you won't be in the public eye."

"But people inside NASA will want to know what we're doing."

"You'll be in Development Engineering, identified as the Flight Operations Design and Test unit. You'll have your own office at Langley and, for now, at the Mercury Control Center at Cape Air Force Station, where we're going."

"And what is NASA's plan?" Tom asked.

"Well, you heard the president announce our intentions to get to the Moon by the end of the decade. The first missions are being planned and details will be announced in the next few months. But everything is still in development and you'll be part of that journey from the beginning."

Chris took a sip of water and continued. "You can expect a few grueling months ahead, and if you pass the tests, you will spend the next few years working at NASA and other defense sites—planning, preparing, supporting, and training. Initially, most of your work will be at the Langley Research Center in Virginia until the new Manned Spacecraft Center in Houston opens, but you will also be assigned to the Mercury Control Center at Cape Air Force Station. That's where you'll train. There will be time at Vandenberg Air Force Base in California, so we are matching our capabilities. Gradually, you'll migrate to the Special Ops launch facilities to, one day, sit on top of the world's largest candlestick for the ride of your life. Oh, and you'll keep your military jets so you can get around more easily and without questions."

The trio looked silently mesmerized at the idea of what had just been pitched.

"Okay, now let's talk about you," Chris went on. "About what this unit is going to ask of you." His eyes pierced the men. "The answer is: probably everything you have to give. There will be no room for distraction. Nor complacency. Every day, every decision will count if we are to win this race. And the clock is ticking. You all know that better than anyone." He glanced around to make sure they understood. "But if you can't, you're free to go." He paused again, scanning for movement, but each of the three sat silently. "The door is right there." He pointed to the front exit. "Well, you're still here, so I'll take that as a yes."

They chuckled and Chris said there was a very good reason he'd chosen to brief on an airplane.

He continued, "You've had the good news. Now the bad." Jim gulped quietly.

"Medicals!" Chris paused to let the word sink in for a good long moment. And sure enough, the grown men each drew a sharp breath and tensed as their minds turned to past private humiliations at the hands of medics. "That will be the next two weeks in Albuquerque, New Mexico, after we get through this one. I'm told they're designed to be, er, comprehensive, shall we say. Apparently they don't miss a thing," he joked. "That's the first hurdle. But you've all been through that before in your military careers," he added with a shrug.

Fred lightened up again and turned to Tom. "A personal examination should be a small sacrifice for some."

Tom laughed and replied, "I just heard you speak for yourself, buddy!"

Jim chimed in. "I'm going to need an extra week for that!"

Chris brought the group back on point a second time. "And, I need hardly say, it's a risky business, and, that it's going to be tough. Grueling at times. You're all experienced military pilots, and you know what that means. Going into space could be a one-way ticket; there's no rescue party up there. You'll be flying covert missions. You might want to think about that before you meet the committee."

Jim saw Fred flinch subtly and wondered if it was the "tough" or the "grueling" that had gotten him. And what did that even mean? Jim sensed that an intense competition was about to brew for a spot on the unit.

Picking up the thread again, Chris added that there were more recruits. "Each of you will face the selection committee. You'll need to be clear about what you bring to the party, so think about it carefully over the next two weeks. They'll want to know that you and your families can handle several years of intense commitment and pressure in a covert operation. There could be enormous risks to your personal safety for the nation. But for all that, you could be one of America's first in space. How bad can that be?"

Chris finished, and despite his penchant for straight talk, Jim felt that he was genuinely pleased to meet the men.

"So, coffee anyone?" Chris asked, sounding as if he'd finished. "Oh, and there's something here you might want to take a look at." He pulled a memo from the Democratic Policy Committee out of his pile of papers and handed it to Fred, who sat closest.

Jim saw the title: *The Russians have left Earth and the race for control of the universe has started.*

"Here's another." Chris handed Jim a *Life* magazine dated *August 24, 1962*, with a picture of a Soviet rocket racing into orbit. The headline read: *Russia's Feat: where it leaves us in the race to the Moon.*

"It's a fascinating read," Chris added. "We've got a couple of hours, so have a look and get to know each other. You'll be buddies to start with, and you might even find yourselves together as a crew at some point. There's more reading here when you're done, and of course you'll get everything else you need at the Cape along with the other candidates."

A short while later, Jim was still in his luxurious wide leather seat, reading the briefing papers. He glanced out the window and saw the sky had taken on a pinkish-blue haze as the plane's wingtip lights pulsed halos against the thin pervasive cloud. It gave him the impression of a featureless dream world outside. His mind returned to the commitment and competition ahead as his head bounced from one idea to the next, thinking that each of these men would pull out the stops to get a spot. And there would be only one chance. It was now or never. And what about Mars someday? Or the solar system beyond? It seemed like science fiction. And how on earth was he going to keep his work a secret? Should he do it at all, when an all-out war was about to break out on Earth anyway? What would JoAnn think of it? He had to tell her, but not on the phone. Would she also be questioned about her ability to keep a secret? "Tell me about a time when you kept a really big secret," he imagined a suit in an office asking her. Could she do it?

Tom came over and interrupted his thoughts. "Wow, incredible!"

Jim looked up again and rose to his feet, then turned to see Chris buried in his papers again, a few seats away.

"No kidding," Fred replied just behind Tom. They high-fived in a ritualistic style, no doubt born at the Skunkworks.

"A shot at space, hey? And maybe the Moon, if the Soviets don't crash the party. What do you say, Jim?" Tom asked.

"Yeah, wow. I'm kind of speechless to tell you the truth. Probably a good thing it's all under wraps," Jim replied. "Can you imagine trying to explain any of this?"

"Who would have guessed, huh?"

Jim sat down and looked out the window again, back at the full Moon, now floating in the hazy pink sky. "Well, there she is," he said, trying to imagine what it would be like up there. His brain simply had nothing to go on, though oddly, pools of stringy cheese came to mind along with a giant rabbit from some fable he'd read as a child.

And intrigued by the whole idea, they all now seemed eager to get onto whatever stage it would play out on. For the next hour or so, they took the opportunity to share their stories (and size up each other), wheeling in notable career moments to establish some sort crude credentials.

Jim went first. He recounted how his life had changed when a uniformed Air Force officer and chaplain showed at his door one day to express deep regret that his father, Lieutenant Commander Cobb, was missing in action and presumed dead. His mother insisted that the Communists must have captured him, although he was never found or returned. He explained that his father had been one of the last of the Army Air Corp to return from the war in Europe. But he'd barely stepped in the front door at home when they sent him to keep an eye on the Communists from bases in Japan.

From that moment on, Jim said it was his life's mission to continue his father's work wherever it took him. He'd signed up for the Navy's Holloway Plan, which they all joked was where students were indeed "hauled away". The plan gave him two years of college, paid for by the Navy. He transferred to the Reserves and learned to fly at Pensacola. Then it was three years as a pilot, followed by two more years as a reservist. He'd hoped that maybe, somehow, he'd find out what had really happened to his father from the inside while he got his own back, but it didn't happen.

The trio swapped stories of training and joked about the screaming Lieutenant clones that showed up on every campus during those years. Jim recalled the copious amounts of water he'd swallowed in the pool, then outside, when they were herded toward the ocean and lined up to dive in. The infamous Dilbert Dunker was not forgotten, nor was aerobatics training, which involved a lot of vomiting. Jim recalled once taking up toilet rolls to mop the puke; then throwing them out of the plane as streamers to fly into just for fun.

Then came the Korean war. Jim recounted the day he was shot down behind enemy lines. He said he'd shared his story with Neil Armstrong, who had also been shot out of the sky in Korea and escaped. He was now in the Gemini program. The UN pulled out of Korea and he returned home feeling that he'd struck back at the Reds for the loss of his father and had somehow managed to survive. Eventually, after Korea, he became an engineer and continued to fight them in any way the Navy wanted.

Fred went next, starting all the way back at his early days as a Boy Scout. He went on to electrical engineering then to the United States Air Force as a Second Lieutenant. He'd spent years intercepting Soviet bombers over the northern hemisphere, but returned to a post in Burbank, California, where he'd first met Tom. He didn't say what he was doing there, and it didn't surprise Jim that the word Skunkworks wasn't mentioned at all.

Tom, too, said he had been an Army Air Forces cadet and had flown sixty-seven missions with the 340th Bombardment Group during the war in Europe. He was an instructor at the time, but when he said the Air Force had sent him to college to study aeronautical engineering, all three wondered how they'd never met before with such remarkably similar histories and ambitions. College led Tom to a stint as a test pilot. Then it was Burbank for him too.

All three clicked immediately, as if cut from the same cloth. But Jim knew there would be a lot of jockeying and one-upmanship to come. He decided to play his best game and try to have some fun, no matter how far he got along the way. That is, if he made it past the *anal panel,* as they called it, followed by the selection panel right after that.

CHAPTER 6 - THE EDGE OF THE WORLD

The same day, Cape Canaveral

The ramp at the Cape's Patrick Air Force Base was a hive of activity when the Gulfstream finally pulled in. Jets of all sizes were parked everywhere, big and small, slow and fast, while others came and went, ground vehicles scurrying to and fro between them. Jim stepped out of the plane and immediately perked up at the smell of avgas as if it were his caffeine.

"Looks like the other guys are arriving, too," Chris said, glancing around and squinting into the sun as they disembarked and walked across the tarmac. "They're coming in from all over the country. Twenty of them."

Jim saw that they'd landed in a remote coastal area of Florida, flat and green with low shrubs dotting the landscape, dissected by chalky white roads and paths interspersed with small industrial buildings. Situated among an array of square and circular rocket launch pads, some of the buildings had satellite dishes pointed up into the clear blue sky, as if communicating with distant galaxies.

They made their way to the Mercury Control Center for the day's agenda, entering a large hangar with a few smaller aircraft parked inside. The first order of business would be a whistle-stop tour of the launch facilities a few miles away; Chris had said that the visit was all about, "making it real."

Jim met the other Special Ops candidates in a conference room inside Building 1385 and saw that they were all military men too. Some were from the Air Force, some from the Navy, and others from the Marine Corps judging by their uniforms. A few the shoulder patches read Vandenberg Air Force Base and others were from the Mercury and Gemini space programs. Tom and Fred wore Reconnaissance on their shoulders.

"Here, gentlemen, is where Project Mercury and Gemini took off, and where Apollo will follow," Chris said. "The pads are just a few miles that way," he added, pointing along the Atlantic coast.

"Atlas rockets go up every month, and the Saturn V rocket, that will take us to the Moon by the end of the decade, will launch from what will be called Launch Complex 39A. The north side, over there," he pointed and continued, "will host the Vehicle Assembly Building, and it will be the largest single-story building in the world. He paused, then added, "I think they should have called it the Very Big Building. It will be huge. Large enough to house a Moon rocket. A track about four miles long will lead out to the launch pads on the shore over there. And a platform with the rocket on top will move at about a mile an hour after assembly inside that VAB. This place is going to be very, very big and construction is ramping up. A similar launch facility will be commissioned at a new site on the West Coast."

They were transported over to one of the pads, which was as huge as the Atlas rocket sitting on it. Jim guessed it was a modified ICBM ballistic missile that had probably started life at Vandenberg with a nuclear payload on top instead of seats for humans.

"This one goes up in two days. It's going to be fueled tomorrow and then burn a million gallons of gas in a couple of minutes," Chris explained. "You can see that it's quietly waiting to fulfill its short and singular purpose in life of reaching for the stars.

"And what about First Class? Well, that's the little capsule up there. Pretty much everything else is just a giant barge of fuel. Your teeth, your hair, and every bone in your body will rattle when a rocket like that goes up. And that's from three miles away."

"The first time my lady saw a rocket like that, she said she knew it had my name on it," joked one of the men within earshot of Jim.

"I hope they remember to change the trajectory of those missiles," said another voice behind him.

Jim recognized the gruff, solid tone immediately, but couldn't place it.

The man added, "I don't feel like dropping in on a one-way state visit to Moscow."

The other guys laughed, then another said, "We'll have to point out the window at the stars when we take off. The guys in mission control will forget there are people up there."

The gruff voice spoke to Jim after another chuckle. "Korea? Fifty-three?"

Jim was startled. He recognized the tone immediately and stopped to think. "Skyraider? Able Dog? From the … Rusty Bucket?" It was the same voice he'd heard on the radio calling for help during a dogfight over Korea, just moments before he was shot out of the sky behind enemy lines. He'd just told Tom and Fred about it on the plane, and now he stood there in utter astonishment.

"Yes. Chuck Moore. It's been a while, hasn't it? I never got a chance to thank you for getting me out of that jam."

"Oh boy, I took one in the ass for you guys that day! I got to see a little bit of the country and I can tell you it was unforgettable!"

Jim found Chuck Moore to be not only one of the older candidates, but also a true military specimen if ever there was one; lean, muscular, action man type and close cut. His tone was even, terse, controlled, and direct.

"Some of us supported the early space missions from the ground," Chuck said. "And we're being selected for this new unit."

"What exactly is that?"

"They're testing pilots for covert operations. You never know what the Soviets are up to up there. We have to be prepared for nasty surprises. NASA officials are confident they can move on to the next phase after Glenn's orbital flight in February."

"The world's just turning upside down right now, isn't it? And boy, is it going to be a monumental challenge to get to the Moon, even if we get there with all that's going on with the Soviets right now," remarked another candidate.

"It's probably safer up there than down here," another quipped as the jockeying continued.

"All we've done so far is spend a few hours in Earth orbit. Now they want to leave Earth for days, maybe a week. That's a huge step. I don't think we have the equipment or anything else to live up there yet."

"Well, the Soviets seem to be doing all right. What about this Gagarin fella?"

"Dogs, satellites, and who knows what's next."

"I think the president needs space more than anything. A great escape, huh? Winning up there might solve some problems down here."

"He has to do something. It must be difficult with his girlfriend, Marilyn, taking her life. He's in a tight spot. Maybe he wants to jump on a rocket and leave all his troubles behind. That's what I would do if I were him."

"I suppose that's one way out." Jim half-laughed.

They walked on, but separated from the group's banter where Chuck headed for lighter waters. "You from around here?"

"Houston."

"Oh, same. Family?"

"No kids. Just me and JoAnn. She's away right now, but she'll be back this weekend."

"You holed up in the Holiday Inn here for the night?"

"Yeah."

"That's the regular place. Nice enough. You should come by one weekend and bring JoAnn. We can discuss a few things I had in mind—once the panel and the medics, and all that's done."

Jim was intrigued. Chuck seemed to know what he wanted. "Well, it's good to meet someone who knows how it works. I might need some advice on how to navigate my way through all this."

"You'll feel right at home, I'm sure. It's a good place."

They walked and talked for the next half hour. Jim got a clear view of the huge launch pads, lined up neatly like giant concrete crop circles along miles of swampy Florida coastline with a multitude of roads connecting them. Everything looked interplanetary in size, and the scale of it all screamed that this whole venture into space would be no trivial pursuit. The pads themselves housed towering red, crisscrossing gantries that seemed to reach for the sky. Acres of huge, echoing concrete ducts, as thick as nuclear bunkers, were sunk deep into the ground for escaping ignition gases from roaring engines. The equally gigantic Atlas stood patiently on one of the moon-sized platforms Chris had mentioned, pointing the way up and just waiting for someone to push the button. Jim imagined the ground beneath him trembling like a massive, chest shaking earthquake, while all the hearts in the area stopped to watch the candle unleash its hellish fire, sending huge, violent plumes of cloud for miles around.

At one point, with a clear line of sight in every direction, he felt like he was standing at the very edge of the world. Whether out to sea and across the mysterious horizon, or up into the vast empty expanse of blue sky, the place felt like a departure point to other worlds. His imagination untethered as he looked out, feeling a rare and deep sense of curiosity that was a million miles away from any mundane reality he'd ever had. This was the big picture. But he could hardly imagine what humanity would encounter up there, and what his role in it might be, if he ever got anywhere near the stratosphere. And what if it was all-out war with the Reds up there? The magnitude of it all seemed unimaginable and terrifying.

And if coming to the Cape first had been an act of persuasion on Chris' part, it had certainly worked. Jim felt reeled in, despite the obvious risk to his life of doing anything with rockets that still blew up as regularly as they worked.

CHAPTER 7 - THE PANEL

Two weeks later, mid-November, 1962

Jim's mind raced and bounced like a pinball during the next two weeks of medical tests. He discovered that they were just as humiliating as the first round at the Navy recruiting station many years before, although fortunately no bodily functions seemed to have deteriorated measurably in the intervening years—or so he was told.

And when it was over, Chris called him at home in Houston one night to tell him that he now had a chance at the selection panel if he wanted to continue. JoAnn was behind it, so Jim said he would.

He arrived at Langley early, dressed in his Navy uniform, and felt like he'd brought all the confidence he could muster to the panel. There was no fanfare. The room was an ordinary large meeting room with an oblong hodgepodge of tables pushed together in the center and basic office chairs scattered about. It could have been a high school classroom. Maybe, he thought, the billion-dollar budget didn't stretch far enough for administrative facilities, especially when they had a million tons of rocket fuel to burn instead.

A seat stood alone at the end, just for him, as if he were

about to enter the dock. He stopped next to it, facing a mixture of military uniforms and civilians sitting around the other side, and reminded himself to keep a cool head, to treat the panel as peers, and not to get ahead of himself. *No unnecessary deference. No yes men.*

The chairman, dressed in a gray suit and red tie, spoke first. "Thank you for joining us this morning. I'm Neil." It was a calm, friendly tone.

Maybe it wouldn't be a grilling after all, Jim hoped, though his legs still felt as if they were preparing to run as fast as they could in the opposite direction. He took a well-practiced deep breath and held it for a count of four.

The seat was offered. He sat down and released the tension with a shallow smile, feeling an immediate sense of calm. *That's it, smile away. Costs nothing.* He spoke his first words. "It's an honor to be here, sir."

The chairman looked down and began to flip through papers on his desk. "We've read about your impressive flying career, Jim. Preliminary physicals show you're in good health, though I see there's one thing the doctors want to take a closer look at. And," he continued, turning the page, "your family has a distinguished military background. No doubt you've been briefed on why you're here?" The man seemed to have ticked a few boxes in his head and paused for a moment before asking, "How do you feel about joining Special Operations?"

Jim had heard the question, but was momentarily distracted, his mind still on the curious one thing the doctors seemed to want to look at. They hadn't mentioned it to him. Did the panel have the right report? The chairman seemed to have let it go, so Jim refocused and said, "Well, sir, I'm very happy to be here. It will be a great opportunity to serve my country and it feels like a personal accomplishment too."

"It could also be a dangerous undertaking," another of the panelists said. "Why do you want to do this, Jim?"

"Well, sir, for the security of our people, for our future. That's my job. And the adventure, of course." Jim smiled at the thought. "We'll be exploring the rest of the solar system soon, and I'd like to be a part of that, if that's what's in store. Isn't that the spirit of adventure?" Jim's shoulders relaxed a bit. It seemed to have started well enough.

"Adventure? You want adventure?" interrupted one of the military men.

Jim stammered for a moment. "Sir, I'm all for security. I lost my father to the Soviets. But in space we will undoubtedly find, er, discover something of our place in the universe when we leave Earth."

"That could be a problem, don't you think?" the chairman remarked. "How would the world take it if there was something else to discover besides our gracious God? Is that something we should know about?"

"Sir, I understand that not everyone is open to new truths. I know that. But if that's the case, I think it's ultimately inevitable for humanity. Exploration is what we do to find the truth." Jim's temperature suddenly spiked and he knew the questions were taking him dangerously off track. He told himself not to say anything stupid like that again and took another deep breath. He had to get back on track.

"It's avoidable," a civilian panel member added firmly. "It's not our job to figure out where we fit into some big picture. Our job is to protect our own little piece of it, so that everything keeps ticking along just as it always has for another eon or two, even three. Against communism and the threat of tyranny. Don't you agree?"

The momentary silence was deafening to Jim's ears. Damn it, he thought. He'd lost his way.

"So, what do you bring to the table, Jim?" the chairman asked.

"Sir, I think my flying career speaks for itself. Piloting spacecraft requires new systems and approaches and experience with flying machines; cramped, little flying machines." Jim smiled. "I've trained and flown in the most difficult conditions for many years, sir."

The chairman looked at him intently and acknowledged the answer before turning to the table to confirm something. "Yes, and that is why you are here. I see you've been assigned to work with NASA's Flight Procedures Group, here on the schedule."

"Yes, sir. That sounds right."

"And one of the teams has requested that you assist in the development of environmental systems as well?"

Jim shifted in his seat. That would be Chuck and his spacesuits. He'd mentioned them at the Cape. "Yes, sir. There's an idea from one of the units."

"Very good." The chairman took off his glasses and looked straight at him. "It's going to be tough, Jim. And all of our people are very strong, as you would expect. But for now, we wish you luck and strength in the further tests to come."

Jim acknowledged.

The chairman added, "Get through them all and we'll meet again in a few months. Is there anything you want to ask us?"

Let sleeping dogs lie. All Jim had to do now was get up and get out in one piece. He'd gotten the buy signal and the deal was done. "No, sir. Thank you."

The chairman ended the meeting quickly, leaving Jim a bit surprised at the suddenness. He looked around and wondered if it was just him today.

Over the next few days, he learned that two of the twenty had either decided not to continue or had failed the medicals, though Tom, Fred, and Chuck were all still in play. But he also knew that the rug could be pulled out from under him at any time without notice.

CHAPTER 8 - SPACEMAN

The following day, mid-November 1962

The bedroom at home was still dim with the dull light from outside when Jim woke at the crack of dawn to get ready for his first day. Chris had called again and said the panel had approved him right away. Jim had paused on the phone for a moment to think about his conversation with JoAnn. Although she was still impressed by the whole thing, other thoughts had entered her mind. Now she wanted to know if it was safe and if the world itself was any more secure against the Soviets who'd backed out of Cuba. She was worried about how they were going to start a family if he was going to be away so much. These were all good questions and he gave her a straight *yes* to everything which she returned. He'd summed that up into a *yes* to Chris, so he could seize the opportunity like the horns of a raging bull about to be released from the traps. Having served his term well, Jim would immediately resign his Navy commission and begin training at Langley.

He turned to see JoAnn still asleep when he woke up, still vividly remembering the end of his dream from a moment ago. He laid his head back down for a quick nap and dived back into the memory of meeting her at a local farm when they were teenagers and about to leave home for the first time to go to college. He'd probably still be there if he hadn't joined the Navy when the Korean War broke out. He wondered why this particular dream had surfaced and chalked it up to the previous weekend when they sifted old photos that had tumbled out of a box while they were finally clearing out the other bedroom to start decorating. The old days seemed infinitely simpler—the war in Europe was over and the world looked like it was waiting for them with open arms. He remembered being mesmerized by her lightness and poise as she approached along the road. Jim had been repairing farm machinery inside a hangar. He'd straightened his collar, then brushed his hair back several times with dirty fingers until they felt clean, still watching JoAnn's every step as she came to the doors. She looked over him and pulled away with a chuckle. He persuaded her to jump in the cab and start one of the farm machines he was fixing. The hangar filled with smoke as she turned the key, then she was in his arms on the way down. Her face softened and she kissed him gently on the lips for the first time. He took her home with a new spring in his step.

Jim came out of his dream feeling the love he had for her, opened his eyes and looked at the clock. It was five a.m. He got up and turned on a tall, sentinel-like table lamp. He went to the bathroom, cleaned up and began to dress in front of a large mirror opposite the bed and above a wide dresser. He glanced over his shoulder, first at the large print hanging above the headboard, then at JoAnn as she stirred. Dark brown furniture and bright orange curtains contrasted sharply with the pale walls. A white telephone sat by Jim's side, a framed photograph of the couple by JoAnn's. A single chair with a circular orange cushion sat at the end of the bed, and a few pillows were scattered on the floor.

"Hey, spaceman," JoAnn said, sitting up in bed, still half asleep. Jim was adjusting his tie in the mirror. "Do I have to greet you like that from now on?" She sounded playful.

Jim walked over to her, leaned forward and kissed her as he tied a cuff. "Yep," he half-whispered in the early hours, his face in hers. "I'm under strict orders to zap anyone with my ... well, my special edition ... light ... blaster." He laughed softly, unable to find the right words. "Just like a Triffid gun, which still needs inventing, of course."

He sat down on the edge of the bed beside her. "So, wish me luck on my first day?"

"You sound like you're going up there today," she toyed. "Don't they have to build a new rocket first and spin you round and round really fast or something?"

"I'll probably meet the other people who will no doubt tell me what to do and that everything will be fine. *Just sit still and keep your helmet on,*" he joked, fastening his second cuff. "I'm sure we'll argue about who sits up front. There'll be, oh, jockeying for position, some backstabbing maybe, a little undermining and so on, I imagine." He laughed it off. "Actually, I have no idea what they want me to do. I'll take it one day at a time."

"Is there a space class today? Shouldn't you know what's out there before you go? I'd like to know where they're sending you."

"Space, hey?" He stood up and went back to the mirror. "I'm sure we'll get to that. But I'm also sure there will be more testing, poking and prodding, shaking and twisting. You know what? I'm so glad this is all under wraps. No media.

NASA usually wants picture perfect astronauts and families," he added, turning to look at her with a raised eyebrow.

Her face turned serious. "Speaking of families, what are we going to do?"

He turned back to her. "Nothing has changed. If I can just find out what's going on with NASA, then we'll see if we can fill in the picture."

"So do you get to try on the spacesuit?" JoAnn asked. "You know, to see if it fits in all the right places? You're probably halfway there if you look the part."

"Let's see what happens. Anyway, have you thought about starting to write again? Will you use some time for that?"

"Yeah. Maybe," she said.

He looked at his watch. "Oh look, I have to go soon."

With a last fiddle of his hair in the mirror, he grabbed a jacket and pocketed a shiny silver Douglas DC-3 airplane lapel pin. His father had given it to him for luck after flying the workhorse during the war to support the Berlin Airlift against the Soviet blockade. "Maybe a haircut is in order. Did you say looks matter?"

JoAnn rolled her eyes. "Did I say that?"

Jim went downstairs to the living room and sat in a white swivel chair in front of the television in its wooden cabinet. The front door of the house was to his right and the wide staircase he'd just come down on his left.

He turned on the set and began flipping through the news channels. They were still reporting on the American pilot who had been downed over Cuba a few weeks earlier. Then came archival footage of warships, nuclear weapons, and malevolent looking Soviet soldiers marching on Red Square.

He reached over to the cabinet on his right and turned on

a table lamp just as JoAnn walked quietly down the stairs in her nightgown. She began arranging bright yellow flowers in a vase, though they were clearly in their dying days.

"I still can't believe what happened to that poor pilot," she said, listening to the TV. "People are upset about all the secret stuff going on. Should the CIA be spying like that?"

"The Communists want to take over the world. That would be a total nightmare."

"It's just asking for more trouble."

"The government has to protect our country. Everyone knows they kill and imprison their own, especially if they have a different faith or belief than the order. Think of the Nazis in Europe. It could be worse."

Jim flicked over again and got President John F. Kennedy, who, he recalled, had warned ominously of nuclear annihilation in his inaugural address in sixty-one. And now, just two months earlier in September, he'd announced the battle for space, likening it to a hostile theater of war and declaring that America would be the first to put a man on the Moon by the end of the decade.

Kennedy might be committed to the war on communism and the space race, but a stack of problems had begun to pile up on the new president's plate. He was making initial preparations to put America on the Moon against the Soviets, just as the CIA bungled an invasion of Soviet-backed Communist Cuba at the Bay of Pigs. He'd also gone to a summit in Vienna to sell Khrushchev on a joint space mission, but the Soviets were having none of it. Things really went south for the president when black activists, the Freedom Riders, intent on testing unconstitutional segregation, were severely beaten and their buses burned by whites in Alabama right under the nose of law enforcement in early May of sixty-one. Jim couldn't help but notice that all of this was in sharp contrast to Shepard's own incredible joy ride into space for the nation the very next day. Some had remarked that a seat on a modified ICBM into space was safer than the same on a state bus for anyone born the wrong color in their own country. Tensions continued to rise, and by January sixty-two, black students were arrested for sit-ins at the Huntsville restaurant where the rockets themselves were made, threatening to keep the entire new space program on the ground. The Soviets, meanwhile, stayed at work and continued their race to the heavens. To some, America seemed to be in a war for freedom against a tyranny at home just as much as it was anywhere else.

JoAnn left the room for the kitchen while Jim continued to flip through the channels. A woman in a long-sleeved sundress stood proudly in her kitchen, holding a plate of cookies in one hand and caressing her new stove with the other. Cheerful children ran onto the screen, followed hastily by their father, who smiled broadly as he pecked the woman's cheek. JoAnn had already argued that women should go into space, but Jim didn't think this lady looked anything like astronaut material—though she would no doubt be a welcome sight for any man lost in space. Even Kennedy, in an interview with Eleanor Roosevelt, had said that a woman's primary responsibility was the home.

Jim remembered the Popular Mechanics magazines he read as an early teenager. Back then, science and technology promised to take aim at the future with the idea of abundant free solar energy which would unshackle mankind from work forever. By the year two thousand, the magazine promised, life would be filled with leisure. Everyone would ride around on jetpacks. And the tyrannies of domesticity would be abolished. Not only would there be cheap housing for everyone, but furniture that could be hosed clean. There would be disintegrating plates. Even cooking would become a relic of the past. He was amused to read that sawdust and underpants would be turned into food. And, thankfully, the diseases of mankind would also be eradicated. All this and more would come just in time for peace on earth for all mankind. But all of that was merely a precursor to on-demand inter-stellar travel that would emancipate man from Earth's gravity. The possibilities and adventures of the future seemed endless at the time, and Jim's childhood ambition was to one day live on a lunar base with a flying rocket car. Now, that future didn't look quite like he'd once imagined.

He flicked over again, to a couple cruising through the California hills in a drop-top Corvette on a sunny day. Buy on credit, the adman urged. Jim was amazed that he could actually buy the car now and pay another day, and wondered for a moment if he should do just that. Everyone seemed to be buying everything they could lay their hands on.

He looked back at the clock on the wall and realized that he had lost track of time. It was just before six and already light outside. He turned off the TV, got up, grabbed his wallet and keys, and headed for the door.

"Don't you want breakfast?" JoAnn called from the kitchen. "I forgot to tell you, I'm on my way to see Eve in Detroit, if you call. She wants to talk about Ricky. He's not doing so well in school."

Jim walked back and poked his head around the kitchen door. "Sunday. I've arranged a barbecue for Sunday. Gotta

57

go."

JoAnn looked intrigued. "Oh, where?"

"Chuck Moore's." Jim disappeared.

CHAPTER 9 - ESCAPING GRAVITY

Moments later

JoAnn went back into the living room, opened the curtains, and heard Jim's car start up outside.

She watched him drive away, then headed upstairs, thinking she'd start organizing the old photos she'd put off for too long. She also needed to spend time figuring out how to be an astronaut's wife. Jim's work would be made clear to him in the coming days and weeks, but even they had not talked about what she was supposed to do. Maybe she'd just go along for now, until she met the other women and understood what it was all about. Her excitement about Jim's new job also felt mixed with an unexpected fear that she'd kept to herself. It had hit her, one night while trying to sleep, that rocket men played with fire.

Returning to the guest room, she took a large shoebox from the closet and sat on the bed. Under the lid were a hundred old photographs piled on top of a medium-sized album with swollen pages. She took it out slowly to avoid spilling it, set it down, and began to leaf through the contents.

The first few pages were photos of her and Jim in the year or so after their wedding. There were shots of day trips around

Texas, in lieu of the honeymoon they had postponed due to his busy work schedule. She turned another page and picked up a photo of her family on a picnic when she was about six, standing on the shore of a large lake, though she couldn't remember which. She and her older sister, Eve, were holding paper windmills in the breeze. The outing was her first exhilarating and frightening experience of swimming in open water.

It was not long after that day that she first noticed a change in her mother. A late-onset depression was periodic and mild at first. She would go quiet for days at a time, two or three times a year, though it became more frequent. The trigger was often an argument with JoAnn's father about his failing business and their lack of money; he didn't want a steady office job that would have given the family a more stable income and he'd get the cold shoulder for a week or more. Her mother finally saw a doctor when she began losing her appetite and weight. A daily prescription pill helped, but it seemed to JoAnn that a hollowness had appeared, as if her mother's cheerfulness had vanished. She spent her life at home going through the motions, and it was clear that she had stopped loving JoAnn's father. He finally got a cubicle job he didn't want and resented the treadmill life he was forced to live every day. They managed to coexist even though he turned to drink, trapped by life.

JoAnn flipped a few more pages of the album, stopping at pictures when she and Jim would have been about eighteen. The Korean War had just broken out and Jim had left home to join the Navy. He wrote at first, but his letters became less frequent during college, and she was heartbroken that he had forgotten her.

She'd moved on, too, marrying a civil rights professor from her college around the time Jim went off to war in fifty-three. It was her big chance to get away from home. He had promised to support her in becoming the journalist she'd always wanted to be. But it wasn't long before she realized she'd made a terrible mistake. Though she had tried, she knew she had never truly loved the man, nor he her. She began writing about her feelings to help unravel the trap she'd fallen into, and around the same time, she was already drafting small reports for the local press, fulfilling the dream she'd had since elementary school. Her idea was to shine a spotlight on society's injustices, starting with personal stories of women who felt trapped in their homes. She moved on to segregation, seeing that although the US had emerged strong after World War II, the new prosperity was far from equal across the nation. Black children had to endure segregated educational facilities. Violence and intimidation, not enforcement, were common against some minorities who wanted to express their rights.

JoAnn paused for a moment to consider where she'd put a letter she'd helped write for Dorothy, a friend and waitress at a local diner, expressing her grievances to the president the previous summer. She rifled through the photos in the box, certain she'd saved a draft, and fished out a small, dog-eared scrap of paper with penciled notes and a lot of crossing out.

Dear Mr. President,

Sending Americans to space is important to you. But I do hope you won't leave some of us behind and forget your people here on Earth.

61

For the second year now, I've applied for college outside of the segregated school system in my neighborhood. But, despite good performances, I, like others, received two rejections because the dormitories were said to be full. I am saddened that they continue to decline my application each year.

Like you, sir, all I want is freedom. Mine is the freedom to an education in my own country. I'd like to be an astronaut too, like the Mercury ladies. It is a shame that NASA will not take women to space.

I hope, in your own words, and with the stroke of this pen, you will free us from discrimination, as you once promised.

Sincerely, Dorothy

As far as JoAnn knew, Dorothy had not received a reply.

And sitting here now, the reference to space in that letter seemed like an uncanny coincidence with Jim's new role at NASA.

Her thoughts turned to the Mercury Thirteen women who had lobbied Congress for a chance at the moonshot Kennedy had announced in September. The press had proclaimed that women wanted their place in space, but the men at NASA had shut them out. One of the Mercury Thirteen, Jerri Cobb, had been on television. A young male interviewer had naively asked her why there was a need for women in space, after she had just said that the Soviets were about to put a lady into orbit. Cobb, wearing a plaid shirt, blond close-cropped hair and large white earrings, asked why men were needed in space, to which the young man had no answer. Another reporter later undermined Cobb in public, questioning her role as a mother who chose to go into space and leave her children behind. It still infuriated JoAnn, and she began to feel hot and bothered just thinking about it. Breaking free of society's norms promised to be harder than escaping gravity itself.

She took a deep breath, put the letter back in the box, and thought about what she had written. It had been her sanity's savior during her difficult first marriage, and it pained her again that her first husband had never done anything meaningful to help. Instead, she'd found him in a college lecture hall, his face half-buried inside a graduate student lying on a desk with her skirt up.

She turned a few more pages in the album and remembered returning home to her parents, feeling like a failure. She spent more and more time there, trying to figure out how to divorce the man before they actually separated.

Then Jim showed up again. She remembered him in a white-and-blue striped shirt, and recalled thinking he was sick and needed a bed when he visited her at the hospital where she was a nursing aide.

It was like old friends talking for the first time in years, about college, about work, about how their parents sabotaged their chances of getting together, and about her moving back home. It was not long after that, that they got married in the little church where they were baptized.

She stopped at a photo of her and Jim on their wedding day, resurfaced, and took a deep breath after sorting through very little of the pile. She felt frustrated that they'd been trying for a baby for almost a year now. What was she going to do while Jim was at Langley or in space or wherever they sent him every week? He might not be home at all, she knew that much. But how long could she be alone, doing very little? It could be years. And what if one day he simply didn't come home from some terrible accident? It happened. Then what? She knew she had to find a way to start writing again, just like Jim had said, or she might disappear in the shadows.

Putting the box away for another time, she went back to her room and got ready for the day.

CHAPTER 10 - BBQ

Late-November 1962

After visiting her sister Eve, JoAnn arrived in Ellington, Texas, on Sunday morning and met Jim on the tarmac next to the military transport that had brought her in from Detroit. It was a balmy seventy-three and almost certainly the last unexpected gift of summer. She'd come in a sleeveless, knee-length white and green floral dress that hugged her slender frame, with light-colored flats to match. Her shoulder-length chestnut hair was held back by shades on her forehead.

Jim's face was relaxed and his eyes warmed like the sun the moment he saw her. She glowed, too, and quickly looked up and down at his red short sleeves with white buttons (which he'd gotten for his birthday), beige pants, and dark shoes.

She gave him a long hug, then leaned back slightly and glanced up a foot and a half at his hair. "What's that?" she asked with a grin, stroking the back of his head. "Smooth as a robin. Nice."

"Well, it's kind of warm out here, so I wanted a close cut." She gave him another bright smile.

"I have to look the part, like you said. Instinct—I need to appeal to instinct," he added.

JoAnn looked surprised. "You thought of that?"

"Well, not quite. The barber was an interesting guy. Had a lot to say. Anyway, I just thought you'd like it," he replied.

They continued through the hangar to the parking lot where JoAnn stopped in surprise, "And a nice car to go with it, I see." She walked over to the drop-top and ran her hand over the smooth paint. "Where did you get this?"

"Corvette. It's great, don't you think? Even has air-con."

She looked genuinely impressed for a moment, then her eyes pressed the question.

"It was the rental company. I said I'd started over at NASA and they upgraded me. Just like that, they said I looked like an astronaut or something. It was after the haircut." He rolled his eyes and shrugged. "All I have to do is mention their first-class service, so I figured, why not?" He dropped her luggage into the back seat and jumped in over the side. "Ta-da! Try it."

"No, no, I can't. Not in this," she protested, tugging at her tight skirt and glancing around for onlookers.

"It's not that high. You'll be fine," Jim replied, turning back to the terminal. "Come on, no one's watching," he added with a cheeky grin.

She stopped, eyebrows raised, then slowly slid over to the passenger side and landed on the seat with a bump and a childish giggle. She leaned over and planted a kiss on him. With another chuckle and a squeal of tires, Jim sent them down the road in the slinky new Corvette toward Chuck's.

Talking over the road noise and holding her hair back from the wind, JoAnn asked about the Cape in Florida and whether or not they'd have to move.

Jim said it had a great beach and a huge launch site and

was a real hive of activity, but explained that most of his work would still be around Langley for now. At some point in the not-too-distant future, he'd be able to work at a new facility in Houston that controlled missions and training and much more. He'd also have to spend time in Albuquerque and Vandenberg on the West Coast, as well as at the Cape. Home would remain in Houston for now; some of the space families were already in Timber Cove and El Lago. They talked about making a second attempt at the honeymoon they hadn't managed the first time. Jim said he'd look at the new schedule and see what was possible. JoAnn had heard that before.

Chuck's rather modest ranch-style suburban home had a medium-sized backyard, half of which was taken up by an oval-shaped swimming pool in the middle. The living room of the house opened onto the backyard with floor to ceiling white louvered windows and wide open French doors in the center.

The sun was out, and some of the men were wearing brightly colored short sleeves, just like Jim, while the women were in equally bright capris and short sundresses. Couples lounged around the diving board and a few wandered in and out of the kitchen. Jim guessed they were all Chuck's space buddies, with probably a family member or two and maybe some neighbors in there somewhere too.

Chuck, wearing an apron and on barbecue duty, stood a quarter of the way around the pool from the kitchen next to a waist-high green hedge.

"Jim, it's good to see you. Glad you could make it," he said. "And good timing. Would you mind helping me with this?" He handed Jim an empty food tray. "I was just going to the

67

kitchen to get some more. Oh, and you must be JoAnn." He put down his utensils and gave her a peck. "Come on in and meet Peggy. I'll introduce you both."

The kitchen, with its pale green units, opened up to the living room, which was recessed into the floor and decorated mostly in white and gray. Several accent lights brightened the corners and edges.

"Peg, honey, come here a minute. This is Jim and JoAnn."

They greeted each other, then Chuck and Jim left the girls and went back outside with more food.

"How did you like visiting the Cape?" Jim asked back at the grill.

"It was good to be down there and see everything. I actually stayed behind to look around," Chuck said. "We're thinking about buying something out there. Optimism is high right now and the economy is looking up. It's easy to get credit, and you never know, space tourism might actually become a reality in our lifetime. It's going to drive investment. Everyone will take a space vacation some day."

"You sound pretty confident," Jim said, picking at the food while Chuck cooked. "You'd need a lot of money."

"There's plenty of that around. Anyway, what did you think of the panel?" Chuck asked. They hadn't seen each other since their meetings.

"I just went in with an open mind. It was hard to know what the right answers would be. But they seemed to buy whatever I said."

"One of the things they'll continue to look for, I'm told, is a stable home life. They don't want people worrying about the plumbing or school schedules when they're developing, testing, and operating a billion dollars worth of space equipment.

Looks like you and JoAnn are good."

Clouds of smoke rose as Chuck seared meat on the grill.

"Well, yeah. It's simple really—no kids, no strife at the moment."

"They'll be trying to figure out what you're good at. What you're *great* at. What you can do for Special Ops. I've looked into life support and space suits, as you know. Any idea what you want to do?"

"Flight and navigation systems, I guess."

"Well, I heard they just made the big decision on Lunar Orbit Rendezvous."

Jim looked puzzled.

"The plan is to land on the Moon with one spacecraft in lunar orbit while another goes down to the surface. No more one big rocket all the way there. Sounds like that's your bag if you can get on the development team."

"I would love to take a ship out of Earth orbit and into space! I can't believe I'm saying that. But, what's up with the Soviets? Defense?"

"We hear they're looking at a system to get some kind of nuclear advantage in space. And they're about to put three men on a flight after the two Vostok's did two at once. They're obviously preparing for the Moon as well. Their N1 rocket requires a crew of three, now that one is going all the way there instead of breaking up in Earth orbit first. One man stays in lunar orbit and two go down to the surface. That's what we're planning too."

"Where do we get all this intelligence?"

"They must have plants. Soviets defect. I read about a couple this year. A physicist or something in London and a couple in Berlin. They must be getting treats for information.

"Well, look, anyway, here's something to get you started, settle you in, and get you going. I could have used something like this when I began. Why don't you work with me to develop environmental support systems first? That's space-suits in English. You'll get up to speed quickly, and once you know what's what, you can decide what's best."

Jim listened but held his tongue. Chuck spiced up the meat again.

"A small company in Baltimore, funded by Langley, has proposed underwater training for working outside a space-craft. They simulate reduced gravity." He turned the food to the fire.

"Isn't there an airplane for that sort of thing?"

"Yes. Falling from the sky is good, but only for short periods between all the ups and downs. But with this new idea you can train for hours. We'll give it a try and report back. What do you think?"

"Sure, sounds interesting. But I'm curious—what if something leaks?"

Chuck chuckled. "I met them for a briefing, and they said they had some interesting moments in the water. He shook his head and laughed. "Imagine, a man going into space drowns at the bottom of a pool. That would be a good one."

"Is that what we consider ourselves?"

"Yeah. We have to work and train as if we're ready for any eventuality. We're preparing for missions on the West Coast."

"And if that eventuality doesn't come?"

"Oh, it will. Space is the new frontier. Our solar system is a big place. We may not be on Apollo, but I'd say we could be on Mars, right behind it. There'll be plenty to keep us all busy."

Peggy and JoAnn poured drinks in the kitchen.

"Chuck and I would probably never see each other if we hadn't moved here. It's not a marriage if we're not together, don't you think?" Peggy said, patting her beehive, the style that was all the rage at the moment.

JoAnn quietly pondered her own thoughts about Jim when she noticed a familiar book on the kitchen counter, *The Navy Wife* by Anne Briscow Pye & Nancy Shea. So that's what Peggy was all about—providing a good home, raising children, and making Chuck proud whenever he walked into a spartan house. JoAnn could do that, but she just needed some children. She flicked her eyes back to Peggy.

"Besides, it's all too easy for the cookies to move in when no one's keeping an eye out." Peggy gave her a knowing look. "I've seen it all slip away. Guys get the itch when temptation's literally knocking on the door, looking for military aces working at NASA buildings. Then BAM! It's a slippery slope right down to the rocks."

JoAnn forced out a thin smile.

"Oh, I didn't want to worry you, honey. I'm sure Jim's a good man. Besides, it's a nice neighborhood. There's a lot of NASA families here."

"They don't live on the Cape?" JoAnn asked as they walked back outside.

"No. That's just where the rockets go up. Most of them are in Houston now. Some moved from Langley. But others live all over. The guys just fly to work during the week and come home on the weekends. See those guys over there?" Peggy pointed. "They're from Houston, too. Those over there, New Jersey. Those, Virginia. All over. Weekend parties and get-togethers are common for people who work here. The community's hard-working and pretty tight-knit."

JoAnn saw another set of beehives reaching for the stars and said, "I don't see a lot of kids."

"Some of them just aren't here today. Some couples are either too young or too insecure to raise children when all this is starting up. But I know that some of the girls need their own now. They just don't know what else to do with themselves. Are you planning a family?"

JoAnn took a deep breath and smiled shallowly. "Trying."

"Well, some of us took a home decorating class, and that's how I fixed up this place. You should give it a try when you find out where you're going to be."

"You didn't want to work?"

"Oh, honey. I wanted to go to college after high school, but my mother said girls should have an M-R-S, not an MSc." Peggy rolled her eyes. "So it's taking care of the house for me. Chuck doesn't have time." She confided in a half-whisper as they approached Peggy's friends, "Some of the girls are a little closed off sometimes. They try to be strong for their partners, but they're really just as competitive as their men," she joked softly. "So watch out."

JoAnn remained relaxed as they walked out. She began to mingle as Be My Baby, a hot favorite by the Ronettes, played on speakers in the background. She was invited to get-togethers at the yacht club, the golf course, and the homes of other astro-wives. Sharing recipes and decorating tips seemed to be a favorite pastime in between raising kids.

Chuck turned down the music and tapped the side of the grill with his tongs. The crowd returned a friendly boo and laugh as he threw up his hands. "Okay, okay. I'm sorry, folks." He raised a glass. "Colleagues, friends, I want to toast us all for this amazing opportunity." The crowd cheered. "And I want to welcome the newcomers to the party."

An even louder cheer went up. JoAnn and Jim looked at each other, both utterly delighted.

"Welcome to all of you," Chuck added. "Now, please, raise your glasses for the best part. Lunch is now served and everything is right here."

With another cheer, everyone rushed to their plates, and for the next few hours, Jim and JoAnn mingled with the rest of the party, sharing hopes, dreams and backgrounds.

Eventually, the sun settled on the horizon and JoAnn sat on the lawn, drunk and draped over Jim. They watched the sunset while he picked at blades of grass.

"So what do you think?" he asked. "He's quite a man, don't you think? Clever too, and already tried to rope me into something." Jim laughed and rolled over on top of her. "I'd better be careful," he added, pretending to be serious.

"They seem like nice people." JoAnn's words turned to a giggle as she pushed Jim onto his back and lay on his chest. She turned around to see a few stars already glimmering in the sky.

Jim also looked up and said, "I wonder what's out there? Aliens with big tentacles?" He laughed again.

"You mean the Hollywood type?"

"Yeah. Maybe something new they can put on screen."

JoAnn stopped and looked at him as his eyes scanned the sky.

"The Cape has got my head going. Is there some unpalatable truth out there? And where does it all end? Or begin ... if it begins and ends at all?"

She took his hand and placed it on her chest. "Right here," she said, beaming at him.

They giggled as Jim tried to roll over again, though it was clumsy.

His eyes returned to the sunset. "You know, Chuck's had a year's head start; he's got all the inside knowledge and so on. And that kind of advantage stays unless something changes. And now he wants me to work with him ... for him, maybe, to test *his* suits." Jim sat up. "Which means playing second fiddle to him, if I'm not mistaken."

JoAnn reached up and kissed him. "Does that bother you? Oh, come on. It's just the way you look at it. You guys are too competitive. You say we girls are complex. Now relax and enjoy the moment."

"I need to be flying, not drowning in a pool somewhere," he added with a chuckle. "I did enough of that in Navy school."

"You're scared of water."

"I'm not scared of water."

JoAnn laughed. "You're scared of water."

"Okay, so I'm scared of water."

Jim laughed back and they rolled over each other on the grass.

"I've been thinking. Why don't we ..." JoAnn looked up at him again, just as his eyes wandered to one of the short skirts at the far end of the pool. She pulled his face back. "I was going to say, lets just have a little celebration now. But promise me you won't forget us."

Jim looked deep into her eyes. "JoAnn, you're everything to me. You always have been. Even when you didn't know it."

She half-laughed and kissed him. "Now let's go dance."

"Who me?" Jim replied. He rolled back onto the lawn with a swig of beer. "I can't dance. I've had one too many of these. I can't get up." He held up the half-empty Miller and looked her in the eye. "But you know what? I'd still fall for you even if there was no gravity."

They giggled like children then JoAnn pulled him awkwardly to his feet. "Come on, up you get. We still have to get you into space."

CHAPTER 11 - DUNKING

December 1962

Sure enough, and as forewarned, the exhaustive and often humiliating battery of physical and mental tests began for Jim. Lovelace's cheerful doctors in Albuquerque left no stone unturned, just as the chairman of the selection panel and Chris had hinted. Over the next few weeks, Jim's blood, urine, heart, balance, and other bodily functions were measured. He received psychological and personality tests for imagination, memory, comprehension, and perception. Endless x-rays and general body physicals, inside every orifice known to mankind, left nothing hidden. Ice water was shot into his ears to freeze the inside and induce dizziness, then they just waited to see how quickly he recovered from the ordeal. This was after he'd already been pushed to exhaustion on exercise machines to test his endurance. They said the results would be used to design difficult missions, to which Jim replied that space travel would have to get a lot simpler if real people were to be involved.

A few weeks later, he walked with Chuck from the locker room to a deep blue pool near Ellington Air Force Base in Houston, still itching bald patches waxed onto his chest for the various machines they'd hooked him up to. Today, they'd try out and report back on the potential for underwater training. NASA chiefs were still skeptical, but said the new guys in Special Ops could do the evaluation, so they could keep their precious Gemini crews safe.

"Did you have to do all that testing?" Jim asked as they left.

Chuck remembered with a smile. "Yeah, about a year ago. But, I think they've found a whole lot more to look at since then."

"They must have drilled a new hole or two where the sun don't shine."

They snickered like adolescent jocks, then Chuck said, "That was just phase one, buddy. There's way more fun ahead. Anyway, come diving in the sea with us on the weekend. The doctors don't follow us down there."

"And what about the high-altitude ejection seat? You had that too?"

Chuck grinned. "They say your spine can afford to lose an inch or two. I'll bet they just want to squeeze in a little more astronaut in each capsule to get their money's worth. Anyway, that's the least of your worries right now," Chuck confided with a grin. "You're about to meet Hans."

They arrived at the poolside where suit technicians were waiting to outfit them in silver Mark IV Arrowhead pressure suits, which were modified versions of a Navy suit worn by the Mercury astronauts. Divers from NASA's Lift Systems Division were already in the water.

As they prepared, Hans, one of the technicians, did all the talking and spoke with a dry Germanic humor. It was his job to manage the work to research and demonstrate the potential for underwater training with the modifications.

"These suits, you know, just have to work. They must be pressure tight. There's no room for error. A leak, no matter how small, will be fatal up there in an instant." He paused for a moment while he worked systematically on Chuck's suit with precision and deliberation.

Jim glanced around the huge enclosure at the rigs and test equipment while another technician worked on him. Everything was packed tightly above and around a huge pool in the center of the floor, its edges marked with yellow lines for moving equipment. The water itself looked like a deep well of crystal clear blue, with an ominously large curved white rocket section that looked as if it had sunk below the surface. Tall diving boards stood at the far end, and he guessed the water must have been twenty or thirty feet deep.

Hans continued. "So how are we going to find these tiny little air gaps? Well, we're going to put you two lucky guys on the bottom of that deep water over there." A wry grin appeared. Jim followed his eyes to the temperature gauge on the wall. "Oh, lucky today. It's a tropical seventy-five. You good?" he asked.

"Sure," Chuck replied. "Jim?"

"Let's do it."

"Don't look so worried, Jim," Hans reassured him with a wide smile. "We'll pull you out if there's a problem."

"Aha. Thank you. Probably good if we come back alive to report," Jim joked, thinking about the bends and the need to surface and decompress quickly if there was a problem. His thoughts were interrupted by a siren echoing around the enclosure.

"Okay, last piece. These," Hans pointed to lead weight belts on the floor, "will hold you under."

Jim felt like an extra child had been strapped onto his suit, and found it difficult to stand up straight as he put on his belt with the help of the technicians.

"You ready to go?" Hans asked. "We'll start with the basic tasks. Walking and using the tools. Find your balance first and set your buoyancy." He held out his hand to Jim. "It's nice to meet you, no?"

Jim chuckled and shook it, and Hans patted him on the shoulder. He and Chuck put on their helmets and gloves and the suits were pressurized to around three and a half pounds above water pressure.

Hans had already disappeared into a balcony office on the first floor overlooking the pool. "Okay. You ready?" he called down.

The two checked that their visors were in place, then hobbled over to an aluminum platform attached to a hoist. It lifted them up and slowly lowered them into the water. Jim was relieved to feel buoyant. The weight of the belt was off his legs once he was submerged.

"Okay, can you hear me?" Chuck asked once they were underwater.

Jim spoke through his mic. "Roger, loud and clear." The hoist stopped at the bottom of the pool. "Twenty-five feet. I'm going to step off the platform now." He pushed his left foot back and placed his right foot on the bottom of the pool, then turned to the big blue void.

Facing at him was one of the strangest but most brilliant sights he'd ever seen. No small mask window to look through, but the full width of his visor underwater. As clear as day, it gave him the impression that he was standing on dry land. Even the divers seemed to be floating in thin air. He

79

took another step, then another, slowly, with deliberate movements, as if walking in space. He quickly lost his footing, but miraculously, he seemed unable to fall.

The suit, which had fit snugly when he first put it on, now felt like a pressurized balloon and was so rigid that it had become almost impossible to bend his limbs. He began to bob up and down, thinking he might just float back to the surface. A diver opened a valve over his shoulder and released a shot of air, then turned a dial on his tanks to lower the suit pressure to one pound. But he seemed to have overdone it. Jim fell to the bottom of the pool and couldn't get up.

The diver tried to raise him, but Jim just rolled sideways, his arms and legs flailing as he struggled to stand. "This buoyancy's a real bummer," he said, looking over at Chuck, who seemed to have figured it out with the other diver.

With another few short bursts of air, Jim began to float up again, stopping the tap early to make sure he didn't overdo it. He inhaled and exhaled a few times, bobbing up on the in-breath and sinking on the out-flow. With another adjustment, the diver found the point of one-sixth gravity, just like on the Moon.

Hans opened the comms link. "Okay guys, nobody's going all the way up there for a gentle round of golf, so here comes the fun. Straight ahead you'll see a device underwater on the other side of the pool that looks like a giant tube. It's an airlock with three hatches at the ends. Jim, you will unscrew them and open them. Get inside, adjust your buoyancy to zero-G, and then maneuver through the tube, weightless, please.

"You'll also see a wire cage containing basalt rocks. Chuck, use the hammer and chisel to chip at it, then try using the drill to loosen the bits. You'll find them nearby, along with a core hammer head. There's a long stem hanging in the water from above. We want to see how you work in microgravity. Your own center of gravity will shift as you pick things up and move. We're also looking for leaks in the suit's seals under load and whether they can keep you cool. You have thirty minutes of air. Okay, ready? Let the games begin."

Jim and Chuck began to shuffle and bounce across the vast blue floor, Jim's ears continuing to adjust to the change in his balance. The rig itself looked like the sidewall of a rocket, with large curved aluminum panels and alternating black and white sections submerged below the waterline. A couple of hatches were also labeled ECS and Fuel Line, just like the real thing, presumably. Directly in front of it was the large wire mesh tube, about four and a half feet in diameter, ten feet long, and suspended in the center of a large rig. This was the one Hans had mentioned. Nearby were the caged rocks and tools which Chuck would contend with.

Jim picked up a ratchet. Near the wall of the pool, he adjusted his buoyancy again, found his footing, and began to turn a bolt holding one of the hatches at the end of the large tube. Chuck, nearby, grabbed a hammer and chisel and began tapping away at the rocks inside the wire cage, releasing a muffled *tap, tap, tap* into the water.

Although the drag of the water helped Jim feel steady, it was not nearly enough. His feet felt like they were on ice skates. "It's hard to stand still," he said. "I'm sliding all over the place here."

"Me too. Phew, you really need to whack this stuff underwater," Chuck replied, breathing heavily. He selected another set of tools while Jim used some muscle to loosen the first bolt on his hatch.

After a few moments Jim said, "One down," as the first thread came loose. "Got the hang of it now. Fairly straight-forward once you find your footing."

"You're sounding pretty buoyant there, buddy," Chuck quipped, looking up at the long drill shaft hanging into the water. "I'm gonna try to bore a hole in these stones here." He sidled over and pulled a drill head from the tool basket, then returned to the cage and attached it to the shaft.

But Jim, in his eagerness to turn a ratchet, had practically turned himself upside down. Blood rushed to his head. He turned it back up, thinking that that rush probably wouldn't happen in space.

Chuck's first attempt at the drill trigger sent him spinning like a top.

Jim looked up and laughed in his helmet as one of the divers took off his mask and released a stream of bubbles to salute Chuck.

"Aha, we were waiting for that Catherine wheel," Hans said. "Steady yourself first, Chuck. If you weren't tethered, you'd have gone flying into space, never to be seen again. Remember, for every action there is an equal and opposite reaction. We got that in school. Keep going."

Jim crouched over the ratchet and pressed his right foot down hard on the pool floor for a firmer foothold. He tried to anchor his left against the rig, spreading both for maximum grip. It was an awkward position, but he pulled the ratchet and the second bolt began to turn.

He'd barely unscrewed it halfway when he paused for a breath, feeling heat and sweat building inside his suit. "How you doing?" he asked.

"Damn thing's stuck," said Chuck, also breathing heavily, trying to free the drill head in the rock.

"Temperature's rising," Hans said.

"Well, I could use a swim to cool off about now," Jim joked.

"Right. I'll get this thing out," Chuck said.

Jim heard a muffled clang!

Chuck's drill had fallen out of his hand and he'd tumbled forcefully onto the cage, going over and sideways as he lost his footing. A nearby diver rushed in as he fell to the bottom of the pool, bouncing up again like a rubber ball.

"Everything okay down there?" Hans asked over the comms link.

Chuck scrambled to his feet. "I can't believe how hard this is. We're not making it look easy," he replied, struggling to steady himself as he floated around like a balloon in the water. He shuffled back to the cage. "Okay, let's go again."

"Sure need to find a solid footing," Jim said.

"What about the suit, Jim?" Hans asked.

"It's holding up pretty well as far as I can tell. But wow, I'm either sweating buckets in here or it's already leaking. I said I wanted a swim but I didn't mean it. It's as hot as hell in here."

Jim jiggled the ratchet on a bolt with his gloved gorilla hands, but it seemed to be stuck. He struggled to free it, then paused to ease the pain. With another jerk, it came loose, though it slipped from his grasp. "Damn it."

He leaned over to grab it from the bottom of the pool, but could barely bend at the waist in his stiff suit. With a little hop, he belly-flopped onto the floor, pushed out a hand to grab the ratchet, bounced on his stomach and back up onto his feet awkwardly in one motion.

83

"You okay there, buddy?" Chuck asked.

"Please don't do that, Jim." Hans said. "The pressure spike could damage something."

"See how that worked?" Jim replied. "I feel like a bouncy sumo," he added, breathlessly, as if he'd just finished an uphill race. His jubilation ended when he pushed off the pool wall again. His helmet's visor gave way on a corner, and a jet of water splashed his left cheek. "Damn it, I got a leak. Guys, there's a leak," he yelled, sinking like an anchor in a cloud of bubbles. At the bottom of the pool, his faceplate blew off and water imploded onto his face.

"Jim, the divers are on their way," Hans yelled.

Chuck dropped his tools and followed. "Hurry. He needs help!"

"The suit pressure's dropping. Pull him out. Quick, get him out," Hans ordered, running down from the balcony to the pool.

Jim was already flat on his back and knew there was no way he'd get up with the weights around his waist and all the air gone from the suit. One of the divers got under his tank and pushed up with all his strength, but Jim wouldn't budge. He held his breath, feeling sure he would drown just as the second diver unbuckled his belt and helped pull him up. Both divers kicked furiously with their flippered feet toward the hoist. Jim was back on it in thirty seconds and out of the pool in a minute, spitting water from his mouth.

He sat on the side as the divers went back for Chuck, thinking it was his first outing to do something and he'd blown it. The show was over. What would he tell NASA? That underwater training was too dangerous, or admit he had screwed up and needed to go back for more data? He released his helmet and leaned forward, feeling a sense of déjà vu as water poured from his collar and sleeves when he removed his gloves. It seeped from his ankles as he unbuckled his boots. He apologized to Hans, then leaned back and poured out an upturned boot, feeling like he was back in Pensacola, and wondering why on earth he had just swallowed water again while training to be up in the sky.

CHAPTER 12 - RIGHTS

May 1963

For the next five months, Jim came home on the weekends feeling like little more than an exhausted hermit. He'd immersed himself in his work and was soon busier than ever inside the NASA training and development machine. It was clear that he had to give it his all to succeed, so it was easy for him to slip into work mode and just stay there. Every day was long, he traveled all week, if not for weeks, and usually squeezed in several hours of grind on the weekends just to stay on top of it all.

At first, JoAnn seemed to be adjusting to the new situation and enjoying the new adventure of socializing with the other NASA wives. She told how a handful of them got together every few weeks at the yacht club, talking about outfits and hairstyles in the latest fashion magazines, how to improve their complexions and stand taller for photos, how to make the perfect deviled eggs, the ideal yellow of custard, how to dress up the house, and how to pretend to be a perfect parent while sometimes feeling like the opposite and hoping not to be found out. Jim discovered through JoAnn that none of them wore red lipstick, but they spent hours discussing whether or not they should.

NASA itself seemed to be fond of women who stayed close to the kitchen. The fact was, things had to be right at home or the men wouldn't get a seat on a rocket. For the wives, that included dealing with the occasional copperhead snake that was discovered in the car or on the doorstep during the summer months when the man of the house wasn't around. That was the deal. The roles were actually perfectly clear to JoAnn, just as Nancy Shea had written.

The women kept their fears of becoming young widows to themselves. One of them had privately shared that she looked up to the sky whenever a helicopter flew by or circled overhead, and said that once, she almost broke down, certain that her husband had crashed in some experimental vehicle, when she saw plumes of dark smoke rising in the distance. It was all because (she was sure) his steak that morning had been well-done instead of medium-rare. Fear was contagious, so the girls just pursed their lips and pretended it was all sunshine and roses within the NASA program.

They complained about having to raise children alone, with all the schooling, the taxi rides, the growing up, the feeding, and the goodnights, because the men were never home. But when pressed, most of them didn't know what else they would do with the time if it were given back. Others were just desperate to get out of a dusty, drafty base and into a home of their own, so they could finally *be* the perfect parents they thought they needed to be in their own perfectly manicured homes.

As time passed, JoAnn cooled to the club. Mercury had come to an end, but Jim and the rest of the Special Ops continued unannounced. There was no public facade to create, and unlike the original Mercury and the new Gemini royal families, who got the fancy invitations and lunches and the *Life* money and the perks, they could be scrappy, imperfect and normal, as long as they didn't fall apart. Still, JoAnn kept her previous divorce a secret in case the NASA men caught wind and grounded Jim for being half of an imperfect couple; they'd do it in a heartbeat. And though she had occasionally babysat other people's children—laughing at the instructions for the first few deliveries—she always pointed out an obvious delta, that she was the only one without children of her own. All she did was cook for herself and figure out how to pass the time and fall asleep alone night after night, week after week. Jim, who was out all the time, just wanted to stay home on the weekends, while JoAnn was desperate to get out.

And now, despite her initial awe at the whole idea, she seemed more and more in limbo as time went on. She became obsessed with having a baby, and after a while Jim sensed, from her growing silence, that something was being stored up for a release. Work meant he'd missed several, rarely opportune moments to try for a new Cobb. But no family expansion was in the offing, and JoAnn began to simmer quietly each month, waiting for the next fertility cycle, distracting herself with housework and what looked to Jim like just filling time. She visited her sister, Eve, in Michigan several times, and after a pause for his help, she finished decorating the guest room practically by herself—though he repainted the ceiling; it would have been a doghouse if he had left that to her. She also began experimenting with writing, though she hadn't shared anything. She searched his diary for a clearing so they could take a vacation as he had promised, though she likened it to finding a patch of blue in an overcast sky and said she was worried that the endless stream of his work was taking over their lives completely.

It was obvious that it had taken her a fair amount of fortitude to live practically alone while he was busy laying down his own necessary tracks. Jim realized he needed to do a better job at home, thinking it was also hers to take care of him and his household and raise a young family. "That's what women do, Jim," he remembered his mother saying when he was young. He was embarrassed and apologized, promising to be more thoughtful and attentive, since his work had practically pushed aside all thoughts of starting a new family except whenever she mentioned it.

Jim jetted himself home in a T-38 early one Friday afternoon to make up. He arrived tired, but pleased with the week's accomplishment of mapping out what a lunar orbit rendezvous might look like with the contractors designing the module. It had been a good week. Astronaut Gordon Cooper had just completed a twenty-two orbit spaceflight, though it had taken NASA more than a year to send him up after Glenn in sixty-two. That didn't seem particularly fast compared to the Soviets, especially after Chris James had said on the plane, the first day they met, that NASA was speeding up its program. Some people even speculated that the whole moonshot didn't look like it was on track for sixty-nine.

JoAnn was standing on the porch with a cigarette and a tipple in a glass when he came up the front path. She looked tired when he greeted her, as if she'd been up half the night. He got only the merest smile, then went inside, took a shower, and got back in the car beside her for a round of grocery shopping. It was "a good way to keep my feet on the ground,' he said, but JoAnn remained tight-lipped and sour as they walked the aisles. Jim guessed that another cycle had come and gone.

He picked up a mud pie dessert to cheer her up, though in truth it was just as much for himself.

"We haven't had one of these in a long time," he said on the way home, his tongue practically salivating as he drove.

JoAnn continued to look out the window with a calm, flat face, her eyes scanning the road as she thought about something.

"When was the last time you had one?"

She held her eyes straight ahead and shrugged. "Can't remember."

"The cafeteria at work doesn't make them." He grinned and added with a cheeky smile, "So it was banoffee instead."

JoAnn remained silent.

"One slice or two? With whipped cream?" Jim asked.

She perked up, but looked a little frustrated. "I won't have any, Jim."

His smile disappeared.

"It's a good one, their best," he said, as if he knew what that was. "I should probably go easy, too. They seem to think I have an irritable bowel."

She finally looked up at him.

"They must have mixed up my file." He looked sideways at her with a grin. "I just told them it never bothered me."

"You need to tell them they were wrong."

"They'd start an investigation, and who knows, maybe I do. Or they'd find something else. They let it go, so I didn't push it or get in their web. Everybody's hiding something, I bet."

She said nothing, and Jim drove on quietly.

A moment later, she revealed that she'd cut dairy from her diet.

"Oh, why? When?" Jim asked.

"It's been over a month, Jim." She looked distracted again.

He glanced sideways at her, though she didn't turn to him. "You never said."

"I did. Your head was somewhere else."

Jim looked at her again. "You did?" When she said nothing, he asked, "Why?"

"In case it got in the way of having a baby."

Jim paused to calculate what she had said.

"Dairy? How is that?"

"It just does. Certain types of fat." She went on. "Red meat prevents ovulation. Some fish have harmful chemicals."

"But babies like milk, don't they? There's nothing like a juicy bottle."

"There's research that shows all this, Jim."

"Old wives' tales?"

"Nutritionists," she insisted.

"Well, mud pie doesn't have anything harmful, does it? Okay, maybe a little fat. But when's the last time we had one of those?"

They sat in silence for a moment. JoAnn let out a small sigh of frustration. "I'm just being careful, that's all. And so are some of the other girls. We have to figure this out, Jim. It's taking too long."

"So are you on bread and water now?"

JoAnn sounded annoyed. "You're not taking this seriously, are you? At least I'm trying to figure it out."

Jim felt knocked for a loop and apologized for being an ass, thinking she was right, that he hadn't been around, that he probably didn't hear her, or that he'd forgotten it the moment after she'd said it. "But won't that affect your health, cutting everything?"

"I didn't cut everything," she insisted. "Just the stuff that prevents conception."

"How do you get calcium? Iron, minerals and stuff?"

"Spinach. I started with spinach. There's some at home."

Jim was concerned. "Is that dinner?"

She finally looked up at him, confounded. "No."

"Did you check with the doctor first?"

"I didn't. It's fine. It's just a few things."

The last two miles were quiet, and Jim knew something was about to happen as they pulled onto the drive.

The approaching storm failed to materialize as they began to put the groceries away. Jim relaxed for the first time in days and began to talk enthusiastically about how the lunar maneuver would work after she asked him how the week had been.

She listened, deflated and quiet, while Jim lost himself in his odyssey, even reminding her that they were all paying for it as taxpayers, as if that mattered to her right now.

Without warning, she regained her composure and said, "In that case, I think I should get a shot at it too ... if we're all paying the price."

Jim grinned at her, then pulled out some plates and picked up a dessert knife. He said he couldn't wait to try it and, amused by what he took as her joke, said it would be a job to convince NASA to bring the ladies along. He added that von Braun, who made NASA's rockets, had been told to increase their payload and said he'd reserve space on future missions for recreation. So, everything was fine.

Looking mildly affronted, she turned up the volume and reminded him of the girls who went to Congress last summer to get their place in the space program. "Well, you saw Jerri Cobb on TV. Then there was the *Life* article. Lovelace told the committee that women have advantages over you. They're smaller, use less oxygen, less food, better in isolation. It's NASA that's holding back. The Soviets are already training women." She stopped abruptly.

Jim saw that she was serious. "Well, they are making it look easy, and I'm sure that doesn't help one bit. None of Cobb and her gang have any experience anyway."

"Experience?" JoAnn replied. Jim was surprised at her forcefulness and wondered if and why she'd been in a simmer over space.

"None of them were military pilots, no engineering background. You need the right head for this sort of thing. Not shiny earrings," he said, realizing immediately from her silence, and his reference to jewelry, that it was belittling. He apologized, thinking he wasn't in the office talking to the guys.

"You know military flying hasn't been allowed for women since they closed the Women Air Force Service Pilots in the forties. Women aren't allowed in Air Force training schools. It's just a blocker so the boys can do their own thing ... and the ladies can stay, well, be kept at home."

"That proves the point, doesn't it?"

She didn't get it.

"Where's the experience, Jo?" He went on, "I guess that's it. It's our way of life, isn't it?" He paused and added lightly, as he took a bite of pie. "We should just ask Glenn. He has all the answers."

She became grizzled. "You sound like you talked to him. That *pioneer* John Glenn, for all his bravery and daring, just followed the NASA line and deflected. He said that roles for men and women were, *all part of the social order*. It looks to me like he and his buddies just didn't want to be upstaged by a skirt. What use will brave men be then? They're the ones who maintain this social order anyway." She finished with a glare.

Jim was a little surprised, although it made sense when she put it that way. He thought she must have been planning an article.

"Anyway, how long can this go on?" she implored. "Is a man expected to fend for himself out there? He can't exactly do that at home. They'd all be floating back down in deflated spacesuits within a week."

Jim was confused. "JoAnn, what's this all about? Are you writing something?"

She ignored his question. "Not that that's the only thing women can do. But, seriously ..." She shrugged at the unfinished point, then asked, "So, how many women are there in this special unit of yours? If I were writing about NASA, I'd start there."

Jim felt mildly encouraged and concerned at the same time, but said nothing. Was she expecting to take a shot at NASA in an article? He pushed a knife through the dessert, feeling a little disturbed by the Friday night debate.

"And anyway, if you see Glenn again, can you ask him a question or two for me?"

"JoAnn? Come on. I have no idea," Jim looked around and shushed her as if he expected the neighbors to hear.

He sliced through the pie, then moved to put the knife in the sink and asked, "Is something wrong?"

JoAnn shook her head.

He knew that meant *yes*. "What's the matter?"

She paused with a deep sigh, then stood up to look out the window. "What's happening to us, Jim? You haven't said a word about us. Not a word. Everything feels on hold. Us, the baby."

Jim turned to her, put his hands on her shoulders and said with a grin, "Well, let's go upstairs and put in a few words, shall we?" She shrugged him off. "Look, sorry. Just trying to lighten things up. It's Friday."

She turned to him and said, "I wish you were closer to home, Jim. I've been thinking about those rockets. They're just big missiles. They used to bomb places."

He was shocked that she had put it that way. Though he knew it was coming, it was the first time she had revealed that particular concern.

She noticed.

"Look, it's okay."

She sighed and asked, "How are we going to have a baby, Jim? I can't do it alone. It's been a year." She looked him in the eye and asked, "And anyway, how do you know?"

"Know what?"

"It scares me. How do you know it's safe?"

Jim saw that he couldn't really refute the concern. Rockets did still blow up. "Look. Okay ..." He gave her a kiss. "Nobody's putting me in a rocket yet. They asked me to do this, so I have to take it seriously. I thought you were okay with it."

"I am, but we also said we were going to start a family."

95

"Yes. So let's keep trying." The truth was that his libido had waned over the past few months. His weeks away had become busier and busier. They'd both noticed. It had been moving in the wrong direction.

"I need you here, Jim." She turned away and picked up a tiny pill that lay next to a small brown bottle on the counter.

It was so small that he hadn't noticed it before. The label read Equinal. With a change of heart, she opened another bottle labeled Miltown and swallowed two torpedoes with water.

Jim was stunned and frowned quietly while she was still swallowing.

She said, "The doctor gave me these. But, I'm not sure they're working."

"Why?"

"It's just hard to sleep, Jim. I feel anxious and you're not home. One of the others said they help." She sighed again. "It's just being around them. Some are so mysterious. And worried too. But their kids distract them."

Jim hugged her, frowned at the bottles and made her sit down.

"Look, would it help if you started looking for work again? Staying home can't help."

With another sigh, she revealed that she had started writing again. "I want to do something about all the protests going on."

Jim thought for a moment. "Why not write about NASA? It sounds like you're onto something. You could do it from here, for ... the *Houston Chronicle*. Just send it in. Everybody wants to know about space these days." JoAnn quietly toyed with the idea while Jim continued enthusiastically, "Let's see what happens. Maybe I can get you the inside scoop. More and more of it will be here at the Manned Spacecraft Center anyway."

"Nice idea, but *Time-Life* has the exclusive."

"I know, but you know: *inside*, inside," he joked with a smile. "I'll put you in touch with the right people."

JoAnn didn't look so sure. Jim wondered what was on her mind.

She reminded him of the letter she had helped Dorothy write to the White House. That was the kind of thing she wanted to do.

Jim was surprised to hear it and asked, "What, are you going to write ... another letter?"

"I'm thinking of writing about civil rights, Jim."

"Civil rights?"

"It's the perfect antidote to space."

"An antidote? Why do we need an antidote?"

"It's about the rest of life that gets forgotten while space gets all the headlines."

"But civil rights, Jo? What's that about? That won't help you."

"There are a lot of issues out there. People need to know, and there's more than enough material. It's a problem the size of NASA's universe."

"Okay, but ..." Jim didn't look so sure. He wondered how this would fit in with his career at NASA, in the military, and working for the government. He was sure it would not. "Who are you going to write for?"

"Local press. I'll send in some pieces like you said. See if I can get published." After a short pause, she added, "I want to cover a group called Students for a Democratic Society."

Jim felt confused. "Who are they?"

"...and equality."

"Okay," was all that Jim could muster. He left an opening for her to explain.

"They're in Michigan. Not far from Eve's. Nice bunch. I met them and I'm going to visit them again while you're gone."

Jim saw that she was serious and had obviously been planning this for a while. "Who are they?"

"SDS? It's a new student group." She went to the counter on the other side of the kitchen and started rifling through her purse. "They fight for democracy ... and protest for people's rights. It seems perfect."

"Perfect for what, Jo?"

She pulled out a pamphlet and handed it to him. He read it quietly.

Join the New Left. We can stop the war and end discrimination in our country. Support the Students for a Democratic Society. We are the SDS! There's a change gonna come. Ann Arbor, Michigan.

Jim was shocked. "Of all things, Jo? Can this wait? I work in government. I assume that's your goal? And you'll no doubt find that the president is not doing a very good job of protecting people's rights right now."

"I want to write about what's really going on out there, Jim. Real lives. For displaced Americans who think the government is no less a tyranny than the Communists seem to be. Anything but space. If we don't fight to right the wrongs in society, who will?"

Jim felt dismissed, but held his tongue. Overlooked, by-

98

passed—was that how women felt?

"I'm going back out there on Monday to do an interview."

Jim said nothing.

"And there's the march on Washington Monument in the summer. I have to cover that if I want to get into the area."

Jim took a deep breath. They ate dinner and not another word was said about JoAnn's crusade or the space program to beat the Soviets.

CHAPTER 13 - VOMIT COMET

July 1963

Jim and Chuck wore cool shades and bright orange flight suits as they walked across the tarmac at Edwards Air Force Base under the bright California sunshine. The affectionately named Weightless Wonder V, all white, and with a large sky-blue stripe running the length of it, stood patiently waiting to perform its unique party trick of churning the stomachs of hardy men as it dropped them from the sky.

"Wow, she's a beauty. Goes up like a rocket and drops like a lead balloon," Chuck said with a grin as he ran his fingers along her belly.

"Our very own roller coaster," Jim gushed. " Zero G, just like the real thing." He glanced along its huge gray underside, big enough to crush them to a pulp if it somehow collapsed over their heads and just rolled over. *Air Force Aeronautical Systems Division* was printed on its side, just behind the black nose and next to an *Air Force Systems Command* insignia; both just below the captain's slightly ajar left seat window. He glanced at a huge parabolic flight profile painted just under it and thought it looked like the side view of an inflated pimple. The briefing room was closed for renovations, so they'd get the mission lowdown on the plane today.

"Yeah, but it's going to feel different than the pool with our buddy Hans. Keeping still's gonna be the problem up there, just as simply moving was in the water," Chuck said.

After a quick walk around the plane, out of an ingrained piloting habit, the two climbed a vertical step ladder that hung from a large square hatch in the side wall, just below the cockpit and forward of the nose wheel.

Jim went up first and entered a small cabin with several passenger seats. Behind them was a three-quarter interior wall, beyond which he could see the long empty tube where all the fun would be. A uniformed man appeared from the cockpit just as he dropped into his seat. "Welcome, folks. I'm your skipper today. Strap in and we'll be on our way. I don't believe I've met either of you before?"

"Nope. It's a first for me," Jim said. Chuck echoed.

"Okay, let's go over our flight plan."

The captain pulled out a scale model of the plane that was about the length of his forearm. He began to explain, "As you can see, this model is the Pan Am version, although paying passengers don't get your kind of fun with just a regular ticket. But since you two haven't personally paid for the ride today, there's work to be done. How do you like roller coasters?" He handed each of them a list of the day's activities.

Chuck leaned forward in his seat and studied it carefully, while Jim began to read what the captain had already started to explain. It was the same as the parabolic diagram on the nose cone.

"We'll climb to cruising altitude at twenty-four thousand feet, during which time you and your instructor, Al—he's in the back there—will get ready."

"There, the plane will pull up at fifty degrees, generating two and a half-G. We'll shoot up to thirty-four thousand feet. I'll cut the engines when you're ready to float around the cabin, and the plane will enter a nosedive. Then, voila, the fun begins. We'll drop back to Earth at forty-five degrees and five hundred and ten knots, pulling another two and a half-G at the bottom. Then it's back to flight level twenty-four. We'll be weightless for about two minutes. zero-G is about thirty seconds. Then we climb back up and do it all over again. How does that sound? We good?"

Chuck looked up, first at Jim, then at the captain, and said, "That makes sense."

Jim began to feel butterflies already, like his imagination had just described floating in space to his stomach for the first time.

"Oh, and one more thing: as you probably know, we have a unique claim to fame. This lady has already produced a few gallons of, uh, churn from her privileged passengers (shall we say), but we'd rather not find ourselves floating around in your breakfast today if we can avoid it. So, I hope it was a light one this morning?"

Jim looked at a seat-back pocket and saw a stack of small brown paper bags lined with plastic.

"If you need to offload anything, half-digested or otherwise, keep one of these little bags nearby." The captain reached into a seat-back and pulled one out. "You'll probably need one at some point, since this is your first time with us." He paused to let the thought sink in. "We don't want to clean up after the flight. It costs a lot of downtime. There's a little box of sawdust in the back if you can't hold it."

Jim leaned over to Chuck and said, "Remind me to tell you

about the Saufley toilet rolls. Lots of puking, but they got me my wings."

Al came in, introduced himself, and took a seat behind them. "We're going to do the parabola about forty times today," he said with a big grin.

Jim looked up, slightly startled. "Did you say forty?"

"It's non-stop fun with us," the captain said, answering for Al. "That's about two hours before lunch ... assuming, of course, that you still want to eat at noon."

"Keep your feet under you when you look down. And keep your head up," Al said. "Avoids nausea."

They stowed everything, then took off, but Jim didn't know whether to be happy or worried as the plane quickly climbed to cruising height. He hadn't thrown up in years, and the last time that happened was during aerobatics training. He really didn't want all that again.

The plane finally leveled off and everyone unbuckled. Preparations for the first zero-G freefall began. Jim got out of his seat and walked across the boarded floor of the fifty-foot empty cabin, almost tripping awkwardly on an anchor point. He looked around at the vertically stitched, cream-white upholstery that quilted the walls, as if they were in some kind of insanity cell. Pieces of equipment with pipes and dials and switches were bolted to various points on the floor, some of them protruding from small hatches where the floor met the walls. Overhead, the lights were recessed in a flat roof, about a foot above head height, each about the size of a letter page. The windows, too, were surrounded by square cutouts, though bits of gray aircraft skin and ribs were just visible at the ends of the cabin. Jim reached for one of the guide ropes that ran from front to back along both sides at head height.

He and Chuck retrieved their Mark IV spacesuits, minus helmets, from the aft stowage, and donned them while Al armed the communications system and checked their air hoses. Once set, they returned to their seats and strapped in again. The captain pulled hard on the stick and pushed the engines to full throttle, sending the massive aircraft into a near vertical climb.

Jim hadn't anticipated the steepness of the ascent as the engine fans revved up and began to rage against gravity. He had just managed to grab his notes as they slipped off the seat next to him, but missed his pen, which clattered somewhere in the back of the cabin along with a number of other small items that had been lost in the folds of the structure.

At the top of the climb, the engines quietened to a whisper until there was no sound but the rush of air. There was a moment of silence as the plane slowed to a stop in mid-air and leveled off imperceptibly. The overhead light came on for the impending dive, though Jim could have sworn they were already falling.

He unbuckled his harness and slowly began to rise from his seat. Chuck followed suit, as did Al, and so did other pens and papers scattered about the cabin. The hair on their heads began to float freely, just as butterflies began to flutter again inside Jim's stomach. He felt like he was reliving a childhood fantasy, remembering the magical flight of a little dog in a story he'd read as a toddler.

The plane's nose dropped slowly and it began to freefall from the sky. Jim looked out the window and saw that the horizon was now almost vertical as the cabin began to creak and bend in protest at the accelerating speed. The wind noise grew until the engines finally roared back to life, pulling the plane out of its suicide dive. They screamed to full throttle once more, taking the men back up the vertical climb for a second run.

Jim was now pressed hard into his seat and felt like an elephant was sitting on his chest. His legs and arms were as heavy as oak trees. Unable to resist gravity and feeling several times his own weight, he let go and relaxed into it, just happy not to be flying the plane.

At the top of the drop, both he and Chuck, wide-eyed and still grinning from ear to ear, felt euphoric, like kids with boundless energy bubbling up from a long-forgotten childhood. They unbuckled together, and for a moment Jim realized that he was actually falling to Earth, with only the force of gravity pulling him down. The plane, and everything else with it, fell in formation around him. Every time he moved, it felt like he was dropping a little faster or slower than the rest of the plane.

Instinctively, he pushed up from his armrests and immediately shot toward the ceiling, thinking he was going to fall up somehow. His hands sprang up to grab something, just as he expected to hit the wall with a painful crunch. Fortunately, the impact was softer than he feared. He bounced off the wall, then tumbled toward the back of the cabin, imagining he was upside down from the look of Chuck and Al, who seemed to be standing on the ceiling.

He wondered if they were simply inverted in his head, then decided that he could no longer believe what his eyes were telling him about his orientation. It no longer mattered either. Chuck, he saw, had stood up (or maybe he was standing down) and found himself in an unintended glide toward the front. It was only Al who showed any semblance of composure as he moved around, ignoring them both. Nice and easy, Jim told himself as he slowed his movements at the next impact and floated away from the wall more gently.

Soon he and Chuck were playing in the air, getting used to the feeling of weightlessness during the next few parabolas. They bounced, jumped, skipped, spun, rolled, walked along the padded walls, crawled along the walls, and waltzed together on the cabin ceiling. Jim grabbed his pen as it floated by unassumingly on its own adventure around the plane, somewhere on round three.

He had lost count of the turns when nausea finally struck. Deciding to keep it to himself, lest something come out and he had to jump for a bag, he began to wonder how much more *fun* he could stomach, especially with all the work still to be done.

"This is a model of an airlock door," Al said from the back of the plane. And there it was, just like the one Jim had seen in the pool, though this time with an aluminum skinned tube about chest high. It was four and a half feet wide for astronauts to pass through, though not quite wide enough to turn inside with a suit on. The rigid rig that held the tube in place was about two yards wide and four yards long on the outside, including the frame and brackets that were bolted to points on the floor. It certainly looked too bulky to be the real thing they were going to send up in a rocket. Al explained, "It'll be a doorway into space on the side of the capsule, so the spacecraft remains pressurized in orbit while you go outside for a walk. As you can see, it's a man-sized tube that you pass through headfirst as if you were going outside. But for this exercise today, you're on the outside and you want to come inside. So you're going to open this outer hatch, jump in head first, close it behind you, then open the inner hatch and go through. When you're done, you're home safe. You're going to lock the inner hatch so you can recalibrate the cabin pressure. Okay, you got it?" The men nodded. "So who's going first? Jim?"

Jim saw that there were no bolts to undo today—just a levered clasp on the hatch to lock and unlock it. The capsule version, he knew, might actually have a wheel to turn a multipoint lock, but that was still in the design stage. The other purpose of this thing, he had learned, was for astronauts to crawl out of one capsule in space and into another, perhaps to a spent hydrogen tank of all places, which would become a living and working space on some kind of orbiting laboratory. It was the hatch of a hydrogen tank that needed all those bolts he had fought with during the underwater experiment in the pool.

He put on his helmet and pressed the voice button on the side to check that the system was working at both ends. Al checked various pressure sensors and accelerometers that were wired into his recording equipment. Finally, Chuck connected the dummy air hose to the suit. The hatches on the airlock tube were checked and secured.

When zero-G started again, Jim opened the unlocked hatch on the airlock contraption and looked down into the cold metal tube as he floated in front of it. He took a deep breath and dived in head first, closing the door behind him as Al had instructed. A flashlight on his helmet illuminated the inside of the cold, dark tube. He continued through it and emerged from the inner door, all without a hitch and not wanting to stay in the confined space a moment longer than absolutely necessary.

"Right, lock it now. Remember to lock the inner door behind you," Al said. "Otherwise the capsule will leak vital oxygen. There's not a drop to spare up there."

Jim grabbed the latch and locked it.

"Okay, now, this time, Chuck, you take the *inside* and you'll unlock the inner hatch to let your buddy *in*. Got it?"

After they had practiced the maneuvers several times, Al marked both of their check sheets to indicate that the practice had been flawless.

Jim noticed that Chuck was already looking tired with dark circles under his eyes. He was also moving a little gingerly. "You okay?" he asked.

"Slight churn. You?"

Jim nodded. His head was now spinning and his stomach was not at all sure which way was up anymore. "It's milkshake in here," he said, looking down at his belly. "Compressed to a pulp one second, floating around and mixing the next! How long have we got?"

Al replied, "Let's do about an hour and see where we are. You good to try it?"

"I'll do my best," Chuck said. "Should stay focused, huh?"

When Chuck was done checking his suit and his lines were connected, the plane dropped again, but shook momentarily on the way down. The men stopped and held on, looking up and around. Jim looked up at the seats at the back of the cabin, but nothing had fallen, moved, or come loose. The large airlock tube was still in place and all the equipment bolted to the floor and side walls were exactly where they should have been. Fortunately, the vibrations stopped.

"Must be hot out there," Al said.

CHAPTER 14 - IMPALED

A moment later

The captain glanced at his cockpit instruments and saw that nothing had moved out of place. Altitude and airspeed were stable, and the gimbal was pointing straight to the horizon as normal. Engine pressures and temperatures were also fine. He looked out the left window over his shoulder and said, as if to confirm Al's thoughts, "It looks like the day's warming up. We're picking up some turbulence."

The first officer on his right glanced at the dials, then out to the pair of engines over his right shoulder. "Nothing unusual. Though number three looks a little warm on the gauge here. We might be pushing it a little hard on the climb."

"Keep an eye on it, will you? We might have to cut the fun short if it gets too hot out here. I'd better let them know in the back." The captain grabbed his microphone and said, "Gentlemen, we hit some rough air back there. The sun is high and cooking the desert below, so we'll have to expect a little more of that, but hopefully nothing serious. I'll let you know if we need to tie down again."

Al looked at Jim and Chuck. They nodded to each other and

started moving again.

Chuck, now suited up, jumped up and floated to the airlock hatch, unlatched it and dived in feet first, catching the edge awkwardly as he tried to get his boots through the hole. Once inside, he reached up to close the door, just when the plane shook again. This time it was more violent, slamming him against the wall inside the tube. Jim and Al stopped and looked around. There seemed to be an inevitable pause on the way.

The captain spoke again. "Folks, I'm afraid we're going to have to level off," he announced. "Please fasten your seat belts until we find smoother air. There's suddenly a lot of movement out there. It's a little unpredictable."

Both Jim and Al jumped to their feet. Jim went to the hatch to see if Chuck needed help getting out.

Al said, "Chuck, are you going to slide out for now? We'll get you back in as soon as we can."

The plane hit another wall of turbulence and lurched violently as if a giant shoulder had rammed it hard from the left while it was still falling. The men were knocked sideways like bowling pins. Chuck bounced around in the airlock tube. "Okay, guys, I'm coming out," he said quickly over the comms, just as a second violent jolt hit the plane again. The open hatch door slammed down hard on his hand, throwing him backward into the tube. He screamed as he held on by one arm. "Guys, I'm stuck. My hand is stuck in the hatch. Get the goddamn hatch open. Get it open!"

Jim felt the plane roll and turn as if it had been dropped from the sky like a toy. It began to freefall in a tightening spin and he knew immediately that the wings had lost lift.

"What the hell just happened?" he yelled.

A loud siren sounded in the cockpit.

"Number one's out," the first officer yelled, struggling with the stick to regain control.

The captain glanced back at the crippled engine and saw a long trail of smoke behind it. He reached down and flipped a couple of switches. "Damn it. Darn thing won't relight."

Inside the cabin, loose objects were already bouncing off the walls as Jim pushed off again toward the airlock tube. Chuck was still inside and Al was right in front of him. But Jim had jumped too hard and, unable to stop himself from floating faster than expected, slammed hard into the tube, winding himself on the metal frame as it slammed into his chest. His fingers, outstretched to catch his body, were bent painfully backward as he instinctively grabbed an outer rail of the tube and wriggled on it like a buckaroo.

Al momentarily lost his grip, but managed to regain it just as two of the airlock's four floor anchors gave way under the weight of the three men inside the spinning aircraft. Jim was thrown off. A metal bolt head, sheared off by the extra weight, flew past him with other floating debris toward the front of the cabin.

He grabbed on with one hand and reached up with the other to pull himself back on. He began to inch his way toward the outer hatch of the airlock tube as the plane continued its nosedive. He pulled at the hatch, but saw that it was stuck tight. The tips of Chuck's white gloved hand were sticking out of the lip. "His fingers are caught in the seal!" he yelled to Al. "We've got to get it open."

The captain pushed the yoke forward to point the plane's

nose down and applied opposite yaw on the foot pedal to turn direction. "We have to stop the spin," he announced to his first officer. He applied full throttle at the same time they were headed for the ground.

"Okay. The other fans are holding," the officer said, glancing at the engine dials to see that they were still spinning.

The engine noise had grown to a deafening roar as Al and Jim struggled to open the hatch. It wouldn't budge. Jim turned around and faced the back of the cabin, then began to inch his way toward the inner hatch on the opposite side of the airlock tube.

He got halfway there. Spread across it, with Al on top and Chuck inside, it broke free of its anchors on the floor and shot across the cabin. Jim saw himself heading for the ceiling first, horrified that he'd be in line to cushion the blow when it hit. He yanked himself sideways just in time as it bounced off the wall and plowed toward the forward bulkhead between the cabin and the cockpit. Al shimmied sideways and managed to avoid impaling his right arm as it made a dent in the wall padding. They both let go and moved to avoid the next impact and other flying debris as the airlock tube continued to hit the spinning cabin in the unfolding chaos. Jim knew Chuck would be rolling around inside like a ball tossed in a can, though he hoped it would be safer inside than out.

The airlock tube hit a first-row seat at the back of the cabin, ripping it off its hinge and adding it to the floating chaos. Just behind that, in the second row, it slammed into another upright seat back, which went spinning into the mix.

"Damn it. It's going to puncture the skin," Jim yelled, but Al couldn't hear him. If that happened, he knew things would get really tricky. They'd follow Chuck out of the plane as soon as the cabin was depressurized. Jim began to pray in silence. He didn't want to be sucked out without a parachute on his very first outing. He looked up at the upholstery around the cabin and wondered if it would hold, since it was only meant to contain the shoulders and elbows of flying men. Rays of sunlight traced the walls through the windows like a giant scanner as the plane continued to fall in a quickening spin.

Moments later, the rotation began to slow, though the plane was now in a near vertical suicide dive. Jim noticed the change in attitude as the plane plummeted and began to buffet with increasing speed. Both he and Al were now drifting upward toward the seats at the back of the cabin where the tube with Chuck inside was teetering. Al twisted and turned in the air, reaching down on his way up. He grabbed a headrest on his way back.

In one sudden movement, everything fell to the floor and onto the seats. Jim's right elbow came down hard first and broke the fall, though thankfully not itself. He knew the captain must have pulled back the stick to regain lift.

Still on a steep incline, Jim reached out to grab another seat, but narrowly missed. He shot down the empty cabin floor toward the front of the plane with a hundred other objects. Halfway down, he looked up and saw that the airlock tube was still resting precariously against another seat above him. It gave way, sending the tube careening across the floor toward him. He shot out a foot, which found an anchor on the floor and catapulted him into the ceiling. He grabbed the guide rope that ran along the length of the cabin and quickly kicked his legs up as the tube shot past underneath him. But he'd curled up too much and his right shoulder had fallen into its path, taking an agonizing blow as the airlock shot past him. Losing his grip, he tumbled after it. Al had also lost his hold on the rear seat and was sliding down the cabin floor right behind him.

The tube hit the forward bulkhead just below them with such force that the hatch opened. Jim fell beside it, holding his shoulder and wincing in pain. Al landed squarely in a seat that had come loose and was now bundled up against the front of the cabin with seemingly everything else that had come loose. The chair flipped over and threw Al right on top of him.

The plane leveled off and the men stumbled clumsily toward the hatch on the airlock tube seeing that Chuck hadn't emerged.

Jim peered inside and saw him lying hunched and motionless on the floor, his white right glove and arm stained with blood that had also splattered the inside of the tube.

Jim pushed in head first and pulled Chuck's arms while Al pulled on Jim's legs to yank them both out.

"He's out of it," said Jim, emerging with a grip on Chuck's arms.

Al quickly looked at Chuck and said, "He's breathing okay, but his fingers don't look good, and maybe his wrist. He's losing blood. The bouncing around in there must have knocked him out." He glanced back at the battered seats in the cabin. "Let's get him in the back. Quickly."

They dragged Chuck, Jim on his shoulders and Al at his feet, onto a row of seats in the back and strapped him in. "I'd hate to take the glove off, but we'd better do it now or it'll congeal and they'll have to soak it. Best while he can't feel anything, hopefully. Can you get me the medical kit?" Al pointed. "Right over there."

Jim jumped to it and pulled the bright green box from its anchor on the wall and spilled its contents onto the floor next to Chuck.

The captain ripped off his headset and turned to his first officer, then jumped out of the left seat of the now stable plane. "Take us home. I bet they're filling the sick bags back there."

He turned and left the cockpit, but stopped dead in the cabin. It looked like a force twelve hurricane had hit. The airlock tube was shattered, and pieces of the broken seat and other debris were piled up against the cabin wall at the front. Jim and Al were in the back tending to a prone Chuck. He rushed toward them, swatting away an empty sick bag that floated in his face from above.

Weightless Wonder V limped back to the airfield with a trail of smoke from the stalled engine number one. Emergency personnel were already waiting at the end of the runway when the plane finally stopped. Chuck was taken away on a stretcher, while the rest of the crew were patched up for minor injuries; Jim had a gash over his right eyebrow.

He nursed his battered right shoulder as he walked over to Chuck, who was already in the back of the ambulance.

"Hey, what happened up there?" asked Chuck, now horizontal and still in his spacesuit, conscious but barely able to speak.

"The captain thinks we hit wind shear. And one of the engines blew at just the wrong moment. Turbulence hit us hard just as things were getting worse."

"It's a hot day. Must have stalled. He was really pushing it up there," Chuck muttered.

"You should have seen everything bouncing around, including you. Anyway, you okay, buddy?"

"Can't feel my hand ... or my arm for that matter." Chuck slowly turned and looked down at the bandages. "They're going to have to cut me out of this thing. Well, at least I didn't chuck!" he joked with a little grin.

Jim put a comforting hand on Chuck's leg. "There was no time with all the action. That's something, huh? Relax now. They'll get you to the hospital. I'm sure you'll be fine in no time."

"Thanks for helping me out of the tube. Is Al okay? The captain and the other guys?"

"Yeah. Anyway, don't mention it."

Jim stepped out of the ambulance and turned back to look at the plane as the driver closed the doors and sped away with his screaming lights on max volume. The plane stood still at the end of the long runway, white smoke billowing from one of the engines, surrounded by firefighters and mechanics. A long, thin scar bulged into the skin of the plane, just behind the wing, as if a corner of the airlock tube had rammed hard against it, bending the ribs from the inside. He was suddenly relieved that neither he nor any of the crew had been impaled. Much of the tail rudder was gone too, and he knew that that must have been the cause of the uncontrolled spin after the plane was first rammed from the side.

He winced in pain and twisted his shoulder into a more comfortable position, then his mind returned to Chuck. He instinctively turned to see where the ambulance had gone and wondered if Chuck was essentially finished with Special

Ops for good. NASA could be unforgiving. Surely an outage now was the worst thing that could have happened to him. There would be no way to make up for lost time, especially with the stopwatch already on NASA itself.

CHAPTER 15 - KING

August 28th, 1963

Jim worked in earnest over the next month to get ahead with NASA influencers in Chuck's absence. He needed to avoid being distracted by life support so he could focus on his own abilities in flight systems.

One evening, after his executive center had already thrown in the towel after a grueling day of mind-numbing psychometrics, he slowed to park his car in the usual corner spot at his hotel in Albuquerque, where he was holed up for additional physicals at the Lovelace Clinic.

But his usual spot was taken. "That's mine, guys. Damn it," he vented, as the frustration of the day boiled over. He sighed and smacked the steering wheel, then looked around. The whole place was full. "What the hell's happening here today?" His frontal cortex suddenly kicked in and pointed him to an open space across the street.

On his way back to his hotel, he passed around twenty national flags flapping in the breeze in front of the two-story building. A fifty-foot green sign read *Holiday Inn of America*, outlined in yellow, with a pointed arrow at one end and a white star at the top. In the center, black text on a large white square read *Hope and prayers of a free world are with you.*

He reached the lobby and was surprised to find several young, scantily clad cookies hanging in the doorway and draped over the couches. The real NASA astronauts must be here tonight.

Jim asked the receptionist, gruffly, if there were any messages.

"Just a moment, sir. I'll check for you." The young girl turned to the mailbox but Jim felt a firm hand on his shoulder.

"Jim, buddy. How are you? Feeling better? You look great," a familiar voice said.

He turned to Tom but saw that he was not alone.

Jim lost his tongue, wondering if the lady on his arm might be a local tequila. Tom's left hand was around her waist and he was drunk.

Jim looked back at the doorway to the group of girls and thought that Tom, of all people, would not be with an escort.

"We're heading out for a beer. Why don't you join us? A little liquid medicine for your head after those psychs have crawled around in there. I know how it feels."

Jim fumbled his words and mustered a spray-on smile. "Thanks, but I'm kind of beat right now. It's been a long day."

"Ah, the psycho's chair—it's enough to drive the sane potty, huh? Gives them something to work on." Tom said. He looked at his companion and laughed at the joke while Jim loaded a question. He was about to speak when—

"Jim, I'd like you to meet my lovely wife, Trudy."

Jim visibly thawed and the color returned to his face.

Tom chuckled. "You haven't met yet, so we thought we'd get you."

119

"Aha, Trudy! It is so nice to finally meet you." He suddenly wondered what on earth he was thinking. Fred? Maybe, but Tom? No way. It confirmed that the day had really gotten to him.

Tom half-laughed in a way that Jim had rarely seen him so relaxed. "She came down to make sure I was behaving." He nodded at the girls in the doorway. "And I was, so she said I had to get out and have some fun!" He burst out laughing.

Wow, Jim thought. "Well, you guys go ahead. I don't want to get in the way. I'll see you in the morning."

"Okay, buddy. Bright and early! You get some rest now."

With a pat on Jim's shoulder, Tom disappeared into the evening with Mrs. Mitchell on his arm.

It was still light outside when Jim went up to his room on the first floor, feeling unusually wound up and still thinking about his unnecessary cursing in the parking lot. He walked past alternating orange and cyan doors toward his own, thinking he'd snapped at the receptionist and couldn't even muster the energy to relax on a night out with Tom and Trudy. He walked past a trio of guys in cheap suits, carrying briefcases and looking like they were checking out rooms. The NASA Gemini men were definitely here somewhere. These salesmen were hawking products and begging for endorsements.

It was also a rare sight that no one was sitting under the yellow parasols around the pool when he arrived at his room, a regular-sized motel hole with beige walls, green curtains, and a blue bed on a mustard-colored carpet. Jim walked past the wood-paneled wall to the bathroom on his left, turned on a black table lamp, and flopped into one of the white recliners next to a coffee table. After a moment, he got up again and turned on the TV next to the walnut dresser across from the bed. He needed a distraction.

"There are rumors today that the US Army is about to confirm that the draft will be extended to younger males," the reporter said. It was another news story about the war. "Sources say youngsters in the bottom half of their class are already being called up to fight as the cost and number of lives in the war over Vietnam continues to escalate."

He didn't have the energy to take it in and flipped the channel.

"I have a dream ..." Jim immediately recognized the voice of black activist Martin Luther King Jr. He was speaking to a huge crowd of mostly African Americans at the Lincoln Monument in Washington DC. Every square inch for a mile seemed to be covered with people in colorful clothing on the Mall and around the Reflecting Pool. He leaned forward and looked for JoAnn, then his mind drifted back to his African American friend, Wilson, wondering if he might actually be out there, however unlikely. He was looking for any sign of JoAnn when the news reel flipped to a pair of men holding a marketing board that read, *March on Washington for Jobs & Freedom, August 28, 1963.*

He flipped over again and saw a shot of an African-American, Ed Dwight, an Air Force man from Edwards, pictured on the cover of a magazine as the first of his race to get a shot at the Moon. Jim instinctively thought this wasn't the show NASA had been asked to put on screen and couldn't see it happening. But the story looked ripe for JoAnn to bite into with her new civil rights crusade.

He had to call her. She'd still be in Washington DC, at the Willard, on Penn Avenue, and near the Women's National

Press Club, which she was also visiting. He turned off the news, plumped up the pillows on his bed, kicked up his feet, and picked up the receiver on the black phone on the left side table.

The operator put him through. "So how was it?" he asked. "Did you stay all day?"

"Amazing. We started at the Monument in the morning, then went to the Lincoln Memorial in the afternoon. King is an amazing speaker. I think he's here," JoAnn said.

"What do you mean?"

"Here at the hotel. But I haven't seen him. He must have written his speech right here."

Jim could tell she was still roused by the day.

"*The time is now*, they all kept chanting. It's stuck in my head. *An end to segregation. Jobs for all.* And it was all very calm."

Jim could feel her energy radiating down the phone line. "So are you going to send a report to the news room? Can I read it?"

"Yes. But I still have to write it. *Houston Chronicle*, I think, but I haven't decided yet."

"So?"

"Well, I'm sure Congress will pass the bill. People have been crying out for freedom. For civil rights. They've really organized this time."

"Did you happen to see my old buddy Wilson? Do you remember him?" Jim asked jokingly.

"Oh." JoAnn laughed. "Wilson? There were maybe two hundred thousand people there, Jim."

He laughed again. "He just popped into my head."

"So? What about you?" JoAnn asked. "Are you okay?"

Jim saw his moment and began to unload. "Well, guess what they discovered today?" he asked, suddenly impassioned for an outlet. "They wanted to know what I like for breakfast." He paused, then picked up again. "What's breakfast got to do with it? And a daily enema right after that. They looked inside my head at my brain waves." He chuckled at the thought and took a deep breath. "The isolation tank—oh, that was bliss—but only for ten minutes. And what do you do then? Answer: Start hallucinating. I've been bathed in ice this week, then baked in a spacesuit in a man-sized oven; I guess they'll have those in space." Jim was still feeling nauseous as he told JoAnn that the spin-dry in the giant centrifuge had been particularly brutal, and that he could barely function at fourteen-Gs, though he still managed to walk away from a temporary blackout. "At least there's some flying involved in the final stage. But, my goodness, they bought a license to see everything. And I mean *everything*." He laughed again. "They just vacuumed up whatever they could find. Dignity is gone. None left. Are you still sure women want to go up there? We should just tell them what it's like, we really should. They'll realize what they have at home." He stopped ranting, then fell silent.

"Well, Valentina, the Soviet lady did just that this summer."

"Yeah. Unbelievable."

"Still, we could have been the first. They did it again, didn't they?"

"You know, I didn't actually see any of the Mercury ladies at the clinic. Does that mean the crusade is over?"

"I'm sure it's not. It's never over."

"But I heard that Johnson asked to kill the whole idea of

women in space after their sponsor, Jacqueline, stuck the knife in their back. She just came out and said they shouldn't do it. Look, anyway, we've talked this to death. Let's not go over it again," Jim urged.

"So, not your average day in an average office. Are you guys having a hard time without the girls?"

Jim didn't know what to say.

"Point proven?"

Jim was silent. He really didn't want to get into the gender debate again either.

JoAnn said, "Normally you'd take it all in your stride. What's the matter?"

Jim raised his right arm and flexed his hand, then narrowed his eyes in pain. "My right shoulder still hurts a little when I get tired."

"Okay, so why don't you come home for a few days?"

"They're having too much fun here. They won't let me out!"

"And how is your buddy Chuck? Is he back yet? Maybe he can help you get through? Didn't he do all this?"

"I don't think he's quite there yet. The fingers are okay, but the broken wrist will set him back, and I think he knows it. Every day counts down here and it's getting as competitive as hell."

JoAnn listened.

"You take your eyes off the prize for a minute, others step into your shoes, and then it's the sideline. I don't know exactly what he's going to do when he gets back."

"You sound like you're saying it's the axe."

"Everything gets the axe eventually. The trick is to survive the game until that happens."

"Can't you help him back in?"

"I'm thinking about what I can do, but I still have to play. And I hate to say it, but one day it could be him or me. There aren't enough seats in a rocket. Everybody's thinking the same thing, I'll bet."

JoAnn sighed. "Just do what you can. But take care of yourself."

Jim took a deep breath.

"So when are you heading home?" she asked.

"Next weekend, but it'll be on a regular plane. My jet is still grounded. I can't fly with this shoulder, so I might be late. In fact, I should probably get behind the wheel and just take one of these new highways that are popping up everywhere. I see them from the air. Then I'll be back here Sunday night." Jim was deadpan again. "So it'll be a short one. And what about you? You know ... are you still feeling anxious?"

She sighed. "I don't know what it is, Jim. It's like all of a sudden I don't even trust myself to lock the door or turn off the lights."

"Have you been to the doctor? It must be the pills you're taking. Why don't you stop?"

"The doctor doesn't know either. Maybe I just have a short memory. He gave me some more."

"More pills? A short memory?" Jim thought for a moment, then said, "Maybe you can just write it down every time you do something."

"What, every time I hang up my coat?"

"Well, if it helps."

"Jim, stop it."

"So go back and tell him you don't need any more pills. He should admit you to the hospital for observation."

"Observation and then what? It's just an expensive hotel that's not very good. I really don't think there's any treatment. And I'm going back to Ann Arbor for a few days. Maybe that will help."

"It's not the money, if that's what you're thinking. Look, how about you get some new appliances in the house—on credit, like everybody else these days. The new stuff does all the work, you take it easy or go out. You'll feel better."

"I'm already getting out, Jim. I'm going to Ann Arbor."

"I know, but Ann Arbor again? So soon?"

"Yeah." JoAnn paused, then added, "Look, I think I just need stronger tranquilizers."

"What's—"

"I just thought, like you said, maybe it'll help me to get away. And, you know, Eve's there. She'll know another doctor. I can get a second opinion."

"Are you writing about the group out there?"

"Yeah, that too. There's something new."

"Look, maybe you should just get well first and then pick it up again."

"And do what, Jim? It makes me feel too much like my mother."

"What do you mean?"

"Her whole world was at home. But I went to college and did journalism, and there are new opportunities for women now. Okay, not the big jobs like editor or going into space, but I'll make some money. I don't really want to spend my time teaching or nursing like everyone expects. I hope one of my articles will be picked up. And I don't write about women or life in the kitchen or, you know, I'm not a sob sister."

"Be careful an editor doesn't just put his name on your

work."

JoAnn sighed, then finished. "That makes me so mad. I was writing something for the SDS, you know? I mentioned them, about Vietnam, about the coming draft and how kids could get around it. The editor of the magazine did a little work and just put his name on it." She exhaled loudly.

Jim was alarmed but held his tongue, silently relieved that she would not be named. The Cobbs could not be associated with a call to subvert the draft.

"See, that's why I have to write about this stuff. Why are there separate jobs for the men and smaller jobs for the girls? You know, some of the ladies here can't even cover stories because they're not allowed in the men's club." Jim knew she was referring to the long-established, male-only National Press Club she had mentioned earlier, which was also close to where she was staying. "It's everywhere, Jim. There's so much to write about. Anyway, you're right, the guys will probably just take my stuff and submit it as their own. It makes me so mad, I might just join one of those protests."

Jim's tone lightened. "You and me both. I'm protesting the invasion of medics." He could tell she was still seething. "Sorry, JoAnn, I know how you feel, but that's the world we live in. The other girls are taking it easy. Just look at Nassau Bay. Why don't you take it easy? You don't have to bang your head against all that, do you?"

"Eve's worried about Ricky anyway, so I'm going there tomorrow, right from here. Remember I said?"

"You did?"

"Yeah. And there's someone she thinks I should see, about fertility."

"Oh, okay. Like a witch doctor?"

"Don't be silly, Jim."

He relented. "You're going to be a good writer, JoAnn. You have fire in your belly."

Having encouraged her, Jim laid his head on the pillow that night, feeling restless and unable to find a comfortable position to relieve the persistent dull pain in his shoulder. He couldn't quite figure out how to resolve the anxiety of his continued absence from home, and it didn't help that JoAnn hadn't snapped out of her general malaise either. And who was she going to rattle with one of her articles? Was she losing her mind? He couldn't understand what had happened to her and was afraid that she might break down just when he wasn't around or in the middle of something critical. And it irked him that she might start writing anti-government propaganda hidden in supposed news articles. How would he fare while he worked on the inside? He prayed that the doctor could help her, even if he was the type who wore a grass skirt.

JoAnn hung up and immediately dialed another number.

"Yeah, tomorrow? Michigan?" she said. Her face lit up. "On campus? Okay, I'll see you tomorrow."

She put the phone down, then sighed in deep frustration, rolled her eyes, and muttered to herself as she stood up, "It's locked. Come on, JoAnn, that's four times already." She went to the door of her room and checked that the latch on the handle was properly closed, then scribbled it on a notepad next to the phone, just as Jim had said.

CHAPTER 16 - GAME OVER

Late-September 1963

"Hi, where can I find Chuck?" Jim asked the receptionist after stepping out of an elevator at the Sycamore Hospital.

"Down the hall, right over there, sir. Third room on the right," she replied, looking down at her notes. "I think he's doing his exercises right now, but I'm sure the physio won't mind you dropping by. How is your shoulder, by the way?"

"Oh, it's coming along, slowly. Still doing my own exercises. And how's he been?"

"Good. The doctor thinks he'll make a full recovery and should be home soon. I'm sure his wife will be relieved with all the coming and going she's had to do. In fact, I think she's here right now."

"Peggy's here? Great."

Jim knocked lightly on Chuck's door, then looked around and called his name. A physio was working on his hand while he sat and read a book with the other. Peggy was sitting upright on the bed, flipping through a glossy magazine.

"Jim, come on in. Come in," Chuck said with a warm smile.

Peggy stood up and pecked Jim on the cheek then offered him a seat. "How are you?"

"Getting there, you know, one day at a time, just like Chuck, I guess. I heard some good news out there."

"Am I being released?" Chuck joked. Peggy rolled her eyes.

The physio sitting next to Chuck put his arm in a sling, then left the room, promising to return that afternoon. Chuck put down his novel, stood up, and slowly walked around the room at a recovery pace. "It's a rare pleasure these days," he said. "I can't remember the last time I read anything that wasn't a technical manual."

"Looks like you're doing well," Jim said.

"My recovery's not complete, but a few more weeks of work on the right arm should do it. Peggy here's a virtual inmate, too."

"I haven't seen him this much since we were married," she said. "He's always off flying or trying to get somewhere. I'm sure JoAnn has the same problem. How is she, anyway? Is she here?"

"No, not at the moment. She went to visit her sister. She'll be back in a week or so." Jim sat on the edge of the bed and said, "She sent a bouquet." He held it up, even though he saw that the room already looked like a flower shop.

Peggy thanked him. "I'll leave you two and go find a vase for these, but I think we already have most or all of them." She giggled.

The men moved to the large window and sat in the bright morning sun.

"You're on the road to full recovery, I heard outside."

"Oh, good. I'm just about ready to get out of here. I count the days when I'm not climbing the walls," Chuck replied.

Jim looked down at the sling around his arm and Chuck noticed.

"These babies were trapped in that hatch," he continued. He lifted his arm slowly and looked at his hand. "Snapped off a couple of fingers flying around inside that thing. But they're still there. At least I didn't have to search the cabin for them," he joked. "Anyway, you?"

Jim nodded, though he still felt a little uncertain. "I'm fine. But my shoulder took a blow and it still hurts. Of course, considering all the tests and all that stuff you know is still going on." He half-laughed. "Believe me, you're not missing anything right now."

"Well, I can't do a damn thing that requires this hand at the moment." Chuck's tone suddenly changed, as if he was preparing to say something. "So how's the program going, Jim? Are they lining up candidates yet? Any missions?"

"I honestly don't know. They don't give much away."

Chuck stood up and looked out the window, suddenly quite agitated. He took a deep breath then appeared to calm himself again.

Jim knew instinctively what was coming. If Chuck was afraid of losing his place in Special Ops, he was probably right. He remained silent as Chuck reloaded, still looking outside.

"I've worked long and hard to get here, Jim. I've sacrificed a few years of my life for this, and I'm so into it, I can smell it." He glanced down at his cast hand. "If they pull the plug now, I don't know what else I'll do. It's all or nothing on this, Jim. You understand that, don't you?"

Wow, Jim thought; here was a different man speaking—the vulnerable Chuck, or perhaps the real Chuck behind the well-rehearsed facade that most NASA crews seemed to carry around.

Chuck gathered himself and was back in character in under

131

a second. "There's just no losing my position." He turned to Jim and added, "Listen, I want to thank you again. You and Al probably saved my hand and my whole arm up there."

Jim noticed that Chuck's guard had come back up almost as quickly as it had been lowered. And for a fleeting moment he felt puzzled by the mercurial man, even though his appreciation seemed genuine. "Don't mention it. It was nothing," Jim replied. "It could have been me or Al in there. Anyway, I was thinking—why don't you let someone else try out those leaky spacesuits for a while? I think you've had your share of the fun," he joked. "You just rest a little longer."

Chuck looked him straight in the eye, as if searching the words for meaning. Jim put on his poker face. Chuck smiled politely and backed off.

Jim turned and looked around the room. "Is there anything I can bring or take? For Peggy, if not you?"

Chuck stood up straight and declined. "We're fine. She'll be right back." His piercing stare returned. "Just let the guys know I'll be back soon, if you don't mind. I wouldn't want any of them to forget."

"Sure. Whatever you need." But Chuck had triggered Jim and he couldn't resist holding the line. "Just rest for now, while you can."

When Jim left, Chuck turned to the window, looked up at the sky and muttered, "I'll rest when I'm dead."

CHAPTER 17 - PORT HURON

Late-September 1963

JoAnn called her sister from the airport in Detroit. "I'm here," she said cheerfully.

"Where exactly?" Eve asked. "Do you want me to come get you?"

"Thanks, sis. But I'm meeting friends first."

"Friends?" Eve sounded doubtful. "The same friends from college? What about the doctor? We were supposed to go see the doctor."

"Oh, yes, the doctor." It had slipped JoAnn's mind. "Can he wait? "Until tomorrow?"

Eve sounded a little disappointed. "Jo, I made your appointment at the hospital. Aren't you coming?"

"I have to do something first."

"Look, don't worry, he'll see you. He doesn't turn people away just because they can't afford it. We're not like those inner-city places where people just walk in and back out because they don't have insurance. You'll be fine."

JoAnn sighed. "He can't do anything about this ... thing, can he?"

"He won't charge you if he can't, JoAnn."

"Okay, I'm ... still thinking about it."

"But where are you going?" Eve asked.

"I'll explain later. It's not what you think."

"Then what is it?" Eve sounded concerned. "JoAnn?"

"On the campus. I'll head home later if I'm late."

"Are you going to get caught up with those people again?"

"I said don't worry."

"I can't believe it, JoAnn. What are you doing?"

"Can you stop it now?" JoAnn looked at the giant clock above the arrivals board and said, "I really have to go now. We'll talk later. I promise I'll be fine."

"Shall I pick you—" was all that JoAnn heard as she put the phone down quickly, not wanting to get drawn into an explanation.

She hurried to the cab stand, then stopped and turned back, mumbling. "Oh, did I hang up?" After a brief pause, she rushed back to the pay phone and realized that she had indeed put the receiver on the hook. She picked it up again and replaced it, just to be sure. "Remember, write it down: it's on the hook now. It's on the hook."

She glanced at her watch and rushed to the nearest cab, her mind wondering whether to turn left or right as she jumped in. She hadn't told Eve exactly where she was going, but with renewed determination she said, "Port Huron."

About an hour later, the cab arrived on East Jefferson Avenue and pulled into the drop-off area of a large rectangular office building called Solidarity House. She paid, got out, and looked around, notepad and pen in hand.

The sun was shining and a group of people had just come out of the building with small stacks of pamphlets, all heading toward the street she'd just arrived on. Others were handing out flyers in shops along the wide avenue in front.

She pulled from her pocket a small, round, white lapel pin with plain black lettering that read *There's a change gonna come.* She looked at it for a moment, thinking she should put it on, but hesitating, put it back in her pocket, reminding herself that she was only here to report. Just as she was about to enter one of the offices on the ground floor, she was greeted with a warm hug. "Hey! JoAnn." A lady beamed at her like an old friend.

"How have you been, Sue?"

"I was so excited to hear you were coming down," Sue said.

JoAnn entered the room. "I'm late." She apologized with a smile. "There's always a delay getting on a plane these days. I hope I didn't miss anything. I came to do a story."

"No, and great. Come and see what we've been up to," Sue said delightedly.

JoAnn hung her coat on a rack and walked across the small office floor, past desks and chairs that looked like they'd been thrown out of buildings with completely different decor. The place was untidy, and the disorder grated as she crossed the floor. She waved to a middle-aged man on the phone at the first desk, then hugged another girl at the third, and sighed back at Sue. "I'm just going to check my coat. I think I hung it up."

"Relax. I'm sure it's fine."

But JoAnn shrugged.

"You're still feeling ...?"

JoAnn nodded despondently and said, "I can't seem to trust myself. Before, it was the phone on the hook. Now my coat. I don't know what it is." She glanced around the room again and immediately felt her body tense again at the disorder.

"I'd better check it out."

"Have you seen a doctor? There must be a pill for that. Those doctors can fix anything these days." Sue suddenly lit up. "You know, Jack and I have been on the new pill for ..."

JoAnn looked unimpressed and her friend paused, although the affliction about to be aired was immediately obvious. For a moment she felt a pang of distress and anxiety, reminded of her own inverse struggle to actually conceive.

"Well, it is good to see you again," was all that Sue said.

JoAnn walked back and straightened her already straight coat, then returned to be greeted by Pete, a thirty-something man with gentle eyes and a warm smile whom she had met the last time she was here; it was a visit she hadn't told Jim about. "It's good to see you again. There are some exciting things happening today." He was clearly expecting her.

Pete wasn't one of the leaders, though he seemed to be working his way up the organization. He was smart enough to have influence, and it was he who had explained to her the goals of the group and who was who. He'd given her some things to look at. An activist in the margins of his life, he was also a family doctor. He explained that he had been persuaded to support the SDS after losing a young friend in Vietnam just two weeks after he'd landed there. Several of his patients had also lost family and friends. Although he said he understood that lives were being lost in the war, he felt that it wasn't winnable, even though he had only been a medic in the field.

Pete didn't attempt a physical greeting, but JoAnn looked up and returned his smile, acknowledging that she was here to get something on the new campaign.

"I'm just going over the last column for the new flyer for Ann Arbor next week. And you can let people know what we're

136

up to. It really helps."

JoAnn was greatly encouraged and asked if she could take a look.

"Come this way," he said.

They returned to his desk where he offered her a chair. She sat down and looked at a proof with the headline *Don't Mourn, Organize and Bring the War Home.*

JoAnn had no particular opinion about what she read, but said, "We have to move fast. My sister said something about college kids being drafted."

"We?" Pete seemed surprised and smiled a little.

JoAnn laughed at herself, though she suddenly saw what was in her heart. It fueled her excitement and vision.

"Yeah, well, no time to waste," Pete interrupted. "Anyway, good, good." There was a short pause, then he asked, "Are you coming outside today?" It was as if he had an idea. "You'll see what it's all about. We're handing out flyers in the neighborhood. You can talk to people and get their opinions for your piece."

JoAnn thought and smiled again. "Sure. Good idea."

He returned it. "Great, great. Uh, you wanna quick smoke while we have time?" He had already grabbed the remaining half of a thin roll-up from his desk before she answered. He took a deep drag and blew a long, thick cloud of white smoke toward the ceiling.

JoAnn didn't smoke and had never considered starting. "Later, maybe."

Pete returned to his idea. "You can ask the locals what they need from us to build support against the war." He nodded quietly to himself and turned back to look at his flyer, just as another girl, clutching a stack of negatives, hurried over

137

from her own desk just a few seats away. "You have to see this reel. It's a good one."

"Is that …?" JoAnn knew they were making new footage about the war draft.

"Yes, it is," Pete said with delight in his eyes. He held out a hand to help her up, though she didn't need it. She smiled back at him for his thoughtfulness.

The lights in the room suddenly dimmed as the blinds were closed. Everyone turned toward a pale, cold projection from a reel camera, as it flashed flickering colorless images across a large expanse of clear white wall through the palls of cigarette smoke in the room.

"We're here to overthrow the government, violent or not, and you can avoid the army," said the clip's narrator.

"I can't," replied a civilian on the screen. "It's my duty to fight for my country."

"No! It's up to you. It's your choice. You have to get out. Here's how you can get a sick note, then you'll be free from the draft."

JoAnn warmed as the movie played out for another two minutes, and as the narrator went on to explain how to actually get a sick note from work.

The room applauded when he finished. Pete reached over the desk and grabbed a stack of new flyers with the headline *There's a change gonna come.* It was just like on JoAnn's lapel pin in her pocket. "Ready?" He said. "Cover us today. We're going out now. Other people are out there already. We'll be on Van Dyke across the street."

They walked out the office door and into the reception area where they met Sue from earlier. She was ready to join them, but they were interrupted by another younger man coming down the stairs. JoAnn knew him as a student at the University of Michigan.

"JoAnn, hi. By the way, did you see the Baker article? Great article. Extraordinary. They loved it upstairs. Your research must have been amazing. He gave you a mention."

JoAnn went cold. "Yes, it was mine." It was terse. Everyone paused in stunned silence, then she added with a smile, "I actually wrote it, you know."

The man paused halfway down the stairs, looked apologetic, then said with a shrug, as if it were some consolation, "Well, the guys loved it."

JoAnn felt like she might explode, though she was relieved that at least her first job had gone well.

The man on the stairs said, "Listen, the guys are interviewing students for Ann Arbor next week, and they asked for coffee."

JoAnn knew that the organization had started a growth drive to capitalize on strong feelings about the draft.

Sue frowned and turned to look out a large window onto the parking lot, muttering something before turning back to the man. "Can't they even make coffee?"

Pete put a hand on Sue's arm and said sheepishly, "Don't worry, I'll help."

Sue sighed in frustration.

Pete added with one eye on the stairs, "Look, I know. It's easier to stop a war, huh? Someday ... I'll help. We still have some time."

"No, you go ahead. I'll catch up." Sue turned to the student halfway up the stairs and barked, "I'll get it then." She hurried off to the kitchen.

Pete and JoAnn left the building, still clutching the flyers.

They crossed the parking lot, then frogged their way across the wide avenue as cars rolled by, making a very slight right, then an immediate left onto Van Dyke. It looked like it hadn't been maintained in years. Small tufts of grass littered the tree-lined sidewalk. The road itself was patched with thin black lines that snaked across the white lines, covering the gray asphalt like stretch marks under the sun.

The first house on the left corner was a white Dutch Colonial. Pete walked up to the door while JoAnn crossed the street to the other side and began making notes about the location and what they wanted to accomplish.

Pete knocked, but no one answered. He slid one of his flyers through the mailbox and moved on to the next house across an adjacent alley. It had two huge columns holding up the second floor. JoAnn walked behind Pete, notepad and pencil at the ready, and stood behind him as he rang the doorbell. This time someone answered.

Pete handed over a flyer. "Help us fight the war."

An older African-American man stood at the door, looking puzzled. After examining both sides of the flyer, he remarked, "I don't know who's fighting who anymore."

"Sir, we are fighting the government to stop the war. You can be sure of that," Pete replied.

The man looked up at both of them and said nothing more. He closed the door. Pete turned to JoAnn and flashed his eyes in surprise, but JoAnn said she had the reaction. "The government's war policy was confusing to Americans," she read from her page. Pete nodded.

They returned to the sidewalk and stopped while JoAnn took out of her pocket the small white SDS pin that had been there from earlier. She looked at it for a moment, wondering what she was going to do, then pinned it to her lapel.

Pete watched quietly as she tucked her notepad under her arm. "Looks like we lost Sue." She looked at the flyers in his hand and held out her own. "Let's take a couple of those." She looked down at her pin and said, "I want them to remember who we are."

Pete looked quietly impressed and handed over half the stack with a smile.

"I'll get some reactions as we go," JoAnn added. "It'll be faster."

They looked down the road, then Pete took the left side, JoAnn the right. They soon passed a community hall that had been converted into a church and crossed Lafayette, passing another group on their way back. They had just finished at a large brown brick apartment building on the corner.

For the most part, JoAnn's interactions with the households were quick and without much conversation. She got what she could, which included fears about safety in the world, parents worried about their children, the cost of the war, and one young woman who said she was going to join the SDS and wanted to know how. JoAnn showed her the way to Solidarity House.

About an hour later, Van Dyke became increasingly interspersed with empty lots and smaller houses. They looked down the road and saw only diminishing returns in exchange for shoe leather, so they decided to turn around and take another road.

The pace had slowed, and they had interrupted conversations about JoAnn's love of writing, her desire to get into mainstream journalism, and the fact that she was actually from Houston, not Detroit. He said he would introduce her to an editor he knew. She learned that he had his own medical practice, had been divorced for eight months, and had a seven-year-old son.

Two hours later, around four in the afternoon, they returned to Solidarity House, drained of flyers. They immediately walked through the office to the kitchenette in the back and made the drinks, then returned to Pete's desk and slumped into chairs among others who were already resting with cups of coffee going straight to their feet.

Sue came up and apologized, explaining that she'd taken drinks upstairs to the organization's leadership just as they were about to watch the same footage JoAnn had seen earlier. It was about dodging the draft. She'd been invited to stay and hear the plan to show it all over the neighborhood the following week.

Pete offered the girls another cigarette. Sue grabbed it first, took a deep breath, and leaned back in her chair. JoAnn took a drag and sputtered. Sue got up and went to the kitchenette to get some water.

"Hey, you know, it's a long drive back to Ann Arbor," Pete said. "Why don't you just, uh, crash here?" He looked at her. When she said nothing, he added, "Go in the morning. It'll be easier."

JoAnn smiled politely. "My sister's waiting for me. I can't." She looked up at Sue, who was already returning in the distance.

Pete continued, "Tell you what, I'll take you back. It's what, an hour?"

"Oh no, I don't want to put you out. I'll be fine."

"Really, it's nothing. It's been a long day. And home is that way anyway."

"Thanks, but I'll take a cab. In fact, I should be leaving soon. I don't want anyone to worry."

JoAnn took some water, then said goodbye to Pete and thanked him for the day. She walked with Sue to get her coat, and at the stand, Sue gave JoAnn a wry smile and said, "Oooh, I think. No, I know," she whispered.

JoAnn frowned at her. "Sue, shush. What are you saying?"

"I'm right," she added.

Laughter erupted and JoAnn's heart suddenly lifted. She felt present, focused, and hopeful with Sue. Whether or not she could change the world, as she now hoped, she knew it would be a lot of fun trying.

CHAPTER 18 - AMBUSHED

November 22nd, 1963

Jim stood at the front of a medium-sized empty conference room at the newly opened Manned Spacecraft Center near Clear Lake in Houston, looking over schematics of a lunar landing design the Flight Systems team had constructed. It had to be in his head before his presentation in a few moments. He thought to himself, if Special Ops bought his plan, it would show that he'd put something significant on the road to success; though in truth, the opposite was not even worth considering. He wouldn't be here for long if he couldn't pull it off.

Speculation was rife about a nefarious Soviet defense machine in orbit, but not enough was known to launch a mission. The race to the Moon still consumed everyone's attention.

He was ready to lay out the specific landing approach he'd been working on with engineers from one of the contractors to test thinking and pave the way for simulator runs. The diagrams showed how a lunar module could drop to the Moon's surface and descend safely under its own power. This approach had been favored by NASA a year earlier, in contrast to the Soviet plan to send a single-stage rocket all the way. For Jim, this was the landmark decision that would clinch America's goal of landing on the Moon first.

The meeting room itself was large enough to seat about ten people, with a long rectangular table in the center and a blackboard on a wheeled stand behind it. The window overlooking a wide hallway was covered with half-closed vertical blinds. He was looking out for Chris and the rest of the Special Ops crew to arrive when Chuck, now back in business, walked by outside with a few colleagues, entered the room, and took a seat.

Some of the group began discussing plans they'd seen for the Soviet space program, describing them as nothing less than a hostile Soviet ambition to dominate the entire solar system. It was amazing how a small team of men, led by a so-called mysterious chief designer—apparently plucked from a Russian gulag where people were usually sent to die—had launched, not only, the first Sputnik satellite into space just a few years earlier, but also the first dog, man, woman, and turtle; the whole room chuckled at this achievement. Another chart, described by one of the team, had ticked off the first of several Earth orbits, including the first two-man crew, and even the first time that two separate missions orbited the Earth at the same time. They knew of a Soviet probe that had already been sent to the Moon, presumably in preparation for the first cosmonauts, not forgetting the two now on their way to Mars and Venus.

"The Soviets have just announced that they will go to the Moon in one stage with three men in their lunar landing capsule. They're not doing an Earth orbit first like we are. They think it'll cost less and they'll get there by sixty-seven, which is two years ahead of us," said one of the team members.

"But I hear there's no more money in the pot. They can't feed their people or build houses. You wonder what they are doing racing to the stars," Chuck remarked.

"Well, they keep putting on more and more grandiose displays. Everyone thinks they're in pole position for the big prize."

"What? You mean that lucky turtle?"

The room chortled, then Jim quietened the team and began to explain his own plan for landing on the Moon, pointing to a diagram on a board. "The proposal is to use two lunar stages in a Lunar Orbit Insertion. The lander will detach from an orbiting stage, the latter remaining in orbit around the Moon with all the fuel and equipment necessary to return home, although we would have dragged it all the way there in the first place! That's in keeping with the LOI principle. If we took it down to the surface in a single stage, the mission might be easier, but we'd have to carry extra fuel just to escape the Moon's gravity on the way home. I'd say it's best to minimize the landing mass. Then, it's a matter of hitting the Moon's one point four kilometer per second escape velocity with a trans-Earth injection on the return trip.

"Backing up for a moment, we'll initiate a Trans Lunar Injection as we leave Earth orbit to put us on a Free Return Trajectory around the Moon, so that if anything goes wrong along the way, lunar gravity will pull us back onto the path straight home without any burns ... well, not exactly straight, if you know what I mean.

"When we get to the Moon, we hit a Lunar Orbit Insertion at sixty-two miles. A complete orbit takes about two hours.

The lunar stage will detach for its Descent Orbit Insertion at eight miles, to survey the surface and avoid mountain peaks and mascons—uneven concentrations of Moon mass which skew the gravitational field and could endanger a landing. There, we take microwave readings for depth.

"The lander itself has four, two-meter telescopic probes suspended under each of its four feet." Jim paused, glanced around the room, and saw that his audience was listening intently, a few of them nodding from time to time. "Just before touchdown, the probes will sink as far as necessary into the dust, which we expect to be a thin layer; just a few centimeters, perhaps up to a meter in some places if we choose a site carefully." He paused for a breath and looked around the room to make sure everyone was still with him.

"When the probes touch the ground, the lander will slow to zero-G for a second, then the platform engines will lower the lander to the surface. If it doesn't settle, well, you know you're about to sink into unstable ground. That means aborting the landing and shooting right back up or moving over to firmer ground. But, all well and good, we then have the engine stop when it's down."

While it all seemed like a practical solution, Jim would have admitted to being a little nervous, knowing that more work had to be done on the risk of it all going horribly wrong. He had no way of testing the theories before presenting them. Aborting the mission could open up a whole new can of worms. And what if the lander stumbled over a probe while hovering sideways for a landing site, as it had done in development simulations? Despite his reservations, he was determined to show that he and the team could think through the complexities and bring others along. He decided to plow ahead, expecting his colleagues around the table to help him work through the challenges later; after all, they were all in this together. "Oh, and there won't be any inhabitants to greet up there, furry or otherwise," he joked to ease the tension. "No stringy Moon cheese to contend with either."

His audience chuckled as Chris joined the meeting and apologized for being late. Jim knew he'd come to see the candidates in action.

Chuck asked, "Can we carry that much fuel to hover over to safer ground? The lander may run out before touchdown. It has to be safe to land quickly."

Jim saw the challenge coming and remained calm. "There's really very little hovering involved. We've tried it several times in the simulator. A safe place will be chosen before-hand and then we'll just need an extra ounce of fuel before touchdown."

Chuck started again. "Like we said, there could be several feet of dust up there, maybe more. What if you just disappear? Vamoose, Jim?"

"How long are these probes?" interrupted Chris, still settling down.

Jim was disturbed by Chuck's insistence. Was he jockeying for position to get back in the game after his absence? Jim faced him to answer the point, "First question first: several feet of dust? That's unlikely." He turned to Chris. "Fifteen feet per probe, I expect."

"It'll work," interjected Frank, another recruit and Navy ace pilot. Jim had already shared the plan with him and knew Frank wanted to try it out first in a developmental lunar lander contraption which was already on the design board. "There's good evidence that the surface is solid. Let's just hear him out."

Jim continued and knew that now was the time to lock in his proposal as the primary option. "Okay?" He looked around. "In this model we're assuming a solid surface—"

"But the surface data that came back isn't conclusive, Jim," Chuck interrupted.

Jim pressed a little harder. "The sonar will read the surface mass and altitude when we're a hundred feet up, in any case."

As he spoke, he could see that Chuck was already reloading and hadn't heard a word of what he had just said. He needed to break the flow and knock Chuck off his train of thought quickly. "Here, take this," he said, unfolding a set of poster-sized maps of the lunar surface and throwing them across the large table. "If you look here, they show crater impacts. See how the dust is spread out in a thin bank around the edges? It's obvious there's a thin layer; no more than a few centimeters for the most part. Like I said, maybe up to a meter or two in some places."

"Whoa, hold on guys. These craters are eons old. They could be under several more feet of dust. That doesn't really prove what we need to know," Chuck shot back.

"Yeah, it didn't form overnight," another replied, building on the concern. "I bet the whole surface is littered with deep bowls of the stuff. Fall into one of those and you're gone forever."

There was an uncomfortable silence as the group waited for Jim's answer.

"The Soviet Lunar probes hit the surface without disappearing," Jim replied curtly, realizing immediately that his words had come across as impatient and defensive.

"And we're sending our own new Ranger probes in Block

3—January and July—to beam back surface data before the first flight. I suggest we analyze what comes back before we continue down this path," added one of Chuck's companions, who had now locked eyes with Jim.

Jim thought the stare was a little long and said, "That seems like a good enough suggestion," though it sounded to him like he was being handed an obstacle to block the proposal until it ran out of steam. He looked around the room to gauge what was going on.

"Anyway, I don't think we can abort that low, can we?" asked another of what seemed to be Chuck's cohort, now taking shape.

It was the moment Jim had dreaded. The inevitable early doubts and unknowns had surfaced surprisingly quickly and taken the stage against an embryonic proposal. He realized he'd jumped the gun and tied himself to the mast before he had enough support. These men could derail the whole thing with the snap of a finger if they really wanted to, whether or not it worked.

Chuck seized the moment. "You can't abort that low, Jim. The only way is to land first, then relight the engines to shoot back up; or not land at all. There are still too many unknowns. I say it's just too risky."

One of Chuck's allies pushed the knife a little further. "I like the idea of the Ranger data. We should see what comes back first. What do you say, Jim?" he urged, holding Jim's eyes again.

But Jim turned the tables. "Well, how would you do it, Chuck?" he asked in a gentle, open tone, his teeth barely stopping the question from flying out like a missile.

Chuck smiled and seemed to enjoy the opportunity he'd

been handed. "We fire a projectile at the surface from above, then take a sonar reading of the depth so we know what we're stepping into—before we land right in it."

The room chuckled while Jim gently rolled his eyes and said, "You're going to carry an explosive projectile in the lander? Isn't that just a ... a lander, on the lander?" He paused and glanced at the crowd, then backed away, realizing he'd walked right into Chuck's trap in his own determination to be right. It was a ridiculous idea, but he suddenly wished he'd kept his mouth shut. What he really thought didn't matter, and now he had lost control of the meeting. The door had been opened by Chuck and the crowd had subtly piled onto him until he'd become the agenda. He calmed down when it dawned on him that he hadn't come prepared to address the group's motivations and had instead focused on the technicalities of the problem.

"Jim, it's a good idea, so let's work on it a little more," interrupted Chris, who had been quietly observing until now. "We can't go all the way there and find out that the assumptions were wrong. That would be a disaster, you know that."

Jim bit his lip, wondering how he was going to thank Chris for pushing the knife home. Couldn't he see what was going on? Was he part of it?

"It might work on a later mission, but probably not on the first one," Chris added.

One by one, the audience agreed to postpone Jim's proposal until the uncertainties were resolved, with five out of seven voting against it, a significant majority. Chris looked around the table, then at Chuck, and said, "Let's develop the projectile idea. But only in parallel," he added quickly.

"Okay?" He looked around the table. Everyone nodded. "End of meeting?"

Jim stood alone for a few moments when they finished, his heart pounding. He realized, like a slap in the face, that they were certainly not all on the same side. He had to get his act together or he'd be thrown out of the game faster than a discus at the Olympics. He stood up and quickly followed Chris out of the room.

"Are you okay?" Chris asked dispassionately as they hurried to their next appointment in the wide corridor outside, passing a ceiling support with a lone, potted green plant against it. It looked as isolated as Jim now felt.

His frustration spilled out. "Chris, you saw what happened. They deliberately derailed a promising idea and played up the difficulties for something ridiculous. And now I have to wait for Ranger's data, which is itself uncertain. All to see if there's anything we don't already know."

"Jim, there's too much uncertainty. That's the problem."

"Uncertainty? Certainty is just ... a lack of dissenting voices. You know as well as I do that clarity only comes as the work progresses. We have to keep developing this, Chris. There is no certainty in this whole endeavor."

Chris stopped and turned to him. "Look, what they asked for is a perfectly reasonable next step."

"It's just a way out, disguised, Chris."

"You're going to have to bring Chuck on board. You have no choice. Spend more time with him in the sim."

Chris kept walking, but Jim stayed still, thinking for the first time that Chris looked like he was fighting in Chuck's corner. And Chuck, he also saw, had begun to work his relationships, which in turn had begun to work for him.

"What was that all about?" Jim asked Chuck, coming up behind him on the way out.

"What's going on, Jim?" Chuck replied coldly, hurrying up a grassy knoll.

"What's going on?"

"Just doing my job, Jim. Something the matter?" They both continued quickly.

"Is there something we need to talk about?"

"Look, Jim. Some people expect a show."

Jim was puzzled and also mildly affronted. "A show? You're a showman?"

"Jim, I think you've got me all wrong—"

"We're undermining ourselves here. It's not a good show if that's what it was."

Now Chuck looked surprised.

"Just saying," Jim added, as if he'd pointed out what was plainly self-evident.

"Jim, look." Chuck held up a reassuring hand. "I can promise you one thing about this place. We don't succeed alone. It's better that we stick together."

Jim paused for a moment, considering what Chuck had just said. The words made perfect sense, but they didn't describe what had just happened.

Chuck stopped and turned to him. "Your commanding officer, Powell, asked me to help you get settled." He started walking again.

Jim was bewildered by the change of course and followed behind. "What? He did, did he? Why would he do that?"

Chuck stopped again, turned to him and sidled up. He looked around and lowered his voice to confide. "There are bigger things going on here that you're not aware of yet."

Jim looked stunned. "Bigger things? What bigger things?"

"It's not for me to say. Just keep your eyes and ears peeled."

Jim paused, confused by Chuck's remark. Cortisol coursed through his veins and he began to think he'd made a terrible mistake. He wondered for a moment if he'd misread the situation completely, though there were just too many unknowns flying around. He realized that he still needed Chuck just as much as he didn't, and his survival in the game was by no means assured.

"The Soviets?" He looked up at the sky. "What? Is something going on up there? Is it their machine?"

Out of the blue, an instinctive, visceral reaction flooded his body as screams erupted from somewhere in the corridor. Jim and Chuck both froze for a moment as people began to spill outside.

"Oh my God! Hey! You've got to see this!" screamed a fearful staff member as though a bit of the world had just been hewn off.

Jim and Chuck followed a small crowd rushing toward an adjacent building. They had all stopped in front of a live television feed of utter chaos.

"The scene over here is one of fear and confusion in Dallas as President Kennedy was gunned down less than an hour ago while touring the city in his motorcade," the reporter announced on the screen. "Police arrested a man, believed to be a Lee Harvey Oswald, who is now in custody for questioning as the president was rushed to nearby Parkland Hospital. Oswald is believed to have fired several shots from the building, known as the Book Depository, as the car rounded the corner and passed below. The president's wife, Jackie, and the mayor, who were also in the car, were spared. At this time, we have no word on the president's exact condition, but sources who witnessed the scene believe that he could not have survived the shots and may have died instantly."

The crowd gasped and stood shocked, silent, and terrified.

Jim could see outrage pointed straight at the Soviets. But what about Kennedy's whole moonshot? Would it go with him? He looked around the room and was sure he was not the only one with that question.

CHAPTER 19 - MENTOR

January 1964

The space program continued, despite Kennedy's violent end a few months earlier.

"I do not believe that this generation of Americans is willing to resign itself to going to bed each night by the light of a Communist moon," said America's new president, Lyndon Johnson, just weeks before the December blood moon.

Jim had decided on humility to help him stay with the program and keep the others' support.

He and Captain Powell walked across the angled gray tarmac strip on USS Ranger's deck—the skipper's next commission—as it sat moored at Hunter's Point, San Francisco, for an overhaul. They walked away from a giant number sixty-one, painted on the side of a fifty-meter tower behind them, its small square windows slanted downward to keep watch over the entire deck. Half a dozen planes were folded and lined up along the narrowing nose of the ship to their right, and just below their view ahead, steel-gray metalwork and pipes were being overhauled below the port side of the ship. The stillness was strange. Yellow tugs that looked like small cars with their tops lopped off under a low bridge were all stationary and silent.

Just the day before, Jim had fired up his little NASA jet to fly across the country to see his old skipper. "We're told the Soviets are concentrating their efforts on defense again. I'm sure they're smuggling nukes up from behind the Iron Curtain. I've heard of some kind of network around Earth. The hornet's nest has been disturbed. By the Soviets themselves? By someone else? Who knows," Jim said.

"America's certainly going to take aim at the Communists for it," Powell said. "They're all still paranoid after Sputnik and Cuba."

"And, space cooperation? Dead? That was JFK's idea," Jim said. "And now he's gone. It's a game of advantage, not cooperation."

"It was Johnson who started our whole program anyway. I'm sure he won't stop, whatever the cost."

They paused to look out at the calm gray Alameda Bay under the overcast sky, then Powell switched gears to ask about Jim's selection panel.

"It was a little strange," Jim recalled. "I think they just wanted to meet the candidates, probably to make sure they had two arms, a pair of legs and a head. And not just another bunch of chimps like in the early days. Evolution of the space program," he joked. "And it's no small undertaking, I suppose." Jim tried, but couldn't recall anything particularly noteworthy about the meeting. "There were no really hard questions. Something about our place in the universe seemed to rattle them a bit."

"From what I hear," Powell said, pausing for a moment to consider his words, "it sounds like you need to focus on building alliances. How's it going with Moore?"

Jim looked away, suddenly feeling the urge to rub his neck. "Chuck? We survived an air incident. You heard about the Vomit Comet, sir? We, er, worked together on life support and he's back now after a spell in the hospital."

"Just what are you trying not to tell me?"

Jim shrugged and clasped his hands as if wringing a neck. "I could just ..."

"Remember, Jim, you're not going to do this alone, like flying in your own little plane up there. I'm sure you've heard that before. Chuck has the experience of playing these circles, and you're one of the youngest. If you use his experience, he'll pull you along."

"I don't need a chaperone," Jim snapped, but immediately regretted his words. He had to try harder to keep his cool and apologized.

"That's not what I said. It's not a game for individuals, but what I'm hearing is that you're playing the lone ranger."

"You heard that? From where? Are you supposed to—"

"There it is again."

"Sir, this is a competitive place. I need to know what's going on, who's saying what, now more than ever."

"This is exactly why you need support around you." The captain took a few steps, then looked out to sea. "Speaking of which, is JoAnn on your side?"

Jim shrugged, then said, "Of course," though he no longer felt one hundred percent certain. Junior still hadn't been conceived, and she was spending more and more time away from home; just like him, he supposed.

"That's important, Jim. Relationships. You can't be looking down when you should be looking up. It's dangerous, but you know that already." Powell looked around the deck, though it was like a quiet Sunday afternoon. Nothing was moving except for a metal grinder to their right.

"There's a lot going on, sir. We're trying to make the best of it." Jim wondered if he should reveal JoAnn's new interest in what he could only describe as reporting on activism. But he was sure it would be an unwelcome revelation.

"Kids on the way?"

"No, sir." Jim wished he hadn't asked.

Powell turned to him. "They give you something to come home to when you're in trouble and you don't know what to do," he said. "Don't underestimate that. They've been bringing men home from the battlefield since the beginning of time."

It sounded like music for JoAnn's ears. And of course he was right. "Well, I'm not quite in a rocket or anything yet, sir."

"Just plan it out, if nothing else. So, are you ready for the next review point?"

Jim was relieved that they were back on business. "Yes. The advice is to focus on the job and avoid strong opinions about Vietnam, God, and so on. Nothing surprising there."

"Makes sense. Those are disagreements you can only lose. And you're not a spokesperson, so leave those questions to others and stay focused, like you said. Off the record, what do you believe anyway?"

"Kennedy wanted to pull a thousand troops out of the war. Terrible, what happened to him, but, we need to keep at the Communists as far as I'm concerned—contain the problem. Let them go and they'll be everywhere like rats. We can't let the Soviets win in space. It would be disastrous. We have to be first. There's no choice."

Powell looked at him with a small grin and seemed to acknowledge the energy in his voice. Jim understood that they were on the same page.

He felt he could now add some deeper thoughts. "And speaking of religion, I suppose I'm curious to know if there's any kind of life and a God up there," he said, a little sheepish after his experience at the panel.

The captain smiled and went with the softened tone, looking up at the sky. "If there is, He's probably a long, long way away, rather than just up there. And, *it's* probably no more than a ball of dust anyway. Though it has been looking a little red for a while now," he added, gazing up at the three-quarter Moon in the sky. "But, you'd know more about that, than me."

Jim kept a poker face about the Moon. He'd had a rough meeting with Chris and Chuck.

"But I guess anything's possible," Powell added.

Jim went a little further. "My father used to think we're *just too small in the universe, even for God*, he used to say." Jim half-laughed. "*Like a grain of sand out there, somewhere off-center.* He used to wonder what all the stuff was for, out there. *Why leave it all empty? Did the grand plan fail somehow, with just little old us?* And *what are the chances of aliens making it all the way across the galaxy just to come here and hide quietly?* my mama said. She's certainly no believer."

"We're going where no one has gone before."

"And who knows what we'll encounter."

"Jim, I'm no newbie to the warnings of life, hostile or otherwise, awaiting us in deep space. Hollywood's been pumping that stuff out for decades." He half-laughed to himself.

"You know that NASA's creating that plaque of peace for all of mankind—one for the Moon and another for Mars. Is that a confession? Who are they expecting will read it? God? It can't be for the Soviets—they're just a phone call away."

"I suggest you don't worry about all that. It's war, as you well know. It's about territory. About security. About making sure those decolonizing countries out there don't choose a Communist future. Our government doesn't pay for mankind's greatest adventure across the galaxy unless there's something in it or something at stake. Even you and I don't get out of bed for any other reason. Maybe someday we'll all be shuttling and bouncing around the stars in freedom, but I don't see it happening in my lifetime, and I don't see who's going to pay for it all. Maybe a handful of idle rich people, someday."

Jim, feeling more and more at ease with Powell, stretched his arms across the vast expanse of sky. "Some people think we just have to explore, that it's in our DNA, that we live for the experience."

"Planet Earth doesn't run on motivation or adventure. Resources, Jim. Security. These people don't understand that we fought a blockade off Cuba, not because it was something interesting to do." Powell looked around the deck again. "Don't let those ideas derail you now. This is where you need cooperation, not just advantage. Stay on task and build your alliances. You aren't protecting liberty without them."

CHAPTER 20 - PENNY

End-September 1964

It was later that year when Jim, Tom and Fred stopped for a drink at *The Spacefarer*, a watering hole along the strip at Cocoa Beach.

The place was spaced out on a long stretch of relatively sparse coast road. The trio entered from the adjacent parking lot, passing a row of palm trees overlooking the pale blue roof above the establishment. The back of the bar opened onto a wide expanse of sandy beach that ran down to the turquoise Florida waterline. The orange sunset illuminated the cream and white facade of the building.

They walked up the stairs to the main deck on the first floor and saw that the place was busy, packed with pad technicians, rocket engineers, other military folks from the base, and regular Joes from the neighborhood, all crammed between high stools and smaller round tables littered with tall blue, red, and yellow cocktail glasses and beer bottles. The local press was there, too, probably hoping to break a story, knowing that some of the astronaut fraternity would find their Cape escape, without a spouse, to be an ideal opportunity to get some cookies.

"I'll be right with y'all," said a passing waitress as the trio walked in together. "Just take a seat over there," she said, pointing to the center, which was already packed with revelers. Fred dropped a few coins into a jukebox and high-fived Tom in a familiar old style.

"Beach Boys—Surfin' USA coming up," he said, just as the waitress pulled up on her skates again.

"First time I've seen you all round here," she said in a teenage squeak. "Are you from over at the space center?"

"Just visiting," Tom replied, unsure of how to say something without actually saying anything; Jim knew several people at work who were natural at that, though not Tom.

"You're new to the beach, I see. And there are some guys with cameras around, so smile when you see them," she continued, just as a flash-light went off somewhere around the edge of Jim's consciousness. "There's a special on drinks just for you."

She continued with the standard spiel. The guys ordered and were soon surrounded by other merrymakers, while others spilled out onto the beach to watch the sunset and catch the cooling sea breeze.

Their conversation ran through the events of the past year. Jim flew back to JFK first, and they all said they were relieved that NASA had kept going. They talked about the first Gemini flight in April, even though there had been no company staff on board that one.

Jim then recounted how close he'd actually come to "moving on" with his previous unenviable job of test flying the first Gemini tow test vehicle out of Edwards for North American. The contraption was strung under a paraglider that opened like a giant parachute wing. The idea was to bring the astronauts and their capsule down to Earth for a controlled landing on solid ground. Gemini 2, scheduled for the following January, once looked like it would be the first time some poor soul would have to try it for real, although that now seemed unlikely.

Tom reminded Jim that just about everyone thought he was crazy to take it on in the first place. Jim said he realized they were probably right the very first day he went up, though by then it was too late—he was already committed. When he'd first seen the machine, he'd wondered if he'd been shuffled off to a cruel sideline by Chris. But it turned out to be worse than that. He thought he was a dead man when, on the first test, the glider hit a gust of wind after being dropped from three kilometers. The Gemini capsule bounced around in the sky like a cork strung under the brim of a hat. He'd managed to straighten the machine with the help of God, but it landed with a bone-crunching thud on the dry lake bed below. He lost a tooth filling when he clenched his jaw at just the wrong moment. The unfortunate choice Jim had made was to say he wanted to do the flying. So that's what he got. They all laughed at that.

But, he went on, that nobody was more worried than JoAnn. She became a nervous wreck whenever he said he was going to fly the thing. At one point, she said she'd rather not know what he was doing and even admitted to checking the insurance policy to see if the company actually knew what he did for a living and if they would still pay out if the worst happened. Finally, in tears, she begged him to do something else, to which he agreed, much to her relief. The project had come so close to its own death several times by then that NASA had decided it was safer to ditch its precious people in the ocean, as they'd been trained to do as pilots anyway. The Navy could fish them out of the water instead.

Ten minutes into their reminiscing, Fred suddenly blurted out, "Hey," his arms outstretched. "Penny!"

The already merry girl planted a long kiss on him and pushed them both back into his chair. When they resurfaced a few moments later, she turned to Tom and Jim. She was very excited and introduced herself with a voluptuous, "Well, hello there. How are you?"

Fred introduced them all. She seemed to realize something and blurted out again excitedly, "Yes! Fred told me about you. It's nice to finally meet you. Glad you could make it this time. You need to get away from it all sometimes, Fred tells me." She turned and giggled at him.

Jim glanced at Tom, wondering why they'd never seen Penny before, not to mention what she'd heard about them.

"These here are my aces," Fred cheered, putting an arm around her and raising a beer to his buddies. "To all the singles in the bar."

"So, are you going to take me up in your plane one day?" Penny asked Jim, clasping her hands in a show of drunken persuasion.

"You know Fred's got one of them too," Jim replied. "But yeah, sure," he added with a laugh.

Then Fred said, towering over her and picking her up playfully, "Come on, girl. Looks like we need to get some air."

"No, no, wait a minute," she protested, jumping off his arms. "I want to introduce you." She reached over to the next table and pulled another girl over. "Hey Susie, come over here and meet the boys. You know Fred, and this is Jim and Tom. They're over at the space center."

Jim's jaw dropped as he turned to face Susie, and she too locked eyes with him. Penny whispered something in her ear, then turned back to the boys. "Fred and I are outside, but you two should talk. Come on Fred," she called. "What are we waiting for? Pick me up and let's go."

"Listen, uh, it's a small world," Jim said to Tom immediately. "Susie and I need to talk. It goes back a long way."

CHAPTER 21 - SUSIE

A moment later

Jim was mesmerized. Was it really the dark-haired Susie from high school standing before him? He followed her to the bar, certain that she was the same girl he'd once had a passing interest in. It was at the same time as a budding crush on JoAnn. She seemed to have blossomed spectacularly beyond recognition in the intervening years.

She smiled at him and asked calmly, "So, are you going to the Moon?" It was as if they'd known each other for years. "I always knew you'd fly something. Everyone did."

Jim was speechless at her transformation from the awkward teenager he remembered. It was as if she had crawled out of a cocoon and spread huge, colorful wings. She seemed thoughtful and softer and more even in her tone, though he couldn't remember if her hair was practically jet black then, like it was now. She seemed a little distant and independent, though direct and confident in her tone.

"So how have you been?" he asked her with his best grin. "And how did you end up here of all places?" he added, still spellbound.

"Parents—my father moved to the base here and we just

... stayed."

Jim continued to grin unconsciously. "I can hardly believe it."

"Me neither."

"And Penny?" he asked, turning to look at the door to see if she had wandered back inside.

"Oh, college. She's infatuated with Fred at the moment, as you probably saw."

Jim wondered if he should break the bad news to her, but decided it wasn't up to him.

Susie caught it. "Does he have someone?"

He did, Jim knew—several, actually, but what could he say? "Oh, I don't think so," he replied. "Just a lot of work to keep him busy."

But Susie caught him again. "It wouldn't be the first time. And it never stopped any of you guys from the base anyway."

Jim rolled his eyes at the man-bashing. There seemed to be a lot of it flying around.

"And what about you? Are you staying here?"

"Well ..." Jim suddenly found himself on the back foot, not having planned for the old Susie to ask him that question tonight. "I'm in Houston. And you? What are you doing on base?" he asked, intrigued.

"I work on the health team. Making sure the guys are in ship shape. Especially up there, where it gets really interesting."

"Good. That's good. I could probably use some of that," he joked. His heart started to flutter.

"Well, come on over. You're not based here, but I'll take a look at you if you want."

Jim heard a seductive invitation in the way she said it.

"Besides. I think you owe me one if you're here again," she added.

Jim was confused.

"You still owe me a ride, I seem to recall."

Jim laughed. "Oh, that? The little plane when we were in school? I never thought that would happen," he recalled. "I had to stop flying that thing for a while. The plane was taken away and I was grounded. Reckless teens."

"They must be faster now. Climb higher? Got a little rocket now?"

Jim laughed, though he couldn't be sure it wasn't just a question that came out wrong. But it seemed too deliberate to be misjudged. "The planes are fast enough."

"I didn't see you in that group on TV."

"Oh, me? You think I'm going ... up there?" He looked up and laughed. "Maybe someday. Who knows."

She thought for a moment, then said, "Yeah, I knew it the minute I saw you. Why else would a fast jet pilot be here? Are you staying long?"

"What? Well, I'm just waiting my turn. Like the other guys. It's not like catching a plane." He laughed that off as well.

"Me too."

Jim wondered what she meant and she caught him again.

"Aren't we all headed up there some day?"

"I think we're all just fine right here, aren't we?" he replied, glancing around at the merry makers. "For one thing, it's going to be hard to find a decent beach bar up there like this. They have seas on the Moon, but it's not really the same—even when the sun's out."

She laughed and gazed off into the distance. "Lying on a beach under a billion stars with nothing in your way. That

169

would be something, wouldn't it?"

Jim was intrigued by a small black and red tattoo on her bare shoulder as she turned to get a drink.

"Black widow spider," she said, following his gaze. "I always thought they were cute. I got bitten here on the shoulder climbing in Yosemite. I sat down to rest and it fell out of a bush."

Is she for real? Jim wondered in awe. "I thought they were deadly," he remarked, taking a closer look.

"Not always. Obviously!" she replied, flashing her eyes. "She kills and eats her mate so they don't all get lucky. And that's why she's a widow. Anyway, I survived somehow, and I always thought it was something special. Like a sign. To get something out of it. I got a tattoo to remember it."

Jim was quietly amused as she took one of his hands. "I can tell you haven't been turning wrenches all these years," she said, running her splayed, slender fingers along the ridges of his palm. "You don't have hands like that."

"Are you saying I'm wimpy?"

"No. Just gentle hands. And precise. No heavy stuff. You know, hands say everything. They make you the person you become," she said thoughtfully.

A primordial subroutine kicked in inside Jim's brain. His thoughts began to ease and he started to enjoy her flattery.

Susie lit a Winston and took a long swig, keeping her eyes on him. "I'll let you in on a secret," she said, taking another drag. She gave him another soft look. "I saw you at the base the other day."

Jim felt a figurative squeeze on his balls from the way she said it. "But you didn't say hello?"

"Actually, I wasn't sure it was you. It's been so long." She glanced at her friends, who were signaling that they wanted her back. But seemingly reluctant to leave, she stayed. "Will I see you again?" she asked, looking into his eyes. They softened behind a well-rehearsed, flattering smile. "I have to get back to the guys now." She reached out and took his hand again. "We're going to another party later. Why don't you come with us? For old times' sake," she added, tilting her head subtly and glancing over her shoulder as she slipped away, one hand inside his.

Jim's mind raced. He stared at her as she gently dropped his hand, thinking that he hadn't done something like this in a long while. He hoped it didn't show and tried to look cool.

A cameraman asked a group around the bar to turn for a shot. They cheered and raised their bottles and glasses, just as—to Jim's surprise—Susie clasped his hand and, with a big smile, nestled herself into his side for the photo. He was pleased and shocked, thinking that there would be trouble at home if the photo got out.

A low coffee table in the middle of a private room at the back of the bar, known as *The Den*, surrounded by equally low, deep-cushioned couches, had the rocket dust on it. Everyone seemed to be getting their fill, rolling up and passing around weed in various sizes.

Jim wondered if he was seeing double with all the pot he'd just sniffed out of the air. Fred had found his fun with a pair of twins—both Penny lookalikes—and was clearly not to be disturbed. It seemed too good to be true and he wondered if it really wasn't.

Susie poked her head through the beaded curtain that separated *The Den* from the dark world outside, and looked around. She caught Jim's eye and he instinctively smiled at her, somehow knowing, from the look in her eyes, that it was time to leave. And numb, as if dreaming, with alcohol coursing through his veins, he clumsily climbed off the low couch, took her hand and followed her to the bar.

She turned and looked up at him, pulled herself in close and said with a soft, nervous breath, "Come with me. It'll be fun. I promise."

Jim had lost his inhibitions by now and found little capacity for resistance. His heart began to pound as he looked down at her familiar face, glowing perfectly in the dim light of the bar, her dark lips and eyes piercing through her pale, warm skin. His eyes fell onto her sheer dress, clinging to the curves of her tightly toned body. Without another word, they walked out of the bar together.

Susie's friends were already waiting by the car when they arrived.

"Hey dude, glad you could make it. Jose's the name." It was one of her buddies, dressed in a colorful Hawaiian shirt and quite cheerful. "Will you open the door, dude?" he demanded of the driver. Jim thought there were a lot of dudes tonight.

"Okay, okay, don't rush me. Relax, will ya?" The other man unlocked the car. They all climbed in one by one, though Jim stayed outside for a moment because none of them seemed sober enough to get behind the wheel. He looked up at the sky, wondering what to do next. The Moon was low and nearly full. His thoughts turned to JoAnn and he silently promised her it wasn't what it looked like.

"Come on. What's going on?" called Jose. "Let's go, dude. Jump in!"

A cool evening sea breeze suddenly blew across Jim's face.

He took a deep breath and clambered into the back of the car and squeezed in next to Susie. But as it pulled away, he noticed a flash of light somewhere behind and to the left.

CHAPTER 22 - DOWNFALL

A week later, early–October 1964

JoAnn was on the porch when Jim arrived home Friday night. He'd called ahead to say there was a storm coming in, so he'd be home later than expected. She wasn't convinced by his story, even though she'd checked the weather report to confirm it.

Her head had been throbbing for an hour as she thought, rethought, and chewed over what to say and how to say it. And now she didn't have the energy to hide her sullen face. She sipped on a shot of scotch and drew a cigarette without a word. She heard Jim sigh a little as he paused for a moment on the steps in front of the door. He came forward quickly and pecked her cheek, then said he had to go to the bathroom and disappeared inside. That told her everything. He'd come home, hoping for a few easy weekend days. No fuss. It had become the norm and was beginning to feel like indifference. But today there was something she needed to talk about.

She walked quietly into the kitchen, telling herself to stay calm whatever came out of her mouth.

Still zipping up, Jim followed a moment later and went straight to the sink, turned on the faucet and scrubbed his hands. She turned away as he gave her a small hug from behind. He sat down at his usual place at the dining table.

JoAnn stood at the stove, heating a pan, and turning just enough to see Jim thumbing through a pile of mail. She opened the refrigerator and took out a wrapped slab of steak and dropped it into the pan, turning off the gas when it started to smoke.

Jim asked for a beer, but she pretended not to hear him over the sizzling pan. After a moment he got up, went to the fridge and pulled out a Miller, took a long swig and asked, " Everything okay, honey?"

"I'm just tired, that's all."

"Oh, what happened?"

"Didn't sleep again." She stirred a second pot of whatever was coming for dinner.

"Why?"

"First light. Gets me up."

Jim acknowledged her quietly and continued to rifle through his mail.

But already she couldn't hold back the words that had been playing in her head all week. "It was the same on Monday. You got up early and parted the curtains to look outside. Then you didn't close them. You do that every week, Jim."

He stopped and looked up. "Uh, I'm sorry. You should have said."

"I already said it. And you left the toothpaste cap off."

Jim shifted in his seat and looked down again, staring straight through the mail.

"And it leaked again."

"Well, you have your sink." Jim replied. "I try to keep mine tidy."

175

"Just put the cap back on when you're done. I don't want half the bathroom looking like a mess when I walk in."

Jim remained silent, flipped open a letter and began to scan it.

"And I put my curlers in the front of the cabinet so I can find them easily. You put your laundry bag in front when you come home every week. I have to pull it out to get to them."

"It's always been there. Where am I supposed to put it?"

"There's room in the closet."

Jim put the letter down, got up again, a little slower this time, walked quietly to the refrigerator and got a plate of covered snacks. He sat down again.

"Well, it's been a rough couple of months and a long week. Does any of this matter now?"

"Oh yeah?" The moment came and she just couldn't hold back. She turned to him and felt her anger bubble up. "Busy doing what, exactly?"

Jim looked shocked. "Something wrong?"

"I said I didn't sleep. That's what I said, isn't it?" She turned back to the stove and turned the steak. It sizzled and smoked even higher.

After a moment Jim asked, "The pills aren't working?"

What? her head screamed. "No." It was short, like a rebuttal, but JoAnn liked it—quick and clean as a gunshot.

Jim seemed to barely know what words were, but he managed to say, "Weren't you going to ask for something stronger?"

She stopped dead, dropped the tongs, and turned to him. "Why don't you tell me what's making you so tired?"

Jim's eyes shifted as he considered what to say. He recounted, warily, that he'd been in the cramped simulator all week, lying on his back for most of the hours God had sent. He had to reach for dials and switches and manuals, which killed his arms and brain.

In a sudden rage, JoAnn dropped his half-cooked dinner in the garbage beside the stove. "Really? That's it? Anything else?"

To Jim's obvious shock, she put the pan back on the stove, walked over to a cabinet and yanked open a drawer. She pulled out a folded newspaper, unfolded it, and slammed it down on the table in front of him, then stared him in the eyes for the next move.

Jim looked at it while she stood a few feet back.

"Well?" she demanded.

Jim continued to stare at the *Florida Times* in shock. A medium sized picture of Susie, holding his hand in a smiling group at the Cocoa Beach bar the week before, stared back at him. Another smaller picture had him in the background with her at the bar.

Jim's face flushed and he looked thoroughly embarrassed. "How did you get this?" he asked. He groaned and rolled his eyes, then looked up at the ceiling. "She just grabbed my hand," he implored.

"She?"

Jim shook his head, then sat back and looked up in disbelief.

JoAnn pressed him. "She? And when were you going to tell me?"

"It was a mistake."

"A mistake," she repeated, mocking his words. She stared at him, silently seething inside. "Were you going to tell me? Is this what's making you tired on the weekends?"

"We were at the bar and she just took my hand. There were

cameras everywhere. They said turn around for a picture and that was that."

JoAnn looked at him doubtfully and with a penetrating gaze, trying not to miss a clue. "Who is she?"

Jim froze for a few moments, still looking worried.

"Who is she?"

"I knew her from elementary school. I was surprised to see her."

JoAnn was stunned, and for a moment a wave of relief washed over her. Then it suddenly hit her that that could be worse. "Oh yeah?" she replied, leaning over to look at the photo. She picked up the paper and studied it, then tossed it back in front of him. "Nobody just grabs your hand. What did you say to her? That you're going to take her up in that rocket of yours? Is that what you tell them? Like you told me?"

"It was a mistake, JoAnn, I swear. I was going to say, but I didn't want to make something out of nothing."

"Hoping it would go away? Well, that didn't happen, did it?"

Jim said nothing.

"It's in the papers, Jim!" she pleaded.

"Look, I'm sorry, I should have said. That was a second mistake." He immediately mumbled something confusing about how Susie wasn't his doing, so it wasn't really his first mistake. "But it was nothing. You know how it is. There are a lot of girls down there just looking for—"

"That's enough."

Jim was silenced, but after a moment he got up and hugged her, even though she wanted none of it. "I'm sorry, Jo. I promise it was nothing. She works at the base, that's all."

"Jim, do you think I don't know what happens out there?

I know what other wives go through. They just pretend it doesn't happen. They'd rather not know."

"JoAnn! Nothing happened. I said it was nothing."

She pulled away and put her hand to her head, scrunching her face and feeling like she had a hangover.

Jim stared back at her as if he'd been caught in the dark by a flashlight.

"I don't know what's going on with us, Jim." She paused, then continued. "I don't think I can do this anymore. I can't go through this again." She pictured herself walking in on her ex-husband as if it were yesterday, and suddenly became angry. "I'm not listening to the others talking about all that again." She paused. "I'm sorry." She remembered his dinner and groaned at the trash. "Oh, what have I done?"

"Look, let's do something next weekend. Take a trip? We always wanted to go to Vegas. Let's do that? Get away. I'll take a few days off."

She considered the idea, then remembered that she couldn't. Besides, he'd broken that promise too many times.

"Well?" he asked.

"I can't."

Jim looked surprised. "Why?"

"I-I can't," she repeated, turning away slightly as if also caught out.

He probed her again.

"I'll be in Michigan."

"JoAnn, that's the third time this month." It was impatient.

"There's another march."

Jim frowned and took a deep breath. "Why are you marching for those people, Jo? I thought you were writing articles. Do it here."

179

"It's not *those people.* They need me to keep reporting. I want to do it." JoAnn suddenly felt conflicted. It was unexpected, and she hadn't seen it coming. It was going to be more than just an article to produce—she hadn't been able to keep herself from rallying with everyone else, though she decided not to reveal any more.

"JoAnn!"

"I said I'd do it."

"Well, do it from here."

She suddenly had an idea. "Why don't you come with me?"

Jim was dumbfounded and stared at her for a moment. "I can't come with you."

"You can. Why not?"

"I can't just join a march against our government," he pleaded. He backed off, then wound up again with his hands splayed as if to hold his ground. "Look, Jo, can't you just put this on hold? While I'm in the running at NASA?"

"How will they know? I'm in the background."

"They know everything. They have ways." He sighed deeply and looked exhausted. "Why are you doing this?"

"I have to do what I can to stop the war, Jim."

"The war? Vietnam? You never said anything about the war."

He was right. She hadn't. "Yes. That's what they're doing. I have to help my nephew Ricky and others like him."

"But it's not your war, JoAnn," Jim insisted sharply. "Those people have no idea what they're playing with. We need to keep fighting in Vietnam."

That surprised her. He'd never lost his temper before. She waited. Jim looked up in thought then barked, "Protesting! The Communists would just love that, wouldn't they! Stop the war! Please!" He paused and shook his head. "I'll bet they're in there somewhere. Protesting to stop the war! While some of us are trying to keep the country safe."

JoAnn stared back in disbelief. Jim had revealed himself. It was clear he wasn't going to live with her protests.

Numbed by his words, she replied, "Yes, it is. If it's your war, it's mine. We're all in it. If we don't do something, who will?"

Jim looked incredulous. "What is it, JoAnn? It's those darn pills, isn't it? We need to get back to the doctor."

"I'm not taking those pills anymore." A moment later she added, "Nothing's going to change for us now, Jim. We were supposed to have a family. It's been over a year. You're not making decisions about us anymore. We … I just keep getting kicked down the road." She continued, feeling tearful. "Meanwhile, you're … you're so caught up and attached to the whole thing. When it's over, there'll just be something else."

"What's that supposed to mean? You're out there protest-ing the war. Whose side are you on?"

JoAnn looked incensed. "How dare you?"

They froze in shock and stared at each other.

"How dare you?" she repeated.

Jim looked shaken and ran his fingers through his hair. He sidled up to her and started to apologize, but JoAnn's fury now saw an opening. She put up a finger to him and said, "No. I'm not staying here to be the talk of the town. Not me. Not me. I'm done with that." Suddenly all the past hurts of her first marriage and her husband's infidelity poured out. She saw that she was still walking on thin ice over what had happened all those years back. She looked up at him and shook her head, repeating firmly, "Not me."

Jim was bewildered when she backed away. "Where are you going?"

"I won't get in your way. You don't need me here. I have to go." She turned.

"JoAnn," he called as she hurried toward the stairs. "Whose neck do I have to wring for this? Was it one of the girls?"

She caught him shaking his fist in the air and heard a curse as he went back into the kitchen, presumably to see if there were any leftovers. Then she ran up the stairs to the bedroom in tears. The front door slammed and a moment later Jim was gone.

JoAnn picked up the phone and dialed her sister, Eve, and asked to be picked up at the airport the next day.

CHAPTER 23 - THE TYRANNY OF BEING SELECTED

December 1964

Jim looked at his watch as he sat alone in his Washington hotel room. It was almost time to leave for the Medical Board. He poured himself a last cup of coffee and thought back to yesterday when he'd ripped open the telegram, butterflies doing triple somersaults in his stomach. He wished JoAnn was with him and regretted what he had said to her in that split second of madness in the kitchen. Somehow, she'd been gone to her sister Eve two and a half months already. He'd crossed a line with his words and it had hurt her deeply.

And it didn't bode well that the panel needed to talk today. He racked his brain again for mitigating explanations against a short list of possible ailments the doctors might have discovered while he was strapped down in Albuquerque. He turned on the television to more news of anti-war demonstrations across the country.

"In growing signs of unrest, the streets were clogged today with angry demonstrators, protesting, sometimes violently, against the drafting of young men into the escalating war in Vietnam. Scenes turned ugly as arrests were made of draftees who came to burn their draft cards in public, right here, today. Shortly after four in the afternoon, tear gas canisters were fired at the entrance and student exits to keep the crowds away, while hardliners were still holed up inside. Though some had been evacuated, the result was clashes and standoffs with riot police that seemed certain to be repeated at colleges across the country."

The reporter on screen cornered a middle-aged woman wrapped in a scarf, hat and thick red coat. She was carrying a picket sign in the midst of a protest that read *DON'T REGISTER*.

"Ma'am, why are you here today?" he asked her.

The lady, clearly energized but tense, spoke firmly. "I don't want my children to go to war. It's pointless and inhumane, and we need to pull our soldiers out now, not increase the numbers and send our children—can you believe it? Our children? Young ... boys who have their whole lives ahead of them."

A bearded man beside her interrupted. "It's outrageous and immoral. We must stop this illegal war now and stop sending our people to their needless deaths."

The two were swept away by the fast-moving crowd and thanked the reporter.

"Well, you heard it here, straight from the angry people of Washington, right in front of the Pentagon. They don't want the war. Now back to the studio."

Jim rolled his eyes, thinking they were crazy, that the only thing these people knew about the war were the casualty figures and the gruesome images on television. It was hardly a balanced view. They couldn't possibly understand the dangers to freedom if the Reds went unchecked, and of course it would be these same people who would protest for freedom if totalitarianism ever took hold. He saw troublemakers in the crowd, inflamed and intent on causing chaos for whatever reason, angry at life, not to be reasoned with, armed with tactics and incendiary words in constructed speeches, and never missing an opportunity to pose for antagonizing images on camera.

He glanced at his watch again and saw that it was eight-thirty. He turned off the TV and figured it would take him about thirty minutes to get to the address, which seemed to be somewhere near the hornet's nest he'd just seen on the news. That was assuming he met no detours along the way.

He wasn't entirely surprised to encounter a roadblock manned by a small group of protesters shortly after leaving his room, though he was relieved to be in civilian clothes rather than the usual military fatigues. He drove slowly through the jeers and taunts, but found himself sandwiched between other road users. Even though nothing obviously identified him as a military man, he wondered if others could just smell the sea air on him. Maybe it was his haircut.

Several demonstrators peered through the windows of his car, chanting slogans, as one protester threw himself over the hood and pounded on the windshield, sliding down the other side and knocking off a side mirror. The mob began hammering on the car. A few of them yanked the door handles and tried to get in even though they were locked.

Jim knew he was pretty much stuck. He pulled into a side street and stopped, extracted a map, and traced a new route along a parallel just a block away. It would take a little longer, but it looked worth a try. He proceeded slowly, then turned left at the end of the street. Straight ahead he encountered an even bigger blockade. In the middle of the road, about fifty yards ahead of him, was a street fire. A few other cars had already backed up in front of it, and about a dozen demonstrators were standing near it, throwing pieces of wood to taunt it higher.

Jim parked again and got out to lock up, estimating that he had about a mile to go. He'd better walk. A young man hurried past him and knocked the keys out of his hand, but turned and waved a postcard in the air with the defiant glee of a lottery winner. Then he ran up the street to a sign that read DRAFT CARD BURNING HERE. ANYONE WELCOME, and lit the card in the flames next to it.

Two police officers wrestled the card burner to the ground, then turned him over and sat on him before cuffing his hands behind his back. But the burner didn't go easily. They dragged him kicking and screaming to a nearby van, where three other protesters jumped in to peel off the officers. More police joined the fray and fought them off, just as a suit walked up to the fire and fished out an unburned corner of the half-destroyed card.

Jim was gripped by the rebellion as he moved quickly past the fire, feeling its warmth against the cold morning air. Picking up the pace to clear the mob before he was drawn in, he slipped down another side street onto the next parallel. He jogged most of the way, finally arriving, breathless, at NASA's Washington headquarters.

Still huffing, he walked up the steps and said to the guard, "Did you see that?"

"Yeah. It's unbelievable to see such chaos around here. Never seen anything like it. Are you all right, sir?"

"Yes, thank you." He looked back down the street. "I bet this is the best place to air grievances, though."

Jim wiped his face and walked through a set of revolving doors into a large, spacious hall. To the right was a reception desk and straight ahead was a huge staircase. Not surprisingly, the building's security alert was on high. The path ahead forked both left and right to the next level, and to Jim, the place immediately felt like a hive of activity and expectation. A lot of people were scurrying around. And it seemed paradoxical that this part of the government, at least, seemed as energized in its own mission as the disgruntled forces were outside. This was the place where, in October, one of the most memorable announcements of the era was made—the names of NASA's group three astronauts, arguably the first of mankind to leave Earth for another world. It created hopes, dreams, lives and legacies.

"Several others have arrived upstairs, sir. But we are a little late," the guard said over Jim's shoulder, walking in behind him. "Make yourself comfortable for now." He took Jim's coat. "Up the stairs and to the left, sir."

Jim felt unsure about the schedule with all the commotion outside, and asked if they were going ahead today. The guard said they were, so Jim went up to the first floor and found himself alone in the waiting area in a high-ceilinged hallway. He passed a couch and went straight to the tall windows to look out at the street again. Several empty police cars were speeding toward the scene of the riot he'd just escaped. Another returned in the opposite direction with a prisoner flanked by officers in the back.

He turned and took a seat just as Tom appeared on the landing. Pleased to see each other, they shook hands. Tom said with a grin, "You'll never guess who's here. It's your buddy Chuck. We're just in the room upstairs."

Jim looked surprised. "By accident or design?"

Tom shrugged and said, "It's hard to know what they're up to."

"And Fred?" Jim asked as they walked.

"I haven't heard from him." That sounded ominous. "You?"

Jim hadn't heard either, and shook his head as they approached Chuck, who was waiting in the hallway outside the boardroom. He hesitated at first, then offered a terse handshake.

"Jim? Tom? Good to see you here." He looked calm, though he had an unusual air of formality. "Interesting that we're here together, isn't it?" he added with a glance at Jim. "No sign of Fred?"

"Too early to tell. Shouldn't guess, huh?" Tom replied in Fred's defense.

"There's room for everyone. LBJ is a supporter of the unit, so it's not going to end anytime soon. I'm told that the meetings with the panel are staggered throughout the week, so it's impossible to know how this will turn out."

"I thought you got a clean bill of health," Jim remarked.

"Let's see in there. Maybe the panel just likes to see me once in a while," Chuck joked.

"Very reassuring, I'm sure," Tom said.

"Well, who knows—maybe we'll find ourselves on a crew together!" Chuck replied.

Jim looked at him. "Be careful what you wish for."

Chuck paused for a moment and then said, "I should let you know that I applied to transfer to the Apollo Group Four pool in June." He stood quietly for a moment while Tom and Jim absorbed the news. "Anyway, this encounter in there is guaranteed to be more prickly than the first. Minds are focused on the difficult challenges ahead. There's less wriggle room and no deferring anymore," he said. "It can't be an easy job."

"I'm sure they'll make the right choices," Jim said, still pondering Chuck's revelation.

The event host interrupted the trio and patted Chuck on the back. "Okay, you're up in two minutes."

"Gentlemen. Good luck," he said. In that, Jim heard a confident farewell. "I'd better get ready. See you on the other side." Chuck disappeared.

"I don't know about you, but what I just heard was every man for himself," Tom said as they both stepped outside again.

"That's just Chuck being Chuck."

They stopped at the top of the building entrance and looked out over the park across the street where a small group of protesters, perhaps twenty strong, had begun another march, cordoned off by police on the opposite side of the street, though this time it looked peaceful. It was not the adrenaline-fueled madness Jim had seen earlier. One of the crowd, in full military uniform and in a wheelchair at the head of the march, looked like he'd seen action in the war and returned without his legs. A woman carrying a large picket board lamented the loss of her son, while several others held up a large banner that read *VIETNAM: LOVE IT OR LEAVE IT.*

"A lady on my street lost both her boys," Tom said, glancing at the crowd. "And she's talking about joining another march in Washington, on The Monument."

Jim was reminded of the previous year. "That King speech for African-Americans brought out the mother of all marches,

189

didn't it? I'll be surprised if anyone can top that. JoAnn was out there."

"Getting civil rights this summer looked like it was going to be easier than getting out of Vietnam. They actually got what they wanted. Anyway, how do you feel about the war?" Tom asked.

Jim hesitated, thinking of JoAnn and wondering if he should say what she was up to. He held back but said, "As far as I'm concerned, we need to stay the course." That was how he felt. He couldn't lie about it. "There's no substitute for victory, said MacArthur. You?"

"It's tearing the country apart. I just hope this whole space program can bring us back together. We need something new to aim for."

Twenty minutes passed and the two returned inside where the host informed Jim that he would be next.

Chuck exited the panel meeting room as Jim stood by, though he was not alone. Deep in conversation with a companion, he neither turned nor stopped to share his news.

"Okay, Jim Cobb? You're up. The room on the right, please, sir."

Jim and Tom wished each other luck and shook hands again.

When Jim walked into the room to meet his fate, he immediately recognized the chairman of the selection panel, as well as another official from when he'd first joined Special Ops. The room was a normal large office meeting room. Once again, he stood next to a single empty chair at the end of a large rectangular collection of desks and greeted the panel while still on his feet.

"Please take your seat," the chairman said, glancing left and right at the other members to make sure they were ready.

"Jim, we're here to review how the recruits have settled into the unit and talk about what's next."

Jim's heart began to race and his breath shallowed, almost stopping for a moment.

The chairman took off his glasses. "The standard is extremely high, as you know from your training," he continued with a conciliatory smile. "And that is why you are here."

Jim's senses sharpened to a pin prick and he began to read into every word. Did this mean all was well? "Sir, it's an honor to be here," was all he said. He was sure he had said the same thing the last time.

"Do you realize the gravity of this undertaking for our nation? We cannot afford to lose this race to the Soviets. There will be no turning back if we do," the chairman continued sternly. "We cannot get this wrong," he added, directing the remark at his fellow panelists. "The cost is too high, so we have to get it right the first time."

Jim thought it all sounded great, but wondered why they couldn't just tell him what they wanted to say first. He began to focus on each gesture, as if it were a ritual dance, as he considered whether to stick to his script or flip it.

"You're an ace pilot," began another of the panelists Jim hadn't seen before. "And a man of faith."

"Sir, I believe in the Lord."

"I also read here that you believe the surface of the Moon is solid. There is some observational data, but it's a leap of faith, isn't it?"

Damn, Jim thought. They knew about the fateful proposal, and probably knew that he hadn't been able to get the others on board. "Okay," he replied, though he was not sure where this was going. "It sounds like you know about something

191

I've been working on for a while."

"Yes. The landing proposal. Your colleagues didn't think it was such a good idea, did they?" the chairman replied, a little pointedly. "And considering that they might have had to risk their lives for it … several people said it was dead on arrival. Wouldn't you agree?"

It suddenly felt like an indictment. All eyes were on Jim, and he'd only just arrived. "Sir, there was a lot of data to support that proposal. It showed up in all the information we had. It was an efficient approach—"

"We know you were ambushed when you presented your case."

Jim lost his tongue, then the penny dropped that they'd been watching his every move, evaluating his every word and every single interaction, probably every minute of every day.

The chairman interrupted his thoughts. "We needed to test your commitment to your colleagues, Jim."

He was shocked. "Are you saying it was staged? Were the others in on it? Who—"

"—*against* your own position, when your chips were down."

Jim immediately felt like a child who had been put back in his stroller.

"That's part of the process, Jim. Remember, we're not taking any chances."

Jim felt disoriented. Was that part of the evaluation too, he wondered, like being spun around in a mental centrifuge at ten-G? Anything was possible here. "Well, sir, does that mean—"

"It simply means the supported proposal will win the day. But that's not for this panel to decide. There are technical committees for that sort of thing."

The chairman took a deep breath and removed his glasses. "Look, Jim, your heart—our tests show it has a murmur."

A what? Jim thought.

"And that's the problem. Jim, I'll get right to it." The chairman glanced sideways at his table. "It's a risk. The medics won't let you go anywhere."

Jim felt floored. He had had a horrible feeling that something would come unhitched when he opened the telegram at home. And of all things, they'd found a what? A heart murmur? He wondered if he'd heard the chairman right. "Sir? Are you saying I'm grounded?" He stared into the chairman's eyes, which read back, *What do you think I just said?* "Sir, I've never had a diagnosis that limited my flying or training in any way."

Jim paused and felt the hammer blow of rejection. His temperature began to skyrocket and his mind raced for a way out, as if he were trying to escape the Korean mountains again in his fighter plane. He asked bluntly, "Am I out of the unit, sir?"

After a moment's silence, the chairman replied, "I'm afraid so, Jim."

He suddenly felt as if his hopes had been cut off at the knees. His head went blank, his ears deafened to all but the beating of his heart, while his eyes searched for meaning.

"Nevertheless, Jim, it is the recommendation of this panel that you remain with NASA and support the astronaut corps."

Jim barely caught the words. *What the hell?* almost flew out of his mouth.

"We want you to continue to prepare and support the Group Fours if they're selected, at least until they find a way to fix your, er, heart problem."

Jim didn't answer.

"The doctors will keep an eye on you," the chairman added.

Nice, Jim thought. He had already spent more time with the doctors than with JoAnn, and she was the one who had been sick.

"We'd like you to stay in the astronaut office, Jim. There's a lot to do, as you no doubt know."

Suddenly, it didn't sound so bad to Jim; not like an outright rejection. The chairman had said the word "stay". But for what exactly? To watch the others do the flying and the spacefaring while he sat in an office? The voices in his head battled for supremacy, though the regret of loss seemed to take the upper hand without effort. He was being offered a sideways move, a holding pattern, a graceful freaking exit until he took the real one, the voice in his head screamed.

The panel sat back as Jim began a plea. "Sir ..."

But they showed no reaction, no accommodation. No one was negotiating, and Jim realized he'd only be digging his grave if he kept going. He got up, nodded quietly and left the room, feeling humiliated in a silence that offered no consolation.

He paused on the steps outside and took a deep breath. Everything looked the same as an hour ago, but nothing felt the same anymore. A vacuum had taken all the oxygen. But what had happened to Chuck? And where in the world was Tom?

CHAPTER 24 - SOUL SEARCHING

The next day

Jim returned home, dropped his bag at the bottom of the stairs, and put his keys on the table. The house felt quiet, empty and cold as he entered the front door.

He walked to the kitchen and looked out the window above the sink into the backyard. Easy viewing, or it would have been if JoAnn was out there, tending the manicured yard—a quiet, predictable life, a million miles away from the relentless ambition of the world from where he'd just returned. An image flashed through his mind of the time he'd picked her up from the flower beds out there and spun her around in his arms. She was full of joy that week in their new house, even though they were covered in muck after clearing a patch of overgrown shrubs.

He wondered what he'd gotten himself into when he walked into his office and saw a handful of mail he'd left on his desk. There, on top, was the fateful telegram that had taken him to Washington. He leaned in the doorway and glanced around the room at the space memorabilia he'd collected over the years, including the model rocket his father had bought him for his birthday just before he disappeared. It stood tall on the table in the corner. His father's old DC-3 lapel badge sat next to it, along with a magazine with a cover showing an artist's sketch of a team of astronauts overlooking a futuristic dwelling in a lunar crater. He felt like he'd seen enough of them, and after a moment's deliberation, locked away the booster and the magazine. He sat down in his chair and leaned back, then turned to face the window. It was quiet outside. Not a soul moved.

His mind went over the panel for the hundredth time. What now? Didn't they say he should go on? They did, but the role looked like second fiddle. He'd get a desk job while his colleagues did the real work. He'd be on the road to nowhere, just waiting for something to happen, only nothing would. He'd spend years in his chair, waiting and chasing an outcome he had no control over. Now that he was out, he was out. JoAnn was right—he'd been a player in someone else's game, hauled in by the pull of it all, though now the gravity had suddenly been turned off. He felt a moment of relief at his own joke, then sighed and wondered if it was time to just leave military life behind. Maybe now was the time to let go and see what else he could do. He had a week or so to think about it. Maybe he should try something else locally so he could be home, just like JoAnn had wanted.

He thought about visiting his buddy Gene, a program director at Rocketdyne (a NASA contractor) who was stationed in Houston to support the Apollo program at the new Manned Spacecraft Center. He was like thousands of other ex-servicemen. Jim envisioned a bustling, noisy construction site where massive spacecraft components and giant Saturn V engine cones were riveted, welded, and bolted together before being shipped to the Cape. Could he trade in the NASA life for a line role in management and production? He wouldn't recognize himself without a jumpsuit or uniform of some kind, and he wasn't even sure he could wear shirtsleeves and a tie every day. And he'd have to tell everyone what happened at the panel.

The idea didn't last. Working in a manufacturing plant meant nothing to him. He had to keep fighting the Reds, even if it was from a NASA office. It was the only thing he'd ever done. How could he give it up now? The war wasn't won, or even over. The Soviets were up there, creating secret terror for the world. Everyone knew it.

The specter of medical retirement crossed his mind but immediately sounded like boredom on a stick.

His head turned to Tom, still in the Air Force, mixing it with his NASA role on the West Coast, and Fred, who he now knew was on his way back to reconnaissance. And what about Chuck? He'd jumped all the right stepping stones and had actually skipped across the pond into Apollo's Group Four.

Jim remained silent for five minutes. Now that he'd been away for so much of the last few years, there didn't seem to be much to do at home. JoAnn had been right about that, and she was gone too.

CHAPTER 25 - SIDELINED

A day later

More soul-searching and a few phone calls later, though still a bit unsure of what exactly to do next, Jim decided to remain at Mission Control in Houston for the time being. He needed more space to think, without making a knee-jerk move until a permanent change, medical or otherwise, forced his hand. He would gather intelligence on the Soviet terror plans in orbit. Staying in Houston might also bring JoAnn back, though that was a bigger issue because he still couldn't reconcile what he was going to do with what she had gotten herself into with all the war protests.

He'd called her with the news. She was shocked and upset for him and offered to come home for a while. He said he was going right back to the office at the Cape Air Force Station to empty his desk; he didn't need to be there anymore. It would clear his head before the holidays. Still numb from everything, he said little more.

He glanced out at the launch pads as usual as his flight approached Patrick Air Force Base, but the dichotomy hit him again, that everything had changed, even though, on the surface, it still somehow looked the same. It should have felt familiar as he walked across the tarmac, but now he felt estranged, with a diminished sense of adventure, in a sidelined role. The nervous thought of being left behind hadn't abated after the panel plus a week to think about it. The bar for the whole endeavor had now been set too high for him. His sense of exclusion had taken root. He wondered if Wilson had felt the same way, though in reality it was probably much worse. It was exactly what JoAnn had been talking about since college with her own inability to publish an article without a man's name on it. And what about Jerri Cobb or Ed Dwight, who weren't even allowed into NASA? But this felt different to Jim. The door had been opened and a very high expectation set, but for the first time in his life, he hadn't been able to get through it on his own. Having the rug pulled out from under him was very different from not having one in the first place.

He entered the hangar where he'd first met all the Special Ops candidates and quickly spotted Chuck, dressed in a blue flight suit and with journalists in tow. "Gentlemen, this is the Atlas Launch Vehicle, modified from the ICBM to carry the astronauts into space. I'm happy to say this rocket is still on schedule. So, if you'll just stand back a little please ..."

Chuck noticed Jim from a distance and stopped talking as his crowd laughed. He asked for a moment of privacy while they gazed at the giant rocket.

"Enjoying the job?" Jim asked him, glancing at the journalists. "You could have done this at the local museum. No risk to life nor limb."

"Look, I was sorry to hear about your heart situation," Chuck replied, not taking the bait. Jim noticed a strange new congeniality in his voice, no doubt from his relatively comfortable position in the new pecking order. "You'd make a fine spacecraft pilot, but these guys won't take any chances. You know that. But I'm glad you're still with us on the program."

"Well, I'm sure there's nothing like being on a roster."

"You always get hit with things you never saw coming. You can't prepare for everything. You have to accept the limits of your control, Jim."

It sounded condescending coming from Chuck. Jim felt like asking him the last time he'd accepted anything he couldn't control, though bit his lip.

"Look, the astronaut office is a good place. You'd have influence over the whole Apollo program."

Just then, unprompted and out of nowhere, and as fleeting as a butterfly in his mind, Jim became acutely aware that he still had a huge stake in what was the greatest endeavor on Earth. Like a serotonin surge in his brain, the impression was visceral, but subtle enough to be missed in a busier moment. He stood quietly for a second, wondering where the feeling had come from and willing it to continue.

"You okay, buddy?" Chuck asked, even though Jim looked distracted.

"Yeah," he replied, returning to the moment.

"It's a big change for all of us. Take it easy."

"I'm fine. Looking forward to the new role."

"Good." Chuck glanced back at the journalists. "I have to go," Jim saw that the press crew seemed eager to move on, so Chuck said goodbye and returned to his tour of the facilities.

Jim stayed where he was. He looked around at the magnificent Atlas rocket standing before him, being prepared for its flight in the last week of December. It would soon be wheeled out to launch pad C-19, fueled, and propelled into the heavens.

* * *

Jim arrived back at the familiar Cape Hotel for the last time that evening. He stood in the parking lot, looking around with his bags in his hands, having gone out of his way to avoid his old place. He had to disconnect now and focus his thoughts on Houston instead.

"Good to see you again, sir. Have you been away?" the receptionist inquired in the lobby.

"I had a little time at home. My wife says I've been away too much," he explained.

He walked slowly to his room and turned on the television. New demonstrations were raging across the country, and it looked like college kids were being drafted into the war.

He flipped through the channels and came across a debate. "The Soviets are facing their own challenges getting to space," said a reporter, as footage appeared of a rocket—probably home grown—which swerved minutely on takeoff when its tail just clipped the tower. It moved a few feet closer to heaven, then turned back to Earth and exploded in humiliation as ground technicians ran for their lives.

One of the experts joked about the Soviet cooperation once discussed by Kennedy, "And what are we going to do? Go up there and have a party together? If you believe the reports, they've lost another rocket and it could be months, maybe a year, before they're ready again, especially if their launch facilities are destroyed. We could have sent the first Apollo mission to the Moon by then."

One of the guests winced at the explosion and said, "That's a lot of money gone up in flames."

"The scary thing is if this signals a change in focus. A turning point. The N1 is now behind schedule. It just seems too big to go anywhere. I believe they have to bury the idea quickly so it doesn't sink the central bank with it."

"What? After all the successes and firsts? Just when they look unbeatable?"

"They cause their own problems, as far as I'm concerned," said another guest.

"What?" repeated the other again.

"Well, it doesn't surprise me one bit. The state consistently underplans food production and people literally starve. There was a famine in the thirties. The planners just don't know what they're doing. How in the world would they know what it would take to get to the Moon? They'd build a rocket that ran out of gas halfway."

The show played canned laughter.

"I think we should grab some of their scientists before others move in. The French and Chinese have nuclear programs. And the Chinese have money."

Jim turned off the TV and unpacked, then poured himself a scotch. Out of habit, he decided to call JoAnn.

His head slammed on the brakes as he picked up the handset. She wasn't home. He stared at the phone, wondering if he should call her at Eve's. What would he say? It would be Christmas soon—couldn't they get together? Do protesters call a truce on a festive holiday? He let it go and tossed the magazine away, then downed the scotch in one gulp. It tasted good, so he got up for another.

CHAPTER 26 - LANDING

Mid-February 1965, Friday

The Christmas holidays were over and the new year had come and gone. JoAnn hadn't returned home. At the side of his desk, Jim had gathered intelligence that established the Soviets were already testing some kind of orbital defense network aimed at disarming America's nuclear response.

His first official task, however, was to repeat his original engineering proposal to perfect a way to land on the Moon that was once embarrassingly lampooned by his colleagues. There were two years of ideas to play with, and fortunately the Ranger probes had since confirmed that the surface was solid, just as Jim had assured everyone. The proposal had been approved for simulation runs and remained, "satisfyingly resistant to attack in its original form," he was delighted to tell a new group. Still, they wanted to see it work before they put it in the air. He might not be able to fly it for real right now, but there was nothing stopping him from proving it in a sim. He swallowed some medicine, changed his approach, and felt he'd even managed to turn around Chuck Moore, his most ardent skeptic.

"Okay, fifty feet, ten feet per second forward," Jim murmured into his headset. He looked out of the lunar lander's tiny window and felt mesmerized by how real the view felt to his brain.

Chuck, standing to his right, looked out of another window shaped like an upside-down triangle. Between them, and practically in their face, stood a tall wall of floor to ceiling electronics. There was barely room to step back. "The ground looks a little rough down there. We can head in that direction instead. It's smoother with fewer shadows," Chuck said.

"This is good. I think we'll be okay," Jim replied. "I'll take it down."

"Tanks down fifteen percent," Chuck announced. "Ground speed is a little high. Looks like the altimeter is picking up soft ground."

"Forty feet, nine forward," said Jim, concentrating intensely out of the tiny window and stealing serial glances at his instrument panel. "Dust flying now."

The lander sank slowly toward the lunar surface in an eerily real and stony silence.

"Twenty feet, six forward," Chuck said.

"I'm going to have to move. There's a bunch of rocks down there."

"Tanks seven percent."

"Bring it down. Avoid using contingency," muttered Jim, reciting a class. "No time for a perfect spot, Jim. Look for a good spot."

"Tanks down two percent," Chuck warned. "Jim, you need to put this thing down."

"Okay, I got it. Right … over … there." Jim's eyes fixed on a touchdown spot. "Home in ten seconds."

Jim felt the lander suddenly begin to drift. "A probe caught a boulder," he said, referring to a stick which dangled below one of the four legs. He held the yoke to straighten it out. "Okay, this might get a little bumpy." He started to feel like he was losing it, but said, "Gonna bring it down now."

A low fuel warning flashed and screamed on the overhead panel directly above Chuck. He reached up and reset it.

"Just a few more seconds. A little too fast," Jim muttered, his eyes locked on the lunar surface out the window. He flared the throttle and saw the lander's vertical descent slow on the panel in front of him. "I'm floating on the engine now."

Chuck's eyes were on the altimeter and he started the countdown. "Twelve feet, three forward ... ten. Coming down fast, Jim. Eight down, two forward ... six, four ... two."

The lander shook gently as it descended and stopped. They looked around and out of the windows to check for distress.

"Dust!" exclaimed a surprised Chuck. "I thought they programmed a dust bowl!"

"The bowl's over there, if you look closely. We did it. We brought it down," Jim said.

The simulator windows suddenly went dark and the lights came on before Chuck could see what Jim had pointed out.

They dismounted the red carpeted steps from the simulator into Building Five of the Manned Spacecraft Center. The contraption they emerged from looked like a pile of huge cubes of half-melted, pale brown fudge that had been dumped into a thirty-foot mound at one end of the hangar. A mass of thick black cables from the simulator hung over a giant hook toward the cabinets. Also brown, chest-high vertical columns sprouted from various points on the floor. A twenty-foot cream-colored control console faced them on the right, manned by controllers looking into three monitors propped up on the top edge, about five feet apart. It looked as if brown had been the only color available, with two more thirty-foot rows of identically colored computer cabinets completing the layout of the room.

"That last descent was a little too fast, Jim. I could barely hold the countdown," Chuck said, walking behind him.

"We bounced on the jet when it hit the ground. It slowed the lander like a cushion and we burned less fuel. I knew we had a margin when the lights flashed. The envelope changes as we get closer to the surface," Jim said, on the last step of the nearly vertical ladder that descended from a small door at the front of the craft.

They walked toward Chris and Tom, who were still in Special Ops, waiting near the sim controller.

"But Jim, it's unsafe," Chuck replied. "If we don't get to solid ground, the engine thrust will disintegrate the surface before it can slow us down."

Chuck still seemed stuck on this dust versus solid ground argument. "I have a suggestion." Jim said. "We can try it again."

"The plan today was to land with ten percent fuel left, Jim. You burned practically all of it," Chris interrupted as they approached. "Chuck?"

"I think we're cutting it too fine." Chuck pulled up a chair, scratched it noisily on the floor, and put a foot on it. "You need a better understanding of the terrain if you want to do something like that, Jim, then train specifically for the mission to maintain a good reserve. We were out of options and I'd say the mission was in jeopardy."

"Come on, Chuck. We didn't fail. It went down. Not the way we expected, but we have to be prepared for whatever."

"Well, lucky you're not the one flying the darn thing."

Chris raised his hand and Jim held his tongue.

"Gentlemen?" Everyone was silent. "Jim. Looks like you're back for another go. Ready in twenty? This time with ten percent left in the tanks," Chris said. "You got that?"

Jim's eyes were averted and he sighed after a moment of silence. He nodded.

Chris looked at Tom and said, "Why don't you give navigation a try this time?"

"Sure," Tom replied. He glanced sideways at Chuck, who remained stone-faced, then turned to Jim. "Can we talk about the docking maneuver first? In orbit?"

"Let's go," Jim said.

They passed the supervisor on their way to the Special Ops office, which was down the hall from the simulator room. "Simsup, can we run it again in twenty minutes, please? And can we have that big light in the sky behind us this time?" Jim asked.

"You're the guy who likes to fly into ocean targets, aren't you?" Tom joked as they walked down the corridor. "Isn't that what a deck landing is all about?"

"Interesting way to look at it."

"You know, docking the orbital module for the trip home seems a little too hit or miss for my liking at the moment, with all the complex dynamics we have to deal with. It seems more often than not that the lander just comes up and misses the module altogether, sometimes shooting straight by or just crashing and poking a hole. There's no glide path up there for reference. We need to figure out how to solve that problem in the sim, and soon."

"Did you talk to Dr. Rendezvous?"

"Who, Buzz? Yeah. He said nobody's going anywhere until this works. He's getting the guys to program it so we can go through it again."

"Okay, just let me know when and we'll give it a try. By the way, I just found out that the Soviets have to climb outside, over to their Luna lander, while they are in orbit around the Moon, and then get inside before they can land. It's a lot of work they've given themselves."

"Doesn't sound like the most elegant solution."

Jim and Tom stopped for a moment as a small team walked toward them—a white male, clearly in the lead, followed by two African Americans: a man in a white shirt and tie and a woman behind him. They looked like they were in a hurry to get from one meeting to the next, although their energy and noise attracted a lot of attention. The lady wore a suit and seemed barely able to hold up a large file of papers under her left arm. "But, sir," she urged, "I've checked and double-checked the trajectory calculations and found that they are half a degree out on re-entry." She glanced down at her stack of papers, almost dropping them in her haste. "The capsule will just bounce out of the atmosphere."

The man in front didn't answer but kept walking.

A pair of technical-looking people stopped in the middle of the walk, ten feet in front of Jim and Tom, and stood staring at the trio as if an alien had just walked into a NASA building. Jim overheard a whisper as they moved on, looking back with a double take. "Talk different, think different, and a woman too? How are we supposed to get the job done around here?" one of the two said as the trio disappeared, one by one, into various restrooms in the hallway: the black man and woman into their respective colored-only restrooms and their leader into the unconditional men's room that practically everyone else also used.

Tom said with a half-laugh, "The funniest thing I heard was people think those two are visiting students from Africa."

"Who, Mable?" She was the lady of the trio, a math whiz from the computer department, and someone Jim had used to calculate the trajectory numbers for his original landing proposal.

"I'm not sure how much Civil Rights changed things," Tom said, shaking his head.

Jim took a deep sigh to shake the blues, then said, "Well, she got a double slam dunk out of it. But I'll take one of them any day over one of those damn adding machines. At least she makes sure nobody blacks out up there."

Tom cringed, then laughed. "Ooh, look who's on fire today."

Jim rolled his eyes. With a grin he said, "I'll have to remember not to say it like that. I'm just glad she's double-checking the trajectory numbers the machines spit out. She's good at catching mistakes. I hear she's trying to get into Marshall's in Huntsville next year on von Braun's rockets. She'll be good at that."

Tom looked up again for the African Americans, "Well, at least they can pee in this building now, which is a step forward. Looks like NASA is taking us all into space together."

"And they have their own private bathrooms while the rest of us crowd into the small ones. When you put it like that, it doesn't sound so bad, does it?"

They reached their medium-sized office, the door bearing an obscure-looking Engineering Design nameplate on the frosted glass window. Six empty individual desks were neatly arranged in two rows at the back of the room, and technical schematics and diagrams adorned the walls. A large window to the right was darkened by night outside.

"Uh, Tom, sorry to interrupt. You're needed for something," a lady said, poking her head in the door just as they entered.

Tom looked up and asked, " For something? We're just about to start."

She gave him a broad grin. "There was a call for you. It's the hospital. You're about to have a new arrival."

Tom froze, then looked at Jim. "Sorry, buddy!"

"Best we call it a day," Jim said. His eyes flashed when Tom didn't move. "Go, go, go!" he shooed.

Tom never looked happier. He grabbed his jacket and disappeared like a rocket.

CHAPTER 27 - PANTHER

The same day

Jim came home from work feeling wired from the Friday evening rush hour on the interstate. He cursed the extra thirty tedious minutes it added to his daily commute to the Clear Lake office. His jet, now gone, flashed through his mind and he realized just how much he missed the days when he could get away from the crowds and move quickly around the country. But those days were over. His life, now largely with his feet on the ground trying to get others into space, meant standing in line on the street with everyone else.

Despondent over the events of that day in the sim, he turned the doorknob and heard complete silence. It summed up his home life for the past few months. JoAnn had only come to pick up some clothes, and he hadn't even been home.

He collapsed on the sofa, then turned on the TV as usual. With barely enough energy to pay attention to another war protest, he turned it off again.

A scotch went down the hole after dinner in the hope that it would help to relieve a lingering headache from the previous night's booze. The upstairs bedroom was a mess. He groaned. Lieutenant Marino from training school would have dragged him outside to do a thousand push-ups for such tardiness.

He began organizing his closet, glancing at a row of hanging shirts, pants, and ties to make sure he had enough for the next two weeks. It was going to be a shirtsleeve and tie most of everyday now, though it still didn't feel natural to him. Visions of inhabiting a NASA spacesuit had faded considerably.

Most of JoAnn's clothes remained, and he wondered if he should just move them temporarily. He needed more space to be able to grab things quickly every morning. Looking deeper inside, he saw years of junk in the back that he'd never been inclined to tackle. Long-forgotten piles of shoeboxes, bags, and wedding gifts were stacked high.

He decided to go with JoAnn's, Japanese sourced, sage advice to clear out, as a way to de-mist his foggy head, though the treatment seemed to be made for domestic directors running households.

Random thoughts from the last few weeks popped into his head as he began to move things around the hangars—how Tom had told him that NASA had sucked up almost all of the country's production of new electronic components called integrated circuits, about Kaputnik—the press named American rocket that exploded when it got four feet closer to space after liftoff, to which Jim had joked that another Soviet rocket also went up. The papers suggested that NASA should send up a grapefruit before worrying about mankind, wondering if America's moonshot was more of a long shot. Tom had mentioned NASA's freeze-dried ice-cream, which Jim said he'd at least like to try.

He was sad that he'd probably see less of Tom and maybe none of Fred now, both going their separate ways, Tom:

splitting his time with Vandenberg in California to work on new launch facilities, though he wouldn't say exactly what, and Fred: back to reconnaissance.

At the back of the closet, he came across some old shoes he'd worn to his wings ceremony in fifty-three and hadn't seen since. He sat in the doorway to recover some energy, thinking that his current life situation felt a million miles off course. How exactly was he on the front lines fighting the Reds?

His mind drifted back to where it all started when he'd crossed the Panama Canal as a nugget in the Navy. It still felt like yesterday when they had sent him to Korea to give the Communists a little payback for taking his father. Fortunately, the first four months aboard the Leyte went without a hitch. He transferred to the Essex when the Navy's first jet arrived, but the F9F Panther felt like a death trap to him.

He'd barely read the flight manual when he was ordered to take out an enemy railroad about a hundred miles inside the Korean mountains. Near Mig-Alley, it was like stepping barefoot on a wasp's nest.

His section was within ten miles of the target just forty minutes after leaving the Essex. Swirls of fog enveloped the pine forests, hiding the narrow valleys as they weaved and skimmed their way through the mountainous contours. A storm of super-bright white and orange tracer streams erupted like flashes from the forest below as they rounded a corner. Small black explosions of big-bore TNT peppered the sky, the flak intensifying to levels Jim had never seen before. He'd never have made it out alive if he'd been shot down here. Still, they blew up the tunnel entrance, the train went up like a gas station, and the section reassembled for the home run.

That's when a friendly Able Dog appeared with five MiG-15s in pursuit from the north. It was Chuck Moore in that plane. A MiG began to blaze at Moore. "He's on my six. On my six," he yelled from the Able Dog.

"Okay, turn left, LEFT," Jim ordered, squeezing out another burst of fire and breaking right. But he'd turned too fast, stalled his wings, and began to plummet to earth. The MiG went up with a loud bang and sparks shot out of its engine. Jim plummeted to the ground after it, knowing he would crash at any moment unless some miracle saved him.

Jim now fell out of his recollection, sitting in the doorway. He took a deep breath and looked around the closet again. He hadn't made any significant progress in organizing. He felt finished, fallen from NASA as surely as his plane had crashed that night in Korea. Just because he'd found his way back to his mission then, didn't mean he would now. A bitter lump formed in his throat. The Soviets, he was sure, were preparing to place nuclear bombs from space, their orbital network taking shape. And here he was, clearing out the closet. He was either going to get a shot at it, or maybe go back to the Navy and jump in the pilot's seat again. Truth was, he'd rarely felt more alive than when he was cheating death in combat back then.

He wondered if he should run the idea by Powell. Yes, that was it—back to the original business, back to flying, which he loved more than anything. Vietnam needed him now as much as Korea had back then; forgotten, but necessary. He'd return to the front lines, holding the Reds accountable again, as they should be. It occurred to him that if he'd stayed in the Navy, none of this space stuff would have occurred to him anyway. But he also saw JoAnn's stony face—back to the Navy might not be as dangerous as space, but they'd be apart again, and she'd say he was perpetuating the war.

The Navy could also pull the plug. He could just see himself being hauled in front of the Physical Evaluation Board, then grounded and retired medically with a heart murmur.

On his way out, he picked up a note Tom had left at the mailbox saying the baby was a boy and they'd named him Jake. JoAnn came to mind again, and he thought she'd like to know, although it would be a tricky subject for a phone call.

CHAPTER 28 - POWELL

March 20th, 1965

Jim awoke Saturday morning with a dull pain in his right side. Though it had been some time since the Vomit Comet, his shoulder pain had flared up out of nowhere. He'd had a restless night, and when the day broke, he was still dead tired and practically ready to sleep by the time the birds started chirping at dawn. But his head wouldn't settle, so he threw in the towel, pulled on a robe, and headed downstairs for an early breakfast.

The doorbell rang while he was making coffee. He tightened his belt, straightened his hair, then went to the door.

"Jim, how are you?" It was Captain Powell, though Jim hardly recognized him in civilian clothes.

Jim, on the other hand, still looked and felt half asleep in his nightclothes. He was stunned for a moment.

"Well, are you going to invite me in?" Powell asked, inspecting the paint around the door and looking like he had time to kill.

"Sir? Oh." Jim half-laughed and stepped aside. "Come in, sir. I can't believe I left you standing there."

"I thought you'd never ask," Powell joked, waving his car

away.

"Give me a moment, sir. I'll go change."

"At ease, Jim. We're not at sea now. I'm on shore leave, in case you were wondering. I have things to do at home, so I hope you don't mind me coming by early."

Jim nodded. They shook hands and walked into the kitchen where he poured coffee for each of them. They sat at the dining table.

"Good to see you, sir. What brings you here?"

"I got word that you were having a hard time with every-thing that happened."

"Oh, the NASA job?"

"Yes. I was sorry to hear that it didn't work out the way you expected."

"Thank you, sir. That wasn't supposed to be general knowledge."

"That's fine—I'm not a general," Powell quipped. He looked around the house. It was quiet and dark, with all the curtains still drawn, though it was daylight outside. "And JoAnn? I heard it didn't work out." Powell looked around again and said, "I take it she's ... not home?"

Jim turned his ear to the house as if listening for a sound. Hearing nothing, he said, "It's empty, sir. Just me."

He lit a smoke and offered Powell one, but he declined. Jim took a long drag.

"I see you started again."

"I forgot how good they were. And, well, a nicotine craving in orbit is no longer my problem." He looked at his cigarette. "The other guys don't know what they're missing."

"So, what's the job in Houston?"

"The Astronaut Office? I develop space systems. We still

have to get the men up there, and of course back, like Kennedy said. But I wouldn't really be going anywhere. And, you know, it's getting more dangerous up there every day. We just can't see it, but everyone knows it's going on."

"Sounds like you're close to the action. Maybe you'll get another chance, don't you think?"

"Everything's changed, sir." Jim looked down at his chest and pointed. "It's this guy. They won't let me near a vehicle. My heart's not ticking right, apparently. And I guess it's physically broken now that JoAnn's gone." Jim stirred his coffee. "They don't miss a thing, those medics. They must take such pride in their work."

"Have you seen a specialist? Don't let it get in your way."

"Yes. But ..." Jim sighed. "I'm a risk to them, sir. And the job in Houston ... to tell you the truth, it's not right. Like pushing pencils. I've got to do something. Go somewhere. If they don't give me another chance ..."

Powell looked surprised and said, "You're not staying?"

Jim became animated. "The way I see it, sir." He shifted forward in his seat to explain. "LBJ's sending more troops to the war. Thirty-five thousand a month this summer. He needs us out there, not here just reading the news. And I can't fight for our country sitting here. I was thinking about Korea, and I feel like I really made a difference, you know? In the war against the Communists.

"I see what you're saying."

"It's occurred to me, sir, that I might go back to the ship. And I've been meaning to ask you about that." He laughed. "Or the other option is to open a club on Cocoa Beach." He grinned. "I liked it there. The space tourists will be coming in droves, I'm told." Powell smiled at the idea too. Jim took another drink. "But seriously, sir, they need us in Vietnam more than anything else. And it's my duty—always has been—to fight the spread. I felt I should never have gotten involved in this space stuff, and what worries me now is being stuck in limbo, impotent, sitting here watching the other guys do it all, waiting for who knows what." He looked up. "I can't sit still, sir. I need to move, to make a difference. In action, sir, not waiting, you know?" Jim went on. "That's just the way my head works."

"You should avoid the whole war here, Jim." Powell got serious and said, "Look, I came to tell you a couple of things. I asked Moore to keep a watch over you, and I know you fell out."

"Yeah." Jim sighed and searched for the right words. "I knew that, sir, but I didn't need him. I just wanted some space to get on with things."

"We talked about support and buy-in before. Cooperation. You were never going to make it on your own."

"Well, he's free of me now. I don't need him anymore."

"He has a job to do. And he wanted this as much as you did. He got in early. He has a lot of, shall we say ... political savvy. Never overlook someone who's got that."

Jim got the point and perked up on the edge of his seat.

"So how about I go back to the ship, sir?"

"Jim, you know the Navy would take you back. You've logged a lot of hours and have an instinct for flying that few can match. You've made Lieutenant Commander like your father. But that's a one-way ticket now. Hang on to what you've got, even if it's hard."

"But it feels like it's over, sir. It didn't turn out the way I thought it would. I know what I should be doing."

"Not so fast, Jim. Bigger things have been thrust into your view. Your perspective will have changed forever—and so will your expectations. Returning to the ship now won't feel quite the same."

"But recon is what my father did, sir. And you're right. I should have just stuck with it, you know, finished the job."

"Sure, your dad was a respected pilot." Powell sat back and thought for a moment, then took a deep breath. "Well, okay, maybe you should continue what he started."

Jim looked at him, a little surprised by the about-face. It sounded like Powell had just agreed with him, but there was more.

"He was looking for Soviet missiles in the early days," Powell said. "And now we have a chance to beat them at the space game. It's the same thing, Jim. We have to. That's what it's all about. That's why you should stay put." Powell paused, then said. "Actually, I came here to tell you about him."

Jim was intrigued.

"I looked up one of the ship's hands when your father went missing."

Jim froze.

Powell took a deep breath and revealed, "He was on the Oriskany the day he was lost behind enemy lines. He looked like he was close to getting home. They could see smoke rising from the woods, about ten miles from the coast. Maybe it was him. They never found out. A search party was prepared, but it couldn't take off. Soviet planes were circling the area and there was no way in or out without escalation and someone getting killed. Obviously it was a wrench for the captain and the crew, but they had to let it go."

"You're saying he was alive? He survived the crash?" Jim looked shocked.

"There's no way to know. But this sailor said it looked like it."

"Who is he? I should go see him."

"He asked not to be identified, Jim, sorry. It's still classified. Maybe some day."

Jim sat back and thought for a moment. "Sir, can I ask you a question?"

Powell nodded.

"What about your family? You never said anything. I saw a picture on the ship, in your office."

"Yeah, there's something else I never told you. I lost my boy to war. He was a pilot, just like you. He would have been about your age now. A lot of people have lost someone to keep our country safe and free."

Jim leaned forward. "I'm sorry to hear that, sir. But that's kind of why I want to get back in the seat. I can't protect our people from here."

"What would your father have wanted for you?"

Jim thought back and said what was on his mind. "You know, he was never home. And the truth is, I don't remember much about him. But it's funny how much I've become like him: never home. It must be in the genes. Cobbs are not made to sit around. But somehow I always felt like I had a wind at my back. You know? I always thought it was him. But now it's turned."

Powell left, saying he'd think about sponsoring Jim back into the Navy if he was really sure it was the right thing to do.

Jim's day continued with domestic matters. After lunch,

a familiar old restlessness gripped him, the way it used to when he was a kid in his bedroom at the end of the day, his mind unable to settle, wondering if he'd said the right thing to Powell. Other than work and television, he could think of little else to fill the time.

The rest of the weekend was more of the same. He listed the things he could do in his head: there were chores, grocery shopping, or television. He applied himself to them, but none of them seemed important. On Sunday afternoon, a deep feeling of despondency took hold, like an old enemy that visited his teenage bedroom when he was alone at the end of the day, waiting for his father to return from the war. His mind began to taunt him about the missed opportunities at NASA and the years he'd lost not fighting the Reds.

He was sure he had to go back, got up and went to the bedroom and groaned again when he saw that it was as messy as it had been every day before. Returning to the kitchen, he picked up the new bottle of Scotch, then stopped, thinking he shouldn't. He put the bottle down. A moment later, with renewed determination and more than a touch of frustration, he picked up the bottle and poured a glass, pausing to stare at it. Just a quick drink, get it over with, then move on, his head said. It would dull the emptiness of today, then tomorrow he could begin to set things right. That would be it for the week. He'd clean up his act.

But he also knew that every tomorrow was another tomorrow. Each weekend had become the next weekend.

A cry suddenly bubbled up from the depths as if a pressure valve had just been opened. His lungs filled like a newly uncorked soda bottle, and he began to sob for his impotence and indecision. He saw a slippery slope ahead. Something had to change. This was not the dream. This was nothing. What could he do, except leave the house and just go somewhere? And where to? And would anything be different when he got back? He felt very ashamed, not knowing where the grief was hidden.

He looked at the half-filled glass again, thinking that he'd already poured it and might as well just drink it. He felt desperately disappointed at his loss of self-control. He was on his knees. He wanted to get drunk. The last one, he told himself, and that would be it. But the unpleasant aftermath and guilt of a hungover morning at the office hit him just as hard as the nectar color and taste of the Scotch intoxicated his mind. And it was getting more difficult to hide. What if he made potentially life-threatening mistakes in the sim? He wouldn't be able to cover them up. He suddenly felt very unsure of himself and desperately wanted his father to walk through the door and tell him what to do, just like Powell had asked him the question.

CHAPTER 29 - TROUBLES

March 24th, 1965

On Wednesday morning, Tom knocked on Jim's door, but there was no answer. He knocked again, but there was no sign that anyone was home. Nothing moved inside the hazy windows. Tom turned the doorknob and sighed for not having tried it first, then opened it and went straight inside. "Jim?"

There was no answer.

He called again and went upstairs.

Jim was still in bed, but stirred as Tom walked in and opened the curtains, cursing softly as he saw a bottle of scotch by Jim's bedside. He looked at the clock and sighed. "You want to get ready? We have to get going."

Tom went back downstairs, and thankfully Jim appeared five minutes later. He apologized and said he hoped the wait hadn't been long.

Tom didn't know what to say at first. He could smell a night's worth of alcohol in the air and asked if everything was okay.

"Yeah. Yeah," Jim said, looking shifty and brushing his hair back with one hand, though it still looked messy. He didn't look like the familiar Jim that Tom knew. "Had a late night and a few drinks. But no problem. I'll grab a bagel, then we'll get going."

Tom also saw that he looked quite pale. "You okay to drive?"

"Fine. Don't worry, I'm absolutely fine."

"I'll ride with you today. And it's me I'm worried about."

Tom explained that they had to get to a management briefing; NASA was still wounded by the latest Soviet victory in space. Russian, Leonov, had made mankind's first spacewalk just a few days earlier on March-eighteenth, and NASA had to act fast.

The neighborhood felt wired as they walked. It was like something else had happened. People were discussing, debating, rushing around, and exchanging mysterious cards over fences, in front yards, and in the streets as if they had just fallen from the sky. Jim grabbed a newspaper from the doorway, then walked to his car with Tom.

"What's going on out here?" Tom asked as Jim unlocked the door.

Jim glanced up and down the street. "We're all off to war. Sons, brothers, everyone." He scanned the front page of the paper. "But it looks like some are trying to pair up. You can bail out if you're getting married. Have you seen the paper?" He rolled it up and threw it on Tom's seat, then got in.

"Too bad for those kids. I was out there in my early twenties," Tom said.

"Yeah, I got shipped off to Korea about the same." He started the car and sped away. "Anyway, I wanted to talk to you about something. Thanks for coming over."

"What is it?"

"I've been thinking—over a drink or two, as you can

225

see—that LBJ's sending in more troops. Thirty-five thousand a month. He needs people in Vietnam."

"Yeah. They started bombing the north to liberate the south."

"I've been thinking about it."

"Thinking about what?"

"You know, doing my part."

"Doing what? You're a civilian."

"Yeah, but it's not over yet, is it?"

"The war?"

"The fight. Communism."

"I don't think it has much to do with that anymore."

"That's exactly what it is. And that's why we have to go on." Jim looked sideways at Tom and continued. "Until it's all gone. All of it. You know, every last bit."

Tom was silent.

"That's the job." Jim looked sideways at him. "It's serious. Look at Eastern Europe. What happened after the war? They were all taken over by the Soviet Union. If we don't stop them, it'll be the same in Asia. Think about Korea, Vietnam, China.' Jim paused a moment. 'If the south goes Commie on us, anyone could be next."

Tom took a deep breath.

"Even Hitler was on the warpath to crush them. In forty-six, Stalin tried to pick up where that madman left off," Jim pointed out.

"That was tyrant against tyrant, Jim."

"And now there's no tyrant to keep the other in check. It's up to us, Tom ... well, we've got some of those ex-tyrants—Huntsville? The Cape? To try and beat the new tyrants into space. Anyway, I guess that's what I'll have to do ... unless my father steps through the front door again.' Jim paused again. 'And, I know what happened."

"You do? How so?"

"Powell. Found someone on the ship."

"And?"

"He might still be alive. Maybe I can find him."

"What? How will you do that?"

"If I re-join the Navy. I think that's it."

Tom looked lost for words, then asked. "You're quitting NASA?"

"I'm thinking about it. I've given it a try. It's time to get back in the air and do my part." Jim lit a cigarette and blew the smoke out the window.

"Are you sure? You'll be missing all that's going on."

Jim sounded a note of resentment. "I've got a second-class ticket, Tom. It's the end of the road here."

Tom backed off for a moment, then asked, "Are you sure? They're getting close to the big launches. Isn't it only a matter of time before they find a solution for your condition? Medicine can do anything. Give it time."

"Another shot in the Navy will prove that everything's just fine," Jim said. "Then I'll see if there's a way back if the Soviets haven't nuked everything."

Tom looked puzzled, scratched his head, and turned away to look out the window.

Jim looked down at his chest. "They'll never let me go anywhere with my ticker, Tom. It's just not going to happen. It's the end of the show. Maybe it doesn't make sense to you, but it sure feels that way to me. I can't shake it. I can't even explain it."

Tom looked at him without a word.

"I have a choice. I can go back to the ship and do my duty by my father. That's my job, Tom. It always has been. It's been my life's work. We must fight tyranny wherever it rears its head. Or I can stay a civilian and let others do the dirty work."

Jim took another drag, paused, then changed course. Tom could see that he looked pale now. Beads of sweat had formed at his temples. "Anyway, I see you're spending more time at Vandenberg now. They treating you well?"

"The facilities are coming together and the rockets are going up. The plan is to start manned defense missions alongside the Cape soon."

"Did the Soviets put nukes up there?" Jim suddenly felt bitter, left out in the cold. He splayed his fingers. "Actually, I don't want to know. Nothing more I can do. See if I can stop them on Earth." He sighed. "Anyway, how's the little guy?"

Tom thought about how to phrase the answer and said, "Perfect!" He chatted a bit about his son, explaining how Jake ruled the roost with a short leash for his every whim, day or night.

"I'm really happy for you. I thought JoAnn and I would be in the same position, but it just hasn't work out. Anyway, thanks for being a buddy. I wish you the best."

Tom didn't let the distraction get to him. "Have you talked to her?"

"I'm still thinking about it. She won't like it."

"You need to talk to her before you decide anything crazy."

"Yeah." Jim glanced sideways at Tom as if to size him up. "Can I tell you something?" Jim wiped his sweaty brow and felt as pale as he looked in the mirror.

Tom was intrigued.

"She got herself into something …"

"Yeah?"

"… that doesn't quite gel. So you have to keep it to yourself." Jim explained about JoAnn's interest in journalism and writing about underrepresented groups. Then, hesitating as if afraid of a bad reaction, he added, "She writes for activists who oppose the war."

Tom looked stunned. "Where is she? Is she okay?"

"Yeah, I think so."

Jim's mind swam back to a moment when they were teenagers. He'd just raced around the neighborhood in a red, stacked-wing, piston-engine crop duster from a nearby farm where the farmer was showing him how to fly. The plane was low enough to strip the leaves from the trees as it swooped low over JoAnn's backyard, where she lay on a sunbed. He called her name as if she could hear him on the ground and yelled, "Happy Birthday," though the noise of the plane drowned it out. She looked up, dropped her still-open glossy and a bottle of sunscreen, and jumped to her feet, waving her hands wildly in the air. That's when he knew she had captured his eighteen-year-old heart.

Now, looking paler than ever, Jim suddenly stopped and slammed on the brakes at a remote roadside. Tom wondered if he had a flat tire. Jim threw open his door and leaned out, retching on the side of the road.

Tom looked around and, seeing no passersby, jumped out and ran around the car to help him up, but Jim's hand came up to block him as he bent over.

"Come on buddy. Let's get you back up," Tom urged.

Jim raised his hand even higher and said, "I'm fine! Just give me a minute."

"Look, you can kiss that competitive, self-reliant bullshit goodbye. I'm taking the wheel from here. You shouldn't be driving this thing like that."

"Tom, you'd better stand back," Jim urged, then threw up again.

"We'll get you back in shape. Just hang in there, buddy."

After a few minutes, Jim relented and they switched seats and were soon on their way.

"Oh, I so needed that," Jim said, the color returning to his face, as some of his troubles—at least for now—were left abandoned on the roadside. He thought quietly for a few moments, then continued, "I disappeared into the Korean War to avenge my father. He took me to the thirty-eighth parallel." After taking a deep breath, he added, "But she brought me home."

"Go get her, Jim. She's your future. Not your father."

CHAPTER 30 - EVE

Later that day

With only the faintest idea what he was going to say, Jim pulled himself together and picked up the phone to call Eve.

"Jim," she answered, her response lukewarm. He'd seen that coming. This was Eve, ever since she thought he'd forgotten her younger sister in Korea.

He simply asked for JoAnn.

"She's not here." That was all she said.

"Nothing like a conversation then," Jim muttered after a moment of silence. "Look, Eve, I just need a word, please?"

"Honestly, she's not here."

Jim sighed then tried again. "Okay, when's she coming home?"

Like a stuck record, Eve simply repeated, "Like I said, Jim, she's really not here."

He was stunned by her insolence.

After a moment's silence, she added, "She moved."

"Moved? Where? When?"

"I'm kidding, Jim. You walk straight into them."

He rolled his eyes and kicked himself. "Well?"

"She's actually out. I wasn't lying about that."

"Come on, Eve. When is she coming back?"

"I don't know. She's a busy girl these days."

"Look, can we just stop this? I need to talk to her."

"I'll let her know you called. Is that okay?"

"I have to talk to her fast. Is there a number?"

"Do you miss her now, Jim, or has something happened?"

"Have you had enough?" He sighed, then said, "Fun over?"

After a moment, Eve said, "I'll give you her number. But to tell you the truth, it's a little weird."

"What do you mean?"

"You'll have to ask her."

Jim grabbed a nearby pen and paper and scribbled down a phone number, then immediately dialed JoAnn.

A young man answered.

Jim frowned. Damn it, he thought. He asked to speak to her.

After a long silence, the man said, "Who's calling?"

"This is Jim Cobb. May I speak to JoAnn, please? Is she there?" He replied impatiently.

"Sorry, who—"

"My wife. She's my wife. Is that okay with you?"

The man said nothing.

"Look, who is this? Can you give her the phone? Are you still there?"

"One moment."

Jim took a deep breath and told himself to calm down when he heard the phone being passed at the other end. "JoAnn?" he asked.

Slightly shocked, she said, "Jim? How did you—"

"Eve gave me the number. Where are you? And who's the guy—"

"Someone I work with."

"Are you okay? I wanted to make sure you were okay."

"Yeah." There was a moment of silence, then she asked, "And you?"

"I wanted to know how you are. Anyway, what's this number?"

"I'm in Port Huron."

"Oh. What's in Port Huron?"

"You know I work here, Jim."

"Oh? What's going on?"

"We're protesting the war."

"Why are you protesting? I thought you were writing—"

"Jim, I'm doing publicity."

"Publicity for what?"

"Well." She explained slowly, as if to a child. "We have to show how the whole thing's another Korea. That we're going nowhere. That we haven't learned anything. Lives and dreams are wasted, young people don't come back. Why? Because they're expendable? While the president gets to watch it all on TV. We need freedom and justice on Earth before we worry about space. We live down here, not up there."

Jim was shocked by her words. They had gotten into her head. It was clearly manufactured. "JoAnn, have you heard yourself?"

"We're going to stop the war, Jim. I have to help my nephew Ricky and thousands like him."

"How are you going to help them?"

"He just got his registration card. 1-A. He's only nineteen. Can you imagine that?"

"Nineteen?"

"They're in the colleges, drafting kids for the war, just picking the ones they want to take away—kids who aren't doing so well, like they're good for nothing just because they're in the bottom half of their class."

Jim took a deep breath. He couldn't deny the travesty of what she had just said. "That sounds terrible."

"His college is probably rioting right now. It's everywhere. I've never seen anything like it."

Jim looked out the window at the events still unfolding on his own street and asked, "Okay, so where are the protests, JoAnn?"

"You'll see them on the news."

"Where's the next one?" he insisted.

She exhaled loudly. "There's one in Michigan."

"Where in Michigan, JoAnn?"

"The university. It'll be on the news."

"What are they going to do? Burn down government buildings or something?"

"You just don't get it, do you?"

"Get what?"

"We're educating people."

"Sorry, but I lost you."

"It's a teach-in."

Jim had never heard of such a thing. "A teach-in? What's a teach-in?"

"We have classes to educate people about the war and how to protest. We have speakers. They tell the students about things they've seen and what to do."

"Be careful now, JoAnn. Don't get involved in anything that's—"

"Jim," she pushed back. "It's okay. It's peaceful. And I

have to go now. I'll talk to you again. Call me tomorrow."

Jim grimaced at the receiver, sighed and hung up. He looked out the window and stood for a moment in deep thought, trying to figure out what to do. A young man, maybe in his late teens or early twenties, was sobbing while his mother talked to a neighbor with a card in her hand. It was undoubtedly one of those draft notices.

He rushed into the bedroom, opened the closet, and began to dress as fast as he could.

CHAPTER 31 - AREA 50-SOMETHING

The same day, unknown location, US

The secret area, known as fifty-one, in the Nevada desert, was no secret at all. Some thought it should be in Mali, since most people couldn't point to Timbuktu on a map. Instead, somewhere truly secret, the most audacious plan to defend a way of life was under discussion.

"Gentlemen, this is about freedom and liberty," the president said. "You'll remember Cuba—Jack was hours away from ending it all; and that was his first term."

A dozen middle-aged, stern looking white men laughed around the long conference table. The secretary of defense was joined by the Joint Chiefs of Staff, NASA's highest command, and other senior personnel from specific military operations.

"There's only one place to go if we all fall face first into the shit down here: the Moon. But we can't sit on the shores of the Sea of Tranquility and look up at Soviet missiles. That sounds like Jack all over again."

The audience laughed.

"Life on Earth could quite possibly become a Communist

style tyranny for everyone for evermore. After Cuba, we were forced to build a contingency for the future of freedom," the president added ominously. He paused for a drink of water and looked at his secretary of defense.

"For one thing, whoever gets to the Moon first will control the natural resources that may lie untapped up there," the secretary explained, sitting at the end of the long table near the president. "We have reason to be concerned about the Soviets putting nuclear weapons up there, and if they do, it will be winner takes all, gentlemen. We can't afford to wait and see what happens with their space program. We're dealing with a totalitarian regime that renounces morality and religion. If the president is right, a Communist Moon could mean the end of God for the American people and the world. The consequences are unimaginable. We're skating on thin ice with the Soviets racing into space."

Chuck, Chris, the military officials and leaders around the table looked down at a stack of papers stamped: *Top Secret: to be destroyed upon reading.*

"At least in Cuba we could see the damn things. But up there? We won't be able to detect anything. There is no higher ground, gentlemen. If the Soviets launch warheads from space, we won't know they're coming, and our major cities would be showered within days, maybe less. We would be powerless to stop them. Gentlemen, we're looking at space supremacy," the secretary added. "The pinnacle of all domination strategies. Lose it and we will be trapped in hell forever."

The gravity of the situation seemed to swallow every word in the room.

"Our adventurous PR message about the space race may be

fanciful, but the reality is that the stakes could not be higher," the president added. "We need the American public to fund space one way or another, and we need to keep them onside for their own security." He glanced at Jones, NASA's new assistant administrator and the president's showman for the organization.

"Nuclear arms on the Moon? How would they get them up there?" asked one of the men to Chuck's right.

"In the age of nuclear obliteration, the impossible has become possible. They'll do it the same way we will. Reusable vehicles. There are technical challenges, but they will be overcome."

"Why don't they just put these missiles into orbit instead? It's easier. Why go all the way to the Moon?"

"It's too dangerous to keep them in orbit long term though they will no doubt try. The amount of debris in space is increasing every day, and it only takes something the size of a pebble to cause a catastrophic explosion. Then there's the extreme temperature fluctuations that make long-term weapons unstable. And of course we can see them in orbit, so they can't hide. We could see for ourselves if they were armed and ready for war. On the lunar surface, say on the far side, there will be absolutely no telling once they start regular missions. They can be easily hidden. There's almost no gravity, so they could put a hundred warheads in a cereal box and fire a truckload at Earth with very little effort."

"Mr. President, as you said, we believe the Soviets are planning to place nuclear weapons on the lunar surface," confirmed Ryan, Commander of SAC, the Strategic Air Command. "Our own design for a space shield around Earth to defend against incoming warheads has also begun. Think of it as a strategic defense initiative in the event of a war among the stars. And we're now designing a reusable shuttle to transport our own equipment, just as you said, sir."

"Good," the president remarked.

"But how is all this going to work?" interrupted one of the audience.

"May I, sir?" Chuck asked. The secretary nodded. "I'm Moore of NASA Specialist Operations. Our plan is to establish a missile base on the Moon if necessary. Warheads will be launched and sent to Earth, taking one to three days. They will operate like ICBMs and rain down on strategic locations throughout the Soviet Union."

The secretary interrupted. "It's probably best if we take a look at the model first. Chuck, would you please show us?"

The team stood and walked over to a large scale model of a lunar crater in the center of an adjoining anteroom as the lights came on.

"Is that what I think it is?" asked the president, with the secretary of defense to his right and Chuck behind him.

"It's a lunar base, sir," Chuck replied. "We're starting to build and test the components here and at other secure locations. The plan is to ship them to the lunar surface. We started eighteen months ago." He paused to let the idea sink in, for this would seem like a bold fantasy.

At the base of the crater model, there appeared to be a dwelling, consisting of a large circular biome with building blocks around it, each connected by tubes, and a handful of larger, irregularly shaped rooms, all spread out over the area of a small village. There were fluid and gas tanks in the back, and a cluster of pods neatly arranged in a circle around the outside of a small circular building.

239

"We expect to place this settlement on the dark side of the Moon," Chuck continued. "Maybe inside a crater or a valley, just like the model, so it can remain undetected. There are a lot of big holes up there."

On the other side of the crater model were about two dozen toy-sized rocket launchers, an apron of lunar vehicles, and a small building in the center that was too small to make out.

"There will be a permanent space station in orbit around the Earth, known as Apollo-X. In the event of a nuclear war, a standby shuttle from Vandenberg on the West Coast would take a crew to the Moon. They say you can survive up there for up to six months," Chuck added.

"That's not long enough for a nuclear winter down here," the president remarked.

"We're working on extending the duration. Maybe the worst will be over in that time. We don't know yet," Ryan replied.

"There's not much light on the dark side of the Moon," Chuck continued. "Though it's not quite as bad as you might think. Two weeks of darkness followed by two weeks of daylight. We get a little starlight, but it's not enough to illuminate the shadows. During the day it will be scorching hot, so we will need the natural cover of the craters. There won't be any radio communication with Earth unless they go to the near side to talk to us. They'll need transportation for that; they can't just walk over the horizon—it's too far, despite appearances. The surface of the Moon's the size of Asia, so we're working on a lunar vehicle with a ninety mile range. All of this may one day be home to some people. We've had technicians live in the mock-up house for up to four weeks at a time. And that's going to increase over the next year."

"So when's our turn?" the president asked. "I could use a place to hide right now."

"I think the White House would be more comfortable, sir."

"I wouldn't bet on it! Those Republicans can really turn the thumbscrews. Then it's off to the gallows," he added, pretending to be strung up.

The group laughed again, then Chuck pointed them back to their seats.

Chris had been quiet so far, but opened his agenda item once they were seated again. "We received evidence last year that the Soviets have also begun to create a space shield. They are already testing anti-satellite systems that could wipe out all of our communications in the event of a nuclear war. They could leave us defenseless. May I suggest you turn to page seventy-six in your decks now, please?"

Pages were flipped in the silence as everyone turned to a grainy image of a Soviet satellite on stilts in a workshop somewhere in Russia.

"Their space chief has been asked to create an anti-satellite system. It's under construction, code-named Polyot. And another, Molniya, which controls the system, is already in testing. A celestial network that will give the Union a decisive advantage and perhaps one day control of our skies.

"What you see there is Polyot, first launched in November sixty-three. It will intercept, detonate and destroy targets in orbit. It is essentially a suicide bomb. It's a clear threat to our military communications network in space. Although man is about to become a space traveler, it's clear that his military installations and equipment are going with him."

"All this heralds a disastrous change of direction. One

minute it's going to the Moon, now it's war in space. Is that what they want?" asked a member of the audience.

Chuck knew it was all frighteningly plausible, given enough time, ingenuity, and resource.

"Okay, so how do we get our program up there? How long will it take?" the president asked.

"I don't think we could do it all that quickly," chimed in another.

"If we look at the model of the whole Moon program, the first stage was Mercury, then Gemini. Apollo is up and running, as you know. Chris James, would you like to tell us where we are?" the secretary asked.

Chris stood up and turned his attention to another scale model of the Earth and Moon. A toy spaceship and a small yellow school bus with a handful of toy rockets were spread out on the table in front of it. "We must secure the Moon first," he explained. "Apollo will pave the way for developing ways to get there and back, to search for water and other materials we need to fuel warheads and create living space for our people. Apollo will establish docking and landing procedures so we can build our defensive position." He picked up the bus. "The second stage will involve several reusable shuttles to transport equipment and warheads, all covertly, for storage on the lunar surface." He grabbed a handful of toy rockets. "The third stage, gentlemen, is the deployment of our own space shield around Earth, its purpose: to knock out incoming Soviet missiles before they land on American soil. All of this, gentlemen, will take ten to twenty years of work. But it is all under way. We must begin now. This may be our final defense strategy."

"Let's say we can do this," said NASA Assistant Administrator Jones. "Where and how do we store and manage the warheads on the Moon? Won't that be obvious to the Soviets?"

"Gentlemen, as we said, the base will be on the dark side. Here ..." Chuck interjected, pointing to the facility just outside their room, "... is where we're building and testing a simulated missile base. It's on your tour today."

A thoughtful voice spoke from the left, breaking the tone. "And how exactly do we choose who goes up there? And come back later if war breaks out?" It was Crandall, head of the Manned Spacecraft Center in Houston. "To live on for mankind if the worst were to happen down here? Isn't that an important question?" He paused. "Who gets to decide? Is it the president, sir? Will the American people choose?"

The room fell silent at the question.

"Soldiers? Will these be the remains of the American people? Of humanity? Soldiers?" Crandall asked.

"We think they are people too," Ryan interrupted.

"That doesn't answer the question," Crandall replied.

"It's a big question. It may be safer for humans to stay on Earth. Maybe deep underground in case of an attack. We're working on the answers," the president interrupted.

"Fighting communism in space or wherever might be the easy part. But who will protect the weak and vulnerable?"

"Whoever has the power. It's always been that way. It's the hallmark of humanity," the president replied.

With no easy answers to the big questions, the delegation left with Chuck to see what deadly secrets were already in production.

* * *

"Sir, a moment to update you on my unit?" Chris asked as he walked with NASA's Crandall after the meeting.

"Let's hear it."

"We have a team and a mission commander. We've kept it tight. Three astronauts are in training now, learning how to operate in zero-G. They're developing the suits and equipment. We have standbys too, but they don't know what they're in for yet," Chris replied as they passed a row of glass-fronted offices.

"What don't they know?"

"We have a team developing flight systems, other procedures and life support. They were in Special Ops, but not anymore. None of them were announced in Group Three or Four, but they are now supporting the early Apollo missions. Some are at Vandenberg."

"Good. So we have options."

They arrived at Chris' Area fifty-something office.

"So, is your man up to it?" asked Crandall, stooping in front of a bulletin board in Chris' room. It was covered with pictures.

"Yes. And there are a few that could make the A-team," Chris replied. He sat down at his desk and checked for messages.

"Who are those guys?" asked Crandall, pointing to some of the head shots on a cork board.

Chris looked up at the wall. "Seven positions."

"Tell me about them."

"The commander, Chuck Moore, who you know; two geologists; a medic; and two engineers. Two of them have built military base camps in various war zones."

"And the seventh? Who are those two guys?"

"They're pilots, to fly the missions, docking and so on. The one on the right is one of the best. That's his forte. He's done more than anyone else in all the groups. The one on the left is about the same."

"So why isn't the guy on the right primed?" asked Crandall. He turned back to Chris.

"He was tipped for prime, but the commander wouldn't commit. The guy on the left is on his mind."

"Wouldn't commit? But you said he was the best."

"The Commander wanted him in the crew. We found out he has a heart condition."

"What's his name?"

"Jim Cobb."

"Where is he now?"

"The astronaut office. He was in the Navy."

"And what about that other guy?"

"That's Tom Mitchell. He's already at Vandenberg."

"Good. Let's have options and keep them open. There's too much at stake to rely on one person."

CHAPTER 32 - TEACH IN

The same day, March 24th, 1965

Jim walked toward the University of Michigan's Ann Arbor campus that evening wearing nothing more than a T-shirt, a thin jacket, and cloth sneakers. He'd flown halfway across the country and still felt groggy as if it were three in the morning, trudging the last dark, frozen mile in ankle-deep snow and cursing himself for not anticipating the bitter cold.

It had driven into his chest by the time he joined a small group of students among a thousand or so people. They'd shuffled to an entrance of the university's great hall and waited to enter. It was nine o'clock and things weren't moving very fast. He looked around for options and hobbled across the snow-covered square to another entrance with fewer people, though there were about a hundred of them. "Great idea," he muttered, wondering how he was going to find JoAnn in the huge crowd. He stopped, cold and tired, feeling reckless at his lack of planning and foresight. Just then, miraculously, and not twenty yards away, he saw the back of her head in the crowd. With a burst of energy, as if his arm had been pumped full of nitro, he called out and went for her, grabbing her shoulder from behind.

"JoAnn? I've ..."

A startled woman turned. She had a fringe over her thoroughly frozen rosy cheeks and recoiled as if she were about to be accosted. It wasn't her.

Jim backed away quickly and apologized, as several people turned to fight him off, then hurried on, stopping again near the doorway of a busy entrance.

He glanced across the crowd and saw that just a few yards to his left, and within earshot, a reporter and his news crew had intercepted a young man standing in line to enter the hall.

The man asked, "Sir, it looks like you're going inside for the teach-in. Can we have a moment, please? Can you tell us why you're here today?"

The man in line turned directly to the camera and smiled, then spoke calmly and deliberately. "Well, to put it simply, I do not agree with the war. We must do everything we can to stop it quickly. That's where I'm going," he added, pointing down the hall. "In there. I'm going in there to stop it." After making his declaration, he nodded politely to the camera, thanked the news crew, and finished with a confident smile for the crowd.

Another man next to him jumped in and added in slurred and intoxicated words directly to the camera, "I'm amazed. This is amazing, isn't it?" He stepped back and glanced around the crowd calmly and, with a look of pride in his eyes, announced to the camera again with a subtle grin, "Tomorrow ... well, tomorrow I'm going to quit my job. He turned and blew kisses to the crowd. His smile widened ear-to-ear. "Yes, you heard it here, on the news tonight."

The reporter waved the camera in for another close-up.

"You're quitting your job?" he repeated. He looked back at the lens as if to check the attention of his audience.

"Yes. I'm quitting … tomorrow," the man replied to the reporter. "Because we have to help these people. Quite simply, it's time to stop living a lie. We have the money. We have the education. We know what's going on. It's not what they're telling us. We're not going to go along with it. I work for one of the defense contractors in town. I won't name them." He looked straight into the lens again. "We can't keep killing innocent people. I'm going to help these great people." Pride clearly swelled in his words, and his eyes were once again glazed with vision, purpose, and alcohol.

The reporter acknowledged the two men as they regained their places in line.

Wow, thought Jim. He'd never expected to see such conviction. Though it had been attention-grabbing at times, it had never felt quite so visceral on television while he was cocooned in his NASA and Navy bubbles. He looked around and saw a crowd that seemed intensely committed to their fight to avert the war.

The reporter turned to Jim, who was standing alone. "Sir, hello. Sir, can we have a moment, please?" he asked. "How about you, sir? Can you tell us why you are here tonight?" He waved his cameraman closer.

Surprised, Jim put his hand to his face and looked away, thinking he couldn't be on the news at the protest. Involuntarily and completely embarrassed, with his face still half hidden, he said into the harsh light of the camera, "I'm, uh, here to find my wife." He couldn't think of anything else to say. He turned quickly and began to walk away as fast as his legs could carry him, though the reporter stayed put for a moment.

The man circled back toward pro-war hecklers who had begun taunting the anti-war crowd just twenty yards behind them.

As he walked on, Jim saw a sign that read *Fight Communism Here at Home,* then another that read *Christ Will Defeat Communism.*

Then, as if on cue, he turned to see a scuffle break out in front of the news crew when one of the jeering hecklers lost his board to an anti-war protester. The man took a snowball to the face, lost his footing, and dragged the heckler down with him. Surrounding taunts quickly degenerated into a skirmish as several more of the crowd fell about and fought in the snow, while more still jumped in to break things apart. Fists came out and tensions rose in the bitter cold as sympathizers from both sides joined in and others began to break up the fight.

"Quick, over there. This could get ugly," the reporter said to his cameraman. He turned his lens toward the commotion. "You got it? Tell me you got it!" The reporter straightened up and spoke into the camera. "As it begins, the protest here promises to be contentious," he said, but apparently unhappy with his opening, demanded, "Okay, again. Let's do it again."

* * *

In a bid to get warm, Jim offered to help a trio of students to fuel a fire in a large drum in the courtyard. He stopped in front of a white girl holding the arm of an African-American man, thinking he'd never seen an interracial couple before. It looked to him like defiance, revolution, and even delusion, though he couldn't decide which was most likely.

The girl puffed on a spliff as if it were the only source of heat, then passed it around and curled deeper into her partner's side. Jim began breaking off pieces of wood and basked in the faint glow of the fire.

The third student, a white man, remarked, "A lot of people out here tonight."

"A thousand, I'd say," Jim replied.

"I don't think they were expecting that many. There just ain't room for them all inside. And, man, is it cold out here." He rubbed his hands a little harder.

Jim kept stoking the fire, but stayed out of the conversation.

The trio looked at him curiously. "Are you from around here?" the black man asked.

Jim hesitated, then said, "I came to find someone."

"Yeah, I knew it. I just knew it," the white man said.

Jim stopped and wondered what the guy thought he knew.

"No place like a rally to get laid and high, huh?" the white man added, clearly smoked out and practically incoherent.

Jim was as surprised by the remark as the girl was. She smacked the man's arm, but he just grinned broadly at his own joke.

The black man feigned disgust. "Come on, dude, are you saying you came here just for that?"

"Yeah," the white man replied, equally baffled by the retort. "Well yeah, but, sure man, there's the war too," he added with another drag.

"It's immoral dude, you know that."

"What? Doesn't everybody want to get laid? Sure seems like a good thing to me. Morality's not in question."

"No, the war, you idiot. The imperialist empire trying to

take over the world."

"Dude, they just have to hold back the Commies. You know that." It sounded like the voice of a party line.

"Do you see any Commies on TV? I don't know about you, but all I see out there is normal people getting bombed. That's not what it is anymore. That's just a cover, I'm telling you."

"Too right, man. Too right," the white man agreed, though the appeasement seemed to come surprisingly easily. The smoke must have lubricated the conflict. "It's our job to rewrite history on this one."

The black man said, "We got Civil Rights last year. At least I can get a job now—even her. So we can end this war too. There's nothing a protest like this can't fix. Mom and pop ain't gonna do a thing except sit back and watch it all on TV. That's what they do. Their way would get us all nuked. We gotta change the game, my reverend used to say."

Jim had just heard a third true crusader that night, and he'd been here barely an hour.

One of them suddenly looked up at him, as if remembering he was still there. "You from around here, dude?" the white man asked. But Jim, unsure how to answer and whether or not he could still pass off as a dude, remained tight lipped.

"Sounds like he's not from around here," the black man added when Jim didn't answer.

Jim looked around. "My wife is here, somewhere. I don't know how to find her. JoAnn. I don't suppose you know a dark-haired JoAnn, do you?" He didn't give the last name and didn't expect an answer.

"What faculty?"

"She's ... uh, actually, I don't know."

"You don't know?" The black man looked surprised.

251

Jim fell silent again, thinking he'd put his foot in it, as he knew he would if he didn't keep his mouth shut.

"Teacher or student?"

"Stu ... dent."

The trio looked at each other as Jim quickly walked on. He didn't need the answer and already felt that he had attracted more attention than was safe by simply trying to do nothing.

A short time later, he found his way into the hall. Still, he decided to keep to himself and avoid another discussion about the what and the why of his presence. As he moved through, he saw that the event had already gathered pace. There were lectures and debates and short films that educated, as JoAnn had put it, about the war and its impact on the Vietnamese people. He stopped to look at a display on the devastating effects of America's infamous chemical weapon, Agent Orange, along with gruesome images of burning Vietnamese villages and their fleeing inhabitants. It looked a lot like Korea to him. Another short film discussed the twenty billion dollar cost of the war that year alone. Soon the discussion groups that had begun in the great hall spilled out into the corridors.

Jim stopped at a television set showing coverage of the event itself. He began to think about how much time he had spent standing in his own tent, just looking out at what the establishment wanted him to see. Now he was in the opposing camp, standing eyeball to eyeball in a world away from the NASA and the military lens. These people seemed as certain of their own views as LBJ was of his own. He tried to reconcile what he'd already seen and heard with his own duty to serve and protect his country, no matter how horrific it might seem to these people. How could they have the full picture? And his job had never allowed for discretion in the matter anyway. As a former naval aviator, he couldn't just follow his own will. There seemed no clear answer, just as there never had been every time he'd been round this loop, though now, for the first time, he could see and really feel the opposition's energy.

CHAPTER 33 - BOMB

Moments later, March 24th, 1965

In a corner of the great hall and next to another small screen, JoAnn and her cohort of SDS friends had prepared to show their own horror films of devastated napalmed villages in Vietnam. She turned on the TV to a shot of demonstrators chanting on the screen, "Hey! Hey! LBJ! How many kids have you killed today?"

She then flicked over to a shot of JFK after Cuba. "In the final analysis, our most basic common link is that we all inhabit this small planet. We all breathe the same air. We all cherish our children's future. And we are all mortal," he proclaimed.

"Well, thank goodness for that," she muttered, wondering what on earth he could have been thinking before that *final* analysis. She switched back to the live report from outside the hall. "Wow! Isn't that amazing?" she said to a companion. "It must be beamed to the other side of the country then back again."

"Filtered for the worst before it gets here," her friend replied.

She chuckled and said, "With a little delay? That's great,

isn't it?"

The two cheered to a news clip of their buddy James, who'd been outside talking to the crew earlier but was now standing next to her inside. "How did they fix you up?" she joked.

He chuckled and said, "It's an hour delay. Plenty of time to fix imperfections."

The group dispersed, except for JoAnn and her friend, who remained, still watching the TV. Her face suddenly froze. *No! It couldn't be.* She stared at the screen and turned quickly to look around the hall.

"What's going on?" her friend asked.

JoAnn turned back to the TV with a furrowed brow and muttered, "That's ..." She pointed at the image. The other hand cupped her mouth. The reporter on the screen began talking to a bystander. "Quick, turn it up! Turn it up!" she ordered.

They both jumped at the volume.

"I'm, uh, just here to find my wife," the man on screen said.

"Oh God!" said JoAnn. "What in the world? Jim?" Her heart skipped a beat then began to pound. Her eyes and ears couldn't believe what they had just seen and heard. She backed away and glanced around the hall again, as the reporter on screen turned toward a scuffle and said, "Just as it begins, the protest here promises to be contentious."

"I have to find him," she said, "Before he finds trouble. He does that. Oh my God, Jim! I shouldn't have said anything."

She searched for him until the early hours, by which time the teach-in audience had already thinned out. She estimated that only a thousand or so crusaders remained as she walked down an adjacent corridor one last time, still chewing on what she was going to say. Exhausted, she paused next to a string quartet playing and felt a moment of peace from the conflict rattling inside her head. A nagging doubt hit her. Surely Jim was here to dissuade her from what she was doing, but she would tell him to go home. And there remained a deeper problem that had crossed her mind several times. Could she continue doing what she was doing and remain his wife at the same time? How long could their relationship go on like this? He'd never buy the status quo and she wasn't going to drop it either. Why should she? What would she do instead? Stay home and do the ironing? Despite the dilemma, somewhere deep inside, a part of her was desperately curious to hear what he had to say. Maybe he had something. The idea of returning home lit a lingering darkness in her heart and she didn't want it to go away. Maybe—just maybe, she thought. Maybe what? Could it work somehow? It was three in the morning and she wondered if she should just call him, even though the wait would be agony. She walked back to the hall, wondering if she'd been mistaken or even deluded. Maybe it wasn't him on the screen at all. And if it was, had he gone home at the sight of the massive crowd?

Just then, an object flew across the hall and past her line of sight. It narrowly missed her and landed no more than ten feet away, close to where the strings were playing. Everything went deadly quiet, then an almighty scream shattered the tension like an ear-splitting wake-up call. "Oh, my God. There's a bomb! Hurry, it's a bomb!" cried a terrified woman.

The disbelieving crowd stood frozen and confused for a moment before panic broke out. A frantic scramble began for the exit at the far end of the long corridor.

"Move! Come on, move!" a man shouted from behind.

The crowd heaved in the sudden pandemonium and JoAnn found herself being pushed along, losing control of her movements. She noticed that the lady in front of her had begun to pray for forgiveness, just as another, further back, began to scream for help. It was then that her heightened senses caught a glimpse of Jim about twenty yards away.

She doubled back and whispered his name in disbelief, forgetting where she was for a moment and almost stumbling in the rush for the exit. "Jim? Jim!" she yelled, escalating each call and waving one arm madly over the crowd. "Jim!"

He'd heard her above the terrified screams and looked directly at her through the fleeing crowd. For a moment, they were in the eye of the storm, and all the commotion around JoAnn faded as she held his gaze for no more than a millisecond.

She screamed his name again and reached out as the heaving mass continued to push her, elbowing its way toward the double door exit like a swarm of insects fleeing a flooded hole. Within half a minute, she was outside, among terrified people, ankle-deep in snow, looking around frantically. She'd lost him.

The long corridor emptied over the next few minutes and security moved in, though the bomb, or whatever it was, hadn't gone off.

Jim looked around, wondering what to do next. He'd been ejected on the other side of the building, and the chances of seeing JoAnn again seemed little better than a thunderbolt with everyone outside now. Many of the hecklers were still there and seemed to be getting more energetic in their taunts at the anti-war protesters who'd been herded out into the cold. New pro-war signs had gone up with the chant, "NUKE HANOI, NUKE HANOI!"

He pushed his way toward the double-door exit where he'd last seen her, and searched courtyards and squares, stopping now and then by fires to keep out the cold. Debates and lectures continued in small groups, and speaker Arthur Waskow added his own speech against the war, which drew cheers from the frozen onlookers.

Finally, he returned to the great hall, looking as exhausted as he felt, having been up for nearly twenty-four hours. He had not found JoAnn. He stopped at a quiet seat near the back of the auditorium and fell asleep the very moment his backside touched the chair.

CHAPTER 34 - ACTIVIST

A short while later, March 24th, 1965

It was only an hour or so later when Jim heard a familiar voice and felt a gentle hand stroke his hair. His cogs were slow to start and his eyelids felt like lead ingots. At first, they simply refused to open. He mumbled something unintelligible from the end of his dream, then almost fell out of his chair with an awkward jolt. He jerked back up and glimpsed at JoAnn, now standing in front of him. She seemed just as startled as he was, and almost as bleary eyed. She stared at him suspiciously.

He managed to utter her name, then stood up with a numb head and hugged her gently, as if she were a house of cards. He sat down again and rubbed his neck.

She looked down at her watch and, with her hands on her hips, finally said, "What are you doing here, Jim?"

"Spoken like a true spouse. You'd be good at that if you were home."

She frowned as he leaned forward and rubbed his face to rouse it.

"I came to find you, JoAnn. I can't believe it took all night." He scratched his head to relieve the tension and looked back at her with a slightly wider aperture. As if they were in one–

sixth gravity, he moved his body stiffly and straightened his hair, feeling completely tongue-tied. How was he going to tell her that he was going off to war, and here of all places?

"You okay, JoAnn?" he asked instead.

"Fine," was all she said.

There was an awkward silence. After a moment, when she hadn't responded, Jim added with a grin, "Well, I managed to take care of myself. Had a great breakfast this morning—yesterday."

"Why are you here, Jim?" It came out like a jab, which she seemed to regret immediately.

"I came to see you, Jo. My head's not quite straight. I've been trying to decide whether or not to stay in Houston." Jim paused to gauge her reaction.

She looked surprised.

"They found a heart problem. And they pulled the rug. You know that. So I've been thinking about other things."

JoAnn waited for him to continue.

"Are you coming home?" he asked. "We can talk about it."

Obviously prepared for the question, she said without hesitation, "I have work to do." After another awkward silence, she sat on a chair a few feet from him and asked, "What are you going to do?"

Jim hesitated but said, "Well, there's the option of maybe trying my hand at something else. You know, maybe something local so I can be home more." He'd already written that idea off, but he needed to see her reaction. He would only do it if she came home. When it didn't grab her attention, he went on. "I put all my eggs in one basket. Big mistake. Never do that. It's time for a change, JoAnn."

She still seemed surprised that he had something else on

his mind and said with a hint of disbelief. "You're leaving NASA? Why? I wouldn't recognize you without a jumpsuit or uniform. You'd actually wear a shirt and tie every day for something else?"

"That's what I've been doing in Houston, JoAnn. And, they do fit. I could get used to it. Maybe it's time to let go and see what else is out there."

Her face turned to intrigue, "Didn't they tell you to stay?"

"Yes. But the whole thing feels like second class, Jo. Like the road to nowhere, waiting for something to happen. It could be years in an office chasing an outcome I can't control. I'm as good as out now, a player in someone else's game. It's like you once said: hauled in by the gravitational pull, but now the gravity's been turned off." A hint of a smile appeared at his own joke. "The question is, Jo, where do I go from here?" He paused, then added, "Where do we go?"

She didn't latch on to his final question but inquired, "And what about the others? Are they leaving too?"

Jim filled her in on Tom, Fred and Chuck and when he was finished he asked again, "When are you coming back, Jo?"

She replied awkwardly, "I'm staying for a while."

"Why?"

She glanced up toward the coffee bar nervously and said, "I have something here now, Jim. There's something I have to do."

Jim didn't say anything.

She looked back at him and went on. "Eve wants help for Ricky. He's trying to get into college for journalism and I'd like to guide him if I can."

Jim listened. It was the help she never got.

"She's also worried about him getting drafted, you know

that."

"There's nothing you can do about that, JoAnn."

"There's still time."

"What can you do?"

"He has a draft card, so I told him to get married to get out of it."

"That seems like an idea. Wouldn't be the first."

"He has someone."

Jim saw an opening and thought about what to say next. "And, who knows—maybe they'll come looking for me too." It was the only way he could bring up what he had to tell her, hoping that she understood something beneath his words, though she only looked puzzled.

Now, certain that what he was about to say would fly right in her face, and still not quite sure how it would work, he explained, "I came to tell you that I've been thinking about going back to the Navy, Jo. Back to the original business."

She looked stunned.

"You know what that means? Fighting in a war, probably. In Vietnam."

She froze, so Jim continued. "I talked to Powell about it."

Dazed, she asked why.

"I figured if I'd just stayed in the Navy, none of this space stuff would have occurred to me anyway. I have to get back into the fight against communism, Jo. You know that. I can't do it in an office." Now he had to admit the truth. "But I also know that going back means we'll be apart, and not for anything so fancy as going into space or anything like that. I came to talk to you. JoAnn, I need to know what's next for us."

She looked confused. "And why did you think I would come

home for that?"

"Well, now it becomes clear," He looked around the hall and noticed a man approaching them and added, "that you're not."

JoAnn looked baffled by everything he'd just said.

The man walked into their stunned silence and stopped a few feet back. He gave JoAnn a warm smile. "Everything okay?"

She looked up at him but didn't answer.

"We, uh, have to open the coffee bar."

She replied gently with a shallow smile, the wheels clearly turning in her head. "Thanks Pete, I'm coming. Just a minute."

The man looked at Jim, then back at JoAnn. "I'll be behind the bar when you're ready." He turned and walked away.

JoAnn looked down at her hands, calculating her words. "Jim. I have something to say."

"What?" Jim's heart tightened. "Tell me what?" He looked back at the man.

She looked him in the face and said, "These past few months, while I've been away ..." She was struggling.

Oh God, Jim thought, fearing the worst. No, it couldn't be. He looked up at the man again. He was already back behind the bar. It was he who had answered the phone when Jim had called the day before. What was she doing with him?

"It's just that ... I haven't been completely honest with you."

Jim steeled himself, not wanting to hear what she was about to say. He looked back at Pete and thought, no, it couldn't be. Not JoAnn for chrissakes. She was the one who had stormed out on him for something he hadn't done with Susie. He looked at her in disbelief.

She looked at him sheepishly. "Jim—"

"What?" He was aghast. He didn't want to hear another word.

"Jim, I joined the protests."

He sat in suspended animation.

"Well, it's marching really," she added.

Jim let go of his breath, looking like he was about to turn blue. He threw his hands in the air. "Marching?"

"Yes. I know I didn't tell you."

All of a sudden, marching was absolutely fine. "Why didn't you tell me?"

"Well ..."

"You were here to write. What happened to the notebook and pencil?"

JoAnn thought for a moment, then said, "I am writing, about Ricky and the other kids and the work they're doing here. Sent things to several papers." She shrugged. "Let's see."

"Why didn't you say anything?"

"I was afraid, Jim. Scared of what you'd say. That you'd stop me."

"So are you an activist now? In the streets?" Jim saw *yes* on her face. "What's that for?"

"For peace, Jim. See, you don't understand. I'm supporting colleges all over the country to fight the war. Starting here, today," JoAnn said.

"Fighting for peace? Does that even make sense? You never said."

"And you never thought to ask. You were never home, Jim."

"I'm asking now." Jim took a deep breath and rubbed his

face again. It looked increasingly strained. She was right. And it hurt. His head began to tumble uncomfortably through the past few years, and he realized how alienated he'd become, trapped in his own world as if it were everything. He had assumed that she would always be there, that she understood the world through his eyes, even though she obviously hadn't. He knew he should have paid more attention to her, but what did he do instead? He'd kept plowing his own furrow.

She stood up. "I have to go now. Go home. Call me. Don't do anything until you call me. Please."

CHAPTER 35 - DOWNED

Moments later

Jim got up, walked to the bar to get a coffee, then sauntered to the other side of the hall.

"Nice girl," someone said out of the blue in a soft voice just behind him.

Jim turned to a large African-American man who was manning a stall littered with photographs, though it lacked an audience.

"No, really. She's quite a girl, but you're up against it, buddy."

Jim felt annoyed. "Oh, really?"

"Yeah, see that guy at the back—"

"Okay, okay, stop right there." Jim held up a hand.

The man backed off and Jim stood in silence again. He looked blankly across the hall, then back to the man's stall to get a better look at the exhibits, though he recoiled at what he saw. Scattered across a desk and pinned to the walls were, what would be to ordinary people, heinous scenes of war with victims killed or displaced. Nothing was held back.

Although he'd been in the military, Jim had no first-hand experience of combat conditions on the ground, except for the time he was shot down in Korea in fifty-three. He suddenly remembered thinking about it when he was supposed to be organizing the closet at home.

He'd landed in a monsoon river in enemy territory, got shot at in the midst of battle, and ran into a Seventh Infantry reservist by the name of Miller while they waited for the Air Force to take out the enemy. His unit had just been killed and he was desperate for Truman to nuke the whole place. Jim also came across a group of enemy POWs, sitting with their hands on their heads, knees bent, shirts off, and surrounded by a small waist-high barbed wire fence. Large white signs hung from their necks like exhibits.

"God picked democracy for these guys," said one of the Marines guarding them. "Hey, little Commie. Want to see some American hospitality?" He raised his rifle to hit a prisoner on the head but stopped short of a blow. A broad grin broke out.

"Yalu River. Yalu River. We kick your ass," the prisoner said with a wide, friendly smile.

Jim was stunned by the insolence, though the man obviously thought humor meant safety.

"Chinks learn good English, hey," the Marine said, laughing back at the man.

"Please, sir. Please, sir. Let us go. We no harm you. Let us go. Come see. We will help you. Missing your mother? Father?"

The Marine swung his rifle at the head of another man five seats away. He recoiled in agony and Jim stopped, stunned by the brutality.

"What's the matter?" the Marine said. "He's a gook. That's the way they like it. Any of you want to try some of that?"

CHAPTER 36 - MR GUM

Moments later

"Photos-o-the-war. All-o-dem, taken in the last year," the chap behind the stall said. It was a loose and lazy tongue, gentle, modest, but not slow.

Jim snapped out of his reverie and turned back to him.

The man waved his hand across the stall, inviting him to take a closer look.

"I wus a photographer with the Army Special Photo Office. Spent six months out there capturing de soldiers, missions, hospitals, locals and so on. Awful stuff, just look-a-here."

"US Army?" Jim asked.

"Wus Army. Then I got injured right here and they told me to retire. Piece of shrapnel right here in ma leg." He leaned forward and pointed to his right knee. "Thought I was gonna need a new one at the time but dey managed to save it. Thank goodness too. Hospitals in ma area not so good. All de good ones springing up outa town, where all the white folk moving to. Civil Rights last year hasn't helped us poor black folk too much. Anyway, ah's not so sure I could have taken more o'dem pictures anyways. I's a nature photographer you see. Birds and that is really what I do. Plenty o'birds in Tennessee.

None of this horrible stuff here, you know."

The man was clearly pleased to have a visitor to share his stories, so Jim looked more closely at some of the less gruesome images of American soldiers in combat, though he found it impossible not to be moved by the less salubrious images of displaced, dead, and tortured Vietnamese (in some cases at the hands of American soldiers), or of children flee-ing battle scenes and even their own burnt or looted villages, naked. It all looked to him as if it had been handpicked to elicit only one reaction: disgust.

The terrified faces reminded Jim of Miller's "gooks," as the man had called them back in fifty-three.

"They's a lovely family," the owner of the stall interrupted his thoughts again, pointing at a particular photo. "They took me in when ah got injured. But the village was torched right here. That's when they got me out. Not sure what happen' to the family. Ah's told they got away. Tha's all I know. But ah went lookin' for them."

"So you take pictures for the US Army?"

"Yeah. This here's my Nikon." He held it up. "She's a beauty. Light enough to pack and sturdy enough for de battle zone. I's real please" to meet you, sir." His hand went out and they shook. "Benjamin's the name, but you can jus' call me Ben."

"I'm Jim. So how did they find you ... for this?" Jim asked, glancing around the event.

"I's here for the rally in a short while. Figured from what ah seen, we need to stop doin' what we doin' to them poor folks out there," he said, pointing to his photos again. "If we can stop this, I won' have to go back no more. But they think ma leg's fine and I's scared I'll be called up for duty once again. Ma daughter said we should try stop it. We got the Civil Rights last year. It was amazin'. You know, I think anything's possible. You jus' gots to try, tha's all."

"Not if you're injured like that."

"Well, I can't be sure, but I gots to do something," replied Ben. "So, you comin' outside? You and I, we should stick together," he added with a grin.

Jim sipped his coffee and said, "I need to ask the girl something."

Ben looked at JoAnn behind the bar. He thought for a second, then laughed and said, "You know, I'd say you two look made for each other."

The comment was equally startling, comforting and wise to Jim, but he said nothing.

As the day dawned around seven o'clock, he walked outside with his new buddy Ben to gather for the teach-in's closing rally, feeling like he was on his first blind date—the scene outside was barely recognizable from what he had imagined in the darkness of the night. The snow had been trampled, and the ground was littered with garbage and charcoal from various fires that had been set during the night. The crowd had also thinned out, so much so, that it looked like only about six hundred of the most determined protesters and persistent hecklers remained.

The two of them stood together for the closing speech. Jim saw that JoAnn was also out with her companions. It occurred to him that, in the cold light of day, he didn't look a bit like a student or an activist. Ben and he were standing among hardliners at a time when, despite the Civil Rights Act less than a year earlier, racial discrimination was still very much evident. Their combined military pedigree must have stunk from a mile away. Jim wondered what JoAnn's cohort might think of him in their sleep-deprived, anti-war state of mind. A government spy? *Saboteur,* he read in some of the eyes.

The rally began, moving through the streets of Ann Arbor to the cheers of supporters who were filled with new energy. Local onlookers stopped in surprise to see what had arrived on their doorstep, while fresh hecklers also began their morning shift. Jim's thoughts of JoAnn and her new friends were interrupted as they walked.

"You like gum?" Ben asked, walking in big steps right behind them. "I likes gum. In fact, there was a time when I could work five packs a day. But, ma teeth started to come loose, you know. You see these two back here?" He pointed to a couple of gaps in his upper right jaw as they walked. "They came loose cus-o-de-gum."

The conversation seemed like a useful distraction, Jim thought.

"In de army, gum's like gold dus' you know. When you out there in de battle zone, you can sell it for whatever you want. One of the only pleasures a soldier has. An' useful stuff too. I held open the shutter button on my camera with a piece'o gum. I was taking photos of me and ma crew, but couldn't hol' de button at the same time. Some gum on a stone an' a few seconds later ..."

Ben was still chewing over gum and cameras when they turned a corner on the street.

"And when you process them photos you can also pin them up with de gum. Takes a lot of chewin' mind you if you taking lotta photos, that is," Ben joked. "That's how I got through most of them packs." He smiled. "Anyway, like I said, you like gum?"

Jim began to wonder if he'd ever stop babbling about gum, and just nodded through his fatigue.

"It's the Big Red ones I like. You can blow the biggest bubbles, but you can't find them out on the battle front. Anyway, all the talk makes me wanna get some. You fancy some gum?" he said, looking around for stores.

Jim relented and nodded as he continued to scan the crowd. They stopped at a small grocery store on the way.

Ben tensed as they entered and Jim felt the frosty reception as well. After a hesitant pause, Ben quickly walked up and down the aisles, browsed the shelves and, to his obvious delight, quickly returned to the checkout with merchandise in hand.

But the middle-aged white man standing behind the counter, wearing a baseball cap, remained as still as a post in Ben's face.

"You done?" Jim asked as he snaked his way back to the front, though Ben still looked uncomfortable. Standing still, he stared back at the poker-faced checker. "I'd like to buy this here, sir," Ben said, sheepishly.

The man stood firm and pointed to something behind him. "You see that up there, boy?"

Ben froze, looking at a makeshift sign on the wall.

"That means you, sunshine. But I don't suppose a nigger like you can read now," he added with a smirk. "So, I'll just show you the door, supposing you can't find your way out. That is, unless you came in for a little playtime." The man laughed and glanced at a couple of thugs in the back of the shop. "No rights gonna serve you in here, boy. We got our own rules," he beamed.

A silence fell and Ben lost his tongue. Everyone stood ready for the next move. Jim looked at the sign that read *Nergos never served here.* He was touched to see Ben blush visibly through his dark hue.

Looking shifty, Ben slowly and humbly repeated his words and stood, ready for an unpleasant reaction. "I just want to pay for some gum, sir. Then I'll be on my way, like I said."

But the thugs, similar in appearance to the cashier, emerged from the back of the store and slowly made their way toward the counter. Jim caught sight of a heckler's board parked in a corner and his heart sank. "Oh shit!" he muttered.

"So, you boys out tryin' to stop the war, huh?" the shopkeeper said. He looked under the counter for something. "Nigger like you ought to be out there, fighting, and *dyin'* for your country—not in here, buying delights." His eyes lit up again and he snickered at his words.

"What's the matter? Can't take a bullet for your people?" jeered one of the others, as they continued slowly toward him from the back of the store. "I'll show you how."

Jim looked out and saw the rally pass by, its marchers oblivious to their situation inside. The store was quiet, and they were outnumbered four to two as more thugs turned toward the door, presumably to block their exit.

Jim shuffled closer to Ben and ordered, "Back off now."

One of the guys grabbed his arm, but Jim anchored his feet, slammed his wrist down and twisted it to free the grip, then pushed the man back. But it was a little too hard. The man lost his footing and fell backwards into a shelf, knocking over cans and food packages. The other man went for Ben, who, still wide-eyed, simply froze.

"Come on," Jim urged. "Let's get out of here before

somebody gets hurt."

They ran out the door.

"No, wait," Ben said as they stepped outside. To Jim's amazement, he turned and dashed back into the store, dropped some coins on the counter, picked up his gum, and hurried back out.

Jim, now with Ben in hot pursuit, ran quickly toward the gathering crowd that was still marching down the street.

"Hey, how'd you do that?" demanded Ben as he rushed behind, limping and rubbing his injured leg. "You ain't no student here."

"Yeah. You're right," Jim replied calmly, continuing to walk quickly and looking straight ahead. "We need to get inside that crowd and away from here."

JoAnn and her cohort, now farther downstream in the march, had their antennae trained on Jim and Ben and saw the commotion outside the store. They turned to join the chase as the store owner ran out with two others. Ben turned to see one of them raise a finger, pointing straight at him.

"This way," Jim urged.

Ben limped behind him into a dim alley on the other side of the road. "They coming. They's lots-o-them now. What we gonna do?" he asked fearfully.

Jim stopped in the middle. "Okay, we can't run far." He turned to face two incoming thugs who had caught up. A scrum quickly ensued. Jim hoisted one of them into a large dumpster and closed the lid, then practically picked Ben up and put him on top to hold the man inside.

The second was a little tougher, but Jim toyed with him,

tossing him like a skittle each time he came back for more. Humiliated, the man ran off down the alley.

"Go, go!" Jim urged Ben, who had also now made haste down the side street. "I'll be with you in a minute."

Jim turned back and saw JoAnn standing at the top of the alley with three of her cohort, presumably from the SDS she'd been talking about. They all looked stunned. Still breathless, he held out a hand as she walked toward him, stopping a few feet away.

"Come back to Houston. I want you to come home, JoAnn."

She still looked dazed, but turned to look back at the rally.

"You can't stop the war," he said.

"Yes, I can. Don't go and perpetuate the war! Go home and wait for my call."

"JoAnn, that was my job. I was a pilot in the Navy, for God's sake. We have to protect ourselves and ... that's not a bad thing, is it? Look, I could still be called up as a reserve—just like Miller. You remember him?"

"It's my job now to help save innocent people and stop our country from going down the drain. We need to get back to a safe—"

"What else do you think we were doing out there? Come home JoAnn, let's talk about it—"

"Jim!" She held up a hand. "I know what this is. It's about your father ... about getting your own back. It always has been. Since the day he disappeared. You gave us up for that. Is it war or peace, Jim?"

Three hecklers from the store now entered the alleyway at the top. Jim looked over his shoulder and saw Ben still waiting at the bottom. He turned to JoAnn and started to back away slowly. "I'll call you. At Eve's. Go to Eve's. I'll call you there."

Jim ran with Ben to the next block, leaving JoAnn still and speechless.

They hurriedly boarded a passing bus that disappeared somewhere into Michigan.

Pete walked over to JoAnn and asked, "Are you okay? Who is that guy? Army?"

JoAnn was still quietly shaken and said nothing. Her own situation no longer felt secure, as Jim had poked a hole in her bubble. She didn't know what else to say, but uttered, "I have to go home. She stomped back to the rally, thinking she had to get to Eve's straight away.

"Thank you, man," Ben said, on the edge of his seat and still breathless while chomping his new gum. "It's good. Fancy one?"

He pulled the pack out of his breast pocket and offered it to Jim, but he declined with a grin. "You get your remaining teeth into those."

"This's good stuff," Ben insisted. "Even if we found it in that trash back there."

Jim stood, looking up and down the road, wondering what to do next. He might still get caught again if he didn't get as far away as possible.

He went for the exit as the bus slowed. Ben stopped chewing.

"So long, buddy," Jim said, jumping onto the sidewalk. "Got to go. Hope you manage to stay out of the war."

Ben sprang out of his seat and hobbled hurriedly to the door as the bus began to move again.

"Hey, come back here," he hollered. "Where'd you learn them moves? Hey? Did you ask her for a date?" He threw the gum at him.

Jim pocketed the pack as the bus pulled away and looked out over the empty streets to absorb the first silence he'd experienced in what had felt like a thoroughly reckless few days.

CHAPTER 37 - GO WEST

The same day

Jim went straight to Detroit airport and arrived in an hour. He didn't want to get picked up by the cops for the mess he'd left behind and thought he should just go home to Houston like JoAnn had said. But now he felt more strongly than ever that he had to stop her from marching. His head spun as he imagined the reprehensible treatment by law enforcement, of all people, that other protesters had faced for years when the establishment didn't like what they saw. Water-hosing, aggressive dogs, incarceration and police batons flew across his mind. He thought back to the escalating aggression he'd seen firsthand in Washington in December. And things would be infinitely worse if there was even the slightest hint of Communist infiltration in any protest that tried to influence the war. Jobs would be lost, careers and lives destroyed, whether or not individuals had anything to do with it. All it would take was one malicious informant to arouse suspicion and start a busy-body FBI witch hunt. He remembered his old neighbor, Wilman, in forty-nine, standing as still as a scarecrow in his window across the street from his mother's house, spying on all the comings and goings from behind hidden curtains. It seemed very un-American at the time, as if he had something to hide by working in the teachers' union office. Senator McCarthy of Wisconsin had already begun weeding out Communist sympathizers from public service when the man disappeared with the FBI, a tactic that didn't seem too far removed from life in Nazi Germany from what Jim had heard.

Inside the terminal, he was still trying to figure out what to say to her. *Okay, JoAnn, we can start over. But I want you to drop the protesting.* That was too direct, like a parent. *I'll devote my time to you,* though that sounded cringe-worthy and he might just throw up saying it.

He dialed Eve's number and got the dreaded answering machine. "This is a message for JoAnn, I'm at the airport. Detroit." He looked up, shook his head and groaned, feeling tongue-tied, but continued. "JoAnn, will you come to the airport? We can go home together. I'll wait for you."

He took a deep breath and hung up. Drained and dead tired, with barely a calorie left in his body, he decided to sleep so he could think straight again. He walked through the terminal looking for a quiet corner and came across a television showing a news clip of a college riot. A few bystanders were watching. Their faces looked horrified. "Well, the Ann Arbor teach-in has certainly inspired a wave of protests at colleges and universities across the country. Just as it was confirmed that the marriage deferment rule was going to be abolished, at midnight Eastern tonight, student protesters at this college in Detroit took over the administration offices and forced out the faculty. Riot police were on hand and moved in to regain control," the reporter announced.

Jim watched in shock and awe. This was JoAnn's work on

the screen. It was what she had said would happen. She was actually doing it. It had made the news and was already driving people in colleges.

One of the bystanders nearby said to another, "My neighbor's a 1-A. He can't pretend to be a homo anymore like some of the other guys. I even know a couple who ran over the border to Canada and got married."

The listener groaned and shook his head. "Common decency has gone."

"I'd just go to Las Vegas. Do it quick and easy. That's what they say on the radio."

Jim had a brainwave. It seemed stupidly audacious. The ace in the hole was getting JoAnn on a plane to Vegas. Yes. That was it. It would be the honeymoon they'd always talked about but never gotten around to. "Anybody know how to get to Vegas from here?" he blurted out to the crowd.

"There's a flight every hour," said one of the bystanders in a work uniform.

Jim began to think. Something like that would show her that he was serious. And it would get her away from whatever she'd gotten herself into. Then maybe their lives would make sense again, like they used to. She was the anchor against which he could make the right choice. A choice he didn't like at the moment, except for *her*. Nothing else felt palatable or certain. He was lost without her.

"What do you need to get married there? Do you need papers?"

"No, nothing. Just drive or walk up, do the deed, and you're done. That's what they say on WEMU. New station at the university," said the homophobe, still looking at the screen with disgust.

Jim wondered how long it would take to get to Vegas and how much it would cost. And how would he tell her? The plan seemed like a hare-brained fantasy, though it promised to be unforgettable if they pulled it off. His head fought against what was probably a hopeless cause, even though it burned brightly in his mind.

He still hadn't figured it out when he dialed Eve again with a mixture of trepidation and hope. His stomach felt like a butterfly farm.

To his disbelief, JoAnn actually answered. It stunned him. He now had to explain himself without sounding completely doolally. "JoAnn? Did you get my message earlier?"

"Jim? Wait, what were you talking about? And what was all that fuss back there?"

"Did you hear my message?" he pressed again.

"Yes, I heard it. What's going on? Is this a game or something?"

"No, JoAnn." He took a deep breath. "I want you to come to the airport."

"The airport? Why?"

His heart jumped into his mouth. "Look, JoAnn, we're going on our honeymoon. Then back home." He paused, half expecting her to vomit into the phone. "Let's do it. Now's the time ... today."

"Jim, are you nuts?"

"JoAnn, just listen. We always wanted to go to Vegas. We should have done it a long time ago."

"Jim! This is crazy."

"Let's make it memorable."

He could just see her rolling her eyes at the other end, catching up to his words. He waited quietly for her to think through the steps.

"Jim, you're tired. Go home, get some sleep—"

"JoAnn—"

"Are you listening to yourself?"

"JoAnn?"

"Jim, you ..." He could see her hold up a hand and squeeze her eyes shut. A tear must have fallen as she paced the floor. "I'm not going home, sitting alone, while you ... you get killed in a war, or in a rocket, or on a plane somewhere, whatever you're going to do. Jim, there were days when I didn't know if you'd come back home, when you were flying those machines of yours. I can't do that again. I'm not going to another funeral."

He took a deep breath and said, "JoAnn, you know that means I'd have to leave everything behind. The only thing I ever wanted to do. To fly. To serve my country."

"Jim, I have work here. It's what I've always wanted, but I didn't have the courage to take on the establishment. Now I do. I have to."

"Okay." He paused and looked up again. "So what if I leave everything behind? Just you and me." He immediately wondered if he could actually say that.

JoAnn paused to think, then said, "I can't ask you to do that. I'm not going to ask you to do that. Don't put that on me. And anyway, you can't just walk away."

"JoAnn, I'm worried about you getting hurt or disillusioned out here. They can mess with your head. I know what you're doing, but it can get ugly, fast. Home is in Houston. We'll figure things out."

"There's nothing I can do in Houston. And why did you suddenly come here with all this?"

"I just want you back, JoAnn. And I saw the news. Everybody's going to Vegas to get married before a deadline."

"What do you mean?"

"They said if a guy doesn't have a kid, if he's not married by midnight, tonight, he's a 1-A or something."

"Oh, my God. Ricky—that's what he's doing. That's it!"

"What?"

"Eve's in tears. He left home with Amy. She said something about him going to Vegas. They're getting married, I know it. That's what I told them to do. Oh, God."

Jim was stunned, but he saw an opportunity. "Maybe ... we'll find them."

"Are you serious?"

"We'll have our honeymoon, JoAnn. We should have done it a long time ago." He stood still and could almost hear the doubt screaming in her head, as if she'd just opened the door to a Jehovah.

His tone softened. "JoAnn, let's find a way. Meet me at the airport? Will you? Let's go tonight. Why wait? I'll buy our tickets." He held on for an answer, but with his last coin gone, the line went dead.

CHAPTER 38 - NUTS

A moment later

Jim walked away, not sure if he was being audacious or just delirious, but he concluded that it was probably both. He felt strangely buoyed about that. That was him, though it was a side which had always weirded JoAnn out.

He bought the tickets and waited at the gate. After a while he changed more coins and tried Eve's number again. Twice he got the dreaded answering machine. He took that as a good sign, but it was also a reminder that JoAnn hadn't actually agreed to do anything and might not be on her way. She had called him crazy and that was all. And, it wasn't quick to get to the airport. She might be stuck. He didn't even ask if she had transport.

He sat, paced, read, and did everything short of meditate to avoid thinking about how easily his outlandish scheme would probably fail. On balance, it was made to fail. They could go another day. But where was the story in that? There was nothing like a big surprise, a grand gesture to warm her heart. She'd always liked that. He had to see her today. He prayed she was on her way.

An hour and a half later, the boarding announcement came

for their flight to Vegas, but there was no JoAnn. He went to the airline counter, anxious to see if she'd tried to check in or inquire about her ticket. As far as anyone knew, she hadn't. He wondered if he should go back to the sidewalk to make sure she wasn't lost or delayed.

Then it hit him, as it should have earlier. She wasn't coming. He wondered if he should get on the plane alone. No, he thought, he should dump the tickets and head back to town and get her. That was why he'd come here. It would be mission failure if he got on that plane now, knowing there was something more he could do. What if the cops picked him up? What then? He took a deep breath and finally decided to get out of town, get some sleep and come back another day.

"Sir, boarding's closing," said an agent, interrupting his thoughts at the gate. He called her again and left a message saying that he was on the Vegas flight, that he'd head home to Houston from there, that he'd call her and they could try another day.

He took one last hopeful look around the terminal and said, "So long."

The door closed behind him and he quickly found his seat, then hunkered down with a heavy heart. Exhaustion took over as he glanced at the terminal and fell into a deep sleep.

* * *

Jim hadn't noticed something that would have dazzled him if he'd looked up from his tiny window seat as his plane taxied toward snooze-land.

JoAnn ran alongside the large terminal window and waved desperately after the next plane to Houston as it, too, pushed back from its stand.

Perhaps weakened by lack of sleep, she'd decided to throw caution to the wind and not worry about her crusade for the day, now that Jim had shown up and messed everything up in her head anyway. He'd come to Ann Arbor to make up for the past. She would do that too, though she'd arrived too late and the plane simply hadn't stopped at her command.

"Is there any way I can get on that flight? I need to get on that plane," she pleaded at an airline counter as the tail turned away.

"Sorry, ma'am. It's already left the gate."

JoAnn looked dismayed. "Did Jim Cobb get on that plane?"

"I'm afraid I can't give you that information."

"You can't what? That's my husband on there," she replied angrily. "We're supposed to be on our honeymoon."

But the agent didn't buy it and continued to work at her desk with her eyes down. It was a convincing pretend deafness, all topped off with a well-practiced standoffishness and a good smattering of indifference. JoAnn wound up again and stared back at her intently, wondering if it was going to be the standard service today.

Without warning, the agent suddenly woke up again, as if her brain could only do one thing at a time. "Do you have a ticket, ma'am?"

"No," JoAnn said, looking very frustrated. She pointed to the moving tail outside the window. "Jim Cobb, on that plane over there, has it. I just said that." She turned away to calm herself as the agent paused in thought, then simply walked away, as if another subroutine had kicked in from some remote control station. JoAnn was confused. "Wait, where are you going?"

Feeling helpless, JoAnn wondered what to do next. She'd have to return home. She could get some sleep and call him. It had hardly cost her a dime to get here, so what did it matter? They could try again.

She looked up and saw the agent intercepting another clone as she passed. They stopped and whispered something to each other, then the two returned to the desk.

"Are you JoAnn?" the clone asked. "Do you know anyone who was on that flight?"

JoAnn was stunned and nodded her head as fast as a butterfly's wings. "Yes! Yes. Jim Cobb. Did you see him get on that plane?"

"No."

JoAnn was stumped and her brain began to recalculate which way was up. "How do you know his name?"

"I was boarding the Vegas flight just now. At the gate over there. The last passenger left a ticket," she said, handing it over. "You were supposed to be on that flight? Honeymoon today?" She added with a smile.

JoAnn was speechless. She could scarcely believe there was a person inside the uniform. "Vegas?"

The agent glanced at her watch and said, "We need to see if there's space on the next flight. Can you come with me, please?"

She looked out of the large terminal window and saw a plane rising westward into the air as the agent led the way. Fear gripped her again, and she began to worry that she would become very depressed if she put Jim back in the driver's seat as he had been before. She needed to get control if she was going to go down that road again. And what about her work with the SDS? How would he live with that? Could he live with it at all? She hadn't figured out if any of it would actually work.

* * *

A few hours later, Jim woke up in his impossibly cramped plane seat when landing was announced, feeling like he'd only just fallen asleep.

He was one of the first off the plane, followed by a steady stream of couples when it tipped out in Vegas. He stopped in a quiet corner, not far from the arrivals gate, to think and wake up, cursing the discomfort for reigniting his dull shoulder pain and thinking that he'd just paid for two miserably uncomfortable seats he didn't really need. And, though it seemed like an awfully long time ago since the Vomit Comet incident, the injury was still there and began to throb. That was the problem with impulse, he told himself—two days of nothing working out because he'd followed his emotions instead of thinking about what he was really doing. He dropped his head and massaged his neck, wondering where he could get his next ticket back to Houston.

He sat for a while and watched the other passengers rush by, most of them young, perhaps in their twenties, with a few middle-agers. A thin, lanky man with a Stetson on his six-foot frame, arm-in-arm with a five-foot partner in a white cabaret dress, caught his attention. He thought they might be father and daughter from behind, though vacation or marriage was also possible. He wondered what would happen if they arrived a minute or two after the supposed midnight deadline. Would they sneak in the back door? And where was the nearest chapel anyway?

He pulled out of his wallet, a small memento, about the size of a credit card, which JoAnn had given him on their dating anniversary. It had the words *I love you* pressed out of rose petals in the shape of a heart. A Cupid's arrow was pointed to the sky like an airplane, but the reality hit him that it had been in a nosedive for some time. He tucked it back in and decided to keep it safe for another day. Now, he needed to get home, then figure out how he would come back for her again. And what would it be next? The Navy or NASA? Without JoAnn at home, Houston felt like game over.

As he stood up, a young, slightly familiar-looking guy with a Roman nose over a square chin and a blue striped top caught his eye. He had a feeling they had done something together, but he couldn't remember what, where, or when. He looked at a dark-haired girl with the man, but she rang no bells. Determined to stop treading water, he walked to the airline counter at the end of the corridor near the exit and bought another ticket home. With almost two hours to spare, he began the second half of his previous night's sleep on a bench.

CHAPTER 39 - VEGAS

Two hours later

Still feeling exhausted, Jim woke to a final boarding call with only fifteen minutes to go. He got up, stretched, and walked to the gate. The terminal was busier now than when he'd arrived. Urging himself to move quickly so as not to delay the plane, he glanced at a row of pay phones with advertisements for twenty-four hour chapels, then stopped to buy some Swedish Fish candy to snack on for the trip. First, he'd call JoAnn one last time.

* * *

JoAnn hurried through the Vegas terminal and glanced at the gate signs, pausing at the Houston board. She checked a scribbled note in her hand, then elbowed her way past the line to the counter. The boarding agent looked up as she demanded, "I need to know who's on this flight."

"I'm sorry, ma'am, is this your flight? These people are waiting," the agent replied. "Please go to the back of the line."

She turned to a row of consternation staring back at her

and said, "No—Yes, that's my flight."

"You will need to wait and have your ticket and ID ready."

"I just need to know who's on there first," she insisted.

"Excuse me, ma'am?" the confused agent replied. "What's your name?"

"Look, there's someone on there I need to find. You have to help me. Please." JoAnn glanced at the upside-down manifest on the desk and saw Jim's name, then blurted out, "Cobb!" Without waiting, she pushed past the line and headed for the jetway door.

The agent reached out to grab her, but missed. "Ma'am, you can't do that. Can you please step aside? These passengers are trying to board." She grabbed a radio from her desk and called security. "We have a problem."

A second agent rushed toward the commotion, blocking the jetway just as JoAnn arrived. He pulled her aside. "You need to stop here."

"Can you just tell me if Jim Cobb is on the plane?" JoAnn yelled.

The last of the confused passengers were being rushed to board as she stood by the door, continuing to plead. "Look, you don't understand. We're on our honeymoon today. He can't leave on this flight. You can't let him leave."

"I'm sorry, but this flight is now closed. Do you have a ticket?" the second agent demanded as the last passenger disappeared onto the plane. He started to close the flight.

JoAnn shoved him aside and bolted down the jetway.

He rushed after her as another agent followed, saying, "Okay, I don't think she's dangerous. Let's just get this over with, quick and easy, so we don't delay or alarm the other passengers. Go tell the captain. Avoid cornering the animal."

JoAnn flew up and down the plane's single aisle, looking to both sides for Jim as the agents stood on alert. She halted with the bewildering realization that he wasn't there.

* * *

Jim stopped at a pay phone and dialed Eve's number for the umpteenth time that day. He picked up a chapel flyer from the booth and glanced at it while he waited for the answer. Somehow he'd missed Eve's household and kept getting the answering machine. "JoAnn? It's Jim. I'm on my way back to Houston. Sorry about everything. It was stupid of me. I'll call you. Take care of yourself. I don't want to see you get hurt."

* * *

"Is there another flight to Houston?" JoAnn demanded.

"Across the terminal," one of the agents said as she glanced at her watch. "But that left five minutes ago. I think you've ..."

JoAnn didn't wait for the agent to finish, but bounded back up the jetway and across the hall to the other gate. It was empty when she arrived. "This one?" she yelled, to no one. "Oh my God!"

For the second time that day, she looked out of a terminal window at a tail inching away in the distance. She stood at the window, stunned for a moment, then cupped her head, leaned over, and collapsed on the floor in utter exhaustion.

* * *

Jim, a little breathless, rushed to the counter at his gate and handed over his ticket. He slapped his head. "Don't tell me I missed it."

"Sorry, sir. Can I help you?"

"Yes. Houston? Hope I'm not too late." He called at the door. "Please, just a moment. I'm coming."

The first agent looked over her shoulder and nodded to her colleague. "You can still make it, but you'll have to be quick. Another minute and that would have been it." She processed his ticket quickly then held up the boarding pass, but hesitated to hand it over as she glanced over his shoulder.

Jim felt slightly annoyed that he had to reach for it. "Said I was sorry, didn't I?"

The second agent unlocked the door. Jim walked up and paused at the threshold.

"Come on, sir. We have to go," the man urged.

Jim's face suddenly relaxed. He forced out a thin smile and sighed with relief. The next twenty-four hours seemed to be clearer in his head again.

The first agent turned back to him. "Sir? Jim Cobb? Could you wait a moment, please?"

He turned to her. "Is there a problem? I bought the ticket at your counter."

"Sir, you're not ... expecting anyone, are you?" she asked, looking at the seating area across the corridor.

Jim followed her eyes and saw what he could not believe at first. There was JoAnn, sitting in a chair with her eyes fixed on the floor. He whispered her name, then stepped out of the jetway and stopped in shock. A short, uncontrolled laugh came out of his mouth, as if he was experiencing some kind of joke or miracle. Almost immediately, his heart began to pound as he slowly walked toward her, pausing for a moment in the middle of the long corridor. She hadn't seen him. Or had she? He turned back to the jetway as the two agents stood watching—the second, with a thumb on the dispatch button and clutching the door handle. The plane would be gone in sixty seconds. He turned back to JoAnn. She was motionless. It felt like another moment of truth was suddenly upon him, its tail stretching all the way back to high school when they were on the farm together.

JoAnn looked up with a tear streaked face and held Jim's eyes across the hall. Her heart began to pound of its own accord as he took another step toward her then stopped. It was like the moment they met at the hospital where she had worked just before they were married. She'd known then, in that moment, that he was the change she desperately needed to start over.

The urge to jump up and do something, anything, surged through her like one of his warplanes on the catapult. Her breath shallowed as Jim began to make his way through the crowd to reach her.

Like a coiled spring, she jumped to her feet and ran toward him.

The world ceased to exist for a few moments as they locked in a tearful embrace in the middle of the corridor. Against all the odds that day, she had found her safe haven again, comforting in this unfamiliar place and the madness of the previous twenty-four hours. She felt vulnerable and open just like in their early days.

He grinned broadly in her face.

"Oh, Jim, what are we going to do?" she asked, tears

streaming down her cheeks.

"Let's start again. Tonight. Now. I promise we'll figure it out. We're here, a million miles away from anything else."

She took a deep breath and said, "You cannot go. You can't go back to the war."

"Will you come home?"

"I have to figure that out, Jim. "Things have changed. I won't live with regret ... like my mom did."

"There is a way, Jo. I've seen it. I've seen how important it is to you. It's been that way for as long as I've known you. How could I not see it coming? You have to tell the world, JoAnn, if it's in your heart. The world needs to know. I've seen you with my own eyes."

She looked at him questioningly.

"It was the same in Korea." She understood that he meant all the suffering of war. "You will be outstanding. You'll show the world what it means."

"I can't believe you're saying all this, Jim."

"JoAnn, I've never lasted long without you."

She smiled up at him.

"And you?"

"I'll take whatever comes."

"Are you sure?"

"There may be slings and arrows along the way. But this is what you want. That's more important." He half laughed and said, "I'm from the old guard, Jo. From a man's world. You're destined to change that. Write about it, Jo. Write to the world. I can't take that away from you. Just, for me, do it from home?"

"I have to be where the action is, Jim, you know that."

He sighed and conceded. "How are you going to be safe?

You need to tell me what you're doing."

She nodded and asked, "No Navy?"

He sighed, shook his head, then said, "No more flight pay, if that's the right thing for us. My place is with you, Jo, whatever that means. That's why I came to Michigan."

She put a hand on his heart as if to heal a wound.

"Let's forget what the world wants for now. This is for us. Let's just take it from here. Why don't we just do it all over?" Jim added.

She waited for more when he had an idea. "Hell, yeah. Let's just get married again while we're here."

She laughed.

"That's it," he said, imagining it all. "Just for the sake of it."

"Can we do that?"

He laughed back. "I don't know ... Well, yeah, sure we can. We can get married in any state in the country, as far as I know. It'll be like starting over. And what would they know or care? Plus the honeymoon. What could be better than that?"

She laughed at the idea. "Jim, you're definitely crazy. What happened to you?"

"We lost being crazy just for the fun of it, didn't we?"

Elated and holding hands, they walked away, past the gate that finally closed on the last plane of the day to Houston. The night would be spent in Vegas, whatever happened next.

CHAPTER 40 - 38TH PARALLEL

Moments later

Jim led JoAnn into a waiting taxi outside the airport. "Let's go downtown and take it from there," he said, when she squeezed his hand excitedly.

The driver looked pleased. "Busy night. You getting married?"

"Yes," Jim said, looking at JoAnn. They laughed together at their little secret.

"Yeah? Well, that's wonderful. They're expecting a flood, so we'd better get going."

"Where is everyone headed?"

"That'll be downtown, where you're going."

Jim grinned at JoAnn again and she laughed at the craziness of it all then turned to look out the window.

"The fifteen's already jammed up ahead, so we'll have to take the ninety-three and the ninety-five. You good with that?"

"Whatever works."

They pulled the doors shut and the driver perked up again. "You've come to the right place. We take care of our visitors here." He kissed a cross hanging from his rear view mirror then put his foot down.

They were already on the highway when the driver said, "It's a good day, you know, to get married, huh?" Jim heard a faint Dutch accent, or maybe it was Nordic. "Are you ready to pay the price?" he asked in the rear view.

Jim thought it was a strange question and felt JoAnn's hand tighten in his.

"But it doesn't cost much here, no," he continued with a shake of his head and a wave of his hand. "In and out in less than a minute and it only costs a few bucks, huh?" He laughed generously at his own joke. "Where else can you get that? Last time we had that was in Tokyo."

JoAnn raised an eyebrow at Jim.

"So have you two been here before?" he asked.

"First time," Jim replied curtly.

With a patronizing grin, the cabbie went on. "This is a lovely city. Have you a few days here?"

Neither answered.

The man nodded. "Ah, I know. I know. Don't worry. I'm not trying to sell you anything. Honestly. No tour. That's not my style, I promise."

After a moment's hesitation, JoAnn asked, "So, what do you recommend?"

The cabbie pounced at the opening. "Oh, so much has happened. Did you know that the Beatles played here not so long ago? You know them? From England? And Viva Las Vegas; you know Elvis, don't you? Did you see that? And there's more on the way, I hear. This place is on the up. Just wait another year, you'll see. All the stars will be flocking here." He glanced at her in the mirror, then laughed again. "And actually, they've already started. Anyway, don't get *me*

299

started. I shouldn't." The man shook his head, but couldn't help but fill his silence. "You know, you two make a nice couple," he added gleefully, though he seemed to sense Jim and JoAnn's bewilderment at his behavior. "No, really, you do. The thing is, I get it all the time. It seems like everyone comes here to get married these days. It's just, well, so easy. There's no planning, no family to worry about, no shopping and so on. And oh, the expense," he lamented. "Weddings cost such a fortune these days, don't they? It's like everyone wants a piece of your wallet on the biggest day of your life. After all, it only happens once in a lifetime ... well, for some," he joked. JoAnn squeezed Jim's hand again. "And it's a great business don't you think? Sometimes I think maybe I should just park my cab." He finished with a regretful sigh and then started again. "So, are you expecting family? Friends or anyone to join you?"

Jim bit his lip.

"I could pick them up for you, too. Would you like that—"

"No," Jim blurted out, not expecting it to come out so forcefully. He asked more politely, "Anyway, how long do you think it'll take?"

"Oh, about thirty minutes, I'd say, if everybody doesn't have the same idea."

The journey was straightforward enough. Both Jim and JoAnn looked out at brilliantly lit billboards that painted the dark suburbs of Vegas as if it were a year-round Christmas. JoAnn remarked that she'd never seen anything like it—casinos, hotels, restaurants, shows, anything and everything. Wedding services seemed to come in all shapes and sizes and were also themed—the Elvis Presley variety seemed popular as were drive throughs in an open top Cadillac. Traditional or glitzy? Cheap or fun? There seemed to be something for everyone. She pointed out one particular ad that read: *Getting Married? License Information. First Strip Exit,* just as the driver exited the two-one-five and took a smaller road to rejoin the ninety-three.

"You'll escape the draft, too," the driver remarked in his mirror.

Neither Jim nor JoAnn spoke, but the man continued to talk like a coiled spring. His tone changed and now he seemed a little inflamed. "But, you know, we have to protect our country before the Communists get everywhere too."

He looked up again for an answer, chewed on something, and began to mutter under his breath. His lips fluttered for a moment without a sound. "I fought in the Korean War, you know?" he said, now serious. "You know about that?"

Neither Jim nor JoAnn answered.

"I would introduce myself properly." He smiled politely as his eyes drifted off into the distance. "Yes. We started the fight at the thirty-eighth parallel. But it was tough in the mountains. I got frostbite, you know? And in the summer it was hot and we had to drink water from the rice fields. But we were fighting evil. That's why we're here today, you and I, enjoying our freedom." He paused and looked up again. "You know that?"

Jim continued to look out the window, quietly dazed. He wondered whether he should butt in, but looked sideways at JoAnn and saw *what the hell* on her face.

The driver continued to reminisce aloud. "Can you believe they fired General MacArthur?" He suddenly pressed a point, "He was right. *He was right. There is no substitute for victory.*"

Jim calculated what, if anything, to say about the war, not

301

wanting to open the man's floodgates.

"There's no substitute for victory. Isn't that right?"

Jim didn't answer.

The man continued. "And it would be unfair to the people of this country if its men did not stand for freedom as others have fought for generations, don't you think?" This time he shifted in his seat and looked at Jim and JoAnn in the mirror.

They looked quietly bewildered, and it seemed to Jim that the man had them completely wrong—that they were here to dodge the draft, like dozens, perhaps hundreds, of other couples pouring into town tonight. Still, he held his tongue. There was no point in getting into such a debate. He wondered what JoAnn was thinking; she wanted to stop the war while this man seemed to want more of it. Jim silently hoped she'd lost her tongue.

The man calmed down and, in his oddly mercurial style, said matter-of-factly, "We had to stop Kennedy from negotiating with them ... from pulling out. It would have been Korea all over again. No victory. Did it ever occur to you that that's why we're in Vietnam now, doing the same damn thing all over again? We can't let it go this time. Where will it be next?"

Jim was sure the man was crazy to talk about JFK, though he had a point about Vietnam.

The man's face lit up, then he spat out his next words, "That's the value of freedom, you know!" Out of nowhere he became angry, remembering some previous disagreement. "It's a choice! It's all a matter of choice!"

Jim and JoAnn were aghast.

Jim leaned forward and finally interrupted. "Hang on, buddy. What's the matter? You want to pull over?"

Strangely, the man remained silent.

"Look, we're already married, if that's what you're think-ing. We came here to have some fun. Just pull over. We can take another ride. You can stop right here." They were now in the suburbs of Vegas and it was pitch dark outside.

He turned to see that JoAnn was alarmed.

"Let's just stop here," he repeated. "I can see you're a little hot under the collar. We're on the same side. We're not here to escape the draft if that's what you're thinking."

The man stared back at him, then spat out a few more words. "They're going to drop bombs on our country, you know. From those things they put up in the sky. They're up there!" he repeated. He looked up for a split second, angry again. "How does that make them feel? Like cowards in their own shoes, huh?"

Jim had heard enough. "Okay, stop the car now."

But the driver kept going.

"You got the wrong people. Just stop the car."

"Oh, likely story. How did I know you were going to say that?" the man said. He rubbed the steering wheel as if preparing to do something with his hands, then pressed the pedal a little harder.

Jim felt the instant acceleration and repeated his command to stop, but the man continued unabated.

"Pull over," Jim shouted as, in a momentary lapse of con-centration, the man looked sideways, then back at Jim, just as the car flew over a bump in the road, followed immediately by a sharp right turn. He was going at least thirty more than he should have been. His foot snapped on the brake and he swung the wheel violently to turn with the road, but he overdid it, lost it, and flipped the car. It rolled several times and landed on its roof in the middle of the road a moment later. The car was immediately hit by an oncoming vehicle with headlights flashing on JoAnn's side.

It spun viciously on its roof.

Then, there was silence and darkness.

Moments later, Jim smelled gas and heard dripping. The car was going to blow. He looked forward and saw that the man's pockets had been ripped open and a chain was hanging low around his neck, just as he was upside down with his legs jammed against the wheel.

JoAnn moaned. Jim called for her but she went quiet and wasn't moving. He saw that he'd fallen onto the roof of the car right next to her. He reached forward and squirmed wildly as a stab of pain shot through his chest and injured shoulder. He screamed as he put his hands underneath her to pull.

"JoAnn? Come on. We have to get out of here."

She remained silent and still as a dead weight.

Jim turned and pushed his feet out of the broken window, then began to pull at her. "JoAnn, come on, move, damn it! We got to move!"

Face down and in agony, with his legs out on the road, he began to crawl backwards as broken glass scraped the bare waist under his shirt.

"JoAnn. Come on!" he shouted again, pulling at her even though she was stuck. A greenish liquid shimmered in the light as it snaked across the street and caught his eye. He crawled back to her face as another set of headlights illuminated everything with a blinding glare, then veered off the road in a cloud of dust. He glanced outside and saw that another car had also stopped farther up the road, its engine steaming, and thought it must have been the one that hit them when they first rolled over.

Someone yelled twenty yards away. "There are still people in there. Get an ambulance."

Jim paused in horror, seeing no movement from JoAnn. He stopped to catch his breath, and soon there were sirens and flashing lights. It felt cold, like an arctic chill. Someone spoke to him. Then everything went quiet.

* * *

A day later

Jim peered past the door of JoAnn's hospital room and stopped, nervous about what he might see. She lay silent, her eyes closed and her skin pale, looking half-bludgeoned, with a jumble of tubes connecting her face to a machine that seemed to be doing all the living.

He limped in slowly, with only minor cuts and a sore knee, and saw that this situation was about to become overly familiar. The medics couldn't tell if he would return for days, weeks, months or even years, only to find JoAnn lost in a deep sleep.

It seemed like a waiting game as he sat in a chair next to her and pulled the blanket up around her neck, even though it was already in place. He held her hand gently, feeling its warmth under her seemingly total indifference to him and everything else. And why should she care about his presence when he had started the chain of events that had brought her here, comatose, just by trying to do the right thing by them?

How would he explain what had happened? And what next,

when—if she came out like a raging bull, at his insistence of going to Vegas tonight? Why couldn't they wait a day? Or whenever? And where to now, he asked himself? What about the future, his precious duty to his country, or launching into space? He'd fought for life, for freedom, but this looked like a new fight. It wasn't the fight he expected. No.

He broke down as the door opened and a young man in a blue striped shirt rushed in with a girl behind him. She looked shocked and tearful. Jim was as stunned as she was.

"Oh my God! What happened?" the man asked.

Jim couldn't speak.

"Mom's on her way. Here, Amy." He handed her a handkerchief, then turned back to face the room. "Jim? I'm Ricky."

CHAPTER 41 - POLYOT

Early–April 1965

Senior NASA and defense officials sat around a table at Vandenberg Air Force Base on the West Coast, waiting for the secretary of defense, the Air Force on one side and NASA on the other.

Moments earlier, Jim had walked into the conference room with Chris. He'd already promised JoAnn he'd stay with NASA in Houston and not go off to war. He returned to work a few weeks later with nothing more than cuts and bruises from the accident in Vegas. JoAnn was transferred to a hospital in Houston but remained comatose.

Chris sat next to Bob Crandall, Head of NASA's Space Task Group, while Jim sat on the other side. He'd been invited to the meeting with the secretary to represent Special Ops in place of Chuck, who was tied up elsewhere. All Chris had said was that there might be questions about the team's ability to put together a mission quickly. What mission? That wasn't clear. They began quietly exchanging news and jokes, while the other side also talked among themselves.

"The Soviet Lunar Module, Luna, is almost ready, and they seem to be on schedule to send the first crew by sixty-seven,"

Chris said.

"You know, I never really saw how they could afford it," Crandall replied. "Khrushchev just kept sinking lots of money into it all. I wonder what the new guy, Brezhnev, is going to do."

"Have you seen the N1 rocket? It's a giant elevator," Jim chimed in. They chuckled. "Must have cost a fortune."

"They're recruiting too. Six Moon men just signed up last week," Chris said.

They all knew that, but Crandall added, "That's good for us. The president wants to make sure the Soviets keep spending what they can't afford."

Knowing this was a controversial point of view, Jim asked, "But can we keep fighting Vietnam and go to the stars at the same time? They must be wondering that too."

"I can certainly see us pulling out of the war to pay for the Moon," Chris mused. "Let's see if the secretary shares his game plan today."

With a grin, Jim added, "I say we just shoot it in Hollywood. *Charlie Chaplin Goes To Space.*"

They were laughing again when the secretary walked in and sat down in the middle of the long table on the Air Force side.

He settled, laid down his papers and the room hushed. "You understand why we're here," he began. "Americans are wondering if we can catch up with the Soviets." He tossed one of the documents from the top of his pile into the middle of the table.

Jim saw the photograph of the Soviet, Leonov, floating in space. It looked like the picture of the century.

The secretary continued, "The public is despondent and

fearful. Here's another one." He threw down a news article proclaiming, *The Reds might be unbeatable,* and said, "Will we one day look up at an omniscient Communist Moon in the night sky? Just as the president feared? Tyranny for all mankind every time we look up, gentlemen?"

The room was silent.

"We know that the Soviets' Soyuz N1 is headed for the Moon in sixty-seven, two years ahead of us. So we have to pick up the pace, or our first trip to the Moon will be an RSVP to the Soviets' party. But we also know that's not the whole story. They have started putting suicide bombs into orbit."

He glanced around the silent table and threw down some more shots of the Soviet program—one of the giant N1 rockets in the Khazak plain that he'd mentioned and that Jim, Chris, and Crandall had just talked about. Another followed, of the Soviet Lunar Module LK-3, which stood on a production floor, presumably in Russia's OKB-1, looking like a giant, spherical, two-story aluminum spider on thin, ungainly metal legs surrounding its guts below. Perched on top was a round, one-man capsule with a huge, circular, designed-in dent. It looked as if the giant ball had been dropped from an awkward hoist to pay homage to the Moon's own cratered face. Then came another report that completed the secretary's pile of exhibits. "The master satellite in their system not only controls the network, but may be relaying launch codes for their nuclear arsenal and may be ready to target our satellites. So we face their nuclear threat on Earth, now partially controlled from space, and their killer satellites are likely aimed at disarming our defenses. They may one day interfere with our efforts to get to the Moon or put that killer network into lunar orbit. Meanwhile, we still need five years

309

to get there. Gentlemen, how do we get this thing moving forward? I don't want to be the one knocking on the door when we get there," he looked around the table. "Ryan?"

"Thank you, sir. As the secretary said, the Soviets have begun to place satellite bombs in orbit," continued Commander Ryan, head of Strategic Air Command, sitting to the secretary's left. His words were calm, deliberate, and meticulously organized. "Codename *Polyot*, that's P-O-L-Y-O-T. We heard of them over a year ago when the first unit went up in late sixty-three. They continue to launch secret missions. Quite simply, the Soviets are building a network of attack satellites around Earth."

From a standard brown CIA envelope, Ryan pulled out a stack of blurry black-and-white photographs and slapped them on top of the mounting pile in the center of the table. The top one showed Soviet technicians standing next to a bare satellite with two circular rings, a large dome at one end to house a warhead, and several struts arranged in a cone with thrusters on the back. Long, ungainly communication whiskers sprouted from the center amid a jumble of tanks and pipes.

"This thing is literally a satellite bomb. They didn't even bother to skin it for a disguise. What concerns us most right now is the risk to our nuclear arsenal from here on out. They could shut down our communications and surveillance network in an instant, launch an attack, and we wouldn't see a damn thing coming."

The next shot was of a Soviet R7 rocket standing tall on the launch pad, waiting patiently to embarrass the US again, Jim thought.

"Baikonur, Kazakhstan," Ryan said. The photos were

handed out for study, so Jim picked one up. Upon closer inspection, he saw men getting out of a small van near a launch pad marked *LC31* on a barren, frozen, snow-covered Kazakh plain. Payload train cars were parked at their final stop on the single track to the nearby loading bay. To Jim, the rocket looked alive and ready to go. He could almost hear it hissing at its tether and groaning with tons of rocket fuel in its belly, shards of ice falling loose as valves vented tufts of steam into the freezing air. Beneath it, a huge blast pit, as if torn from the ground by God-sized claws, sat still, waiting for the rocket's inferno for warmth. And just behind it, a gigantic metallic arm had grabbed a second R7 lying on its side and hoisted it upright by the scruff of its neck.

Another photo circulated, of a white-coated Soviet technician in the Russian OKB-1. He was typing at a small gray console in an even grayer, circular, windowless control room with large screens in front of him. Not unlike NASA's own control room, the desks were strewn with disposable coffee cups and a small, probably greenish-screen cathode ray tube monitor, surrounded by uniform clusters of backlit buttons, knobs, and switches. One of the men leaned forward, peering into a small telescopic sight through a circular viewing hole, while another held a manual, both surrounded by several large electronic towers with huge knobs and vertical dials. The walls were decorated with protruding pipes between another set of towers.

"Defending our country has become a new ball game," Ryan continued. "We have to understand what we're up against and neutralize that threat if necessary." He looked around the table. "The stakes are too high." He picked up a report and continued. "These pages also talk about the master satellite that controls this system, known as Molniya. The Soviets claim it's for television, but this report tells a different story, just as the secretary said. They began sending these into orbit last year along with the Polyots, and so far two have failed. A third is flying above us right now, but our reports indicate that it's also out of control. They're already saying the malfunction could trigger an accidental wipeout of our communications. What's more, another Polyot unit has just been sent up. They've started to expand the network and it's unstable."

"Excuse me, but why are we having this conversation?" asked Bob Crandall.

"We believe that these Molniya satellites are military command and control units. They direct this network of orbiting bombing units. Someday, they may find their way to the Moon and could have the potential to launch weapons. This directly affects the NASA program, not to mention the defense of our country.

"Lunar weapons?" Crandall replied in disbelief.

"That sounds far-fetched, doesn't it? But our own people are already working on nuclear detonations on the lunar surface." He looked at Chris. "Project A-119. Special Ops knows about it," Ryan continued. There was a small murmur in the room. "Although we're not sure, it's believed that this third control unit also malfunctioned. The Soviet Cosmonaut, Leonov, who first went outside in March, may have tried to grab it and retrieve the launch relay. But his suit malfunctioned, we're told. It's clear that Soviet equipment is unpredictable, but that makes it all the more dangerous. We could spend a lot of money and energy defending against hardware that won't work anyway. Either way, we need to know more and neutralize the threat."

"Hold on. With all due respect," said Jones, NASA's assistant administrator. "Our job is to get men to the Moon and back, and that's all."

"Sure," the secretary added to complete the sentence.

Jim jumped in with what he knew to be true. "This network of satellites is funded by, and resides within the same Soviet program that controls all their other space activities. It's OKB-1 in Moscow. It's the same people."

Ryan stepped back in. "These are offensive weapons, and our sources say it's the same design bureau that sent turtles and ladies into space. Their space chief is the head of this killer satellite program and we're very concerned about what looks like a disastrous change in direction with this new development. It's clearly turned offensive and is now aimed at attacking the United States. All this other stuff may have been a diversion from their real intent all along.

"This master satellite, Molniya. M-O-L-N-I-Y-A is also fission powered. They've been testing small nuclear reactors in space for some time, presumably to give their equipment a long, maintenance-free life without the need for external power. That might even work on the Moon."

"But the Soviet spacewalk: as far as we know, that was just a ... spacewalk," Chris said.

"Well, let's see." Ryan picked up the official Soviet statement. "It's very revealing. *A person equipped with a special space suit is capable of living and working in space,*" he read.

The room waited for the rest, but it didn't come. Chris had nothing more to say.

"That's it! That's their statement. The less said, the easier it is to hide whatever it is they're hiding," Ryan said.

"Gentlemen, we can't allow such a threat," the secretary interrupted. He looked around the table. "So the question is: can we defend ourselves, or disarm this killer network in orbit now, before it gets out of control or takes us out of the game?"

"Why don't you just shoot it down? Or tell the Soviets to take it down. Isn't that what Vandenberg does?" asked NASA's Crandall. "Isn't that why we're here today?"

"We need other options. Shooting it down could be considered an act of war. And we can't just say please," Ryan replied. "So, launching a strike from the ground isn't an option, although Vandenberg is on standby if it comes to that. The Soviets will deny everything, of course, and just claim it's a civilian TV satellite we're targeting. We'll have the whole world on our backs."

"So what exactly are we saying? I'm lost," asked NASA's Jones.

"We need to confirm for sure that this Molniya is what the intelligence says it is," said the secretary.

"Then we disarm it in whatever way is appropriate," Ryan added.

"Just to be clear, are you saying *we* have to go get it?" asked Jones. He looked at Chris and Crandall for a reaction. It was clear to Jim that *we* meant NASA.

"Gentlemen, let's remember that we're not doing all this fancy space stuff just for a nice weekend on the Moon. NASA is a defense program, and right now this Soviet development is a significant threat," the secretary added.

"Hold on. Hold on. We can just tell the Soviets that putting this network up there will itself be considered an act of war," protested NASA's Crandall.

"We could, but there's nowhere to go but conflict. And we can't risk confrontation at this point," said Ryan.

Maxwell, a brigadier general and the commander of Vandenberg who headed the 30th Space Wing, had been quiet until now. He'd seen his cue. "We can intercept it. Right in orbit. Out of sight. We can salvage what we can. Maybe kill it if we have to. The Soviets would probably just see it as another one of their regular equipment failures."

"Sabotage?" asked Jim.

"Defense," replied the Brig.

Jim bet he used that word regularly to cover everything. *He'd do well in the CIA.*

"But our men will be on American television. World television. We can't expect our guys to do this in public. Even the Soviets will be watching," Crandall interrupted, in defense of his own men. "Did I hear you right?"

"We knock it out of orbit. Off camera. But first we take a good look to recover what we can." Maxwell looked around the table. "The attack code relay is the key component. Right here in an earlier report the CIA received from the Soviets about a year ago. There's a way to get our hands on whatever hardware they're using, and decode and jam their transmissions. Code breaking all over again, and all out of sight. Remember what the British were able to do with the German codes in the war? This is another opportunity we can't afford to miss."

"Well, defensive or not, I don't want our men looking over their shoulders every time they're in orbit," Crandall said.

"Gentlemen, imagine for a moment the value of the intelligence. If we can get a look at the equipment or find a way to disable it ... they'd never even know in space," Maxwell added.

Defense again, Jim thought.

"Can we do that?" the secretary asked quickly, as if to close off any possibility of backtracking. He looked NASA's Crandall in the eye for an answer, then glanced at Chris and Jim. "Can your men do it?"

"Too dangerous. We haven't even gotten out yet," Crandall said. "The Soviets just did it."

NASA's Jones jumped in. "The press will be all over this. If this goes wrong, how do we explain it? It would stop the whole show."

Crandall fired again. "The Soviet, Leonov, almost got killed out there. We'd be courting disaster."

"Well, *our* spacewalkers are ready, aren't they?" the secretary asked with a straight face.

"Sir, I am in charge of our Manned Spacecraft Center," Crandall replied, trying to ease the tension. "The equipment and men are almost ready. The first launch is scheduled for Gemini Four."

"Too late."

"Too late?"

"Too late. The Soviets could take this thing down themselves before we've had a chance to look at it. We think it's already malfunctioning," the Brig said.

"Problem solved," Crandall replied.

"Gentlemen, all we're saying is get your men up there and take a look at it," interrupted Ryan. "If the Soviets take the lead and seize the high ground in space from now on, we have absolutely nowhere to go. We cannot let that happen. You understand that."

"Gentlemen, gentlemen," the secretary interrupted, holding up a hand. Both sides immediately fell silent. He turned to the NASA men. "Remember, we're not gallivanting around the universe here. Isn't that what the English say? I like that." The group half-laughed as he turned to the Air Force men. "How fast can we launch a mission?"

Jim almost swallowed his tongue in the silence.

"From where? The Cape?" asked Crandall.

More silence.

"It'll have to be in the dead of night to avoid attention, if that's even possible," added NASA's Jones.

"No. We launch from right here. Vandenberg," Brigadier Maxwell interrupted.

Crandall and Jones appeared to turn cold. Jim began to wonder if Strategic Air Command was here simply to bend space back in their direction, just as Einstein said was perfectly possible.

"We're already launching Titan from the West Coast. We're going to identify the mission as an unmanned test flight. And we've already modified a Gemini capsule as an orbiting laboratory; the MOL, as you may know it. That's the vehicle," Maxwell said.

Jones was silent and it became clear to Jim that they'd already thought this through.

"As soon as the men are up, they can take a look at it and kick this Molniya satellite in the ass—whatever is best. Meanwhile, the eyes of the world remain on the public NASA program on the East Coast. That's our cover. This is more or less how the Soviets operate. They tell the world about the chimps and women, but behind the scenes they're clearly preparing for war.

The Air Force men nodded, and it seemed the idea had

already been bought.

Jones cringed. "We can't do this, can we? It feels like we're courting war."

"It is war. And the rules have changed. We have to do whatever it takes as far as I'm concerned," Ryan added. "The price is too high. Like we said, they kill and imprison their own, so why should they spare us?" Ryan turned to the secretary. "Sir, this is exactly why we need to develop our manned capability at Vandenberg now. We can't expect NASA to do this alone."

The NASA men sat in silence, and Jim's mind reeled at what they were asking, though he didn't have the pay grade to say it outright.

"Okay, so who's capable of doing this mission?" the secretary asked NASA's Jones. He looked at Chris and then at Jim. "You've got the rocketeers."

Jim saw the cogs behind Jones' eyes begin to spin, though Chris didn't dare answer or pretend he could make such a commitment. He glanced back at Jones who was clearly thinking *no way*, then at Crandall, who spoke for them all. "Our first spacewalkers, White and McDivitt, are out of the question. But," he stammered, "there are other possibilities." He looked at Chris, who said, "We have standby crews that are out of the public eye. Special Operations, but they're not trained for this mission yet."

Jim realized that Jones had anticipated this. Why else had *he* been invited to this meeting?

The secretary leaned toward Crandall with interest, then looked at his watch. "Okay, everyone?" He glanced around the table and stood. "Bob, I think we've answered your question. You now know why we're here. SAC supplies the hardware, Special Operations provides the men. Get them trained. I don't need details right now, but both sides put the mission together. I'll brief the president now, but give me the details when you're ready. As far as Vandenberg is concerned, this will stay hidden within the MOL Development P9 line. We'll fund the men through a separate budget. I'll take care of that. Except for preparing the equipment and men, keep this between you. Is that clear? Gentlemen, we have to pull this off and find out what they're up to. We can't just let them threaten our defense with a military installation out of reach above our heads. It'll be the end of us all."

CHAPTER 42 - EVA

The following day

Chris went to Chuck the next day to present him with the challenge of preparing a Special Operations mission for SAC. He'd told Crandall the day before that there weren't many options and that his front runners wouldn't necessarily go along with it, though he'd try to get them on board.

After Chris had finished speaking, Chuck took a deep breath and got up from his seat. He began to pace the room, thinking about what he'd just been pitched.

Chris sat and waited for a reaction, then heard what he was expecting. Chuck sighed, shook his head and said, "I don't get it."

Chris was prepared and jumped right in. "You two have worked together the longest," he said. "You know him better than anybody here."

"Yeah, but ..." Chuck turned back to Chris and cringed like he was reliving a tooth extraction. "Have you even talked to him?"

"He was at the meeting you couldn't make. And I wanted your opinion first, otherwise there's no point."

"Well, maybe you should ask him. This is not a good time

for him, you know that."

Chris held up a hand and said, "Assuming it is ... for a moment, we first need to agree how it will work so I can put it to him. He may have seen it coming, or maybe not ... with JoAnn."

"But where's Tom? He's your man, isn't he?"

"You know Tom's not available to us right now."

"Why don't you make him available?"

"He's supposed to be testing the LLRV and we can't touch that program. They're behind schedule," Chris replied. "And Jim is one of the best pilots we've got. He's been developing orbital maneuvers from the Astronaut Office with everybody else. That's what this is all about."

"Are you saying that Jim is right for this just because he's available? And therefore Tom isn't?"

"No." Chris took a deep breath, then said firmly, "What we're saying is that Jim is the best person for the job, right now—right now—if he wants it. And yes, if you like, he is kinda available too."

Chuck looked stunned. "Kinda available? He's out of the unit. And, not ready for walking out in space. He's not trained for that. I'm not trained for that. It's not been done yet, by any of us. Only one Soviet has tried it and he didn't fare too well as far as I've heard."

"Jim's back in if he has to be." They stared at each other in silence, then Chris continued. "The equipment is ready. You and Jim know the suits and Tom doesn't. And you'll have time to train for the mission; not much, but enough. They're getting White ready on the equipment for G4. You'll join his training. Work out a program and you'll be fine."

"But Jim has a heart condition. That's why he was out. We

all know that. Has he recovered? It's a risk. Whose crazy idea was this?" Chuck demanded.

"Straight from the top. SAC's pulling the strings. And our guys are piling on a lot of pressure to keep control of this."

"Strategic Air Command? How do they get to pick our crew?"

"They supply the equipment. We have the men. Look, the Air Force wants to invest in Vandenberg for national security. They've proposed this mission to demonstrate their readiness in space. The East Coast is way too public for what they want to do, and we're not going to stop it, so we're either in the tent or out. We have to play a role in this or the whole thing will just fly off in its own direction like one of their rockets.

Chuck frowned and said, "*I'm* East Coast."

"Okay, yes, we'll get to that in a moment. But back to your point, Jim has a condition and this will be a good test for ... the other missions. We have to rule him in or out now. Once and for all. The medics might not agree, but I reckon he'll be fine on that score. There's time for him to make a full recovery. We can't lose a good man to an if, but, or maybe he'll be okay. I'm sure some of the others are hiding something. We would have lost half of them by now if they were found out."

Chuck continued to pace the room silently, as if projecting what this would mean for him.

"You know the crew life support systems better than anyone, Chuck. You've been suiting buddies. And there's not enough time now to prepare another crew. Put Jim to the test and learn to work together for real. Not in a simulator anymore."

Chuck sighed again. "Okay, so I've come to know him

better. But, oh boy, are you saying what I think you're saying?" he implored. "Am I leaving Group Four for all this?"

"Listen, Chuck. Not if everything goes according to plan. But, you must know," Chris' voice softened. "This may be your only chance in space. Things change very fast and we don't sell tickets for this stuff."

Chuck froze, his face pained.

"Jim can do this if he wants to," Chris continued. "But this is your mission. Work together and get the best out of him." Chris sighed. "And you'll be together on the base missions. We expect him to make it and you'll be his commander."

Chuck whispered to himself, "*The big one*, hey." He paced and looked up at the ceiling, then recalled, "The lunar base."

"You put him on your list, remember? So now's a good time to do something smaller first, together."

"I put Tom in pole position for this because we weren't sure what the medics would say about Jim. Anyway, that's a whole different ball game, landing an orbiter on the lunar surface; even if he had the right idea originally about how to get it down. We put him through the grinder."

"Chuck, I know. He's one of the youngest, but he'll learn fast. The Soviets are racing ahead and it's a threat to our country."

* * *

The next day, Chris and Crandall entered a meeting room at the Manned Spacecraft Center five minutes late. They sat next to Jim, who was here today in his position for the Astronaut Office. They were to discuss how close NASA was to being spacewalk ready and whether or not the upcoming Gemini

IV would be green-lit for an Extra Vehicular Activity, or EVA. Chris had said they needed to talk right after this meeting, and to Jim that meant only one thing—he'd be preparing someone for the Special Ops mission the secretary had asked for. The one described today would probably be the template.

Other NASA leaders were already sitting around the table, thinking about their own first spacewalk mission. But to Jim, they still seemed uncertain: their press release was timid, with only half of the ninety-one page Gemini mission brief referring to a *possible* outing.

Glen from Flight Operations explained, pointing to a diagram showing G4's flight pattern, "Right after liftoff, the first stage is jettisoned right here. The second stage is right here, then the capsule is in orbit. It will circle Earth sixty-two times in four days. McDivitt and White will conduct eleven experiments. When it's time to come home, the capsule will re-enter, the parachutes will deploy here, and we'll pick them up in the ocean about four hundred miles south of Bermuda, right over here."

"And the EVA?" Crandall asked, taking charge of what seemed to be the big question of the day.

"Right now, we're planning to do a stand-up in the cockpit when the doors open on G4," Flight Ops Glen replied. Jim knew exactly where he was going.

"Why go all the way there just to stick our heads out?" asked the man from Public Affairs.

"Full egress is scheduled for G5," Glen said.

The room looked like it had just heard the wrong answer.

"I say we give the go-ahead for full egress on G4 so we can pick up the pace with the Soviets. The EVA equipment is ready. Am I right?" asked Public Affairs.

"Pretty much," Glen replied, seemingly surprised by the insistence.

"See, the point is, everyone is impatient. The American public needs to see something. The Soviets are taking all the credit, and it scares the shit out of them. I need to give a good story this time. And no more E-V-A. Can we just call it America's first space walk? It has to be interesting."

"Let's just stick with EVA in here, please," Crandall said. "SAC's starting to put missions in their pipeline, so I need to know if we're ready."

"We're waiting to find out what happened to the Soviets first. Their man barely made it back alive from what we've heard," Glen explained. "We certainly don't want the Soviets to have the first success and we get the first casualty. Luck doesn't play ball. So, when's the SAC mission?"

"We'll say more when we know." Crandall paused to see if he was being heard. "So, what does an EVA involve?" he added more gently, bringing it back.

Glen relented and Joe from Crew Systems took the baton, demonstrating the equipment with a mock chest-pack on his torso and a hand-held maneuvering unit on the table. He turned to an illustration of the floating astronaut on a wall panel.

"This hand-held unit has two oxygen bottles. Our man pulls the trigger here and gets a little push from the cones, right here."

Jim asked, "May I, Joe?" He leaned over and picked up the HHMU and pulled the trigger while looking down at his wheeled seat, though it didn't roll as he expected.

The room chuckled and Joe apologized that the device wasn't charged.

"It would have thrown you through the window if it had been," Crandall joked, drawing a laugh.

"It's much gentler down here. Up there, very little thrust will move a mountain," added Crew Systems' Joe. "It's made for space. Remember, there's no friction up there. Now, breathing is provided by this twenty-five-foot umbilical tether, and our guy stays connected to the ship. There's also nine minutes of emergency supply here in the chest pack."

"Is the umbilical ready?" asked Chris, finally speaking.

"Yes, it's ready. We've even gold-plated it to keep the heat out. No expense spared. So don't leave it up there and don't take it home for your plumbing either."

Flight Ops Glen was still chewing on his own thoughts and couldn't resist another interruption. He turned to Crandall and Chris and asked, "Who runs the SAC missions? Who's training them? We need to know all that."

Chris held his tongue for a moment.

Jim waited for a signal—a glance, a nod, anything—about why Chris needed to talk later, but nothing was forthcoming.

Chris replied, looking down at the table. "We have a couple of men from NASA Special Ops lined up. We'll know in the next day or so, but we're briefing them right now. All you need to know is that there's an altitude test at McDonnell, then you'll manage their training on the equipment."

Crandall began again, while Chris now stole a momentary glance at Jim as he scanned the room. Suddenly, Jim knew. Chris was going to ask him to do the SAC mission. "This will give us a chance to test the equipment and procedures. The Soviets were not on TV. They didn't even inform the men's families in case things went wrong. But White will be on the screen, so there's no room for error. That way we might get a chance to test everything off-stage." Crandall looked around the room while Jim sat frozen, thinking about the secret spacewalk. It sounded like fiction.

"If all goes well, we'll have reason to move White's space-walk up to June. Public Affairs: Happy?"

Silence pervaded the room, even though Moscow's OKB-1 had just launched another rocket, this time in Houston.

CHAPTER 43 - MISSION

Later that day

"Chuck! What? Chuck? Are you kidding me? Tom's in a better position to command this thing. And he's already at Vandenberg. Why Chuck?" Jim was stunned at the idea that he had just been sold, but predictably he couldn't help but protest. He couldn't be stuck with Chuck for several days in a capsule no bigger than a refrigerator.

Chris' face flushed. "Look, this is Chuck's mission. It's a done deal. Then there's Tom, or I'm offering it to you. Though, I apologize if I overstepped given your situation. I'm not looking at a lot of options."

"No, it's not that. You know, Tom and I started as a crew together. We've been training together all along." It appeared that Jim could see it all very clearly. "Chuck doesn't—"

"I'm sorry. If this doesn't work for you, I apologize for asking. But thank you for coming to the meetings."

Jim stopped and thought for a moment, then said, "I'm just saying—"

"I heard you, and I'm sorry. I thought you were right to do this, and I respect your circumstances. But this is important for national security, and I thought you'd want a chance. Excuse me, Jim."

Jim cringed and looked misunderstood. "No, that's not what I'm saying. Look, what I mean is that Chuck—"

"Not quite how you'd like it? Chuck's not what you had in mind?"

"You're putting words in my mouth, Chris."

"Well, what are you saying?"

Jim paused and slowed his head. "Tom and I were training orbital maneuvers. He developed the docking procedures with Aldrin, and that's critical to this mission. You can't just make this stuff up. I'm advising you that Chuck doesn't know it."

"But you do. And that's the point." Chris relented. "I hear you. But Chuck's experience far outweighs Tom's in command. And that's his role."

"And he's in the public Apollo program. How's that going to work?"

Chris sighed. "He'll be off the public program if he chooses. He can come back to it, but ..."

"Off?"

Chris nodded. "Between the three of us, he knows he has to take this. And you have to understand, too, that it's either Tom or you, with Chuck in command." Chris glanced at Jim to make sure his point was clear. "Although Tom has other priorities right now."

"Other priorities?"

"Yes," Chris jabbed firmly with a furrowed brow. "Other priorities." He'd already been through this with Chuck.

Jim flared his own. "Well?"

"That's classified."

"Classified? Look, this isn't a trip to the park. What's classified? I've been to classified meetings," Jim said. He stared back at Chris.

"No one's going to let Tom do this."

Jim froze in thought, then said, "Oh. Is that it?" He suddenly saw that they weren't going to risk Tom's life as a new father for a mission that had the possibility of death written all over it.

Chris held back.

"That's it, isn't it?"

Chris shifted in his seat and held up a hand. "I'm sorry I asked. I felt I owed it to you. I know how hard you worked for this and you were dealt a bad hand, that's all."

"He has a family. Is that what you're saying? And I don't? I'm expendable if this goes south? Is that it? What about JoAnn? She's gone too?"

"Look Jim, I'm not going to lie to you. You know how things work. It's not just capability. It's circumstance. All of that makes you suitable or not."

"Oh, well, I'm Jake's godfather. Does that count?" Jim sighed deeply.

"Sometimes in life the strangest factors work for you and sometimes against you," Chris continued. "Think about it for a minute. If all goes well, this puts you back in play for bigger things at NASA. The medics will have been put to rest about your condition. Back in their crib. If you want it, make it work."

"Bigger things? I wish everyone would stop talking about bigger things," Jim lamented. "What bigger things are we talking about? This program? That program—"

"If you get through this, prove to the medics that you're

good, assuming you're up for it," Chris replied. He looked at Jim's chest. "I'm on your side. Then we can talk about those bigger—sorry, other things."

Jim stopped again.

"So what do I tell them?" Chris asked. "I understand if now is not a good time. But I also know that you have always wanted to protect our country. This is a race against communism. It may not be what you expected, or maybe it is ... even though things aren't good for JoAnn. But she's in good hands." Jim wondered why Chris had suddenly turned pale. "I know I'm meddling, but how long has it been? What do the doctors say?"

Jim didn't answer.

"This may be your only chance. The timing is far from perfect, but if you want this, you have to work it out with Chuck. I've done my best to help you. Think about it, but I'll understand if you can't."

Jim looked Chris straight in the eye and said, "Okay. But what am I going to tell her? I said I'd stay put."

* * *

Jim walked into JoAnn's hospital room and paused at the window, placing both hands on the sill and taking a deep breath. Visitors, some wheeling patients, were milling around outside in the sunshine, while just behind him, JoAnn remained cocooned inside her coma, looking like she hadn't moved a muscle in months.

The room was silent, except for the life-support machines whirring in the background. It occurred to him that he hadn't quite gotten used to being so completely invisible to her.

There had always been a steady flame, no matter what their circumstance, always a place to come back to. But now he couldn't see it burning.

He turned to her and took a seat beside the bed, leaning over to straighten the flowers in the vase. He pulled up the blanket as he always did before holding her hand.

"I came to ask you something." With a sigh, he decided to dive right in. "There is a mission, JoAnn. I came to ask you what to do." He straightened the ruffles in her cover as he continued. "It's a mission to protect peace. I know how important that is to you. You were right all along. What we need here is peace on Earth and in our skies. And that's all my father was doing when he disappeared all those years ago. He wasn't dropping bombs or anything when they got him. He was out there trying to keep the world safe in his own way." He paused for a moment. "But, you know, peace has to be fought for. Isn't that what you were doing?" He paused again to think about what had just come out of his mouth. "It's what we do. It's in our DNA, in the DNA of every surviving thing on Earth. It's in our past, it's in our future. It goes everywhere we go. I have to do this for our people. For us, for you and for me."

He looked up at her face and wondered if she had heard a word he had said. Maybe she had. But she hadn't burst out laughing or wondered what on earth he'd been smoking. "Squeeze my hand, JoAnn, if you can hear me. Go on, squeeze it," he urged, looking down for the slightest movement. "Help me figure out what I should do."

He waited, but there was nothing. He shuffled forward onto the front edge of his seat, feeling a little teary. "See? You don't talk to me. What am I to do? Should I go and try to continue what he started all those years ago? Maybe I can just pull it off this time. Who knows? I have to try. I might just be able to prevent war up there so the world's a better place down here. For all of us. We might still get a chance at that promised future when we were young. Remember that? If we don't fight for it, we don't have a chance. It doesn't happen by itself."

He took another deep breath. "I have to be honest. It isn't assured. It's never been tried. There's no manual. It might not work." He paused again to think. "But, I don't know if you'll even realize I'm gone, JoAnn. But if I am, I hope you'll wake up in a safer world where you won't have to protest injustice. You'll be safe again. Safe like you couldn't be, like your mother couldn't be."

Jim wasn't sure what else to say. He looked at her bedside, at the special photo that used to be on the TV at home. It was here now, next to her bed. He got up to leave but turned back to her and said, "I'm gonna do what I can for us now, JoAnn. You know how long I've waited for something like this. I can't lie to you. This is my only chance. It's the wrong time for us, but don't judge me too harshly. I'm made to explore for what's just out of reach, not to sit in an office or a comfortable backyard. I know I promised to stay, so I'll be back. You rest now and hold on. Just hold on." Jim sat down beside her again, took her hand and leaned forward so that he was almost face to face with her. Then, grinning at what he was about to ask, he said, "Let's make a deal: you come back, and I will, too. Then we'll be together the rest of our days."

CHAPTER 44 - VANDENBERG

Late-May 1965

An optical tracking station on Tranquillion Peak picked up a great white, swimming in the surf next to Vandenberg Air Force Base at the Western Test Range. Home to the 30th Space Wing, the scrub desert plateau on the California coast waited quietly to launch its next spy satellite—or America's nuclear arsenal, if called into action for the first and probably last time. Atlas, Titan, and Minuteman ICBMs stood ready, each one large enough to obliterate the Soviet city celebrated on its nose cone. A few minutes and the word was all it would take to destroy the entire Union and everything within its reach.

The hellish firepower seemed deceptively still and quiet at dawn as Chuck and Jim were driven past a track-side sign to launch pad 2-West, better known as Slick Six, with a Titan IIIC ready for its "unmanned" test flight, as they would call it.

A lethal cocktail of adrenaline-fueled excitement and cortisol-driven fear coursed through Jim's veins as he sat quietly, wondering how his Soviet counterparts must have felt at this point on their own journeys into orbit. He read everything there was to know about Russia's Leonov—the first man to walk in space back in March. He had never imagined that Soviet rockets could inspire less confidence than America's. The Titan engines ahead of them could just as easily kill him and Chuck, if another one of a thousand dangers didn't sneak up and do the job first. And like today, the Soviets had no fanfare, no nation to cheer them on or wish them luck on their journey into the new frontier. Neither platitudes nor red carpets were rolled out today; giant metal plates hiding buried silos were the only things that covered the ground here. All the Soviets had was life-threatening danger for company, hidden behind a closed Iron Curtain in case things went badly wrong. And unless it all went south today (followed by an inevitable cover up), all of this would become nothing more than denied access personal memories. Jim pictured his father strapped into the seat of his plane, taking off on his own solitary, secret journey into hostile territory, never to return, no explanation, no goodbye. Just poof, into thin air.

He glanced at Chuck sitting in front of him, dressed in a white space suit that was now almost entirely of his own making. He looked out over the base with his visor up as the transport passed a row of empty gantries in the distance to the left, each of them pointing skyward and housing thermonuclear ballistic missiles under their giant arches. Today, he and Chuck would be the payload on top of their own modified ICBM, where deadly uranium would normally sit.

The ride was silent and internal as the launch facilities, like giant oil refineries somewhere in the desert, began to thin out. The transport turned south and joined the remote track to Slick Six, and within five minutes they'd arrived, disembarked, and stood in the shadow of the mighty Titan, silently steaming in the cold morning air.

If Jim had looked out to sea, he might have noticed the great white shark still thrashing wildly in the North Pacific; as if the big fish knew that smaller ones were about to climb out above them and might not make it all the way. Pad technicians checked the emergency escape systems one last time to make sure the men weren't about to become its breakfast.

Chuck glanced up at the capsule on top of the rocket, then came out of his thoughts. He pulled out a small cross hanging on a chain, kissed it, and said, "The Soviets sent one of their men to walk in space. Well, how about a quick stroll around Earth today?"

Jim looked at the time on his Omega Speedmaster Pro, chosen to withstand twelve-G's—though the watch would be the only thing that made it back if things got that bad. He reached up to the sky, feeling as if he could almost touch the wisps of low, angry cloud that were now rolling rapidly across the plateau. The sky had already begun to clear, revealing shifting rays of light. He unzipped a small suit pocket and glanced down at a photo of JoAnn next to his own little cross and DC-3 badge, then zipped up again and began walking toward the gantry lift to take his own first small steps toward the heavens, wondering if it would be anything like he'd dreamed of as a boy.

He couldn't help but feel a little nervous about the million pounds of liquid oxygen and hydrogen just below his rear as the pad technicians began to install and strap him into his cramped little seat. A rush of liquid somewhere south of his butt foretold that the Titan was being pressurized with its explosive fuel. Later, he would feel slightly bemused at having to sit still like a sack of potatoes as each engine and launch system was checked and armed, one by one, over the course of nearly two hours—the Soviets would have closed the show by now and just hoped for the best. The cabin became a silent cocoon, and other than the chatter among the controllers and the occasional mechanical and pressurization sounds from fifty or a hundred feet below, the deeply insulated enclosure seemed like the quietest place on earth. There was nothing around for many miles in all directions. It felt like the first real isolation he'd ever experienced, because nobody was crazy enough to come near a fueled rocket. Jim's thoughts began to wander. He was glad that Mable at the Marshall Space Flight Center had checked and double-checked the numbers. He also wondered why, in the year since the Civil Rights Act, he was still hard pressed to notice much of a difference for her. His eyelids felt heavy and they closed as the checks continued in the background. He'd lost a lot of sleep over the past few days, and while the powers that be were still happy to put him in the driver's seat of a billion-dollar rocket in that state, they'd never allow him behind a wheel like that.

When he woke up again, the forty-minute countdown had begun.

Then, other systems were checked.

Chuck had snoozed too, and they joked about a launch delay because the crew had fallen asleep on the job. Chuck even suggested that they send one of the poor pad technicians to knock hard on the window when it was finally time to go.

Eventually, the final countdown began and the candle was lit. Chuck snapped his hand back from the abort handle with a sideways glance at Jim, clearly not wanting to be the one to accidentally blow the mission. In less than a second, a huge inferno and deafening noise erupted from below, as if a seemingly infinite force was shaking and pulsing the rocket's vector violently; left, right, back and forth like a pencil being stabilized on a giant fingertip. The two of them were thrown about in their seats like ball bearings being tossed around inside an aerosol can. The noise subsided as the rocket cleared the tower, its searing flame as bright as the sun and with no off switch.

The blinding plume quickly disappeared through a perfectly timed ring that opened like a passageway in the dense cloud above. Then, on cue, new clouds closed behind it, melting away the twisted, smoky evidence of a launch. Within a minute, the roar of the engines had subsided and dissipated somewhere in the sky, allowing the plateau to relax again.

Jim breathed a sigh of relief as they quickly cleared the Max-Q danger zone, where he knew the dynamic pressure was most likely to tear the rocket apart. Fortunately, it continued to accelerate toward the great light in the sky.

Jim could no longer hold back his words, even though his bones still shook like a bag of skittles inside his skin. "We're doing it. We're finally doing it!"

The first stage fell away and the sudden deceleration threw him violently against the harness, his arms flailing in front of him as if he were about to fall forward. A moment later, he was thrown back into his seat just as hard when the second stage thruster ignited, his left hand snapping back into his helmet visor with a sharp crack.

The deafening roar suddenly disappeared at twenty-four thousand feet as if someone had turned off the rocket's engine.

* * *

A lone satellite drifted silently around Earth; perhaps dormant or dead, or perhaps abandoned or forgotten, for no one patrolled space. The sun had already set. Down below, great swaths of Earth were indistinguishable from the deep darkness that surrounded the planet, save for the city lights that outlined the wealthier continents.

Out of the darkness, a handful of beeps began to pour into an airtight chamber at the heart of the contraption. They stopped when it gave no reply. A moment later, a small electric fan inside the machine awoke and began humming softly inside a sealed chamber. Electronic equipment suddenly began to play its own series of beeps, and after a brief silence, a second stream arrived and a conversation began in gibberish. A tiny ticker lit up next to the fan and displayed code for no one to see; the machine, whatever it was, could just as well have been conversing with Mars.

The dialog stopped abruptly as a small thruster cone fired at the front of the satellite, slowing its orbit. It dropped imperceptibly to a lower altitude as several other cones fired rapid bursts of hydrogen peroxide in sequence, spinning the satellite on its vertical axis. A handful of pyrotechnics pulsed in unison, ejecting pins along with other debris in all directions. Several of them hit the *CCCP Polyot* inscription on one of the struts. Inside the chamber, the jolt from the small explosions ignited a wiring loom behind the ticker. It blew, leaving an imprint on the screen that read *Molniya*. More beeps came, perhaps to check if it was still alive, but the satellite did not respond. They looped again, but to no response. Instead, large rear thrusters came to life and fired a short, sharp burst, propelling CCCP forward into a new orbit. Polyot was on the move.

* * *

Chuck and Jim's Gemini B capsule had already separated from the top of the spent Titan and began its final short climb to orbital speed and height. The two inside, delighted with their weightless limbs, were ecstatic like children again as they began their first full orbit around Earth with helmets and gloves off. They could barely tear their eyes away from the small porthole windows overlooking the world.

The cabin space was already cramped, but Jim felt certain that the squeeze was somehow tighter than on the ground. He must have expanded an inch in every direction in the eight minutes it took to climb into orbit. His head felt slightly swollen and congested, which was a perfect recipe for the headaches and nausea he had to avoid like the plague. He told himself to stop thinking up versus down just like in training—wherever his head was facing at any moment would be his up, and that would help him avoid chucking.

They traversed through bright daylight, then through the total darkness of nighttime in space. The first orbit passed quickly and uneventfully while Jim checked the flight systems and Chuck looked over the navigation equipment. And while they worked, they both stole glances out of their tiny windows to marvel at Earth in all its brilliant blue-green majesty. Jim's heart raced as he wondered what it would be like outside, without the tiny frame in the way and without having to shield his eyes from the blinding sun that was already breaking over the horizon.

Chuck unbuckled and removed his harness, then unfolded a set of navigation charts in the small space in front of him. "Time to find the intrepid target. It's moving at seventeen thousand miles per hour and in a highly elliptical orbit." He pressed the microphone. "Ground, are you sending coordinates?" *Beep.*

"Roger that. They're on their way," beeped the reply.

Jim looked out as Chuck maneuvered around the tiny cabin. He glanced out another porthole, then back at his charts to get a location. "It'll climb high over the North Pole, right here," he pointed out, "for an extended period." He craned his neck to the window again and looked down at Earth, then out at the thin layer of atmosphere on the horizon, and just stopped.

Jim saw his face relax and his eyes glaze over as they focused on something. "What? Do you see it?"

"Then ... I was going to say ... then it swings back down and goes around the South Pole and out again like a boomerang." Chuck looked frozen, floating gently in place. "That was an incredible sight, wasn't it?" With a shake of his head, he turned back to the charts and glanced at his own Speedmaster, an exact clone of Jim's. "We'll catch it on its way in. Once every twelve hours." He nodded softly, like he had just weighed something in his head. "As if by magic, that means we're right on time and right where we need to be." He smiled. "With any luck, we should see it any moment now. We'll catch it in the north and then follow it around to the south, just like we planned. Perfect!"

"Well well, speak of the devil," Jim replied calmly a few

minutes later, with a piercing gaze out of the hole into the distance. "Right on cue, I'd say."

Chuck scrambled back to his window.

"I think that's it." Jim pointed to a shimmering speck in the distance. "See? Right ... over ... there."

Chuck hopped up beside him and peered out his tiny window, the two of them wide-eyed like rabbits staring out of a hole. The satellite, directly above and ahead of them, was closing in on Earth like a small shooting star.

"Ten miles? Judging by its size," Jim said.

"Yeah." Chuck weighed. "Give it half an hour or so. It'll enter a Low Earth Orbit." He pressed a button on his headpack. "Vandenberg, this is Liberty One." *Beep.*

"Roger Liberty, this is Ground. Go ahead." *Beep.*

"We have a visual. We're gonna chase it down the LEO from the north and around to the south."

"Ground, roger that. Go get it. Looking good from down here."

The men jumped back to their seats and strapped in to intercept the Soviet Molniya satellite.

CHAPTER 45 - MOLNIYA

Moments later

Jim was at the wheel. He steered the Gemini capsule into a lower orbit. "We'd better get going or we'll miss it. It'll be a long while before we get another chance."

They raced up behind the target from below. Chuck unbuckled his harness and looked up through the porthole. "Half a mile. A minute and a half, tops, at our closing speed."

"Okay, I got it," Jim replied, looking into his viewfinder and aligning his eyes with the glass marks. "Easy now. Steady, steady ..." he whispered, focusing intently on the target in his crosshairs. He pulled back on the throttle a little. Liberty gained altitude and slowed. In the distance, he saw the satellite's six flat panels spread out in a circle with its cylindrical body hanging below. It spun slowly on its axis like a rotating fan, pointing an ominous cone toward Earth, looking like a giant space gun about to fire a deadly beam of destruction.

"Solar cells?" asked Chuck, looking up at the circular panels.

"Or maybe this thing is beaming codes down to the Soviets; encrypted, missiles being readied," Jim replied as he looked down at Earth. "There's no way of knowing. Not until a flash of light goes off somewhere down there."

"It looks dead, doesn't it?" Chuck said. "Nothing moving as far as I can see."

"I hope you're right. And there doesn't seem to be a way to dock either," Jim replied, still glued to the crosshairs.

"We'd better not get in its way, whatever it's up to."

"Easy now." Jim coaxed the capsule toward Molniya.

"Move in slowly and we'll be able to lean out and grab it," Chuck said with a grin.

Jim brought it all the way in. Less than a minute later, Liberty finally touched Molniya with a gentle bump. They looked around the wafer-thin skin of the capsule to check for damage. Everything looked intact.

* * *

Somewhere out there, the Polyot satellite ambled silently over the horizon and emerged from its cloak of darkness behind Earth.

In the distance, perhaps only fifty or a hundred miles away, its target, Molniya was lit up like a shining star against the jet-black sky.

It locked on, then dipped into a lower orbit and quietly picked up the pace again.

* * *

Jim shut down his engine as Molniya hovered in tandem, just above Liberty.

"Okay. What are we gonna do with this thing now? It's as

large as a bus," Chuck said. "Slow it down and let it crash and burn? Or sling it out into space?" he wondered aloud. "Either way, the Soviets should be none the wiser. Want to get out and stretch your legs? See what you can find out? Give me some space in here?"

Jim glanced down at a handful of pictures of Molniya from a file stowed under his seat and began flipping through various intelligence reports. Some of them were copies of pages that had obviously been translated from Russian, though they still had snippets of the original text pointing out and describing equipment locations on the satellite. "According to these pictures," he said, stopping to look out and around the contraption, "I can't see the panel. It could be somewhere on the other side in that mess of pipes over there." He pointed a finger at Molniya's nose cone. "And that, according to these," he looked down again, "that must be where the code box and the transmitters are. Just like in these diagrams. Maybe I should take a look."

"Think you can get to it?"

Jim continued to survey Molniya, though his view was obstructed by two tiny portholes. "I really have to open the door and get some air—from the bottle, that is. I have my tool kit right here; it's ready. Let's go take a look." He glanced around outside and said, "I don't think anyone's looking."

"Okay, let's do it," Chuck confirmed in a commanding officer's voice. "I'll jump in the seat and keep you in close." He opened a storage hatch, then half-laughed at what he saw. "You'll need this." Jim turned to look. "Ta-da! A good old-fashioned tow rope." Chuck pulled out and held up the coiled tether with strong metal eye hooks at each end. "No lasers, no beams—just simple time-honored genius."

Jim laughed. "I bet they found a way to spend a million dollars on that. Although it does look a lot like the one at the local hardware store back in Houston. Cost two bucks, ninety-nine."

"At least it can't go wrong. Look, there's no on-off switch," Chuck replied.

With the mocking done, they both put on their helmets and checked their suits to open the hatch. And Hans was right there in Jim's head, his voice loud and clear. "Your own personal spaceship, complete with atmosphere and bathroom. Well, sort of. A second skin, a shield to keep out the sun's rays and keep your eyeballs from boiling and then slowly ionizing. Just follow the instructions and you'll be safe," said the imaginary Hans.

Jim checked a glove as the man continued talking in his head. "Micro-meteoroid protection—they come out of the darkness like shotgun pellets, Jim."

"What's the temperature out there?" Jim asked.

Chuck looked at his instrument panel and said, "A pleasant two-fifty right now. So try not to be too hasty with the suit," he joked in a Hans voice.

"You got him too?"

"Yup," Chuck said with a chuckle and a nod as he jumped into the flight seat and flipped a few switches overhead to maneuver Liberty. The cabin depressurized with a rush of air and stopped after twenty seconds. He glanced up at a screen showing the view from one of Liberty's external cameras, then tapped Jim on the shoulder. "Okay, buddy, it's time. Just fifteen minutes, then back inside. We need this thing hooked up and ready to meet its maker in twenty. Got it? Let's keep our reserves."

Jim suddenly felt the first pangs of space nausea. He'd known it was coming and had decided to bite his lip when and if it reared its unwelcome head. He looked at Chuck and wondered if he was hiding the same thing, knowing that other pilots and astronauts would almost certainly have kept it to themselves rather than risk losing the mission and getting an unhelpful reputation, not to mention a grounding. The stakes were too high. He nodded subtly, then floated gently toward the hatch in the cramped cabin. He grabbed the wheel on the door. Anchoring his feet on the wall, he gave it a gentle heave. The door unlocked with a few slow turns, which he confirmed to Chuck.

"No airlock, huh? After all that practice in the Comet and underwater with Hans," he said inside his helmet. "Just a front door into space. So glad all this electronics just takes care of itself. Okay, well, the comms are good."

Jim decided to focus on the work at hand and forget about his sickness as he stepped out into the vast emptiness of space, stopping to look around and wonder if something unexpected might happen. He saw neither a porch nor a doorstep.

"I see the door opening on camera," Chuck said.

Jim looked back at Chuck for the last time. He pulled down his outer visor to shield his face from the sun and, after a little hop, floated headfirst through the hatch, inching out slowly until his feet were out of Chuck's view. "Okay, I'm going to close the front door now."

"Come back and see us sometime, will you?" Chuck said.

Jim pushed away gently while Chuck secured the hatch from the inside. "I've got you on the screen," Chuck added. "I'm back in the seat now and your white NASA helmet is on TV."

Jim's heart raced as he scanned the orbit from a kneeling position on Liberty's shuttlecock-shaped black and gray surface. The nausea remained, but now a touch of vertigo seemed to be the new danger. He glanced back at the door, realizing he was locked out, then looked down and thought it was an odd place to be kneeling. He got to his feet and stood upright, then took a slow, tentative step off the capsule. "Come get me now if you're out here," he muttered.

Floating freely and tethered to the capsule only by a thin tube, he felt terrifyingly vulnerable and exhilarated at the same time. "What a sight," he said into his microphone. "Men have imagined this for eons. But no experience can prepare you for this."

Inside Liberty, Chuck looked at the colorless, grainy image of Earth beyond Jim's helmeted head and sighed. He looked longingly at the hatch for a moment before turning back to the screen and flicking to another camera. All it showed was static. "Looks like that lens is the first casualty of the mission," he said, switching back to the flickering image of the first. He paused and stared at the screen in awe, his eyes forming a shallow smile. "What's it like outside the window frame, Jim? All good out there?" he asked.

"Just fine and dandy. I can maneuver freely," Jim said in a breathy, low-fi reply.

Chuck pressed the microphone on the panel and announced, "Er, Ground? This is Liberty. Cat's out of the bag." *beep.*

"Roger, Liberty. Looking good from down here, over." *beep.*

Now hovering about a foot above Liberty, Jim pulled the

trigger on his handheld maneuvering unit and immediately spun out of control as a small jet of thrust sent him tumbling backward over the ship. He'd pulled too hard. Even though his mass was the same in space as it was on Earth, there was no inertia or reactionary force to hold him in place. Even a small pup could have hurled him out toward Pluto.

"Jim, what's the matter? Are you okay?" Chuck asked, peering through a porthole.

Jim guessed he had heard a thud overhead and carefully fired another jet to break his fall, followed by a second. He got back on his knees and stood up slowly, saying, "Yeah, good. I didn't realize how powerful this thing is out here." He looked down at the tether and said, "Everything looks fine. But it does feel weird standing sideways on a spaceship like an insect on a leaf looking down at Earth."

Chuck signaled something through the porthole, but Jim didn't get it. "What's that?" he asked.

"I'm going to repressurize the cabin now," Chuck said.

"Okay. Well, time for me to take a hammer and sickle to this new star out here."

CHAPTER 46 - WALK

A moment later

Having found his footing, Jim stopped in awe of a sight more spectacular than he could have ever imagined. Earth now covered his entire field of view in every direction, so much so that he couldn't turn his head far enough to see it all. It seemed alive, radiant and warm, with super-bright blues and whites that contrasted sharply with the inky black of the empty space around it. "There are no words invented for this," he said. "There's been no such experience."

Even the word gigantic didn't seem big enough for it all. Awesome? No, he thought—that was just everyday scrambled eggs. Majestic? No, that was just tiny humans parading around like demigods, as if the world hadn't managed without them since the dawn of time. But this new perspective, he knew instinctively, had the potential to change everything. And it occurred to him that the powers below might not like that at all.

Greenland and Iceland passed underneath, and such was the speed of their orbit that northern Canada appeared a moment later. Then Siberia and the Arctic were at the edge of his vision, though he still couldn't lift his helmeted head far enough to take it all in.

"Okay, well, I'm north, looking down. But I'm also, well, upside down, looking up. Actually, there's no up, nor down ... up here; well, there's no up, here, nor down. Except well, down ... there, of course," he muttered, with a grin.

A few moments later, the Northeastern United States appeared, and tears of pride filled his eyes. His home and everything he'd ever known was all he could see for a few precious moments. He thought of JoAnn, then his mother and father, then those who had paved the way for him and relied on him to be here now. He thought of the war raging on in Vietnam (and at home) and felt, oddly, that Earth just looked too big for nukes to destroy; though surely life couldn't survive a fallout. But Earth itself would simply move on from humanity, a mere blip in its history. Wow Jim, where did all that come from? he asked himself, overwhelmed by his thoughts and disoriented by space. He refocused his attention and raised his right arm to salute home, then glanced once more from horizon to horizon to take it all in.

A sudden realization hit him that there was little time left and a job to be done. He hooked the end of the tow rope into one of Liberty's mounting and hoisting points, expecting to hear a clank, but he heard nothing, knowing full well that, unlike in the movies, there was no sound without an atmosphere. He took a deep breath, then slowly pushed himself away from the capsule and looked up at Molniya, now just ten yards in front of him. With his head up and his shoulders tight, he folded his arms at his sides, then flicked the switch on the hand-held device more lightly this time. Its tiny jets propelled him upward. He let go of the trigger and began to float silently through the void, but with the

351

immediate feeling that he was falling toward Earth at great speed. He silently thanked the globe for reciprocating in kind so he wouldn't actually crash into it.

"Twelve minutes," Chuck said. That didn't seem like much time, but Chuck was hell-bent on maintaining a healthy reserve to leave plenty of margin.

Jim reached Molniya and grasped the polished aluminum frame. It took a slight jolt and, unbelievably—as vast as it was—it began to turn slowly at the merest touch. He hooked the tow rope onto a strut with another silent clang, and the line was taught, this time tugging at Liberty. He paused for a moment to check that everything was good.

Jim saw Chuck looking out of the window at Molniya, now gently spinning in the sunlight like a giant rotisserie.

"Okay, we're tethered," Jim said, already a little out of breath. He arranged his snaking Gemini umbilical to keep it from wrapping around him, then glanced up at the underside of Molniya. "I'm going to take a look inside before this cable winds us in. There should be a code relay box right up there, according to the schematics and pictures." He looked down at his kneepad with the images stuffed inside, then crawled across Molniya and began searching for hardware panels. Two minutes later, he stopped at something familiar. "This looks like it. Bolts here ... and here ... holding the cover plate. There's quite a few. This could take a few minutes."

"You have about ten. Can you do it?" said Chuck. He really wasn't playing around with that margin.

"I'll give it a shot." Jim crept up to the panel, then stopped in surprise. "Looks like there's some damage around the faceplate." He poked at it with a gloved finger. "And a couple of plastic seals around the edges ... they look like they were badly installed or even cut ... or burned."

Jim reached into a shoulder pocket and pulled out a small tool kit. He took out a wrench and replaced the pouch. "If the ratchet fits, as they say ..."

Anchoring his feet as he'd trained underwater, he began to turn the first bolt. "Déjà vu, anyone?" He continued to heave the bolt heads. "Luckily, this is a little easier than I expected." The first screw came out quickly. "Okay, one down. About a dozen to go."

"Keep me posted," Chuck said.

The fixings came out one by one and Jim had them linger playfully in space in front of him. He flicked the fourth and watched with great amusement as it floated, spun, and flickered away in the sunlight. "Oh, I shouldn't have done that!"

"What was that?" Chuck asked.

"Nothing. Though it might come back to bite someday," he replied, with a hint of regret for the debris he'd be leaving in space for someone else to deal with on a future mission. He hoped it would fall to Earth and burn up in the atmosphere.

Inside Liberty, Chuck took off his helmet. He grabbed a water bottle and snapped at the round, amoeba-like globs of liquid that floated around the outside of his mouth, though his fun was interrupted by another tug on Liberty. He slurped what he could from the air, then looked back out the porthole to see that Jim had slipped and fallen against Molniya. The tow rope had tugged again and a wrench had flown from Jim's hand. It was floating on a line.

"Yeah, we've seen that before," Chuck remarked with a grin and a wince. "You practicing your swimming out there again?"

Jim sat up, his legs astride Molniya's nose cone, which pointed toward Earth with its solar panels spread out in a circle behind him.

"Oh, I see. You gonna ride that thing home, or just pointing at some pretty girl down there?" Chuck asked.

"It'd have to be a cute Russian girl," Jim said, looking up. "I don't think ours would appreciate this kind of hardware."

"Looks like you're about ready to invade there, buddy."

Jim worked quickly to loosen all the remaining bolts, but his fingers began to slip with sweaty palms inside his gloves. His suit had already stiffened, inflating like a tire with the pressurized air, just like underwater. A bead of salty sweat trickled past his temple and down his nose to the corner of his mouth. He stopped to catch his breath as he looked up at the blinding sunlight through his visor then raised a hand to shield his face. "Phew! It feels like I'm broiling in my own sweat out here."

Chuck glanced at Jim's temperature gauge on the dashboard and saw that it had begun to rise. "How you getting on?"

"Halfway," Jim replied, his chest heaving for air, his words breathy. "Six to go, then ... we'll get this cover off ... and see what we got inside."

"Er, Liberty. CAPCOM here. Looks like you've got something on your tail, over." *Beep.*

Just as Ground spoke, Chuck saw that Jim had stopped and seemed to be focused on something in the distance.

He looked at his screen and said, "Ground, Liberty, what was that you said?" *Beep.* He moved to the porthole opposite

Jim's side.

"Liberty, Ground. Looks like another satellite. There must be a dozen of them up there," CAPCOM replied. "Do you copy?" *Beep.*

"Yeah," Chuck replied, looking out. He could just make out a speck as faint as a star on Earth's horizon. "Something out there in the distance." *Beep.* "Jim?"

"The sun's hot ... and it's hard to see, but yeah, there's something out there. One of ours?" replied Jim.

"CAPCOM? How fast is it moving?" Chuck asked.

"Closing in on you. We're calculating the trajectory. Stand by." *Beep.*

"Okay ground, looks like we got company," Chuck said. "Jim, you need to hurry now in case we have to move out. Our situation here could change very quickly."

"Yeah," Jim replied after catching his breath. "I see it. What is it?"

"Ground's on it. And how far have you got?" Chuck asked with another glance through the window at Jim.

"The bolts are out and I'm peeling off the cover plate now. I think I can get it open. The damage already here should help."

Jim peeled off the plate and peered at the wiring looms, electronic components, and circuit boards underneath. "I can't tell what's what in here. It's all charred. Hard to believe any of this still works."

"If there's nothing to salvage, start working your way back. CAPCOM, anything?" Chuck asked.

"Wiring's been cut clean here," Jim added. "It's all very strange." He fumbled with the electronics in front of him, then reached into a pocket and pulled out a pozidrive. He began unscrewing a large rack of circuit boards and a gray box as fast as he could.

Chuck turned back to the other porthole and watched the mysterious object that had already closed in. "I think we need to move. CAPCOM?"

"Liberty, we're working on it. I suggest you get ready to shift your position, just in case." *Beep.*

"Okay, Jim, we're going to close the show for now until that thing out there passes us by. You heard CAPCOM. Gather everything you've got and get back inside. We've had it if it collides with us. Let's get ready to toss that Soviet piece of shit out to nowhere, unless we get lucky and get another chance. It's not our problem now. We may have a new one."

"Just a minute," Jim said.

"Jim, this is CAPCOM." *Beep.* "We heard you, but as Chuck says, you need to get back inside now. Whatever's on your tail is closing in at three miles."

"Just a few more turns and I'm done. This is it," Jim said, continuing the effort. "This ... is ... the ... rack. If I can just pull it out, we'll have the brains of this thing we've been looking for." Jim stopped and flexed his right hand. "Damn it! Can't get a grip." He tried again, but felt his hand almost gone. "Oh, ouch," he exclaimed.

"Jim? What just happened? I'm looking at your gauge," Chuck said. "Your suit temperature is in the red. Are you okay?"

Jim stopped and stared down at the boards and the gray box. A sudden, intense itch began to spread over his body. After a momentary shock, a deep sense of foreboding washed over him like a wall of fog thick enough to blot out all daylight. "Chuck, are you okay?" he asked, expecting to hear of some unspeakable horror inside the capsule.

"Yeah. What happened, Jim? Are you okay?"

"I don't know. I got an electric shock or something. Holy shit, maybe this thing is still alive. Can that happen? Is a shock possible out here?" Jim knew he was wrong the moment he said those words. He wasn't grounded in space, so there was no way he could have been a conductor for a potential difference to an earthing point. He'd known that since high school.

"Okay, leave it where it is, or that thing will short your suit if it's booby-trapped," Chuck urged.

Already worried, Jim looked down to see that the half-out boards he'd pulled earlier seemed to have slid back into the compartment on their tracks. What was happening? Was he seeing things? He looked down at his chest pack to check the oxygen level and was sure he was out of air, though everything looked fine. "What the hell's going on?" he muttered.

"What was that, Jim? I didn't catch you."

Jim was still puzzled and said nothing.

"Pack up and get back inside. That's an order, Jim. *Now.*"

Jim grabbed several large circuit boards and gave them a sharp tug. Screws flew in all directions and a fistful of boards came loose in one hand, leaving a number of empty slots in the large bay. "Okay, I'm not sure what I've got here, but I've got a bunch of them. I'm heading in now."

"Remember to disconnect the tether, or we'll end up floating around in space with the damn thing," Chuck said. A moment later, he added, "That intruder seems to have slowed.

I saw what looked like forward thrusters firing. It's been at the same distance for a few moments."

"Yeah, we estimate it's about two miles out now," CAPCOM replied. "And it just climbed to your exact altitude. Zero relative speed and same heading. Looks like it knows you're there." *Beep.*

Jim grabbed his tools as fast as he could with his gorilla hands, but found that they wouldn't go back into the pouch easily. He untied the wrench and tossed it into space, then looked down at his umbilical cord and back at Liberty where it was attached. Everything seemed intact.

Out of the darkness, a bright flash from the object on the horizon caught his eye. A moment later, a shock wave emerged from where the flash had occurred. "Oh my God. Did you see that? That thing just lit up. Did you see that?"

"I'm looking at it," Chuck said. After a moment, he mumbled, "That's not ... That's a Soviet Polyot satellite. Ground, is that what I think it is? Jim, where are you? I'm looking at Molniya now, but I don't see you. Did you throw a switch inside that thing? Anything that looked like a tamper device?"

Jim looked at the boards in his hands in horror. "Maybe this thing is rigged. Oh, my God. I touched some electrics. Damn it."

Ground suddenly cut in. "Liberty, CAPCOM here. The satellite's stopped moving, but we can see there's something else headed your way. Impossible to tell what it is." *Beep.*

"Roger, CAPCOM. Looks like that thing just launched something," Chuck replied. He looked up and out the porthole. "Jim, get inside, now. *Now!* It looks like we're under attack.

CAPCOM, can you confirm that object is a Soviet Polyot satellite destroyer?"

"I'm heading in. I'm coming now," Jim said. He hurried and panted his way back along the line to the hatch.

"Jim, come on, move it."

"I'll disconnect us at the other end," Jim replied as he scrambled frantically along the tow rope.

"I'm de-pressurizing the cabin to let you in."

"Okay, thirty seconds. I'm gonna ring the doorbell," Jim said, his lungs heaving. He looked up at Polyot again, just in time to see it explode in a second, massive fireball.

Sweat flooded Jim's face as he struggled to loosen the rope against Molniya, but it was tight and his hands were already gone. He flexed his fingers to ease the pain, then tried again. "Damn it. I can't get a gr—"

Suddenly, a shockwave hit. Liberty lurched violently into Molniya, knocking Jim across the void. He lost his hold on the tow rope, tumbled backwards across Molniya, and slammed into the solar array on his back, just managing to grab one of the panels with an outstretched arm. His hand grabbed something, but whatever it was, crumbled like a thin wafer in his fist. The other arm immediately snapped around and grabbed a strut, but slipped and caught the solar panel. "Chuck! Get out of here!" he urged, not realizing that the jolt had actually sent Chuck bouncing around the capsule like a bearing in a canister to a chorus of deafening alarms.

Jim was swinging from Molniya like a monkey from a tree as the satellite began to spin wildly against the tight rope.

"Jim? Do you need help? Don't let go, do you hear me?" Chuck yelled.

"My hands are weak," Jim replied, still hot and breathless as another panel crumbled in his fist. His other arm swung around again and grabbed a rib of metal. "Just get out of here. Go! I see something else heading this way," he added, peering at a debris field about two miles out.

"Good God," Chuck muttered. "Jim, that Molniya's yanking us around and our speed's dropping. We're starting to fall. Are you holding?"

"I'm reeling myself in." Jim began to wind the tether around his arm, then wrapped it around a strut to spread the weight and pressure over several turns, gauging that it should hold even though it wasn't meant for that.

"I'm not moving with you outside. I'll come get you," Chuck said.

"No time now. Move, Chuck. I'll hold on. Move it, or we'll be spinning as fast as a Ferris wheel and I'll go shooting off into space. Fire the engine. Get us out of here. Something else is on its way."

"Jim, that's debris heading this way. It might hit. Fifty-fifty. You're going to have to brace yourself. I'm looking at the altimeter and we're dropping like a meteorite. The instruments say we'll start re-entry in two minutes!" Jim heard Chuck slam his fist on the panel and curse. "Okay, I'm firing the thrusters to take us back up to height. We'll have to steer our way out. Are you sure you can hold it?"

Jim was already sweating profusely, and now he was dizzy, his head spinning like it was inside a washing machine. He clambered clumsily over Molniya, expecting to be tossed like a buckaroo at any moment as disorientation and nausea took hold.

"CAPCOM, this is Chuck." *Beep.* "That thing out there

detonated and sent a wave of shrapnel before it exploded. We got hit by a shock wave. More coming this way, but we're tied to our special Soviet friend out there. The extra weight is pulling us out of orbit. I'm about to fire the main engines to maintain altitude. Jim, well, Jim's still out there. We have a couple of minutes, if that." *Beep.*

CHAPTER 47 - DEATH

A moment later

The Gemini Mission Control Room was the size of a small theater, with four staggered rows of cream and light green consoles, each with cathode ray monitors angled upward and surrounded by flashing white, red, and green illuminated buttons. A dozen or more white-shirted operators with black headsets sat behind the consoles, poring over a pile of mission papers.

FLIGHT stood guard at the back of the room, where he could see everything and direct all his men. And CAPCOM, who like everyone else had his own name tag on his personal console, sat in his swivel chair staring at a pair of giant screens at the front of the room. One of them showed a map of the world with Liberty's trajectory superimposed in yellow.

FLIGHT looked at an American flag planted in the corner of the room to his right, then walked over to CAPCOM's shoulder and leaned in to look at his small screen. What he saw made him stand up straight. He ordered the control room doors locked. "No one comes or goes until we get those men home," he announced.

* * *

Jim saw bursts of propellant firing from Liberty's thrusters and knew that Chuck was now dragging Molniya into a higher orbit around Earth. They were still tied together. Strangely, he felt nothing to indicate the additional acceleration in space that had lasted almost two minutes.

"I'm going to fire again to slow us down and stabilize the movement. Jim, hold on."

The capsule slowed and the tether began to flex as Molniya's continued momentum seemed to be pulling Liberty still farther along its new ascent.

Jim felt a sharp tug on his umbilical. The jolt pulled loose the tools from his pocket along with Molniya's boards. He stretched for them but reached too far. His umbilical separated from his abdomen. His right arm instantly snapped around like a Venus flytrap to grab it, but he lost his grip on Molniya. His left arm went for one of the boards, but while it caught the umbilical, it missed them again. The horror of his predicament dawned as the air pressure in his suit began to drop without his tether.

He stopped and looked up at the spinning horizon as sweat began to seep into his eyes, stinging like acid. His nose was choking. "The scrubber's gone. There'll be carbon dioxide in here soon," he barely managed to say, as if he were being strangled. "Chuck? We're heading for the dark side. I need to get in or I'm going to freeze out here. My air is cut off. My suit's contained at the valve, but it won't last."

Chuck glanced at the panel and saw that Jim's oxygen gauge had dropped dangerously low. His temperature was skyrocketing. Chuck pressed the microphone to talk to ground. "CAPCOM, this is Liberty. Jim's in trouble. He won't make it on his own. I'm going out to bring him in. Stand by." *Beep.*

There was no response. Just static on the radio.

"What the hell?" said Chuck. "Ground? Over." *Beep.*

Still nothing came back.

He put on his helmet and fastened it, then connected the oxygen to his stomach and began to depressurize the cabin. He opened Liberty's small hatch and eased out, crouching on the slowly rotating capsule. Looking around, he saw that the light outside had already faded and they were now heading into the night. He looked to where Polyot had been on the horizon and saw a new cloud approaching like a giant sandstorm. Crawling quickly to Jim's tether, he grabbed the tow rope and began to pull himself toward Molniya. "Hang in there, buddy. We'll get you back inside."

Out of the darkness, something super massive hit like the detritus of a giant nail bomb, in a second strike.

Molniya took it in the face first, sending a thousand splinters into a maelstrom of debris. Chuck ducked, but it was too late. A fragment flew into his visor, shattering the glass and hurling him backward over Molniya.

Jim lost his grip and swung out into deep space as Molniya and Liberty began to spin against each other like a giant propeller.

* * *

FLIGHT was standing watch in the control room, waiting for news, when the screens suddenly went blank.

"Sir, they're passing around the other side," said CAPCOM.

"Comms are gone. Liberty seemed okay from what we saw, but we'll have to wait for them to come around again."

* * *

Chuck's gloved fingers caught something as he slid face down over the satellite. He groaned in pain as his fingers reawakened a lingering weakness from the Vomit Comet incident; they'd been caught and nearly broken off. He stopped and glanced up as a field of debris passed around him, this time catching the outer edges of Liberty.

His eyes began to water. "Shit!" he exclaimed, realizing that the anti-fog coating from his cracked visor had peppered his eyes. He looked down at Earth and just managed to see what resembled a giant flock of racing birds hurtling past at great speed in a lower orbit below. Dozens of them detonated in small explosions, lighting up the sky above the bright blue planet like a giant minefield.

His eyes began to well up as he continued to crawl across Molniya in search of Jim. Within a minute they were flooded and he had little idea where he was. "Damn it! I can't see a thing! My eyes are streaming like the Niagara Falls. Jim? Are you out there?" He held out an arm. "Take my hand if you can reach it."

Another brief rumble of shrapnel struck like the last gasp of a dying storm, giving Chuck an unexpected sense of relief that he couldn't see its carnage. Liberty and Molniya spun faster around each other as he continued to crawl blindly. "Jim, I have no idea where I am! I can't clear my eyes or see anything! We're going to fall to Earth on the dark side soon. We'll burn up after freezing if we don't get inside! Move it and get your ass back to the capsule! Grab my hand if you can see it."

Already feverishly hot and with virtually all his calories burned, Jim fumbled to reconnect his umbilical. His peripheral vision caught something in the dim light on Molniya. "Chuck? What the hell is that?" He rubbed his visor and checked his oxygen but it was almost gone.

He looked up again and froze in horror, unable to comprehend what he saw. In front of him, and not ten yards away, a humanoid-like figure in a stiff and pale, massively inflated spacesuit was crawling across Molniya toward him. "Chuck, are you there? Chuck? What the hell is that?"

The humanoid figure, now crouched on all fours like a hound from a nightmare, turned to look up at him. A red *CCCP* was inscribed on its white helmet, just above the blackened visor that covered its face. Its torso looked frozen white, like something that had died in the cold vacuum of space.

"Chuck? What is that?"

Just as he hung there, paralyzed with fear and utter confusion, a flying object no bigger than a baseball came at him. It narrowly missed and exploded somewhere in space. "Chuck, is that you?" He rubbed his visor again. "Chuck!" he yelled. "I'm out of air! Damn it. I don't know what's happening. Oh, God. Hypoxia set in. Chuck?"

"Jim. Say that again. You're not making any sense. I'm on Molniya looking for you." Chuck became more insistent. "My hand is out. Come on. Take it. Reach out. We don't have time!"

"Do you see it?" Jim asked again.

"See what? I don't see shit! Come on! We got to go!"

Jim's heart began to pound in his ears as the fiendish apparition continued to crawl toward him. It reached out a hand and tried to grab him. Then, out of nowhere, a second one appeared from the other side of Molniya.

"Chuck, what the hell? They're coming ..."

Jim was suddenly distracted by an intense itch across his head and realized his lungs were gasping for air. He tugged on the hose and fumbled to reattach it, but could not find the connection.

"Jim?" Chuck yelled.

Jim couldn't answer. He began to choke on the pools of sweat swilling around inside his helmet. Now panting like a steam train, he dragged himself toward Molniya. A third Soviet fiend appeared before him, also on all fours. He continued to crawl frantically, aiming straight for Liberty's hatch as the first two creatures began to climb the tow rope toward it.

"Jim? Where the hell are you? Say something, will you?"

Jim saw that he'd lost the race back to Liberty when the first of the fiends appeared beside the hatch, as if beamed there. It grabbed the open door and slammed it shut, trapping them all outside. Jim turned with all his might and aimed his legs directly at the nearest ghoul, kicking furiously but missed. He kicked again and connected the second time. It tumbled backwards, taking a boot to the helmet, but caught an anchor and stopped.

Chuck spoke again. "Jim? What the hell are you doing? Did you just crash into me? What's going on?"

"Chuck," Jim whispered in horror. "Was that you? I–I can't breathe. What are they? Get out of here. Go!"

He squirmed and gasped for air, feeling like his head was

367

still in a spin cycle as a pool of sweat continued to slosh around his mouth. His hand opened and the umbilical cord still wrapped around his wrist began to loosen. He looked down again to see a fiend waiting at the foot of his tether, though the trio had stopped moving. His body began to relax and his eyes closed. Just then, he was startled with a jump start. A familiar hand stroked his hair. He'd felt this before. His eyes opened wide.

"Take my hand, Jim," said a calm, familiar voice that seemed to be everywhere.

He looked around and felt completely bewildered. "JoAnn?"

"Come on, Jim. Take my hand," she repeated a little more forcefully.

What? he thought. Where was he? And where was Chuck? He looked down at Liberty and saw the fiends fading away like demons at sunrise. Then they were gone altogether. He looked for his hose end, but it was now floating somewhere out of reach. "JoAnn? Chuck? Oh, God," he whispered, still alarmed. "What's happening?"

But neither answered.

Out of the fading light, a faint ghostly image appeared, shimmering in space twenty, maybe thirty feet away.

"Where am I?" he said, floating silently. He suddenly felt completely alone. "JoAnn? Is that you?"

She didn't answer.

"Chuck?"

There was more silence as the light grew brighter.

Then Jim got it, and a pang of acute remorse washed over him. "I'm sorry," he murmured. "Are you ... dead? JoAnn?"

There was still no answer.

"JoAnn?" he cried in frustration. "I'm sorry." He began to sob. "We talked about this. I talked to you, but you didn't answer. What was I supposed to do? You weren't listening."

But whether in his head or out there, she remained silent.

"Jo?" he yelled. "Is that you? I know it's you. Talk to me!" he demanded. "I thought we were in this together. We were going to do it. And then it went wrong. And here we are." He looked around. "Are we still together? Am I gone too?"

A feeling of desperate isolation lingered. Jim felt as if he were floating on the edge of the earth, like a prison from which he might never escape. "Is this it? Are we staying here now? Stuck? Forever? Dead? Is this what happens?"

His eyes returned to the shimmering images, the hazy glow of Earth's surface illuminating them from behind. He imagined he saw flickering flames. "Candles?" he said. "Why the candles, JoAnn?"

She didn't answer.

His eyes closed and his breathing shallowed as he fell into a gentle, oxygen-starved slumber. He dreamed of home and smiled at its ease. The sun's halo began to fade over the horizon and the ambient light dimmed as Liberty and Molniya moved silently and imperceptibly into the dark side of Earth.

CHAPTER 48 - LIFE

A moment later

New images flickered before Jim's eyes as they opened again. Whether in his mind or in space, he did not know. First a huge mushroom cloud appeared from a detonation, then images of naked children fleeing a battle scene were projected, like the ones he'd seen at Ben's stand in Ann Arbor. He squirmed in fear, then relaxed as the images faded into a serene Earth. Then they disappeared completely.

He felt another presence. His head shot right, then left, but he saw no one. "Daddy? Is that you?" he asked, laughing uncontrollably as if he were completely drunk. "It's you!" he gasped with joy. "I know it's you. Look, we got them, didn't we?"

He laughed again. "But it looks like they got us too, doesn't it? Both of us now!" He paused for a moment to catch his breath. "I know you like it up here. I'd like you to meet JoAnn. She's here too. You might remember her. From back home. We used to play ball in the yard." He paused again, reliving the first time he'd met her when they were seven. She was overjoyed to find a playmate to swing a bat and ball against the wall. Later, he wondered if he had been in love at that very moment, but had never known it. "I have JoAnn now. So I don't think I'll be joining you."

He stopped and reached up to unzip a small shoulder pocket and pulled out his father's DC-3 lapel pin. He looked at it in his white-gloved hand and, after a few quiet seconds, slowly slid his fingers back. The badge floated in space before him. He continued to stare at it silently for several moments. Then, as if on a current of air, it slowly moved away, out of reach, glittering like a tiny jewel in the sunlight. A minute later it had disappeared into the vast blackness of space.

Jim's eyes closed and he felt as if they might never open again.

JoAnn called, her voice now filled with a new urgency. "Come on, just reach out. Take my hand, Jim. Let's go inside."

His eyes opened with a start as he hung limp in the middle of the hose. It had floated back and wrapped itself around him. The wafer-thin halo of the atmosphere had all but disappeared, but he felt awestruck, imagining her face against the stars, smiling, like that day at the farm when they were teenagers. Jim had lifted her into his arms. She kissed him softly on the lips. It felt natural and he knew exactly what it meant.

"Do you think you could live on a farm like this?" he asked her a few moments later as they walked home, still flushed.

"What do you mean, Jim Cobb?"

"Oh, that came out wrong. I didn't mean to—"

She laughed and met his eyes. Then he saw that she was heaven-sent for him. He felt that the future over the horizon had opened up and in that moment everything in his dreams seemed possible.

Now JoAnn spoke again. "As you said, Jim, it's time to come

home. The door's right here. Let's go. Let's go together."

To Jim, the door, once a familiar object, now seemed like a strangely unrecognizable idea. He could no longer understand what he was seeing, although he knew it had once had meaning. It was as if his brain had been wiped clean of everything he'd once known, except that he'd once known them. He could find no word or association for it and looked around blankly, then muttered. "Just a moment. Can't you see I'm kind of stuck here?" He laughed again. His eyes closed. His hands relaxed again, and he wondered if he'd just imagined the whole show that had happened, feeling sure that JoAnn had bitten the bullet in the hospital, just like his father in the plane. Chuck must have gone too—he hadn't said a word. The fight against the Reds had finally wiped them all out.

With a last reserve of energy, he reached for a wrist pocket and unzipped it. A small white pill drifted out slowly. No packaging, no water, just ready to go. "This mission had my name on it, didn't it? You see? I don't mind. I don't mind going with you, JoAnn. Is this home now? It's peaceful up here, isn't it? Yeah, it is, except when someone's trying to kill you!" He laughed again. "But, I'm dead already, ain't I, so this won't hurt a bit. I don't exactly know what I'm doing up here, so I'll just finish off a few things before it starts to get real cold, if you see what I mean."

He reached for the pill, but his hand knocked it away. In a fit of anger, he snapped at it, but it tumbled and disappeared into space, just like the lapel pin a moment earlier. "Damn it, JoAnn. Did I have to do that? Now, I'll have to walk through the ice. Will you wait for me?"

Suddenly, the mild annoyance of the disappearing pill

sparked a battle inside his head. With all his options gone and the back door out of his situation closed, there seemed to be no more choices to weigh; nothing to avoid or delay the inevitable end now staring him in the face. No way out this time. No lift in his wings like Korea. His eyes longed for final closure.

It was then, when things couldn't get any simpler, that an instant visceral clarity appeared before him, like a ray of sunlight in a dark tunnel. His next words just floated out. "We're not alone, are we, JoAnn? That's it, isn't it? We're in this together. And that's all there is. Nothing else ... matters. In the end, none of it matters." He laughed as a clear, unadulterated purpose opened up in his head like a spark from a plug. It felt like the brakes had been taken off. He just had to get back home, back to his beloved JoAnn. Clear and simple, no option, no doubt, no something else first, no expectation, no interpretation, no consequence, no explanation, no story—just home. A shot of energy appeared from somewhere deep inside, hidden and released from a secret chamber, made just for this very moment at the edge of life.

Without a thought or care, he yanked the hose and fumbled to plug it into his belly. But it wouldn't engage. He tried it again but couldn't get a fit. It seemed to be the wrong connection. How could that be? He stopped and knew he was not going to make it. He was out of time. It was all over. With a jolt of energy, he clambered a few feet onto Molniya and sank to his knees.

After a moment of silence, he looked up. "JoAnn. Help me." He felt her gentle hand on his face.

He looked down at the connector at the end of the hose, then at the port on his suit, and tried again. Turning sideways, he angled it, but it wouldn't fit.

Still on his knees, he looked up again and stopped, listening to his last breath. "JoAnn?"

He waited, unable to move.

A silent eternity passed.

Last chance saloon, he glanced down and twisted the hose to reposition its teeth.

Miraculously, it clicked.

Utterly dazed, he held still, not wanting to lose it.

A few seconds later, he pushed it further and turned it clockwise. It locked.

He stopped dead again, dropped his head, and began to pray that he hadn't imagined it all.

Another twenty lonely seconds passed.

A sweet, dull ache spread through his legs and forearms, as if they were being pumped with nitro.

He looked down and tugged gently on the connection to make sure he wasn't dreaming.

It held, and he saw that the port was sealed.

Exhausted and still on his knees, he continued to breathe slowly to re-pressurize his lungs. A minute later, he took a deep breath to fill every corner of his puffer, then clambered up to haul himself along the umbilical toward Chuck's calling voice.

"Jim. Didn't you hear me? I called a hundred times. What the hell's going on? Go, go, quick. I'll follow. You have to stop the spinning," Chuck urged.

Jim felt the explosive energy of oxygen pulsing through his arteries again. It was like he'd swallowed a jug full of NASA's rocket fuel. His movements became less labored as he slowly scrambled along the tow rope back toward the spinning Liberty, just as Chuck had instructed. A faint orange glow lit the darkness softly, like little candles, creeping and shifting around every edge and corner. "Oh God, those aren't candles," he muttered. "We're dropping!"

He reached the open hatch and hesitated for a moment, looking around for the fiends he'd seen earlier. Seeing no sign of them, he plunged in headfirst and paused for a moment to regain his strength. Refueled, he braced himself against the sidewall and called out for Chuck, then staggered to an instrument panel and located a single button among the myriad controls.

"Hang on!" he said, then pressed it. A small thruster fired, rapidly slowing the capsule's rotation. He flipped another switch to pressurize his oxygen tank with extra air.

Outside, the tether began to bend with the slowing rotation. Molniya bumped into Liberty and Chuck began to crawl along it. He piled into the hatch on top of Jim two minutes later.

Chuck slammed his helmet with one hand and cursed, still unable to see. "I've got to get this damn thing off. Close the hatch so we can get the hell out of here. Let's throw that Soviet piece of shit out into space."

"I think we're too late for that." Jim was still breathless. "We're on the wrong trajectory. I've got to go back out there and untie it. It'll have to face its own fate." Without waiting for approval, he hobbled back outside.

"Where the hell are you going?"

Jim was already slithering back over the tow rope toward Molniya. "I'm going to the remaining boards first."

"What? Jim, are you crazy? You're out of air."

"Yes, but you're not. I joined our tanks."

375

"Jim. We need a reserve! What is it with you and blowing your reserves?"

"And I only need a minute. We came all this way. Risked life and limb already. I need to cripple this thing ... for all our sakes. I'll salvage what I can."

Already familiar with the environment, Jim surprised himself with how quickly he was able to return to the open electronics bay on Molniya. He pulled out two remaining circuit boards and a gray box, then crawled back to Liberty to untether it from the Russian satellite.

"Damn thing. It's as tight as a sailor's knot with all that spinning." He glanced up at the darkness that had descended upon them and saw that some of the orange glow he'd seen earlier was still there. "It'll turn to flame soon. We can't stay in orbit much longer."

Jim crawled back to the hatch and jumped in, pulling the door shut behind him. He turned the lock wheel to repressurize the cabin, then Chuck removed his helmet and, drenched in sweat, breathed a huge sigh of relief. Jim lifted his own visor and coughed and spluttered, gasping for air as he tried to unlock his own helmet.

Chuck was already flushing his eyes with water. "Not yet," he urged. "Wait."

But Jim had already done it.

Chuck recoiled as a half bucket of sweat poured from Jim's collar and spurted from his mouth around the cabin.

They both stopped speechless and looked around the panels for electrical shorts. Chuck sniffed the air as Jim's sweaty fluids splashed over his face and chest pack. Jim just looked on, unable to respond.

Seeing exhaustion in his face, Chuck helped him back to

his seat.

Jim recovered quickly and had already regained his breath and a little strength.

"The tether—did you disconnect it?" Chuck asked.

Jim looked out of the porthole. "It was too tight and I was too late. I had to leave it."

"What? We're still tied to that piece of shit?" Chuck nearly flipped. He ran a hand through his hair in thought.

"We were spinning like a top in all directions. It wasn't until you hit that button and straightened us out that everything slowed. But I got the boards loose. Look," Jim said, glancing down at a large pocket on his chest.

"Okay, well, we're falling now and probably way off-course while we're still tied to that thing."

"It's a million dollar rope. It should burn through quickly."

"We need to figure out where we're going," Chuck said.

They jumped to their tiny stations and began preparing for re-entry. Switches were flipped and hatches closed. But Jim stopped when he heard an unexpected rush of air, as if a balloon had just whizzed around the cabin. Nothing seemed obviously wrong.

Chuck glanced at his dials and stopped as well.

"What?"

Chuck pointed to a needle on the panel. "The oxygen in the cabin—it's rising. You of all people should be relieved to see that!" He glanced at the hatch, then back at his instruments. "That door's not closed." He unfastened his harness and jumped over Jim to the hatch. "We need to seal it before we pump the air with pure oxygen. We'll light up like a new star in the night sky with the heat of re-entry."

Chuck struggled with the wheel, but it wouldn't budge. Jim

jumped on it too, spreading his feet on the ceiling. They heaved together and pulled it tighter. The airflow eased and the oxygen gauge slowed its rise. They scrambled around each other and buckled in again when it stopped moving.

Chuck reached for the control panel and pressed a dozen buttons in sequence. "Landing procedure initiated. Hopefully, this will steady things."

But nothing happened. He cursed and pounded the button with his fist, but there was still nothing; the capsule continued to rotate quietly, like a spit on a fire. "The explosion must have damaged something," he said. "Okay, plan B. We'll have to fire up the engines. We could end up anywhere."

"Bottom of an ocean? Drop in on some cannibal state for dinner?"

"Not the way you smell, buddy."

"I'll bet we taste heavenly."

Jim hurriedly pulled star charts and maps of Earth from a compartment in the side wall and began making calculations. Chuck looked out of the porthole and fired the small thrusters to stabilize their motion again. He pressed the comms on his headset and said, "Ground, do you read me, over?" *Beep.* There was no answer. "We took a hit from the Polyot satellite, but we're ... okay." He looked at Jim. "And we're still tethered to the Soviet Molniya. We've lost the landing procedure, so I'm maneuvering to slow us down. When we're ready, we'll jettison the Command Module right at it, and hopefully that'll break the tether and throw the thing into space ... which will get us home." *Beep.* Chuck paused for an answer while continuing to look at Jim. When there was no reply, he pressed the microphone again. "The main engine is low, so we only have one shot at this. It has to work first time. Do you copy?" *Beep.*

Jim pointed to a spot on the map. "Here. Looks like we're coming down somewhere in this area. We might end up in the Northern Territories, maybe Canada. Much longer and we'll land in Europe."

Chuck pressed the microphone again. "CAPCOM, do you copy?"

They both heard nothing but white noise. Chuck continued. "It looks like our landing equipment took a hit. We're in a spin and I'm going to fire up the main engines to see if we can correct our course. Come look for us in the, uh, Pacific?" He looked at Jim for confirmation, then glanced down at the map. "Or the Rockies, maybe. And while you're out there, I suggest you try ... the Atlantic. You know, it's probably worth stopping in, uh, Paris, just in case. Actually, why don't we just call you when we get somewhere. Over." *Beep.* He looked at Jim. "We're on our own now, buddy."

* * *

In the Gemini control room, CAPCOM listened intently into his headset and breathed a sigh of relief. "I think they're back online," he said, turning to FLIGHT. "Something's happened."

He held up a hand to silence the room and listened intently then pressed the microphone on his control panel and said, "Liberty. Ground here. We hear you. Glad you're back online. Stand by."

FLIGHT stepped closer and stared at the large display on the wall. "Alert the Navy and Coast Guard and have them send up aerial reconnaissance. Looks like they're heading for the northeastern Pacific. But they could still land outside our waters."

CAPCOM spoke into his microphone again. "Liberty, we've got you. We're tracking you. We're sending in the rescue teams, over." *Beep.*

* * *

Chuck glanced at Jim as he held a finger over a button on the control panel. "Okay, ready? Go." He paused for a moment for a final mental calculation, then pressed the button all the way. To their relief, the main engine fired, slowing the capsule from the speed of a bullet to a crawl in just a handful of seconds, pushing them both hard into their seats. Pyrotechnics fired and ejected the Command Module, leaving only the conical capsule of Liberty with the men inside. It took another shuddering jolt that sent it bouncing off Molniya with a neck-breaking tug through the tether.

Jim watched the screen intently as the module spun and floated away into another orbit, like discarded trash, knowing it would lose power and fall to Earth, then burn up as it entered the atmosphere. Had the tether to Molniya been severed with that last jolt? His relief was short-lived as the capsule began to spin again. The navigation gimbal went wild as Earth spun around outside the window. And now it was impossible to know exactly where they were going as the capsule began to fall silently toward Earth like a giant pebble.

Jim continued to look out the porthole window as the capsule plummeted through the upper atmosphere, a brownish-orange glow permeating the sky, as vicious white-hot flames coiled up and darted past the window at great speed.

"Has that thing separated?" Chuck yelled over the growing din.

Jim craned his neck to look, but he could barely move against the force holding him in his seat. He yelled back, "Something's wrong!"

"We're still spinning too much," Chuck replied.

The capsule began to shake and rattle violently as a plume of super-hot plasma roared and curled past the windows like a raging flame. A minute later, everything turned red and Jim's vision blurred. He blinked and moaned in pain, as if a handful of needles had been jammed into his eyelids. His left eye began to drip and itch, but now was not the time to open the visor for a desperately needed rub. A drop fell on his lip and he tasted blood. He looked up at a dial on his instruments and saw what seemed unlikely. "Is that Ten-G? My God, Chuck, this thing's a damn pressure cooker!"

CHAPTER 49 - SO LONG

Moments later

A lightly bearded man, topped with an ushanka and wrapped in warm winter clothes, slipped down an embankment in heavy leather boots on a bitterly cold but crisp and clear sunny day in deep frozen northern Russia. He paused in the snow-covered field to catch his breath, then took off his thick gloves and pulled a pair of binoculars from a satchel. He scanned the landscape through the lenses but saw nothing notable except undisturbed picture-perfect postcard beauty. The entire forest lay under a pristine blanket of snow, and the bright sunlight cast long shadows off the tall, slender pines in every direction as far as the eye could see. All sounds were hushed, as if the landscape was in deep hibernation. He raised the binoculars and scanned the sky, stopping only to sip water from a small hand-held canister.

"что-нибудь? *Anything?*" another man asked in Russian, coming up behind him.

"ничего. *Nothing,*" replied the first. He dropped his binoculars and swallowed another gulp of water, then wiped the drips from his chin with a sleeve.

The second man looked up with his own standard KGB

lenses and traced the sky, stopping on a blurry sight some-where in the vast expanse of blue. "Wait," he said. He rubbed the condensation off his glasses and looked up again. "What is it, Leonid? Do you see it?" he said wonderingly.

Leonid looked more closely. "Two?" He refocused the image and saw bright fireballs streaking across the hazy sky, each trailing a long plume of smoke and flames, perhaps fifty or a hundred miles high. "One of them is on fire. Look, it's burning," Leonid exclaimed.

* * *

Inside the falling Gemini capsule, Chuck was still strapped into his seat when he saw something unusual rush past the porthole window. It happened again. Then again. He leaned forward as far as he could and looked up. "It's that damn rope. Maybe it did cost a million dollars. It's still there, God damn it! We're hauling that Soviet hunk of metal across the sky like a tow truck!"

"It must be dragging us back to some Russian gulag. They got us."

As they waited impotently, Liberty and Molniya continued to spin around each other like a centrifuge, twisting and turning and tugging at the tether as their speed continued to increase.

"The heat shields won't protect us like this. The fire will get in and eat the damn oxygen!" Chuck yelled.

Just as he spoke, it seemed that the fires of re-entry were already searching for an opening on Liberty as it hurtled through the sky. The blaze, which had vaporized every last piece of the falling Command Module, was now on the verge of obliterating Liberty with the men inside. It would simply burn up and disappear with neither trace nor witness, as a stark reminder that men were made to keep their feet on the ground. There would be no welcoming open arms in space. There never were and never would be.

The tether between Liberty and Molniya—valiant, reluctant and foolish in its persistence, was now ablaze like the stream from a flame thrower. The camera mounts on top of Liberty melted and blew away into the trailing blaze which continued to try, mercilessly, to break through the weak seal around the hatch. Just a little more. Just another minute. Liberty couldn't hold. It would explode, then fire would devour the capsule before it disappeared without trace from the CIA, FBI, SAC, NASA, KGB, ABC, XYZ, or any other acronym that cared to set up an investigating committee.

Then BOOM! it went.

* * *

"Did you see that?" exclaimed Vasili on the ground, awestruck at the display of fire which scattered across the sky like a giant firework.

"They exploded? Both of them?"

* * *

CAPCOM in the Gemini control center looked over TELEME-TRY's shoulder as one of the blips on his screen suddenly disappeared. "It looks like one of them just, well ... it's gone!" exclaimed TELEMETRY. Everyone stopped.

"Gone? What do you mean, gone?" FLIGHT asked. "Check

the systems."

"Which one's gone?" one of the controllers shouted across the room.

"I can't tell—not yet. They're still inside the fire. I can't communicate," replied CAPCOM. "It looked like they came down together, sir."

"Where are they now?" FLIGHT asked.

"Of all places, sir, somewhere over the Soviet Union." He looked up in disbelief at what he'd just said.

"Both of them? They must have come down together. Do we have a trajectory?"

"TELEMETRY indicates they'll land somewhere in the northern Boreals. But that could be anywhere within several thousand square miles."

FLIGHT winced and turned sharply to the MEDIC. "Does it look like they made it?" He looked thoroughly afraid to hear the answer.

The man replied. "The heart monitors are still showing a strong signal." Quickly, to no applause in the room, he added, "But that could just be latency."

"Trajectory?" FLIGHT demanded impatiently.

"A better guess would be the Arctic. As far east as ... the Barents Sea. As far west as the Northwest Territories. Right now they're heading somewhere in the North Pacific, sir."

"Okay, alert the Navy to standby. Let's move it gentlemen. They might end up in a bowl of borscht whatever their condition!"

"Sir, I'm told the Ranger is already heading north up the Bering," confirmed TELEMETRY.

"Good," FLIGHT replied. "Keep me posted."

* * *

An elderly American lady was sitting in a high-backed chair in her living room somewhere in the north of America. She wore a scornful expression as she watched *US Armed Forces Information Film Number 5* on her monochrome television. The room, a small place with aging forties floral décor, opened up to the small kitchen immediately behind her seat. She glanced at a large clock on the wall, then at the door, as if waiting for a visitor.

"In recognizing a Communist, his physical appearance counts for nothing," said the narrator on screen.

"Did you put the cans in the shelter?!" she shouted across the room to no one. There was no response, which seemed to infuriate her.

"But there are other Communists who don't show their real faces," the narrator continued, as the image shifted to a picket board at a May Day parade. *The Communists enslave*, it read. An American daughter was being escorted from her father's home at gunpoint by Soviet soldiers.

"She's been brainwashed to defect East. Frightening isn't it?" said the suited reporter as he walked up to the camera, surrounded by sandbagged checkpoints on a busy American city road.

"Herbert?" the woman screamed, now looking thoroughly anguished. "Look! It could be the kids next door. Did you see them yesterday? Coming and going at odd hours of the night?"

An old man limped into the room and stood behind her. He tore off a greenish-gray US Army gas mask from his face. "Quit yelling, would ya? You sound like they're 'bout to invade. And they're just college kids from next door, and college kids stay up late. Hell, we've known them since they were in diapers, dear."

"They've been acting strange. And for a couple of years now," she said, still pained, pointing a finger through the wall toward their house. "They used to be good kids, they did."

Herbert sighed as if he'd heard it a hundred times. "They're teenagers now, dear! That's what happens."

"Did you put the cans in the shelter?" she demanded.

The old man rolled his harried eyes. "I just went down there, dear. Everything's fine." He sighed again and looked at the TV. "Can you turn that thing off now? It's making you all worrisome again. Quit watching now, would you?"

The woman ignored him and turned back to the set. "They'll be dropping those ..."

Unable to finish her words, she turned to a deep rumble outside the house. They both looked up at the walls in horror, as if an earthquake had struck, then the lady, startled, noticed something outside the kitchen window. Her eyes almost popped. "Oh my ... they're here!" she gasped as a large fireball shot across the sky. In sheer terror, she turned to the old man then got up and prodded him stiffly to get moving. "They're coming. Oh my! What did I tell you? Come on!"

The two of them limped toward their fallout shelter like old turtles on the run. "Quick, Herbert. They'll be knocking at the door. Quick!"

CHAPTER 50 - HOME

Moments later

The ravenous flames of re-entry burned the tether that held Liberty and Molniya together, throwing the capsule on a tangent and beating, by a mere few seconds, other fires that had banged on the hatch like it was the front door to a hot party.

The incessant spinning began to slow, and the capsule quickly regained its composure, its heat shields thankfully down. The prize—the oxygen filled Liberty—was now beyond reach of the flames. They raged hot, having pounced on the second prize: the free-spinning Molniya, which had also attempted to flee into the darkness. But determined not to allow another escape, Jim could see the flames ambush it, devouring it until it could take no more. It burst into a ball of fire, the explosion giving Liberty a final jolt, the fireworks perhaps the largest Jim had ever seen. Molniya's charred carcass careened helplessly toward Earth as the men inside Liberty began to regain their senses.

Fortunately, their G readings continued to drop over the next few minutes. Eventually, the drogue deployed, releasing a giant parachute that gave them as large a tug as any on the mission so far. The capsule slowed from a thundering freefall to a gentle descent in an instant.

"I think my body's broken," Jim said, decompressing and growing a new spine.

"Yeah. No pussying for spacefarers," Chuck replied. "I'll be selling that house in Florida."

Seeing that the inferno was over, they clasped hands in relief. But the elation was short-lived. "Where are we?" he asked, unable to see outside.

Chuck looked out the porthole and saw only eerie darkness. "This makes no sense. Where's the ground? The clouds? The sky? And the stars? Did we hit water?"

"I didn't feel anything. We can't be submerged."

"We're on the night side. So it should be dark, right? We must have missed the target completely."

Jim pointed to the altitude gauge. "Fifteen thousand feet. We're getting close."

"I don't know about you, but I have a bad feeling about this particular homestretch."

Liberty's final descent took less than a minute. The parachute dropped them into a dense mountainous forest, startling a flock of birds resting in the trees. They flapped in terror as the capsule's heat shield struck the unyielding canopy, then tumbled sideways through thick branches, throwing the men hanging by their belts in their seats. A moment later, it slipped through and punched a hole down to the lowest branch until it, too, gave way. The capsule dropped violently, snagging the parachute cords, then landed with a thud on its base on thick, compacted snow. It began to bounce and slide down a steep mountain slope like a giant puck. Pulling free of its cables, it finally came to rest against an unwelcoming tree, twenty yards along and two yards short of a rocky cliff edge.

Everything stopped and the forest fell silent, as if stunned by the uninvited guest. Silence filled the capsule for the first time since its fiery launch atop the Titan rocket the day before. After circumnavigating the globe several times and surviving the inferno of re-entry, this was the end of the line; the commute home was over; the mission complete. All was dark and still inside the spacecraft again.

* * *

"Okay, it looks like we have a good fix now," said TELEMETRY in the Gemini Control Center.

"Where exactly?" asked FLIGHT.

"Alaska." TELEMETRY looked relieved.

A murmur and a sigh of encouragement spread through the control room, and FLIGHT reflected it with a faint smile. "Good," he said. "Get the coordinates and alert the search crews. Find it, wherever it landed. CAPCOM, anything?"

The man shook his head. "No response yet. Maybe they took a hit. Channels are still open."

"Keep trying. We need that capsule and our men alive. Everyone got that?"

CAPCOM and the MEDIC walked over to FLIGHT. "Any news?" he asked.

The MEDIC shook his head and said, "I'm afraid their sensors have stopped transmitting."

"That could mean anything," CAPCOM interrupted. "We're on it, but we can't tell what happened yet. It's like looking for a needle in a haystack, sir."

TELEMETERY stood and joined the trio. "They broke up on re-entry, and it looks like a sizable chunk landed somewhere in the Soviet Union. A second part fell somewhere south of the Yukon between the Northern Territories and Alaska—we're pretty sure of that. There's no beacon yet, but the search is on," he added, pointing to the location on a map. "We're trying to triangulate Tongass right now. Hopefully they just missed the Pacific. But it's mountainous out there, cold, and pretty inaccessible this time of year." He shook his head. "At worst, it could take a few days."

"Okay, we have to move fast. SAC leaders are pushing for answers, good or bad. Our people are out informing the families. I'm sure you understand this has to be managed, gentlemen."

* * *

Tom had woken early that day and was scheduled to be at the newly opened Lunar Lander Research Facility at Langley Virginia to test an experimental flying machine. He'd already made quick progress out of Ellington and was across the Texan border and over Louisiana when he trimmed his plane for a straight cruise, leaning back to take in the view below.

His mind continued to sift through the beginning of the day. Trudy had been nauseous after a restless night, probably knowing he was leaving again. He revealed that things had changed in the program, that Vandenberg was going to start launching and that he had to begin preparing. She didn't look at him but he knew her face would have fallen while it was turned and out of sight. There was no mention of a visit to the doctor, but he already knew it. She was probably worried that he'd have a momentary lapse of concentration and kill himself in a cockpit somewhere, thinking about home and another baby. But without a word, she'd said it all. He'd driven to work, passing a row of T-38s on his left (one of which was his own) as he entered the base, and parked his car in the usual spot. He walked in for his briefing, greeted familiar faces along the way, and stopped to suit up. Next was the manifest before he boarded his plane. It seemed like an uneventful start to work. Nothing out of the ordinary. Trudy needn't have worried.

Now, relaxed in the small cabin of his plane, a faint green light began to reflect numbers on his visor. He looked down at his ticker and saw a message scrolling across the black communications screen. He pressed a button on the side panel and read:

<ALERT: DIVERT TO EDWARDS AIR FORCE BASE. REPORT TO BRIEFING ROOM CHARLIE UPON ARRIVAL. MISSION BRIEFING BEGINS AT 1430 HRS. END>

Without delay, he entered the new coordinates and turned the plane around, landing at Edwards an hour later. He walked quickly to Briefing Room C, stopping only to pick up a package from the mail room, which he tore open and glanced over. Inside were a map, flight plan, and briefing papers, though he was puzzled by the instruction to stand by for a mission to Ranger.

A phone rang behind the mail desk as he glanced over the papers. The attendant answered and said, "Sir, it's for you." Tom was surprised, but picked up the phone and found himself talking to Chris.

He listened for a moment and asked Chris to hold while he took it in the booth. He went in, closed the door and sat down. "I just got here. What happened? Weren't we supposed to be at Langley for the LLRV?"

"Yes, but there's been a change of plan. Looks like the men are back."

"Oh, great. Where?"

"Somewhere north, as far as I know. They came down off-track. There's a search going on. Apparently the descent went all wrong," Chris said. "There's a military transport waiting for me outside." Tom could hear the props growling behind Chris on the phone. "I'm being flown to Ranger off the coast of Alaska to meet them."

"I guess I'll see you there. I have Ranger on my briefing as well," Tom confided. "I suppose a familiar face or two will help, though I'm not sure I understand the whole story. Is there more?"

"Let's just say they're not exactly sure where it came down ... or their condition."

CHAPTER 51 - SNOWBALLS

A moment later

In the still dark Liberty, Chuck stirred and opened his eyes first. Disoriented from the fall, he looked around and then up, noticing water dripping on his head and shoulders. He heard it pooling somewhere below and slowly reached up to turn on a dim cabin light to illuminate the silence. There was indeed water gathering at the bottom of the capsule. He looked around for damage and at the jumble of manuals, pens, and other items that had fallen out of their stowage during the landing. There was no movement from Jim. He looked up at a porthole but the glass had fogged over. "Where the hell?" he muttered, taking off his helmet.

Jim must have heard him, for he now stirred too. Chuck was obviously relieved to hear him moan. "Are we at sea?"

"We're not rocking." He looked around. "But there's water everywhere. It's coming in from somewhere. We have to get out."

"Oh, well, so glad we're not spinning anymore. I'm totally centrifuged. No more Ferris wheels. Never again," Jim said.

The capsule suddenly shifted.

"I think we're about to sink into something. Get that hatch

open!" Chuck urged, as he fumbled quickly to unclasp his harness.

They crawled to the door and tried the wheel together. It was stuck tight.

"What if it comes gushing in?"

"Get ready to hold your breath and swim."

"Goodness. A watery ending after all. They must have known what they were doing. You don't know how much of it I swallowed in training," Jim said.

They turned away from the door and crouched as far back as they could in the cramped space, then Jim hit a switch that fired a series of bolts that set off small explosions around the edges of the door. Black, acrid smoke filled the tiny space, quickly dimming the already dull light. The hatch, however, remained resolutely in place. They stopped to look.

"No water?" Jim said.

Chuck was puzzled. "Could be the pressure holding it. You ready? We don't want to suffocate on our doorstep and then drown."

They re-anchored and kicked the door hard until it eased. To their surprise, it fell out and down, disappearing from sight as daylight flooded the capsule and cleared the air.

"Where did the damn thing go?" Chuck asked.

"I didn't hear it fall."

"Me neither."

"That wasn't part of the training. So glad I didn't sign that darn disclaimer to say we were properly trained. Did you?"

"Not a chance," Chuck replied. He cautiously approached the opening, watching for any shift in the capsule's balance.

Jim felt the frosty air from outside as Chuck peered sheepishly over the sill.

"There's no water. But where's it coming from? Ice?" Chuck sniffed a large wet patch on his forearm and looked at Jim with a sinking realization. "It's your fluids!"

"Yeah," Jim absorbed it. "Probably froze and condensed on re-entry." He joined Chuck at the door and looked down and around at the densely packed trees outside. It was a gray, overcast day and there was not a murmur. The capsule had come to rest on the ground, wedged between a clump of closely spaced spruces. The hatch had disappeared into the deep snow.

Big smiles grew on both of them.

Chuck balanced himself in the doorway and jumped down, sinking a foot or so. He laughed in awe as powdery flakes rippled through his fingers. Unable to resist, he picked up a handful and threw it at Jim, who jumped forward to avoid it. Jim landed on his back, picked up a pile, and threw it back at Chuck. An impromptu snow fight ensued.

Moments later, both out of breath, they were lying in the powder in their spacesuits, looking up at the trees. Jim glanced at the scorched capsule with the charred white *Liberty 1* call sign just outside the hatch. "This thing's not going anywhere. Okay, maybe to a museum—by road."

"We might as well be on some strange ice planet," Chuck replied. "There's no life here that I can see."

They got up, each on shaky legs, and dusted themselves off. Jim turned toward the track they'd sledded down with the capsule, but immediately fell over, feeling as if the balance in his ear had been turned up several notches too high. His muscles hadn't kept pace with his head. He pulled himself up and saw that the track led up an incline, beyond which lay the severed parachute cables and the hole they'd punched through the trees. The chute itself lay splayed across the tree canopy, and beyond it, in the distance, the surrounding mountains were dotted with rocky outcroppings and sheer cliffs of snow and ice.

They clambered back into the spaceship and armed the homing beacon under a floor panel. They rifled through its contents, finding flares and a series of maps, with the goal of getting to higher ground to figure out where they were.

Within twenty minutes they were trudging up steep slopes, around thick branches and over fallen trees. Jim was grateful for the warmth and perfect coverage of his white spacesuit in the deep snow.

It was not long before they were standing on a ridge, looking down into a deep white valley.

"Up there," Chuck said, pointing to a high mountain on a ledge. "We should be able to see what's around if we get a little higher."

They climbed another twenty minutes and came to an unobstructed opening overlooking the entire terrain, but it gave them scant joy.

"Not the snow palace mirage I was hoping for," Jim said, looking through the misty air at the jagged, snow-covered peaks.

They walked a little farther but found more of the same on the other side of the ridge. The sky had darkened and a deeper fog had settled in as it began to snow again.

"I don't recognize a thing," Chuck said. Jim, too, saw nothing more than an obscured view. "And we also can't go on. The temperature will drop quickly. Guessing where we are, roughly, I'd say it's the end of the day. The sun will disappear soon." He scanned the forest while Jim looked up at the sky, holding out a hand to catch falling snowflakes.

"You're right," Jim said. "We don't have long. Remember the way back?" He turned in the direction they'd come from.

"Barely," Chuck replied. "We can follow our tracks if we move quickly before the snow covers most of them."

They started trudging back toward the capsule. "We need to stay inside. A rescue party might take a day or two, even if they know where we are," Chuck said.

Jim was relieved that their path remained visible on the way back, although that was not the only thing they encountered. Chuck bent down to check paw prints that crossed their tracks from less than an hour before. He looked upstream and took a few more steps, then bent down again. "They're leading from the capsule."

Jim peered into the forest.

"They've marked their territory." He pointed to some scat farther ahead.

Jim walked over and took a closer look. "And still warm. They must have been right behind us," he said, looking in the direction of the capsule.

As the men hurried back to Liberty, the snow thickened and the sky darkened faster than expected. The trek in their heavy, inflexible spacesuits became arduous, and sweat began to slosh around Jim's well-insulated toes. The air temperature dropped and his nostrils began to ache from breathing the freezing air.

"We're going to have to hunker down for the night. Let's hope the snow doesn't bury us," Chuck said.

"We can spread the parachute on the trees above the capsule to keep the snow off."

When they reached back, Jim climbed up the nearby slope

and tugged at the parachute lines, only to find them tangled in the branches and already frozen in place. He lost his footing and slipped onto his front, sliding face down like a puck on the ice track carved by the capsule when it landed.

Chuck couldn't help but laugh. "Leave it till the morning. The search team is more likely to see it up there anyway."

Jim just grunted, got up, and jumped into what would be home for the night.

CHAPTER 52 - NEEDLE

The same evening

Liberty brought precious little comfort. The cramped space offered no place to lie down or stretch out, while a cold Arctic breeze brought snowflakes in through the hatch, which remained a gaping hole into the forest. They found the door, but there seemed to be no way to reattach it without its heavy weight pulling it back off the hinges. They broke and gathered whatever branches they could find to cover the opening as best they could, then prepared for the night.

When the snow finally subsided, they retrieved a pair of machetes from the compartment floor, along with whatever meager food rations they could find, and sat down to dinner while there was still a modicum of daylight.

"Welcome home," Jim cheered as he sat in the opening, looking out over the darkened forest.

They paused for a silent prayer, then began to eat, though Jim was no longer hungry. He took only one tiny, reluctant bite and threw his unfinished silver foil packet into the snow.

"Is that for the forest creatures out there?" Chuck asked, sitting in the back of the capsule.

"They're welcome," Jim replied, focusing on a stray

snowflake that had blown onto his lap. He half-laughed, then added, "I don't think they'd be too impressed. Besides, I can't eat any more of this low-residue packet stuff. It's time for something home-cooked ... and whatever comes out with it. I'm not going to Mars or anywhere else until the powdered scrambled eggs improve. It feels like it's been many days, doesn't it, since, you know? You knocked one out?"

"Well, don't hold back now. And don't look at me, I'm not hiding anything."

"It's gonna come out like a raging bull when it does."

"Horns first."

They laughed without a care for whatever might be listening, then silenced themselves.

"Those guys would have you eat that all the way to the next galaxy," Jim said.

"As long as we get ice cream, I don't mind what state it's in. Hang a duffel bag outside the capsule to keep it cool." Chuck started rubbing his arms to stay warm.

"So what was it like, Jim?" he asked. "Walking in space?"

Jim was surprised by the question. "Well, I guess it was about the same as yours."

"It wasn't quite the fun I expected."

Jim searched for a way to answer. What should he say? That he felt like he'd died out there, whatever that meant? Anything he said now could ground him the next time—if there was a next time. He'd already been sidelined once, and he was not about to hand it to anyone on a plate again. He realized that the meaning of the whole episode hadn't really sunk in yet, although the next thing he remembered was the little white pill that disappeared when he tried to grab it. And there was no chance of him saying anything about the oxygen starved hallucinations—if that's what they were—without blowing himself right out of NASA's own atmosphere. "What's left to do now? Walk on the Moon? Another planet? It'll be hard to find anything as memorable down here now. Everything else has been seen, done or said and just repackaged as new. Isn't that what they say?"

"Don't let your expectations get the best of you. Honor your humanity. Life can be small and you don't have to be a spacefarer to make the best of it. We are born humble," Chuck said.

"But once our eyes are opened, there's no turning back." Jim thought again and continued. "It felt a lot like falling ... and just falling." He frowned at his childish words, then looked up at the shimmering stars now appearing in the clearing night sky. "Earth had a reverent glow with nothing but darkness and emptiness around it. A kind of lonely planet. It was a lonely orbit."

Chuck paused, then asked more specifically what had happened out there, but Jim didn't answer. "You were fighting something. I took a boot in the face."

"I was out of air."

"Oh, then what happened?"

Jim shrugged. "The boards. They flew away. I tried to grab them."

"Not the boards. Something happened."

Jim thought again. "It's weird, but I don't think I was supposed to have them."

Chuck looked at him questioningly.

"It's hard to explain. A feeling, when I pulled them out the first time ... the next moment they'd snapped back into place.

I'm sure of it." After a moment, he added, "Must have been out of air."

Chuck was silent, waiting for more.

"And I didn't expect to meet anyone else out there!" Jim went on, deprecating his own words. "But I, uh, I got the sense of the Soviets ... and of JoAnn ... and my father," he added sheepishly. "Maybe not so surprising. He went missing in the early days of surveillance, looking for Soviet missile and ICBM sites. Probably trying to prevent a nuclear strike."

Jim revealed the moment a uniformed Air Force officer and chaplain had come to his mother's house. At first she refused to let them in, as if to avoid the impending bad news. The officer's eyes were already streaming as they entered, but he said that Jim's father was, "presumed dead while on a mission over Communist airspace." A memorial service was held when Jim was already in college and starting his Navy training. That was the last thing his mama wanted, but there was no stopping him. He was going to fight the Reds and that was that.

Chuck listened.

Jim sighed, then shifted and added more boldly, "I certainly didn't expect to find Soviet technicians up there fixing their broken hardware." He knew it was an odd thing to say, but he wanted to hear Chuck's reaction.

"Jim, you are a patriotic son of a bitch," Chuck replied. He hadn't realized what Jim had meant.

Relieved, Jim shrugged and said, "Thanks. It's good of you to notice. We now know what that thing does—did. It's crippled, hopefully, and burned up on the way down. But the thing is, I'm sure it was already dead when we got there."

"It can't be easy to get something like that into space intact. Soviet equipment hardly ever works, we're told. And my teeth were almost shaken out of my jaw on the way up in our own rocket. I'm surprised my bones aren't a pile on the floor. How do they get sensitive equipment up there?"

"Yeah, probably vibration damage," Jim said. Chuck listened again and Jim added, "Do you believe in benevolence? Protecting Earth and its people?"

"Sorry, but that thing looked more like malevolence to me." Chuck pressed him again. "So, back to all your fidgeting. What was all that?"

Jim shook his head and looked down. He poked at his breastplate. "It was this suit, like I was floating in one of Hans' goddamn swimming pools up there."

Chuck looked down at Jim's crotch and raised an eyebrow. "Oh, inside the suit, you mean? Yeah. So, did you, uh?"

Jim looked up in protest. "No. No!"

Chuck grinned.

"Don't you go saying that I peed in here. I was out there sweating like a Laika."

"Oh, really? Two liters? From Laika? That's a mighty big dog."

Jim knew he was backed into a corner.

"And I got your two liters in the face," Chuck said. "Like a gift from inner space!"

Jim shushed him. "Something out there's going to sniff us out," he joked. "Anyway, it was hot and it's still soaking wet in here." He rolled to the side and stuck a hand down his chest plate, then put his finger to his nose. "Ugh," he exclaimed, scrunching his face. "Better get this off or I'll be a sweat popsicle by the morning."

CHAPTER 53 - JEWEL

The same evening

A thick layer of crisp white snow blanketed the ground and covered the Boreal pines from head to toe on the Stikine Icecap in Alaska's Tongass National Park. Every last branch of the perennials was encased in thick white ice, and only the occasional stream or small lake that hadn't frozen over, dotted the white landscape with murky black holes in the ground. The sky had cleared, and its blue and pale pink-orange hue just above the horizon provided the only color in the frozen wilderness.

National Guardsmen alighted from their trucks with a search party to secure the Gemini capsule, while a US Air Force helicopter circled high above.

"Up there," the crew chief pointed, looking straight up at the summit. He glanced down at his map, which showed the circled drop zone, and said, "The vehicles won't be able to cross the terrain from here. We're on foot now. It's less than an hour, so let's move."

His companion looked up at the sky and replied, "It's getting late. The sun is almost behind the mountains."

"Make sure the crew has packed enough food, medical

supplies, and clothing for the men. Let's keep moving." The chief held a radio to his ear, looked up at the noisy chopper again, and yelled, "What?" He turned away from the rotor noise and covered his open ear with a finger. "Sorry, did you say they haven't found the beacon yet?" He listened. "Maybe it broke on the way down." He listened again. "What? Wait till morning?" He paused. "We're getting close now." He looked back at the chopper and saw that it had already turned to head up the mountain. "Look, don't worry about the beacon. I think we got it on the map. Stand by."

He stowed the handset and began to stomp after the search party.

* * *

Chuck and Jim began to de-suit, both shivering as they stripped and wrung out their underwear, which they left to dry on a branch. Jim propped one piece up on a stick as a flag of truce, then ripped out the soft lining from his suit and put it on.

Soon, as night fell, aurora borealis began to dance across the sky, like supermassive flames stretching from horizon to horizon, shifting between pale greens and blues with flecks of yellow and shades of orange.

"The sun was as bright as a magnesium flare in the total darkness," Jim mused, looking up. "And Earth? It glowed with a kind of ... reverence in that pitch-black, vast emptiness. Like an oasis," he added calmly. "It's still very vivid in my mind."

Chuck dropped his eyes from the sky and looked at Jim, clearly surprised by the outpouring.

Jim looked back at him, laughed and said, "Well, I can't think of any two cent words for it!"

Chuck acknowledged the sentiment. "If only we could do more of that, more often."

"How long were you out there?" Jim asked.

"Five minutes, maybe ten," Chuck said, looking up at the celestial light show but sounding despondent about his experience.

"And?"

Chuck sighed. "I saw very little of anything. And what little I did see made me feel insignificant."

"Insignificant?" Jim asked. "There are oceans of water and a warm atmosphere, and only here, of all places in the galaxy—probably. Is that simply no more than the best fluke ever? Why insignificant?"

"Because it might just be. Any other explanation is just a story. A wish, perhaps. A hope? An industry. How are we to know?"

"We have a new perspective now, Chuck."

"A new perspective? I think you'd have to go a long, long way from Earth to get something like that. And when you get there, Earth probably won't even show up, it's so small. Anyway, as long as we stay on this planet, history doesn't have to change, does it?"

"Well, that makes us very lucky. Blessed. It's a jewel."

Chuck looked surprised at Jim's insistence.

"And we have our own special corner of the universe," Jim added. "And it's ours. Anyway, don't you see? This changes everything. Humanity, for the first time, is getting out of its own head and seeing Earth for what it really is, not for what serves *interests*. We may never stumble upon such a defining vantage point again. Not until someone spots alien life. And, boy, would that change everything.

"Earth seems to me more like a needle in an infinite haystack. And, *re-defining* isn't really what *they* want, now is it? How useful is that to the powers that be? The earth has been carved out and humanity doesn't really need this new perspective for anything. Where is this new perspective going to go? It's here that we live. Then again, it's hard to make sense of it all. It's all new to, well, nobody yet."

Jim sighed and thought for a moment. "You sound like my father. You may be right, but you know, I've always thought that it's all nothing more than a choice. You can choose to live with or without faith in our special place. Makes no earthly difference either way, except how you feel—because you'll never know. So why would you choose to live without it? To what end?"

He held out his hand and shook Chuck's firmly. They finished the remaining rations and carefully covered the gaping hole with branches again.

They both fell into a restless sleep for the first time in days, just as life in the forest began to wake up to whatever had dropped in.

* * *

The American search team finally arrived at the burned-out carcass of an intricately designed machine as night fell on the Tongass mountain wilderness. It lay still and smoldering in the glare of a light show coming from the south. First, spotlights were flown in from above, then a second helicopter joined the search. Head mounted torches began to appear in the distance, surrounding the small area.

"What the hell happened here?" muttered the search leader, his eyes filled with disbelief at the utter devastation. "This looks like the wrong show. Are they still inside?" he asked, hurrying down to a mess of broken and charred remains buried in a deep gouge in the ground and surrounded by piled up snow. He bent down and looked closely at the car-sized metal cylinder, running a finger over its sooty black shell.

"Sir, you might want to take a look at this," said one of the searchers on the other side of the wreckage. He pointed to a half-burned, formerly red *CCCP* inscription on one of the struts, beneath the blackened exterior and near where the device's electronic guts had spewed out. Several handling tags were also in Russian.

Obviously startled, the head stood up and stared at it for a moment. "What is this? And where are they?" He looked around for footsteps in the dirt, but saw none. "Search and secure the area." He looked back at the smoldering remains. "Were there Russians here? Where did they go? This doesn't make sense."

* * *

Tom was still at EAFB when he was awakened from broken sleep in the small hours by the news that Jim and Chuck's capsule beacon hadn't lit and that he would have to go look for them; that's what his U2 did. He quickly got dressed and went back to the mail desk to pick up a new brief, thinking the Boreals stretched halfway around the northern hemisphere. It seemed like an awfully large haystack in which to find a needle.

His thoughts quickly turned to Trudy and he called her to tell her he'd be off the radar for a few days.

"Be careful. We love you," was all she could say, wanting to know more but understanding that she couldn't ask a single question about his whereabouts. It was just too risky. *They* were probably listening, because that's what *they* did. He returned her love and said he'd asked someone to look at the leaky faucet in the bathroom and that the repairman might call. It sounded like normal domestic banter, but she'd get the gist of what he was trying to say. They said good night and hung up.

He went for a full physical, then downed a plate of steak and eggs, and with only an hour and twenty to go, donned his pressure suit, which was just like Jim and Chuck's space variant, but with a diaper included. It was pure oxygen for the last sixty minutes before he climbed aboard his new Ranger-ready U2G, as black as the night itself.

Tom pushed the throttle to eighty percent, glanced left and right at the fighters that would escort him to a safe altitude, and released the brake; the last thing anyone wanted was for this American hardware to fall into the wrong hands while the CIA was still insisting that it didn't exist. The wingtip pogo wheels dropped, he pulled the nose up to seventy degrees at three hundred feet and, careful not to roll back over, climbed at a steady one hundred and sixty knots, clearing ten thousand feet by the end of the runway. He disappeared under the cover of darkness to find his buddies.

CHAPTER 54 - OUT OF THE PAN

The same night

Dogs baying, their sharp teeth bared. Leashed by men—soldiers. They're hunting me. No faces. The dial's spinning. The plane's falling. Freefalling. Leg hurts. Which way? The forest. Up the incline. Up. Suit's torn. Wreckage, over there. Must go. Move. Move! They're coming. Paralyzed. Snarling dogs coming. Go! Go! Move!

Jim roused in the middle of the night to the deafening noise of panic inside his head. Adrenaline pumped through his muscles and he felt ready to run, the moment his eyes opened. He'd heard his own groan, startlingly loud in his head, awkward and embarrassing even, and he was sure that Chuck had heard it too.

He sighed, wondering why he was frozen in the dream? And where was he? What happened next? The moment never came in the recurring nightmare after his father went missing.

He reached for his Case machete, but his thoughts were almost immediately interrupted by something moving on top of the capsule. The temperature inside and out had fallen dramatically—whether ten, twenty or thirty below, he simply

411

couldn't tell the difference.

Jim lay perfectly still, peering through the tiny gaps in the branches over the hole. It looked as if the snowfall had stopped and the Moon was out, casting a pale, cold light over the forest. He looked up and guessed that the sounds must have been melting ice falling from nearby branches, so he put his head back down and reassured himself that it was all in his head, that he must have been shaken by the dream. He felt his heartbeat slow, his grip on the machete loosen, and his eyes close softly.

Almost immediately, a shuffling, scuttling and rustling of twigs, a few feet outside and to the right, broke the illusion. His heart began to pound as he remained perfectly still and alert like a compressed spring. He held his breath, feeling sure his pulse could be heard by whatever was out there. He wondered if he should just plunge straight out of the hole knife first.

Perhaps sensing his fear, Chuck awoke too, his own blade ready and trained on the opening. Jim silenced him with his knife to his lips, then quietly pointed to something above, one to the left and another to the right. He flicked his knife back toward the hatch as the movement outside became a restless scurrying. He moved slowly to peer through a gap in the branches above the doorway, his machete twitching with every pulse of blood in his veins.

It became clear that the capsule was buried in two or three feet of snow. Not more than a few yards away, Jim could see a pack of wolves sniffing the air and prancing in front of the half-buried Liberty. One of them, he could just make out through the holes, was sniffing the drying underwear. He glanced around the forest as some of the pack moved nervously in the outer area. The closest wolves turned to look at the strange structure in the snow, while another looked straight up at the small dark opening of the capsule, now covered by a strangely tidy arrangement of branches. It approached sheepishly, pausing to look around for reinforcements, while pawing the snow for courage.

Jim kept as still as a dead twig. He felt like a sitting duck with his knife trained as hard as he could on whichever animal would come through first. A second wolf, obviously unable to resist the temptation, began to creep closer. Another jumped down from the top of the capsule and turned intently toward the hole. It growled at its companions with raised hackles, and now, just a few feet from the opening, the closest of the trio crouched, seemingly ready to leap at the scent of Jim and Chuck's terror lurking just inside.

The horror of their predicament suddenly dawned on Jim.

Without thinking, Chuck grabbed a flare stick they had kept in case of a rescue in the dark. He pulled the cap, slammed it to the ground, and jammed it into a hole in the shroud covering the doorway, expecting it to shower the animals with hot streamers. But, like a wet firecracker, it simply sparked, then puffed, releasing little more than a thin wisp of smoke. They jumped when it popped like a small cracker and thrust itself backwards. It rolled back into the underground compartment from where it had come.

Jim sensed carnage, whether inside or out.

A moment later, a burning smell grew pungent and intense inside the capsule. He looked down for fire. Smoke rose silently from the storage compartment in the floor and filled the capsule, blocking out the moonlight. This was it, he thought. They would either suffocate inside or be mauled outside.

It grew thicker and began to pour out of the gaps in the doorway. Jim held his breath when he heard a whimper from one of the younger Omega wolves, further out. It looked up at the thick black smoke billowing from the capsule, silhouetted against the pale white snow, and began to back away as the closest of the trio growled loudly just outside the door. Another, second Omega, whined. The pack stopped.

Jim saw a pair of young wolves retreat into the trees, but the trio in front stood stubbornly, waiting to pounce until one of them broke ranks and scampered away.

Neither Jim nor Chuck could hold their lungs any longer. Jim threw caution to the wind, for death would arrive one way or another. He turned on the light and scrambled to pull up the panel in the floor. Unable to hold his breath, he put his head against a hole in the covering and took a lungful of air. Chuck did the same. They tugged at the floor panel and lifted it aside, not caring for the noise they made.

"Good God!" Jim said, seeing that the flare was now streaming into the compartment like a super bright candle.

Chuck cursed, coughing for air. "It's going to set everything on fire."

Jim trained his machete on the door as Chuck kicked away the temporary shroud. The remaining wolves scampered and the air immediately began to clear. Chuck grabbed a handful of snow from the sloped ceiling of the capsule and piled it on top of the burning remains, but it made no difference. "We've got to get it out. Get it out!"

Dancing to avoid the streamers, they turfed the torch from the floor panel with their knives, careful not to push it onto the others stacked in their mounts.

"The boards! Get the boards!" Jim shouted, ousting smoldering papers and manuals. Chuck booted the burning torch and embers into the snow.

They waited a minute to make sure the wolves were gone, then looked down at the smoking pile outside. Half-burned Molniya schematics, a bunch of star charts, a Gemini space-craft quick start guide for astronauts, and the half-burned, charred Molniya boards sat next to the sparking flare, now damp and dying again.

Chuck cleared the air with his hands and looked at the floor panel. It was still smoking. He checked the beacon. "Damn it. I can't believe this. I sure as hell hope they've found our signal."

Jim looked back from the doorway and said, "Unfortunately, I think *they* did." He turned back to the wilderness to look for the wolves. "They'll be back."

Chuck looked out, too. "Daylight's coming. Must be, what, four in the morning? I think we're okay for now, but we need to get to safety as soon as possible. We can't stay here."

* * *

Chuck woke Jim to the sound of a helicopter in the early morning.

They quickly donned their suits, then rushed out into the clear day, looking grizzly, with days-old stubble. They scanned the pale blue, hazy sky for the chopper, though tree cover obscured much of their view. The sunlight was blind-ingly bright against the snowy terrain, which had muffled almost every sound, making it impossible to hear where the rotor noise was actually coming from. They pulled sunshades out of their survival kits and packed their knives, then began trudging toward the clearing in the forest along the route they had taken the day before.

"Right there," Chuck exclaimed when he spotted it. He waved his arms wildly in the air. Jim fired the first of the two undamaged flares into the sky. Fortunately, it went up with a red trail of smoke and arched over the forest like a small rocket. A moment later, to their delight, the chopper turned toward them.

The pilot, sitting to the left of the small cockpit, pointed his machine at Jim and Chuck on the ground. "Вон там. *Over there.*"

"Вспышка? Они должны быть альпинистами, потерянными? *A flare? They must be climbers ... lost,*" yelled another crewman standing behind him in the cargo bay. He pointed to the red and white parachute stretched across the trees about a mile away. "Cosmonauts!" he shouted in Russian, looking amazed at their discovery. He peered back down at a map in his hands. "Look, there's something down there!"

The pilot glanced over, then shrugged and said, "I can't land there. Not even here," he protested. "Too many trees. And the snow is deep." He continued to look for a place to set down. "It must be flat. I need somewhere flat," he said, gesturing with his hands.

The crewman paused for a moment, looking down at the men through the mist of snow from the open cabin door. "Okay, we'll use the rope ladder. I'll throw it down. They can climb up."

The pilot edged closer to the men, staying as far away as

possible from the maelstrom of powdery snow kicked up by the rotors, and brought the helicopter to a hover thirty feet above the ground.

"Lower. You have to go lower," the crewman shouted.

"I can't. Look at this!" the pilot protested.

"They can't get on. Lower, lower," he insisted.

The pilot swore in Russian and shook his head, then began to maneuver more precisely into position.

Underneath, Jim and Chuck stood waist-deep in snow. Chuck reached up first, but, barely able to see, he missed the flailing ladder as it disappeared in the blizzard. He tried again when it reappeared and managed to grab hold. He put up a leg to get a foothold, but his stiff, heavy space suit held him down and he tumbled back into the snow. He stood up and prepared to grab it again, this time managing to get one foot on the bottom rung. He hauled himself up on one leg and looked up at the crewman with a friendly thumbs up.

A moment later he stopped, as if he'd just seen a ghost. He said something barely audible.

"What?" Jim yelled.

The helicopter crewman had also frozen, looking down at them with glaring eyes.

Chuck lost his footing and fell back into the snow again. "The rotors," he shouted over the din. "Something's wrong! Where the hell are we?"

The air cleared for a moment, and Jim saw that whatever was hovering above them didn't look like the American aircraft he'd expected. The rotors were thin and gangly, like the early helicopters in Korea, and there were more of them on this chopper than he expected to see in this day and age.

It was clearly an ancient machine.

The pilot saw something in the distance straight ahead, not more than half a mile away. A pack of wolves that had been resting in the sun had turned to the sound of the helicopter that was now echoing through the wilderness. Aggressive and irritated, the Alpha looked up and sniffed the air, then began to move toward the beacon in the sky with his pack in tow.

"Look!" the pilot shouted to the crewman, who seemed deep in thought.

"Look! Look!"

"Americans!" the crewman replied.

"What?"

"Americans! Americans!" He pointed down at the men.

The pilot seemed puzzled for a moment. "I don't care who they are. Tell them to run. Run! Look!" he shouted, pointing at the pack. "Go, go! Now!"

The crewman caught sight of the wolves already racing down a rocky cliff. Shocked, he backed up against the cabin wall, frozen with fear.

Jim saw the man leaning out and screaming something in Russian as he pointed up the slope to their right. They were to clear the area. Maybe, Jim thought, he'd found a place to land. He knelt down to help Chuck back to his feet and said, "Looks like we're going that way. You okay? What happened?"

Chuck looked up and said, "They're Soviets! We've landed in goddamn Communist territory."

Jim looked up and saw that the helicopter crewman was still yelling at them, though he couldn't hear the words. The man kept pointing at something in the distance. Jim followed his hand and stopped in horror. It was the gray furs from the night before, moving among the trees. "Oh my God, those damn creatures are back!" he cried to Chuck. "He's alerting us. They're coming."

Chuck turned and pulled out his machete, as did Jim.

"Hey!" Chuck yelled at the chopper, standing up quickly. "Come on!" he demanded, trying to grab the rope ladder. But it was too high and out of reach. "Lower! LOWER!" he yelled, but the chopper began to inch away.

"We need to get out of here. Where to?" said Jim.

"Just run—that way," Chuck replied, looking in the direction of the capsule.

"Okay, there's another flare if we make it back. That might do it."

They were about to run when a small black object fell into the snow five yards away. Jim jumped for it as the chopper pulled back and the air began to clear.

Chuck, already on the run, stopped a few yards ahead and turned around. "What's that?"

"A pistol. They dropped us a gun," Jim replied, holding it up.

Chuck took a few steps back to examine it. "I presume they work the same as ours."

Jim turned the barrel. "Four rounds. Let's go. Go! Go!"

The pilot had already turned toward the wolf pack and was flying in close. His rotors kicked up snow in their path as they crossed another rocky outcropping. But the wolves, on their home turf, changed course around the blizzard. It maneuvered again, but they, too, shifted and pelted undaunted, disappearing beneath a clump of foliage. Blinded by bloodlust, they leapt over obstacles and weaved through trees, darting along forest paths they seemed to know well. They raced downhill toward the base of the foothill, only a half mile from where the men had run through the snow-covered opening.

"Quick, that way," the crewman shouted to the pilot. "We can head them off on the other side of those trees."

The pilot slammed on the throttle. He had a minute before the pack reappeared in the open. Jim and Chuck, he could see, were now at the bottom of the clearing and about two-thirds of the way back to their red and white chute. It would only be a couple hundred yards up another incline, then across another clearing before they were back under the trees where they'd landed. "They better have a plan," he said.

Chuck glanced up at the chopper, circling like a giant vulture, its noisy whirring echoing over the forest. "Come on," he said, catching his steaming breath in the cold air. "Just up there, then through the trees ... or they'll catch us and pass where we were a moment ago."

With a last look back, they began to bound furiously across the snow again. They were now in a race for their lives, having believed only a day earlier that they had beaten the odds and returned home alive.

The chopper turned quickly over the forest and stopped in a hover at the edge of the trees. The tall, snow-covered pines swayed angrily in its wake as the wolves reappeared and paused for a moment to correct their course. A second later, they began charging feverishly across the deep snow toward the clearing where the men had been standing under the rope ladder.

"We have to do something. We can't stop them," the crewman yelled at the pilot. "Kamikaze!" he demanded, indicating the maneuver with his hand. "Go up, then come down fast!"

"I don't know," the pilot replied. "Americans. They are Americans!"

"What do you mean? We can't leave them."

"I've alerted the base. This is not our business. They will close my business. My family ..."

The crewman looked horrified and conflicted. "I know they're the enemy, but we can't leave them. They will be torn apart."

"What can I do? Look." The pilot pointed to a nearly empty dial on his instruments. "Fuel! We have to get back to base across the sea. If we run out, who's going to get us? Them?"

They both looked down and saw that the wolves had stopped to sniff the ground, though some were already moving again.

"Five minutes. That's it," the pilot demanded. "That's all I have."

CHAPTER 55 - FIRE

A moment later, the same morning

Sixty thousand feet above the Soviet border, Tom looked down at Siberia after his night in the U2. "See you at home, boys. We got you." He turned off his surveillance radar and punched in Liberty's coordinates for Ranger to pick up.

The only thing to do now was to stay high and avoid the coffin corner at the edge of the atmosphere until he was over the Gulf of Alaska. That way, he would escape Soviet airspace quickly and undetected. Once outside, he would drop like a bomb on a northerly route and circle down in a slow vertical stack in full view of anyone watching.

He pressed the button to transmit Liberty's location, along with a packet of digitized aerial photos of the surrounding terrain. They would go up to an American satellite first, so nothing would be heard from him down below. He turned off the transponder in case someone was listening, then took another look down at the gentle curvature of the Earth, figuring he'd be safely alone until he got within twenty miles of Ranger's landing pattern. He looked up at the sky and felt close to his buddies who had been up here not so long ago, when an alarm, with the worst sound they could have dreamed up, grabbed his attention like a hungry Jake at two in the morning.

Two surface-to-air missiles had been launched from somewhere down below, and their sniffers were locked on his tail. According to the blips, a pair of Soviet MiGs were out there somewhere, too. He looked down again, but couldn't see them. They had melted into the sky somewhere out of sight. Okay, so the MiGs shouldn't be a problem, he knew, but the SAMs? Powers had faced the same odds and hadn't been lucky. Damn it, he thought—he'd almost made it home without a hitch. He looked down at the scope again and saw that he was not far from the border, though not close enough. "Okay, Dragon Lady, let's get home now. Stay high. Up to seventy thousand feet. That's our weapon."

Down below, and not for the first time, two Soviet SAMs were already spiraling upward in formation like little rockets in search of the U2.

"International waters any minute," Tom muttered. And, though it seemed comical, he imagined the SAMs might just turn back on program when they hit the boundary which they should not cross. They weren't supposed to touch him above sixty-thousand feet either, but *what the heck,* the Soviets must have thought—*the plane didn't exist.*

A second alarm screamed at him. A Sidewinder missile had been fired by one of the Soviet MiGs, now visible as specks in the distance.

Tom felt like a flying duck as SAM #2 sniffed the air and turned toward him just as MiG #2 launched a second Sidewinder. Sidewinder #1 began to chase SAM #1 and the two started a thirty thousand foot vertical climb toward Tom.

He looked down again and saw the race in the distance. He

turned on a dime. Pushing the throttle, he climbed again, holding back just enough to keep from blowing the wings off.

Smaller and lighter, Sidewinder #1 had quickly caught up to SAM #1, both now heading for the same piece of sky Tom was occupying. And it looked like SAM #1 would arrive first, and perversely, he realized he'd begun to pray that Sidewinder #1 would speed up if it could.

He turned again. The missiles failed to match him. A moment later, to his relief, about a fifty yards away, the two collided in a fireball. A burst of shrapnel peppered the sky. Several large pieces shattered Tom's tail as he yanked the stick to avoid the blast. It punctured his elevator. Somewhere below, SAM #2 pounded MiG #2 just before Sidewinder #2 plowed into the fireball behind it to finish the job.

Tom saw MiG #1 turn home without his wingman. He leveled out again, thinking the SAMs must have auto-launched, for they wouldn't have sent their airmen up at the same time. He trimmed the plane and engaged the autopilot, though it wouldn't fly straight. He pushed the stick to the left and looked at the instruments. He wasn't in the coffin, but the plane was now practically impossible to steer.

He pulled it a second time, but got a muffled response again. Pushing it forward, he looked to the left wing, thinking he was about to stall and fall out of the sky. Glancing back over his right shoulder, he saw that the rudder was stuck off-neutral; the plane was crabbed left into the airflow. He stepped on the pedals but got little back and knew immediately that he was in trouble. What was he going to do? Drop to a lower level and risk his cover? He activated the microphone in his helmet as he looked around the plane for damage. "Ranger Control, I have a problem here. I took a hit and I'm heading back to Edwards. I seem to have lost a control surface. I'm diverting back to base, over."

There was no reply.

He pressed the mic again. "Ranger Control?"

"Roger that. This is Ranger. Turn south east, flight level fifty for ten miles, then we'll hand you over and get you home, over."

Tom breathed a sigh of relief, though his comfort was short-lived. He looked back and saw oil streaks trailing down the left wing. It had splattered the fuselage above the elevator. He began to descend rapidly, but managed a slow turn south with a hard push on the stick.

"Uh, Ranger. I'm leaking fluids ... on the outside, for now."

The U2 continued to descend over the sea, but there was no land in sight, and with a thousand miles to go, short of a magic carpet ride, Tom realized there was no earthly way back to Edwards or the ship.

He glanced down at the map and reconsidered Ranger, then pointed to the Alaskan Bush Archipelago in the Bering Sea. At least he'd stay cloaked and salvageable there, if he could just find a way to land on one of the islands.

"Ranger control. Scrub Edwards. I'm gonna drag this thing to, er," He looked at the map again. "Shemya Island. That's fifty-two north, one-seventy-four east, over."

"Roger that. We'll put Shemya on alert and hand you over to approach control."

Tom punched in the coordinates and maneuvered the plane as best he could on a westerly route to the desperately remote Pacific island, though it was also back toward unfriendly Soviet airspace.

* * *

The wolves had made it to the bottom of the clearing where Chuck and Jim had previously stopped to catch their breath in the Siberian forest. They sniffed again and locked on.

A hundred yards ahead, the two limped across the deep snow in the open. But Chuck tripped and fell, and breathing hard, he turned to see that the pack had emerged from a clump of trees at the bottom of the incline. They now had a clear line of sight.

Jim, also out of breath, stopped and leaned on his thighs when a strong sense of déjà vu hit him out of nowhere. "Wait a minute," he said, standing as straight as a post. He looked around, thunderstruck.

Chuck looked puzzled. "What?"

Jim scanned the forest, then it dawned on him. "It was a hunt, my father's last moments. He was hunted in a forest just like this—at the hands of the Soviets. He fell from the sky. But what happened? Did they get him? I have no idea where it ended." Jim now felt like he was in a similar bind. "We have to go!" he growled, pulling Chuck back to his feet. "I'm not going to let this happen again. Not again!"

Chuck still looked puzzled.

"I'll explain later." Jim glanced back at the wolves. "We need to move."

Chuck scanned the path ahead while he caught another breath. "Just another hundred yards to the edge of the trees. Then a fifty meter run, flatter, right under those ones over there."

In a sudden rage, Jim held up the pistol, cocked a round, took aim at the wolves, and fired. The shot narrowly missed, hitting the clump of trees. The pack disappeared from view behind a bank of snow.

"Come on," Jim urged. "I have no idea where they're coming from now. Three rounds left."

Jim and Chuck pushed on for dear life across the deep snow again.

The chopper arrived above the pack. They had changed course and were now racing furiously along a deep run carved into the snow like a meandering tunnel, about fifteen yards parallel to the men's direction. At their speed, it was clear that they would pass them and strike at a point farther ahead, just inside the clump of trees where the snow was thinner.

"They don't stand a chance," exclaimed the crewman. "The wolves are going to head them off."

The pilot dropped to just a few yards above the run, his fierce rotor noise echoing off the walls of snow. But the wolves were simply driven on. The Alpha at the head ducked and ran furiously toward his targets.

"Lower!" the crewman shouted.

"I can't! I can't!"

"Turn! Turn in front of them!" he demanded with one U-turned hand, blocking it with the other. "Head them off!"

The chopper skidded through the air toward the trees, looking as if it would hit if the pilot did not pull up immediately. He slammed on the throttle and yanked on the stick, then slammed on the left rudder and turned the chopper sideways as it passed only a few yards above the pack. The wolves were suddenly engulfed in another blizzard inside the run. The helicopter swung around and slowed to a stop just twenty yards from the edge of the trees, blocking their path.

The crewman pumped the air in exultation as the pack, now dazed and angry, halted, unable to continue into the maelstrom ahead. They pranced, looking for a way out. One of the pack jumped the side wall, but fell back. They turned, and about halfway down, one of the young Omegas tried a shallower climb. It also tumbled back. Another larger male jumped in and clawed furiously at the snow, grabbing hold and pulling itself up.

"No! Look—they're getting out," the shocked crewman shouted. "Go. Again. Go!"

The pack began to spill out onto the snow, one by one, and were already running feverishly across the clearing toward Jim and Chuck.

"I can't stop them now," the pilot yelled, looking down at the Alpha. It had already joined Jim and Chuck's tracks in the snow. "We're out of fuel. We have to go back for help."

"Look, we have an axe," the crewman urged. "Quick!"

CHAPTER 56 - DEAD

Moments later

Jim and Chuck had already made it back to the edge of the forest where the snow on the ground had thinned. They dashed through the trees back to the capsule and approached it gasping for breath.

"This place will be no refuge. They'll tear us apart on our doorstep!" Chuck said.

"Let's see what we have to work with." Jim climbed into the capsule and searched the floor compartment for the last flare, while Chuck rummaged through the survival pack.

He sighed deeply. "There's little of use in here—though plenty of bandages. I said they should have prepared us better for a place like this."

"Well, this is it," Jim said. He pulled out the cartridge. "We've got to get out. They'll look in here first."

"The trees?"

"Let's hope they don't sniff us out and wait till we drop dead. Can wolves climb?"

"Depends when they last ate."

The two looked up through the doorway as the chopper circled back. They ducked, startled, at a loud clank. Jim slowly stuck his head out and saw that a new object had fallen on top of the capsule. Another object lay in the snow nearby.

They clambered out as the chopper pulled away again.

* * *

Relief came to Tom about twenty minutes later when a string of islands on the edge of US waters became visible in the distance. Soon Shemya's runway appeared. He was very low and his airspeed had dropped to a point where the plane felt unsteady. "Come on Tom. Just push it over the line. Push it over," he cajoled, looking around for an uninhabited area. But there was little to work with. "A lot of sea down there," he muttered. "All the way in now. No stalling. No falling. Come on."

The plane continued on the glide path, but the rate of descent increased. Just ahead, he saw a Northwest Orient Airlines Boeing 720B, probably bound for Asia, getting ready to leave after what must have been a refueling stop. Beyond the top-ups, he guessed, this place didn't really exist. Passengers probably couldn't even pee here. A US bomber was also standing quietly. Wailing sirens were already waking up the remote airfield after the emergency services had been scrambled to meet whatever Tom dropped in with.

"Shemya Approach. I can't hold it—meaning that, if this thing goes down, I'm gonna bail. You'll have to come find me. Stand by."

"Copy that. We see you now," the tower replied. "We have your landing lights."

The nose dropped and Tom pulled back on the stick to increase his attack then began preparations for exit. He flicked the flap setting, but there was no response. The U2 was as good as dead. He aimed it squarely at the airfield and switched to autopilot, hoping the electronics would take him in. But seeing the worst was about to happen, he sat bolt upright and leaned back hard against the seat. He grabbed the handles on either side and squeezed until his knuckles turned white. A moment later, he closed his eyes and clenched his jaw, then flipped open the plastic cover on the eject button. His right thumb hovered a moment before he pushed it in all the way.

The plane's nose dropped again as pyrotechnic bolts shattered a jagged pattern in the glass canopy above his head. Rockets fired his seat through the hole like a missile. His brick of a plane picked up a little speed as it fell like a stone, the tail just clipping his ass and spinning him like a top as he rocketed skyward. That was lucky, he knew—a nano-second sooner and he would have come down in two halves.

While still in the air, he looked to his left and saw the black, pilotless plane spinning rapidly into a nosedive. It plowed into a depot just short of the airfield, causing a massive explosion that leveled several other buildings. A huge mushroom cloud rose hundreds of feet in the air in front of him, throwing splinters at his parachute.

Tom hit the east road hard. He'd bailed out low, and the rocket under his butt had barely lifted him to a safe altitude before his canopy was punctured. His seat came loose and shattered into a thousand pieces on the tarmac as he hit the ground like a ton of bricks dropped from a great height.

The local fire chief in Shemya looked up at the smoke billowing from the burning buildings. "There's ammunition in there," he muttered in disbelief, pressing a finger hard on his radio button. "That way. Everybody, quick, move," he urged into the microphone, pointing toward the fire.

"He's there: the pilot. Right there. I got him," someone radioed back from somewhere on the ground. "It's a major malfunction."

"That's a big fucking understatement. Now move!" the fire chief yelled back into his handset.

If Tom could see, he would have noticed that the four-mile island was awash with every available siren when only one would have done. But he was still and silent on the tarmac as the emergency services reached the east road. Now, for the first time in his life, he wasn't sure if he'd get up, look around, and wonder how he'd gotten away with another close scrape.

* * *

JoAnn had, all along, remained unconscious and oblivious to Jim's plight and endeavors, in her solitary hospital bed.

A nurse checked the tubes sprouting from her face and arms and decided they were secure. She took JoAnn's temperature, then moved to the foot of the bed and quietly marked a number on the clipboard indicating that the last intravenous drip had gone down without waste. JoAnn began to move as the pen left the paper. Her eyebrows stirred and furrowed deeply.

The nurse looked up at her and froze for a moment, mouth agape. She put the board down and held out her hands after turning her eyes to the sky in reverence. "Hey, you hold on there. I'll just go get the doctor!"

She rushed out of the room and returned a moment later with paramedics, as if through a revolving door. They raced to check JoAnn's vital signs on machines and pieces of paper to see if a miracle had happened. JoAnn suddenly opened her eyes and looked straight at the far wall. "Jim?" she whispered.

The nurse stared at the doctor. He looked down at his patient, then leaned forward and asked, "Can you hear me? Ma'am?"

JoAnn turned with a shocked face and stared at him blankly.

"Okay, try not to move too much right now. Do you know what happened? Do you know where you are?"

A tear trickled from her right eye. "Jim?"

* * *

Tom was barely conscious as he was hurried down the hall to the emergency room, though he could just about feel the multitude of wires and tubes connecting him to a plethora of life-support equipment. He also heard the beeping machine churning out its quota for the day, while the lights in the ceiling rushed by like a lit up central reservation at nighttime on a highway. It reminded him of snoozing in the back of his father's car at the end of a long day's family road trip when he was a kid. The beeps turned solid by the time he arrived at the theater. The ceiling lights simply blurred into one and stopped moving. Then they melted away completely.

Tom saw, from a top corner of the room, that the beeper was stayed while the tubes on him were discarded. The jump starter was fired up, and in a last desperate attempt to revive his body, the medics gave his chest a good ironing. He bucked in violent protest against his concluding dilemma: should he stay, or should he go?

Two military policemen burst in. A young medic's face saw them, but turned back to Tom's body and tried again, then again.

"It's over," one of the military officers said as Tom saw his body lying completely still. "We'll take it from here." He walked the medic out the door and requested the he heed the solid call of the beeper.

"But this isn't protocol," the doctor protested, looking back over his shoulder at his patient's door.

"Look, it's national security. It's okay. He's in good hands now."

* * *

In the Siberian forest, Jim had seen the wolves coming from his high branch. He tried not to move a muscle. First they prowled the ridge near the edge of the cliff to see if the men had scampered away, then, with a thirty-yard clear line of sight to the capsule, they stopped among the trees and prepared to ambush the hatch. It was covered again, as it had been the night before.

Jim slowly pulled up the flare gun, then kissed it and said a silent blessing. "Don't fail me," he whispered, aiming the muzzle squarely at a dark spot in the snow. He took a deep breath and squeezed the trigger.

The forest lit up as the super-bright magnesium flare shot through the trees like a torch and detonated in a massive explosion half a dozen yards ahead of the pack. A blinding light cast tall red shadows over everything before it faded quickly.

Chuck dropped from the trees and landed in front of the wolves with his space helmet on. The broken visor was open. He growled at them through the smoke for all he was worth, and waved the Soviet axe in the air like a raging psychopath.

But the Alpha growled back and began to run at him. Several others followed.

Jim raised his pistol and took aim at the front runner as Chuck turned and scampered back to his tree. He scrambled straight up it with a new ease that hardly seemed possible for a grown man.

The Alpha jumped at him no more than a few feet up. Jim squeezed the trigger. His shot rang out across the forest, but narrowly missed its target, splintering a tree and spraying the Alpha in the face.

Jim fired a second shot, then a third. The Alpha yelped and reeled as the last one hit. It fell to the snow. The rest of the pack recoiled and whined as the downed animal lay still. They began to scatter back into the forest.

Chuck glared at the dead wolf.

Jim watched, motionless and utterly startled.

CHAPTER 57 - RELATIONS

The same day

Ranger arrived in the Chukchi Sea, north of Alaska and east of the Soviet Union, ready to hoist Jim and Chuck aboard.

Chris, who had landed in a Navy shore transport, met Captain Powell for the first time. They shook hands on the deck and walked to the bridge.

Powell crossed the blue floor and jumped into his equally blue high chair in the front left corner of the small cocoon, as if it were an office. He looked out through square windows at the nose of the ship. Gray bridge equipment was tucked just below the glass, along with a few outlets and circuit breaker boards, a handful of small round scopes, and a bank of flares hanging on the wall to his right. A glass-top ledge also sat in front with a map inside, and bridge hands, mostly in light brown short sleeves and Navy caps, manned their management posts while other blue shirts steered and navigated the ship.

"Mitchell's on his way, too," Powell said. "You both know the men. I want you to meet them and debrief them when they get here. Check them out and make sure everything's okay. There's no telling what the Soviets might do to their heads if we don't get to them first. You're going to have to take care of them for a while so we can deal with a possible escalation. This may turn ugly before it gets better."

Chris had clearly missed the news while he was in the air. "Soviets? I thought they were in Alaska."

The captain turned to him. "The beacon was located on a remote island on the edge of Soviet waters. I'm told more than one piece came down, but they don't think they broke up. A signal has been found. Your man Tom's flying in from overhead somewhere, but he's incommunicado right now."

"But where exactly are they?"

Powell pointed to the horizon and said, "Just over that water over there. East Siberian." He stood up and walked over to a bridge map with Chris and circled a location in the New Siberian Islands with his finger. It was already marked in red. "Right here. It's a snow-covered mountain range in the northeast. Aerial reconnaissance images were transmitted from the air. They just came in. They show difficult terrain. The men appear to have landed miles from anything even remotely civilized."

"You said we were going to pick them up. Won't the Russians get there first?"

"It's so far from anything, we're counting on them not knowing exactly where or what happened fast enough. But we're on standby right now and can't sail any further. Excomm is meeting this morning, so we could be in play any minute if the diplomats can't agree a solution. Let's hope they find some common ground. If not, God help them."

"But they only have provisions for two days at the most. They're going to freeze out there. How long are we supposed to wait for a decision? They'll die before anyone gets in."

"We've already prepared a landing mission."

After a moment of silence, Chris said, "I should go too."

"I beg your pardon?"

"I'll go too. Whenever we get the go."

"You can't just go out there. You'll get killed or captured. I have soldiers standing by. You're a civilian."

"And so are they." Chris said. "Look, I'm a familiar face to them. It'll make a big difference. They're going to need help, not just a rescue."

Powell stared at Chris thoughtfully.

"Look, I sent them up there," Chris added, then pleaded, "I have to go get them." He took a deep breath. "Besides, the Soviets are less likely to harm a civilian like me now, don't you think?"

Powell sighed deeply, looking like he'd just bitten into a liver sandwich. "And I sent Cobb to your program. So you and the boys go get them home safely. We sure as hell don't want to deliver fateful news to Mrs. Cobb a second time, not to mention JoAnn and Peggy."

They looked at each other for a moment, neither of them able to articulate the thought of Jim and JoAnn being laid to rest together.

But Chris had heard the word. He suited up, then waited in the belly of Ranger with the launch team. Maps were out, coordinates and routes plotted, then, with a final equipment check, he knew they'd soon be dropped into the shit to clean up, with or without access from the Russians.

* * *

The Soviet ambassador to Washington was a well-built, squat

man, barely able to drag himself out of the back of the limousine parked outside the Truman State Department in Foggy Bottom.

He'd just heard that an American U2 had crashed somewhere in the Pacific. "Did we shoot it down?" he asked his aide in disbelief while still in the car. "Now a third?"

"We don't know yet, sir. A surface-to-air missile was tracked and automatically launched near the border, but the Air Force claims they were able to intercept it before the American went down. They lost a plane."

The Ambassador rubbed his forehead as his eyes searched for a story. "I didn't come here to face the Americans for something like this." He squeezed out of the car and demanded to know what had happened. "Pull me out of the meeting if you have to." He turned toward the stairs, then swung back to the car and peered into the window again.

"Have we signed the safe return treaty on, er ... activities and the proper use of space, or something, whatever it's called?"

"Not yet, sir. But soon, perhaps."

The Ambassador thought for a moment and looked around. "It won't help us to hold their men. No doubt we'll need our own cosmonauts back some day. We will be in the same situation. But maybe there's still time to get what we can out of it."

He turned again and disappeared up the stairs into the department. There, he was led straight to the secretary of state's office in the recently built New State, which he'd only seen once before.

The walk took him through the plush, regally styled, cream and wood paneled office, across a massive blue and warm pink rug, toward quaint period furniture and a large American flag flying under age-old chandeliers. The secretary and his aides were already seated. He took a place in a white-and-green striped chair at a walnut coffee table, just a few feet away from them. No sooner had he settled in than he felt the urge to launch in. "You have our property," he opened nervously. "I came to ask for it back."

The secretary looked surprised at the lunge and asked, "What property is that?"

"I think you know what I'm talking about."

The secretary looked around at a bunch of oblivious-looking American faces. He leaned back, opened his hands, and said, "Pray, tell."

"One of our satellites was tracked falling into your Alaska. Well, it was ours, but okay ..."

The secretary kept a blank face at first, then said, "I'm sure whatever it was has been destroyed. Just what are you looking for? That is, if we find anything."

"We lost a television satellite that fell out of orbit. And it landed here, in the United States. It was tracked to your Northern Territory."

The secretary leaned forward again, looking speechless. "You came here to tell me you can't watch television? Because your satellite is broken? Is that it?"

The Soviet shifted in his seat. "The people in the north are up in arms because their children can't watch their favorite shows. That is true."

"Television?"

The ambassador began to explain. "That leaves a lot of unhappy people. Unhappy with Americans—they think it's meddling. Television is important, you know, in a country our size. More powerful than your missiles in, er," he looked down at some papers in his hands, "Vandenberg. People learn from television what to vote for and what to support. They get the information they need to make the right choices. It's not just a television satellite. It's important to us, as you can see."

"*Not just a television satellite?*" the American repeated.

The Soviet took a deep breath as a deafening clock on the wall chocked up an uncomfortable silence.

The secretary feigned incredulity and asked pointedly, "Have you been *spying* on us?"

"What, with a television satellite?" The ambassador half-laughed. "Actually, I don't think that's technically possible. I'm offended that you would even suggest such a thing. But look, how can we resolve this amicably so that you can return our property?"

"You can start by telling me where our men are."

The Russian looked back at him blankly and said, "I'm sorry, but I have no idea what you are talking about."

The American sighed and jabbed his index finger firmly on the desk. "Let's just cut the bull, shall we? What's that in Russian, hey? A spacecraft landed on Soviet territory."

The secretary and his aides stared at him, but the Russian hesitated, then said, "Okay, well, I've heard that something fell somewhere ... in the wilderness to the northeast. Novaya Sibir, I think the place is called." He shrugged as he continued. "Siberia, perhaps. I'm told it's probably just a piece of our satellite. Apparently, the locals said a fireball came blazing across the sky over the hills, then passed out over the sea. They thought it was an American atomic bomb." He laughed. "But they were told it couldn't be or the US would be a pile of

441

ashes by now." He grinned. "Anyway, it fell apart. I'm afraid they're still learning how to make them properly. I know we're leading the way into space, but it's still early days, even for us." He finished with a smug smile.

The secretary leaned forward with a stony face. "Those are our men you have there. You understand what I just said, don't you?"

The ambassador glanced down at what looked like a roster in his hands. "We only know of one, er, unmanned test flight of your rockets." He flipped a page and looked more closely. "According to the schedule I was given here."

The American stared at it upside down. The Soviets clearly had a detailed inventory of everything the US was doing in space, whether it had been published or not.

The Ambassador pressed his fingertips together and leaned back in his chair. "That's all that's been made public. So ... what kind of men are you talking about? Climbers?"

"They're not climbers."

"No?" The Russian looked surprised. "Okay, so if you are right, how did they get there, may I ask?"

"They were attacked."

"Attacked? Attacked by what? Bears in the forest?" He laughed.

"By your equipment."

"Ours?" The Soviet looked confused. "Sorry, I don't follow."

"A pair of our men landed on Soviet territory," the American demanded again.

"So there was a *manned* mission, you say?" He looked down at his papers again. "Well, that's news."

The American was silent.

"And what are your people doing in Siberia? That's Soviet territory, you should know that—"

"We know that."

"So?"

"A mission suffered a failure."

"A mission?" The ambassador looked down again. "I don't see a mission with men here. Ladies? No. Have you stopped putting them on television for the people? We like to watch them in Russia too, you know." He smiled and gave a conciliatory laugh. "That's why we need our satellite back, you see. It all makes sense now."

The secretary was silent and impatient.

The Russian took the cue to come to the point. "Look, you know, Siberia is a very dangerous place for Americans to be—if you are right of course. It's unbearably cold this time of year. It's really not a good place to get lost. If it is as you say, well, the place is very difficult to reach." He then acquiesced. "A search is underway, but it will take some days, maybe weeks, to find whatever it is. The terrain is difficult and, look, we're trying to do what we can, but there are carnivores this time of year. It's mating season and they get very aggressive, so it's dangerous." He finished calmly, smiled again, and leaned back in his chair.

The secretary continued to stare at him intently.

"And now, suppose we find your men on this ... unmanned mission. What were they doing? Should we ask them? Or would you like to tell me first? As you can imagine, time may be very short for them."

The secretary didn't answer.

"As for our television satellite, which you will agree to return to us ..."

443

The secretary kept a straight face.

"Look, as far as I know, we were tending to our own problems. I admit our equipment doesn't always work up there." The Soviet half-laughed again. "So, we have ways to fix it, if you understand what I mean. This time one fell here. It's of no harm to you. But I still don't understand how your people are involved in all of this."

"Fixing it? What, by blowing it up? Is that your solution?"

The Soviet took a deep breath and loosened his collar, then spoke firmly. "You know we will protect our equipment in space, just as we protect our borders. You should expect no less. You shouldn't let your people stray or interfere. It's far too dangerous for both of us."

The secretary sat quietly, but the Soviet continued with a change in tone. "Between you and me, we've known each other for a long time. We both know that this will be embarrassing for you if it becomes public."

"Embarrassing for us? On the contrary, I think the American people will appreciate evidence that you have spy satellites trained on us. And that you're holding American astronauts after trying to kill them in space. If you're right, we'll find some proof now, won't we?"

The Soviet scratched his head and shifted uncomfortably in his seat, feeling his ass eating his pants.

The secretary continued. "You are reminded of the Convention on Human Rights. Find them, take care of them, and return them safely. Or this will get ugly. Neither of us wants that."

CHAPTER 58 - NEWS

Moments later

The Americans had the carcass of Molniya lit up like an alien ship that had just crash-landed on a Hollywood movie set in the mountains of Alaska. A scientist was excavating the remains with scrapers and tweezers when the leader of the search party walked up behind him.

"Be careful, it's radioactive," the scientist warned, protecting his specimen. "There's a fission power supply in there."

"Crown jewels—I just want to know if you found the money."

"There's nothing here as far as I can tell."

"Nothing?"

"The electronics bays and hatches were blown off on re-entry. You can see it's scorched all around. So, nothing. This compartment here," he pointed to it, "looks like it had components inside, but they're gone. We might as well send it back."

The leader thought for a moment. "The Soviets don't know that, do they? All they know is that we have their machine—whatever it's supposed to be. Let's see how badly they want it back. That should give us an idea of what it is."

* * *

At Tom's house, Trudy and Jake sat at the breakfast table. Tom's usual place was neatly set, though it was empty. What made it *usual*, begrudged Trudy, after he had disappeared somewhere into the night, was that he hadn't called by breakfast like she had hoped. It bothered her now that she'd never learned to turn it all off in her head the way she wanted to and even pretended to. Still, couldn't he just find a moment to pick up the phone?

Her mind kept looping on the problem as Jake jumped out of his seat and toddled his plate over to the sink. The TV was also talking about Ed White's upcoming first American spacewalk.

"Daddy," he exclaimed, ripping off his napkin with the renewed energy of a hungry toddler just fed.

"Is that your daddy?"

"Daddy," he repeated with glee.

"Is daddy going into space?"

"Moon," he replied, thrusting both hands into the sky, tugging up his shorts and tee-shirt.

"Well, I hope not," she muttered. "We'd like him to stay here with us, wouldn't we?" Jake was still mesmerized by the images on the screen when she added, with a hope and a prayer, "Your daddy's on a plane. He's safer there. Let's keep it that way, shall we?"

They finished eating, cleaned up, and made their way to the door. A pair of suits got out of a car across the street as soon as Trudy opened it. She saw them immediately as she stepped out of the house and stopped in the doorway, slowly closing it behind her. She hesitated to lock it. Jake ran and skipped across the yard, brimming with energy.

The men crossed the street toward her. She knew to open the door again and led Jake back inside, saying he needed to go play in his room for a minute. One of her hands held her navel to calm a growing bump inside, and to stay her own nerves, but the silence of the men dawned on her before they could say a word. The back of her wrist covered her eyes as she bent over and began to cry furiously.

They said nothing but helped her back inside. When she looked up again, Jake had run out of his room and stopped dead at the top of the stairs watching her, half collapsed in the hallway with the door still open.

* * *

In the Siberian forest, Chuck hobbled back to the capsule and scanned the area, rubbing a hand over one knee. "It's a damn shame that cognac bottle had to go up. I guess there's not a drop left to keep out the cold. Damn that fall—I came down a little too hard."

"We've got to get out of here." Jim looked down at the gun. "Empty." He turned to scan the woods. "They'll be back." He sighed. "My father disappeared in a place like this, and he was alive. I just know it. And he never came home. I'm not going to sit here and wait for the same thing to happen to us," he growled.

"But we could be anywhere, Jim. Russia's a big son-of-a-bitch." Chuck unfolded a world map on the capsule floor in the doorway. "Given the terrain and last night's light show, we're obviously somewhere very north. With our trajectory, I'd guess somewhere around here." He circled the vast northeastern region with his finger.

"I saw what looked like water in the distance from up on the clearing. If we head toward it, we might be able to build a raft or something and get somewhere. We need to find civilians before the army takes us prisoner. Be prepared to be paraded and traded like prisoners of war if we do not get out of here. Anything could happen if we don't find people," Jim said.

Chuck looked at him. "I wouldn't count on it."

They both understood that behind the Iron Curtain they would probably get a Tsar's beating and maybe even termination—the Russians would just blame it on injuries from their landing or wolves.

Chuck scanned the distance. "It could all be frozen, just like this place."

"Well, we're a little short on options. But look, we might be able to get downstream to, I don't know, anywhere. I say we do it and see. I'd feel better if somebody knew we got here in one piece. That's our only option other than to stay put. We're just sitting ducks if our guys don't find us. You know we don't stand a chance on our own."

They looked around the forest, but it was completely still and quiet now with the chopper gone.

CHAPTER 59 - RED HANDED

A short while later

Chuck turned to Jim and held his leg. "Now or never. It'll be dark and we won't have a chance."

"Let's go. There's no time to wait." He looked down. "Will you be okay?"

Chuck winced at the question. "Shouldn't have jumped from so high. All that adrenaline. Anyway, no choice now. Let's go. It'll have to be fine." He went back to the capsule, reached for the control panel and flipped a few switches. "Let's try the radio in case they pick us up." He pressed another button and spoke into the microphone. "Mission Control, this is Liberty 1 inside the Soviet Union—brought to you by the free people of America. Can you hear me?" He waited, then continued. "We think we're somewhere in the Siberian mountains. Jim and I are fine. We're heading out to see if we can find a way out of this miserable place, to find some people, in case you come looking for us." He hung up the mic, obviously not expecting an answer.

They slipped away from the capsule as inconspicuously as possible, and once they'd left the landing site, began to trudge back to the high ground. Back on the ridge, they looked out into the distance, and sure enough, there was water, hazy in the distance beyond a coastline, just as Jim had imagined he'd seen. But that was not all: a dozen or two people were moving up the valley ahead of them, about two miles down.

"Locals?" Jim said.

"It's the Russian army. Looks like they found us after all. I'll bet those people in the air pinpointed us. Damn it, we're too late."

"And they're between us and the coast. So we can't go that way. What now?"

They heard dogs barking down the slope. "We won't get far. Not like this," Chuck said, looking down at his heavy space suit. "We need to protect the capsule now. That's our priority."

Farther down the incline, the Red Army had landed on the island's shore and was already climbing the mountainside. They found the trail left by Jim and Chuck in the clearing where the helicopter had been, while dogs sniffed excitedly at a rare mix of frightened man and distant cousin wolf. The Soviet commander ordered his men around both sides of the parachute, which was just ahead and above the clump of trees.

From inside the hole in the capsule, Jim saw an individual in civilian clothes approaching ahead of the others. The man looked up in awe at the solitary, cone-shaped spaceship sitting quietly with its mysterious, dark opening. He smiled at another man, also in civilian clothes, as he saw an American flag planted near the hatch. The dead wolf lay on his right. He raised a hand to silence his Red Army companions. They stopped and listened to the forest. Then he stepped over a mound of snow and crept slowly toward the opening, with his friend behind him and the intrigued soldiers at the rear, their weapons trained at the hole.

Chuck, inside the capsule, sighed and held out a hand, then shoved away some branches.

The nearest man froze twenty yards back as Chuck, followed by Jim, climbed out of the hole with their hands raised. They jumped to the ground and stopped, looking around at their visitors with equal surprise.

The front man smiled nervously, took a few more tentative steps forward, and was now no more than ten yards away. He paused and raised his hands in the air, then slowly walked forward again, crouching in front of them. Glancing up into the open hatch, as if looking for a nasty surprise, he dropped his hands and looked back at the Soviet commander to signal the all-clear.

He still looked astonished when he broke the silence. "You two—live in *here?*" A broad grin spread across his face at his own wit. The soldiers within earshot laughed.

Neither Jim nor Chuck replied.

The second man came a step closer.

Chuck pulled out his machete.

The first man froze and his hands shot into the air again.

"Stay away now. This is United States property," Chuck demanded. "Do you speak English? Do I have to repeat myself?"

Still crouched, the front man recoiled and looked around, half-turning toward his companions. He laughed and announced something in Russian with one eye still on Chuck's knife, "Они думают, что приземлились на маленьком кусочке Америки" "*They think they have landed on a little piece of America.*"

451

The soldiers laughed and followed with a short murmur.

He turned back to Chuck. "Don't worry. I speak English—sorry, American." The soldiers chuckled again. "Leonid," he added, pointing at himself. "Vasili," he indicated to his companion with a double point. "They," he pointed behind him, "think Russian is better."

Chuck and Jim stood quietly as Leonid continued, "You came, from America?" He looked up at the sky. "Or perhaps Mars? To be with us? Today?" He sighed. "But this is not the best place to see our country."

When he crawled a little closer, Chuck trained the machete a little harder, then stepped into line to protect the hatch. "Stay back now."

Vasili smiled with a sideways glance at the troops and spoke for the first time. "You know, I've never been to your country. I just want to see what it looks like … inside. No?"

Out of the corner of Jim's eye he saw soldiers dressed in white creeping out from behind trees on all sides. Chuck, already looking exhausted, dropped his machete as the Soviet commander radioed something to base.

Just then, a small gust of wind blew a handful of papers on the ground in front of the capsule toward Leonid. He picked up one, which Jim could see was a half-burnt diagram. Original Russian writing was interspersed with English translations. His face fell. It was the damned schematics of Molniya they'd kicked out with the torch. They were finished, caught red-handed with the enemy's secrets.

CHAPTER 60 - END OF THE LINE

A moment later

"What are these?" Leonid asked, picking up a fistful of half-burnt diagrams and schematics. "Where did you get these?"

Jim and Chuck remained silent, their eyes on the ground.

"Is it possible that you have something that belongs to us? What are you doing here?" demanded Vasili. The friendly tone had gone. He drew his gun and walked around the side of them, cocked it and demanded that they drop to their knees. Outnumbered, they could do nothing but comply.

"Returning an old favor," Jim muttered to himself, still looking down.

Vasili stopped in surprise and glared at Jim's insolence. He laughed and asked again, "What was that?"

But Jim didn't answer.

Vasili moved in and put the muzzle to his head. "You better answer me, American."

Jim tensed.

Vasili continued. "America loves war. But we're good at it too, American. Do you want to die here, or will you answer me? We can make sure you never return to our skies."

Chuck gave Jim a sideways glance.

Vasili raised his gun and demanded again, "What are you doing here? With these?" He held up the burned-out diagrams.

"Fire that pistol and you'll go home empty-handed. That wouldn't look good, now would it? So ask nicely," Jim said. Even though he was exhausted, he seethed, thinking that his father must have been in exactly this position at the hands of the Soviets.

Chuck tried to get up, but fell back to his knees as Vasili kicked his legs from behind. He just managed to turn around and look back up into the capsule.

Without warning, Jim lunged at Leonid, now only a few feet away, and wrapped one arm around his neck. He jerked it hard until it looked like it might snap, then pulled out the Soviet pistol they'd gotten from the chopper. He jammed it into Leonid's temple, though he knew it had no bullets. At the same moment, Vasili, reciprocated on Chuck, who was still on his knees.

They stood in stunned silence, waiting for the next move, when an incoming message sounded on the commander's radio. He raised a hand to stop everyone and listened intently.

* * *

Captain Powell was still on Ranger's bridge with Chris, his binoculars trained out to sea. "Excomm's green-lit the rescue, but we have to stay here for a few moments. That's a Soviet Foxtrot attack boat, last seen patrolling the waters around Cuba during the missile crisis. They're a rare sight, thankfully, but we know shit's going to happen the moment it disappears again. There's probably an Echo-1-class nuclear cruiser down there somewhere, too."

He handed the glasses to another officer and told him to keep watch, then walked down to a room off the deck where the SEALs were waiting like coiled springs. Dressed in all black, they huddled for their leader's final briefing.

"The beacon last transmitted from an island in New Siberia, just inside the Soviet border." The leader held up a handful of grainy aerial photos developed from the last digitized bits of Tom's U2 transmission. They showed Liberty's parachute just visible above the snowy, mountainous winter landscape, though the capsule itself remained hidden under tree cover. "It's uninhabited as far as we know, very rocky terrain, cold and deep in snow, but close enough to the coast. We'll climb over the East Siberian to flight level thirteen, then drop to five hundred meters when we cross the border. Then on to the coast. It's a five-mile hike to our objective. Our job is to secure the site, the men and our property. We're to form a perimeter as US territory until the diplomats come to pick us up. Understood?" He looked around but saw no relish on any of their faces.

They put on their masks and climbed into the transport on Ranger's deck. Chris jumped in as well and they sped toward the island.

The black helicopter skimmed the water below radar, like a giant dragonfly on its way to the East Siberian Islands. There, the SEAL team dropped onto a remote shore to prepare weapons, agree coordinates, and synchronize radios. The helicopter turned back to the ship as the team moved quickly up a snowy incline less than five miles to Liberty's last known transmission.

When Ranger forces arrived at the landing site, the last

thing they expected to see was Jim and Chuck sitting around a campfire with a Russian army that wasn't the least bit surprised to see them.

Chuck explained that they had looked ready to shoot holes in each other when the Soviet commander got a radio instruction and, to his obvious disappointment, told his army and the two thugs to stand down immediately, that Jim and Chuck were not to be harmed, that the Americans were coming to get them. Leonid and Vasili looked as if they'd been ordered to throw a prize catch back into the sea. Leonid kicked Jim's knee, got out of the headlock, and the two had a quick scrum in the snow as if to make up, much to the delight of the Russian soldiers. Vasili kept the diagrams of Molniya they'd found, and the Russians set up camp thirty yards back, leaving Jim and Chuck practically to themselves.

The commander allowed American sentries to be positioned to secure the capsule.

The sun was already setting over the wilderness by the time Jim and Chuck decided to forgo the space rations in favor of something more palatable, courtesy of Chris, who'd brought the first real food they'd tasted in days.

Another Soviet helicopter also arrived with a load of supplies as they packed up for the evacuation. A civilian, wearing a cozy looking winter fur hat, came in with it and seemed to be very curious about the capsule.

"That one calls himself Vasili," Chuck said, glancing at the Russians in the distance. "But they're no soldiers."

"Reporters?" Chris asked.

"No. Not with guns in their pockets."

"Almost certainly KGB," Jim remarked.

"Well, we don't have long now. We're going back to Ranger

within the hour." Chris said.

"And the capsule?" Chuck asked.

"Another transport is on its way to pick it up. Time to get your things together."

Jim stood up and offered to check the spaceship one last time.

"Looks like they didn't find the boards or their gray box. What the hell did you do with them?" Chuck asked.

"They were inside a panel. Must have thought they were spare parts or damage or something," Jim said. "Guess they didn't think there could be a bigger haul in there."

The new Russian who'd arrived by helicopter walked over. He had long, dark, curly hair, was quite built, and had a gregarious face. He turned to Chris first and said, "I'm glad to meet you. And I apologize for the treatment you received from our people. We are usually more welcoming to our visitors." He held out a hand to shake, but Chris held back, surprised at the unexpected congeniality.

"I'm not a soldier. I'm Aleksi." His hand was still out, but no one took it. "For me, this is all such a miracle," he went on, glancing at the capsule just ten yards over his right shoulder. "It fascinates me. Everyone in Russia is captivated by space." He beamed at the thought.

There was a silent pause.

"But it's a shame that you have to visit our country like this. You are heroes," the man told Jim and Chuck. "Even here in the Soviet Union." He looked up at the sky. "Maybe we can be friends out there someday?"

When the American contingent remained silent, he continued. "You know, we've also started training six new spacemen ourselves. To go to the Moon." He shook a triumphant fist. "Are you going to the Moon? I came to ask for an autograph." He searched his pockets. "Too bad, I don't have a pen or a camera."

"Are you from the Soviet program?" Chris asked.

"Who, me?" He looked flattered. "No, no. But I have wanted to fly to the stars since I was a boy." He looked up at the deep blue winter evening. "It started with Sputnik. You must remember that? No? The little beeps? We thought they were secrets. Even, I." He laughed and pretended to scribble notes on a hand. "I wrote it all down." He shook his head. "I don't think they'd let me go anywhere now. But our people—we will get there. Then maybe one day it'll be a vacation for people like you and me," he added, clearly delighted. "We'll have to sit in the back," he joked with a broad grin. He paused to look at the one lone bright star in the evening sky that outshone the rest. "Fifty years from now, we'll be flying across the entire solar system. I hope I live long enough to see it. It's a new era, don't you think?"

"It's a race, isn't it?" Jim said.

"Well, yes," Aleksi admitted. "What was it? Sixty-nine, your President Kennedy said? To the Moon?" He thought for a moment, then added. "But you should see our rocket. It's bigger than yours, huh?" He laughed, though the joke was not shared. "It's unbeatable."

"I think everyone can see it," Chris countered. "Must be heavy in a single stage."

"You'll see. We will colonize the planets, starting with the Moon, in that rocket."

"And we'll fly for the freedom of the skies," Chris added. "You can take that back with you."

Aleksi looked surprised and offended. "Freedom? From

what?"

When Chris didn't engage, Aleksi insisted, "You know, the Russian people have built a large industrial might. It's because we sacrifice now and invest in the future so that one day there will be abundance. You will see. We were peasants and farmers, but Stalin made us great. We're taken care of and we have jobs and medicine and recreation and it's all free. Even our women have jobs in space," he joked. "And our power destroyed Hitler and we saved the free world. So we are for freedom. And now we conquer space."

"Our democracy is real freedom," Chuck chimed in.

Aleksi turned to him. "Freedom? A handful of people make all your decisions and throw out the scraps. You stay on a little mouse wheel." He waited a moment and said, "You see? We're not so different. We just don't practice illusion."

"And our faith is in God," Chris added.

The man could see that his congeniality was not shared. He cast some furtive glances at the capsule, then turned and left without another word.

Within the hour, flanked by US Navy SEALs and within a wider path of Soviet soldiers, Chris, Jim, and Chuck were skiing down the hillside toward the coast for their return trip to Ranger.

CHAPTER 61 - TRUST

A week later

Jim and Chuck, after first being decontaminated and physically examined for the effects of space, then debriefed on the mission, handed over the boards, which they neither saw nor heard of again. They were told that Molniya had fallen somewhere in Alaska and that it was returned when *Liberty 1* was recovered, though Jim said he would have liked to see it again.

Tom's body was flown back for the funeral, and per normal military protocol for new widows, Trudy was already packing to move out. San Francisco is what Jim and Chuck had heard. She'd be gone in four weeks.

Upon release, Jim immediately made a beeline for JoAnn in hospital.

Although he knew roughly what to expect, he was a little unnerved to see her in a wheelchair when he arrived. He jumped into her arms as soon as he entered the room, then knelt down in front of her and held her hand. In awe and with a broad grin, he said, "You kept your promise."

JoAnn looked confused.

"We made a pact, you and I, when you were sleeping." He

shifted on his knees to look into her eyes and explained what he'd told her about the mission, about how they'd both come back. She listened quietly, though she looked tired.

He put his forehead to hers, looked into her eyes and said, "If it weren't for you, I don't know if I'd be here right now. That's twice."

She still looked puzzled.

"Korea. And this time you brought us both back. I won't let you get away like that again."

She nodded subtly and gave him a deep hug, then said softly. "You know, I may be in this chair for a while, maybe from now on. I can't go anywhere."

"Then I'll just have to get used to wheeling you around." He looked at it and added with a wide grin, "We'll strap a spare booster on it!"

They laughed, then he got serious and apologized for leaving without her knowledge, though he wondered if she had even heard him at the time. She replied that he was in her heart all along.

She asked if he was leaving again.

"Maybe I've done my part. Although there is a new program." He paused to see her reaction, then went on. "Chuck talked about something he's been working on."

"But you've been fighting it your whole life."

"It was my father," Jim replied, thinking of all his years fighting the Reds. "But I knew up there that it was time to let go." Jim's eyes turned to the sky. "He's still with us." He turned back to her. "And we have each other now. His days are gone. These days are ours. As for the Reds—well, maybe the whole thing is just a monumental clash of ideas about life, a misunderstanding of each other. We don't have to agree, we just have to protect what's ours. Maybe some of them are adventurers like us."

JoAnn smiled and put her hand to his lips as if to stop his words. "It's okay. You know, sometimes I wished you were a just regular mailman. It would have been easier for both of us. But I understand. I want you to do what you're supposed to do. You came back for me. You were always mine. That's all I needed to know. I'm okay. And we've already made a difference. I wanted to show you something."

Jim looked intrigued.

"My piece I told you about? It's being published," she added with a modest smile.

He looked delighted. "Fabulous. Where?"

"In one of the broadsheets, the Texas Post weekend magazine. It'll be a first edition."

"Wow! I'll have to check it out."

She reached into a bedside drawer and pulled out a proof.

Jim scanned it. *America's Fight for Peace and Democracy,* by JoAnn Cobb. He was elated to see her own name on it.

"It's staffed by women," she added.

Jim looked at it and felt awed by her accomplishment. "The future is yours. I know you'll save our country, somehow, someday."

Please Leave A Review

If you enjoyed *Liberty One* as a purchased ebook, please swipe to the very end and leave a rating and review now. Just a couple of words will do.

I want to hear from you, and reviews help others discover and enjoy the book too.

You can also tap a link at 60strategies.com/LibertyOneReviews or scan the QR code below.

Discover the real story!

Visit 60strategies.com/BobbyMehdwan and get the real stories behind *Blue Panther* and *Liberty One*, as well as book extracts, exclusive deals and updates! Be the first to know about the next exciting adventure.

About the Author

Bobby Mehdwan loves nothing more than writing a pulse-pounding, thought-provoking action thriller, with a heart-warming romance inside. His creative head escapes into history, the future, space, technology and Einstein's universe. He studied rocket science (honestly!) and designed military jets, so knows the territory. He also writes non-fiction professional and personal development, and is a corporate business leader by day. When he's not writing, he's probably climbing a real mountain with his family, enjoying a long bike ride or out running. Tap the links for more.

60strategies.com/BobbyMehdwan
tiktok.com/@bobbymehdwanauthor
twitter.com/bobbymehdwan
facebook.com/BobbyMehdwanAuthor

Also by Bobby Mehdwan

Read the prequel to *Liberty One*.

BLUE PANTHER
The Reds are spreading their twisted shadow across the globe. Can he hold freedom's line and avoid a fatal crash-landing?

60strategies.com/Blue_Panther